MURDER IN CONNEMARA

"Veronica O'Farrell was murdered. I think you should see for yourself."

That didn't make sense. Tara wasn't a guard. "Why me?"

"Because you're our quickest link to identifying her."

"Okay." Was that the only reason? "She was here to make amends. I have her guest list."

"I'm going to want that as well, like," Gable said.

Tara picked up Veronica's list. She hadn't mentioned her design book to Gable. She didn't want to give it up. Would the list be enough for him? What about Veronica's additional notes? Why didn't Tara mention them? Darn it. She couldn't keep it from him. She had to turn over everything. But was there any harm in taking photos of every page so she could recreate it? As she snapped photos, thoughts jumped out at her:

Stole the love of her life
Some people aren't meant to be parents
A piece of work
Hasn't created
Accused her of stealing
Injured, might be faking it

This was no longer just an amends list. And everyone seemed to have a motive. These people thought they were coming here to accept a grand apology, and now it was looking like they were all going to be suspects in a murder inquiry . . .

Books by Carlene O'Connor

Irish Village Mysteries

MURDER IN AN IRISH VILLAGE

MURDER AT AN IRISH WEDDING

MURDER IN AN IRISH CHURCHYARD

MURDER IN AN IRISH PUB

MURDER IN AN IRISH COTTAGE

CHRISTMAS COCOA MURDER
(with Maddie Day and Alex Erickson)

A Home to Ireland Mystery

MURDER IN GALWAY

MURDER IN CONNEMARA

Published by Kensington Publishing Corporation

Murder
In Connemara

CARLENE O'CONNOR

KENSINGTON BOOKS
www.kensingtonbooks.com

First Kensington Books Mass Market Paperback Printing: August 2020

ISBN-13: 978-1-4967-3077-0
ISBN-10: 1-4967-3077-1

10 9 8 7 6 5 4 3 2 1

Printed in the United States of America

This book is dedicated to Kevin Collins. Every book he asks me: "So how do I die this time?" To the friendship that still makes me laugh. Cheers!

Acknowledgments

Thank you to my wonderful hosts in Ireland once again: Eileen and Kevin Collins, Susan Collins, Bridget Quinn, Seamus Collins and the wonderful James and Vincent, and James and Annmarie Sheedy. Thank you, Ann O'Shea, for the use of your sofa whenever I get back to New York. The Clifden Station House was a wonderful hotel, despite the coffee I spilled on the bed (sorry). For those who think you can't travel Ireland by bus, my father and I found it rather easy and fun.

Thank you, Carl Carter, for all your support and the trip we'll always remember.

Thank you, Pat Carter, for your ongoing love and support. And thank you, readers and friends, those who take their time to write to me, or message me—your support means everything.

And of course, a big thank-you to my agent, Evan Marshall, and my editor, John Scognamiglio, my publicist, Larissa Ackerman, communications manager Michelle Addo, production editor Carly Sommerstein, the man himself, Steven Zacharias, and countless others at Kensington Publishing, who do what they do so we writers can do what we do. *Slainté!*

Chapter 1

The stunning drive through Connemara made up for the month Tara Meehan feared for her life (and those around her) during her driving lessons. Roundabouts, jerky stops and starts, and the instinct to drive on the other side of the road had proven formidable obstacles, but now, taking the curving roads on N59 in her shiny red Jeep, surrounded by a mountainous paradise, she was grateful for facing her fears. *Just do it*. A delicious bit of advice. The scenery literally made her mouth hang open. Massive round mountains stacked in the background, rolling green pastures dotted with fat rocks (and sheep, and cows, and horses, and donkeys), a glistening bay twinkling in the distance, and patches of vibrant wildflowers completed the postcard-perfect scenes. There was no other word for it, she was experiencing pure joy. Nature was the antidote to feeling sad in this world.

She'd been wondering if moving to Ireland had been a mistake and feeling homesick for New York City: the hubbub of Central Park on a Saturday afternoon, toasted everything bagels with cream cheese and tomato, exchanges with the flirtatious Spanish men in her corner deli; but now it was all forgotten as she concentrated on the curving roads. According to her handy navigation app, the old stone house she had come to see was within a few miles. She needed to find a place to pull over. Her phone dinged that she had reached her destination, and just then she looked up to see it—the remains of an old stone house sitting at the apex of a hill. The sun shone directly behind it, almost setting it aglow. Dated to the 1800s, and supposedly up for sale, she was dying to have a look around it. She wasn't sure if she had Danny O'Donnell to thank for leaving the tantalizing flyer at her soon-to-be-open shop, but someone had definitely steered her right.

Up ahead, gravel delineated a tiny parking lot at the side of the road, (or at least that's how she was going to interpret it), so she pulled over, hoping if she was wrong she could still get away with parking here for a spell. The beauty of being in the middle of nowhere was the conviction that no tow trucks would be sweeping by here anytime soon.

The Jeep shut off with only a slight shudder, as if it knew they were in for another day of punishing heat. Unusual for Ireland, August had been tortured by the sun and nobody here knew how to handle it. She'd tried to make it here before noon, but she'd been too afraid to speed on these winding roads, so it was already half past. She grabbed her camera, took one more swig from her travel mug of coffee before pulling a bottle of water out of the glove compartment and dropping it into her backpack. She looped the strap of her camera around her neck, and nearly squealed with joy as she set off for the old stone house. The sign was only visible when she was halfway up the hill. It appeared homemade, a scribble on poster board: FOR SALE with a mobile number, taped to a piece of wood stuck in the ground. Must be the owner. She snapped her first photo of the beautiful, abandoned house.

How much would it cost to rebuild this stone masterpiece on this achingly beautiful hill? More than she could afford, that was for sure. But it was never too early to dream. She snapped more photos, already imagining one blown up and hanging on the wall of her loft in Galway.

She was nearly to the remains of the doorway, and admiring the variety of gray and blue shades in the stones, when a yelp rang out. She stopped short. An animal—but what, and where? It was a tone that in any language was a cry for help. The yelp sounded again. A dog. Obviously injured. "Hello?" Her voice carried into the air, sweat trickled down her face. Was the poor thing just suffering from the heat? She was ready to share her water. "Hey there." She scanned right and left for a dog. The yelp turned into little barks. *Help, help, help, help.* "I'm coming. I'm here." *Where are you?* The barking morphed into a heart-tugging whine. She reached the entrance to the remains of the old house and there, just inside on the dirt and grass floor, a terrified pug quivered.

"Hi, baby." She sank to her knees and reached for the bottle of water. He was the color of sand, and his tiny body was vibrating. Tara held out her hand. "Hey.

Hey. It's okay." The pug lifted its big brown eyes to her sky-blue ones. Had some horrible human being abandoned it here? Danny O'Donnell wasn't trying to give her a dog, was he? It wasn't his style. Had someone else left the sale brochure and map underneath the lion's-head door knocker to her shop?

"It's okay," she cooed as she inched closer, taking it slow so the poor thing wouldn't dash away. Instead, it lifted its right paw as if reaching for her. She nearly melted on the spot. It had been a long time since something little and vulnerable had needed her, and she eagerly scooped the dog up and held it to her chest. Its heart beat rapidly against her as she stroked it. "It's okay, it's okay. I've got you. What happened?" It was wearing a bright pink collar. She continued to stroke it as she held the water bottle up to its mouth. She glanced and discovered the *it* was a *she*. "Poor girl." She drank greedily.

Tara was used to such heat back home, especially in August, but her Irish friends and family had taken to spending much of their day indoors, occasionally lifting the blinds with a bewildered curse, then retreating into the shadows like vampires awaiting nightfall. Tara gently checked the pug for injuries but found none, and the yelping had stopped. The poor thing was simply frightened out of its mind. She examined the pink collar. In the center, crystal letters spelled out a name: SAVAGE.

"Savage?" The pup swiveled its head and locked eyes. Tara laughed again. "Are you? Savage?"

An owner who buys a glitzy pink collar and gives a dog an awesome name like Savage hardly seemed the type to abandon it in the middle of nowhere on a blazing day. Savage happily tucked in her arm, Tara stood and traversed what used to be the inside of the old house, now missing a floor and a roof, and stared out at a magnificent view of the bay. She wasn't sure what bay this was, so many of them in this area, all leading out to the Atlantic Ocean. Imagine waking up with this view every day. It was a small house, but what did she need with a big one? She was already re-building it in her head: dark wood floors, a fireplace crackling with a basket of peat, fresh wildflowers in an old pitcher brightening the room up, and an old farmhouse sink underneath the massive window overlooking the water and the mountains.

She plodded to the other side of the space, by-passing what must have been the bedroom to the right, for she wanted to move closer to the water, where there was a bit of shade from a large tree. If there was anyone around to see her except the pug and farm animals, she knew she looked quite the sight. Boots and shorts, and a tank top. A bandana around her forehead. Sunglasses. An overeager ex-plorer. Today was a good day to get dirty. She exited the house on the opposite side, eager to see the view. Instead, she got the shock of her life.

A woman was splayed out on her back in the grass, and Tara had nearly tripped over her. As Tara cried out, Savage peddled frantically in her arms, scratching to get down. She leapt to the ground and began racing around the woman as Tara knelt next to her. "Hello?" Was she passed out? Tara fumbled for her backpack, talking to her as she dug through it for her cell phone. She'd forgotten to charge it and only a little power remained. As she dialed 999, she noticed the woman's lips. They were blue. *Oh no.* Tara's hand shook as she tried to find a pulse on the woman's neck. The skin was stiff and cold to the touch. She leaned down to see if she could sense any breath coming from her. No. Tara found the woman's wrist, knowing she was gone, but wanting to make sure. There was no life left in her. The woman was gone, and from the stiff, cold feel of her, she had been for a while.

She appeared to be in her late sixties or early seventies, with short dark hair streaked with white. Her purple and white tracksuit looked too heavy for the heat. Had it been cooler when she ventured out here? How many days had this heat been raging? Savage continued to scramble around the woman, barking right next to her ear. "She's your owner," Tara said, the pieces clicking into place. Savage whined, pawing at the woman's face. Tara's heart tugged as she gently tried to keep the pup back.

Tara scanned right and left, desperate to see another human being, then realized she hadn't connected to 999. She dialed again. An operator promptly answered and asked her location and what services she needed. As Tara stared into the eyes of a large cow, she explained she needed an ambulance, then clumsily announced the woman had already passed, and stuttered as she fumbled for the flyer so she could give them the address. The operator assured her help would be there shortly. Several feet away, sheep and a donkey moved closer, as if drawn to the drama.

Tara checked the woman's pockets, but found nothing. Not a scrap of paper, or a coin, or even a stick of gum. She had no jewelry, no rings, or earrings, or watch. What had happened to her? Had she come with her dog to look at the old stone house and died of a heart attack? Was she robbed? There were no injuries, no blood, no blunt instruments tossed in the grass. Tara gazed out at the bay in the distance, but apart from a small rowboat bobbing near the shore, there wasn't another soul in sight. "I'm sorry," Tara said. *Had someone left her the flyer in hopes she would find the body?* Tara shook her head as if to toss out the thought. *There was also a map. Leading her right here.* It was just an odd coincidence. The flyer came with a map because who would find this house in the middle of nowhere otherwise? She thought again of the very unprofessional for sale sign stuck in the ground. Was it all a ruse? Had someone *lured* her here? Outlandish. No one could have known for sure that she would decide to make the trip. The heat was warping her thoughts. *The guards are on their way. Do not panic.* Tara stood, staring out at the mountains, wishing the hills really did have eyes, so they could spill all of their secrets. What was going on out here? This section of Connemara was a gorgeous but lonely place to die.

Chapter 2

Tara waited at her Jeep, fearing the guards would never spot her if she remained up on the hill. In less than fifteen minutes (which felt like fifteen hours), three blue-and-white guard cars flanked her red Jeep. Soon a yellow ambulance pulled in behind, as a tall guard emerged from one of the cars. Something about shock was making Tara categorize everything by their color. Perhaps it was the interior designer in her, reverting to what made her feel confident and safe.

The tall guard approached. "Are you the woman who called for help?"

Brief introductions were made and then Tara pointed up the hill to the old stone house. "There's a woman lying in the grass on the other side of the house by the bay. She's . . . no longer with us."

His gaze traveled up to the old stone house. "Are you sure?"

"I'm afraid so. Her lips are blue. She's cold. There's no pulse or breath."

"Did you administer any type of aid?"

Tara suddenly felt guilty despite knowing that aid would not bring a woman back from the dead. "I was going to give CPR, or water—but it was apparent that she's been gone for a while." The way the dog quivered and drank, Tara guessed it had been alone for at least a day. "I'm sorry there was nothing to be done."

"Did you know the victim?"

"No." Tara lifted the pug. "I think this might be her dog. I found her huddling in the doorway of the old stone house. Before I found the poor woman."

The other guards and paramedics emerged from the car, and the guard who spoke first held his hand up as if to stop them as he put on gloves. He called out a number to them, which must have been a code for a deceased, for the paramedics stopped unloading their stretcher. Tara had learned, through earlier unfortunate circumstances, that bodies in Ireland were not moved until the state pathologist arrived or gave instructions for the body to be sent to the hospital morgue, where they could do a postmortem. "What brings you out here?"

"I came to see the house for sale."

"House for sale?" He sounded as if he thought she was spinning a lie.

"That one." She pointed to the stone house in the distance. The crude FOR SALE sign flashed through her mind, along with the flyer and map left at her shop. This wasn't the time to burden him with her uneasy feelings. "She's lying on the left side toward the water."

"Is there anyone else with you?"

"No."

"Do you mind waiting here for a minute while we have a look?"

"Of course." Tara gave them directions and four guards headed up the hill, followed by the paramedics. She turned the AC on in her Jeep and placed Savage inside.

Tara was too keyed up to stay in the car, so she hovered outside it. The ambulance driver stood outside his vehicle, head tilted back, gazing at the sky. He righted his gaze and shook his head. "This blasted sun. We've had heat strokes, severe burns, heart attacks. No doubt our insides are probably boiling with cancer."

"Sunscreen is key," Tara said.

They stood for a while, all small talk evaporating in the heat. Tara hadn't realized a guard had stayed back until the door to his car swung open and he stepped out. He clicked off his radio. "You're free to leave, as long as you write down your contact information. Are you on holiday?"

"No," she said. "I live in Galway."

He nodded and handed her a notebook. She dug into her purse and retrieved the new business cards she'd made for Renewals, her new architectural-salvage shop in the heart of Galway city. They were a lovely mint green with a treasure chest embossed in black, and RENEWALS sprawled across the top. She'd paid extra to have the treasure chest pop out, almost in 3-D, and it had been worth every penny. On her website, an identical treasure chest was featured on the home page. To enter the site, you clicked on it and the chest sprang open. She was thrilled to discover her interior design skills could be applied elsewhere.

"Here." She handed him the notebook along with her card. He glanced at it and nodded before jotting something down. From the direction of his gaze, she presumed it was her license plate number. *Number plates* as they called them here. Tara was fascinated by the tiny differences in phrasing between the United States and Ireland.

"Can I see your registration and motor license?"

She retrieved them from the Jeep and waited while he continued to scribble. "What about her dog?" Tara felt a twinge of panic at the thought of them taking her.

He glanced at the pug. "Do you want the name of a pound?"

"No." *Not on your life.* "I'd like to keep her until . . . can you have her next of kin contact me?" She held her breath, praying he wouldn't say no. There was no way she could leave without this pug. The poor girl had suffered enough. The guard glanced at the dog, then waved her away with a nod. "Come on, Savage," she said. "Let's get you home and fed." She smiled and nodded at the guard, although the truth was, if he had tried to take the pug out of her arms, Tara probably would have bit him.

Exactly one week later, Tara stood inside Renewals, sweat trickling down the back of her neck as she watched a pair of hungover lads try to mount her antique crystal chandelier to the ceiling. The rickety ladder didn't look strong enough to hold the lad climbing it, nor did the one bracing it seem to care. He was too absorbed in his mobile phone. "Perhaps you should check your phone later." The lad snorted out a laugh but shoved his phone into his pocket. "What are your names again?" Uncle Johnny had recommended them, and Tara was starting to doubt his judge of character.

"I'm Curly," the one with his phone in his pocket said. "And that's Moe."

The ladder jostled, the chandelier swayed, and Tara's heart lurched into her throat. "Please," she said, letting out a little gasp. The one bracing it gave her the side-eye while the one attempting to bolt it to the ceiling laughed, causing the Irish wolfhound and the pug (posing as a rug and a tiny pillow in front of the fire) to lift their heads and bark a chorus of disapproval. The barking caused the two lads to jump, the ladder to jostle, and the chandelier to sway all over again. *Please, please, don't let it fall.* Curly and Moe were going to be the death of her.

The stunning light fixture was from a thirteenth-century Irish manor house, and had survived too many turbulent times in history to be taken down by an unreliable ladder, a pair of cranky dogs, and hungover Three Stooges fans. "We won't work any faster with you gawping at us," Curly said.

Tara sighed, and headed over to her coffeemaker. She poured herself a cup, pretending she couldn't hear them laughing behind her back. She needed to think about something else. Anything other than the woman she'd found at the old stone house. It was hard to believe an entire week had gone by. Already ignoring her own advice, she went over to the counter where her laptop was perched, and typed the woman's name into the search engine, but there was nothing beyond what Tara already knew. Her name was Nancy Halligan, she was visiting from Dublin, and staying on Inishbofin Island—a forty-minute ferry ride away from where Tara had found her. She'd been taken to University Hospital in Galway where the state pathologist had yet to rule on the cause of death. Tara assumed they were awaiting the tox screens. She'd been gone at least twenty-four hours before Tara discovered her body. Tara had yet to receive a call about Savage, nor did she have any updates on the woman's family or friends. They had her information and all Tara could do was wait.

Waiting was something she was painfully familiar with.

It was now a mere ten days from what she hoped would be the grandest of openings. Located just off the pedestrianized Shop Street, Renewals, (an offshoot of the larger salvage mill Irish Revivals) was starting to take shape. Five hundred square feet of hand-selected treasures, and a back patio to boot. *Gratitude* had become her favorite word. She stood near the French doors to the patio as she watched them work. Her eyes landed on the opposite wall, painted a lively shade of mint green, where she had proudly hung the framed newspaper article:

NEW BEGINNINGS GIVE BIRTH TO RENEWALS

The local newspaper reporter had been kind to write the article. Tara's second chance in Galway, she liked to think of it, given how rocky her first few months had been. The ladder jiggled, and Tara cried out. One lad laughed, the other cursed.

"Relax," Moe, or maybe it was Curly, said to Tara. "Have a smoke in your garden."

"I don't smoke." Also, it wasn't a garden, it was a patio with a small fountain and a few potted flowers, but she wasn't paying them to quibble with her so she kept that mum.

"You might want to start," he added with a wink as he barely braced the ladder for his partner.

Tara eyed the chandelier. Then the ladder. "It doesn't look steady."

"Neither do you," quipped the one screwing her precious crystal commodity into the ceiling.

He was right about that. She needed air. But instead of disappearing onto the patio, Tara escaped out the front door and onto the soon-to-be-teeming Quay Street. It was early morning and the City of the Tribes was still sleeping. A pair of familiar figures emerged on the footpath, Uncle Johnny and Rose. Holding hands, they made their way toward Tara. Rose's black hair was twisted into a bun on top of her head. Today she was wearing a flowered dress. She lived in a caravan by the Galway Bay and read fortunes to tourists. That included Tara. She had been skeptical at first, and there were times when Rose was slightly off, but several of her predictions were eerily on the mark. Tara was now a loyal customer; hardly a week went by that she didn't pay Rose to read her cards. Mostly, she had come to enjoy sitting in the eccentric woman's caravan, taking in the African violets on the windowsills, watching the Galway Bay ripple out the window as Rose concentrated on her cards. She could use some of Rose's wisdom today, as long as it was good news. Would her permit be in the mail today?

Uncle Johnny, in his usual denims and flannel shirt, looked more like Rose's stalker than her lover. His wild beard blew upward in the wind. Tara often imagined taking cutting shears to it while he slept. "How ya," he called as they drew near. In his hands he held an old Viking helmet. "For your opening," he said, hoisting it in the air.

"I love it," she said, taking the helmet. And she did. Uncle Johnny was a little rough around the edges, a bit of a wild man, but he had a keen eye for treasures and she'd already learned a lot from him.

"It's antique, but it's a costume. Real Viking helmets are difficult to source."

"Oh." Tara had so much to learn, but she was looking forward to the journey. "Why is that?"

Johnny shrugged, although Tara had learned that wasn't a stand-in for *I don't know*. The shrug was simply a warm-up to his take on things, his version of *take what I'm about to tell you with a grain of salt*. "Iron would have been heavy to wear, so perhaps a limited number of helmets were forged, but there's also a theory that only the upper strata of society wore them. Those trained to guard the king."

Rose came to an abrupt stop and put her hands on her hips, then swiveled her head to the sky as if reading a message written in the gathering clouds. "Guard the queen," she said.

"King," Uncle Johnny repeated.

"I'm getting queen." Rose continued to stare at the sky, so Tara followed suit. Heavy clouds hung in the distance, slowly marching their way. The heat wave was over and Ireland was back to its normal weather. For Tara's morning walks that meant a comedy of errors. Hat on, hat off, jumper on, jumper off, raincoat on, raincoat off, hat back on, hat off, sunglasses on, sunglasses off. The skies seemed to change their minds every freaking second, driving Tara a little mad. It was also part of its charm—as if even the Irish weather carried a good dose of sarcasm and mischief close to its heart. Lately, everyone had been hoping for a longer dose of rain, as if to permanently wash away all memories of the heat, and it looked as if today might be the day. The River Corrib had been rough this morning, a sure sign of turbulent weather on the way.

"A visitor," Rose said, pinning her dark eyes on Tara. "A very strange visitor indeed." Rose and Johnny already knew about the poor woman in Connemara, so she must have been picking up on someone else. *Or making up someone else.*

Tara gestured to the shop. "If you mean the lads hanging my chandelier, it's too late, they're already in there."

Rose shook her head. "No." She drew closer to Tara, her eyes cutting into hers like a precision laser. If it was all an act, Rose certainly had it down. "You shouldn't be left alone."

"What? Like a toddler?" Tara tried to keep her voice light, but a shiver went up the back of her neck. When Rose went into psychic mode, she had that effect on her.

Rose doubled down. "Today is not a good day for you to be alone."

A picture of Nancy Halligan in her purple tracksuit, lying all alone on the hill, flashed in her mind, and she shoved it down. "I'm not alone. I have you, Uncle Johnny, two fools calling themselves Curly and Moe on a ladder in my shop, Hound, and a sweet little pug named Savage." She placed the Viking cap on her head and grinned. "And this," she said, pointing to her head. "An antique Viking helmet, be it part of a costume or otherwise."

"You look ridiculous," Johnny said, flashing a grin. "It suits you."

"Tank you."

He frowned at her imitation of an Irish accent.

"This is not a good day," Rose said, shaking her head and folding her arms across her colorful dress. "Close the shop and take the day off."

"Gives me hives just thinking about it," Tara said, looping her arm around Johnny. "But you're here now. The more the merrier." The lads emerged in the doorway, hauling their ladder with them.

"She's a beauty," one said, as they passed.

"And the chandelier isn't bad either," the other quipped.

Was that it? Was it hung? "It won't fall?" Tara yelled after them.

"Not unless you swing from it," came the reply.

"Call me if you do," the other called out. Johnny's laugh rang in the air, along with the cheeky lads', but Rose continued to frown.

Tara held her breath as she stepped into the shop and fixed her eyes on the chandelier. It was perfect. An iron base, and just enough crystals not to be obnoxious. It gave off a beautiful glow, casting curved shadows up the far wall. "It's stunning." She turned to get Uncle Johnny and Rose's reaction, but they were nowhere to be seen. She ran back outside, only to see them retreating in the distance.

"Where are you going?" she yelled after them.

"Just came to give you the helmet," Johnny yelled back. "Rose doesn't like the vibe."

"Seriously? She didn't even step in."

"Take the day off," Rose repeated. And then they were gone.

Tara headed back into the shop and looked around. The vibe felt good to her. Bamboo floors, special cabinets to display her hand-picked items, old Guinness signs hanging at varying heights on the walls. White orchids topped surfaces, sculptures stood in every corner, and fireplace accoutrements were set up near the small working fireplace. On the mantel, she displayed antique brass and iron candleholders. She'd personally chosen every single item in the shop. Pottery from the 1800s was gathered in one section; vases, tiles, and antique fixtures in another. Stone lions, which she priced high enough that she wouldn't sob if anyone bought them, flanked the fireplace. The cabinet by the register was filled with antique jewelry. A small section of crystal glassware occupied shelves in the middle. Old doorknobs and decorative knockers were laid out on an old wooden barrel with JAMESON carved on the side.

On the patio, larger architectural items, such as old wrought-iron gates, were stacked up against the back of the building along with garden sculptures and fountains. She loved her shop. *Bad vibes.* Rose was out of her tarot card-reading mind. It had a fantastic vibe. Maybe today was the day she would get her permit. She'd been watching her mail like a hawk. The city was taking forever. Everything was hurry up and wait.

"Looks like it's just you and me," Tara said to Hound and Savage. Hound rose to his feet and padded to the French doors leading out to the patio. Savage remained rolled into a ball. He looked like a Cinnabon. For a much younger dog, he slept a lot. "What's the matter?" she said to Hound. "You don't like the vibe either?" He whined at the door. She sighed and let him out. "Just me and the bun then."

She turned to set the Viking helmet down on the counter, and in doing so knocked a paperback book to the floor. It landed near Savage, who yelped and shot up. The pug's eyes seared into Tara's, and she swore the dog had so perfected the scolding look, Tara wondered if she'd met Tara's mammy in a past life. Nothing could silence Tara from across a room like one of her mam's looks. She let Savage out on the patio with Hound, then turned to pick up the book, wondering if one of the handymen had left it—Curly or Moe? It certainly wasn't hers. She propped it on the counter and stood back to take it in. The white cover showing a torn map with a winding road running through it was intriguing, but it was the title, in large black letters, that caught her attention:

PLACES TO SEE IN IRELAND BEFORE YOU DIE

Chapter 3

Were Curly and Moe messing with her? Was it a gift, or a joke, or something forgotten? It was shiny and new, with no markings or name scribbled in the front pages. Joke or not, she'd leaf through it later. After all, there were plenty of spots she was dying to see in Ireland. She laughed at her pun, then set the book on the counter and went to dig for her to-do list. She couldn't officially hold an opening party until she'd been granted her permit, but she could at least start planning it. Just then, the front door swung open, and a striking older woman strode in on a gust of perfumed wind. Behind her loomed a large bald man dressed head-to-toe in black. Tara had forgotten to lock the front door.

The woman wasn't tall per se, especially next to the giant in black, yet her presence loomed large. *Star power*. She held court in a peach silk dress and matching stilettos. Her thick white hair was cut in a stylish bob. Tara pegged her to be in her seventies, but she looked like a movie star. From her white-gloved hands to her perfectly made-up face, the woman made an impression.

Strange visitor . . . Tara felt a little tingle in the back of her neck and she wished Johnny and Rose had stayed. "I'm sorry," Tara said. "I'm not open for another ten days."

"Dat's good," the woman said, removing her gloves and placing them in a matching purse. "Because I want this place all to meself." She moved into the room as if she owned it while the man in black remained by the door.

"Sorry?" Tara was at a loss for words. Who was this woman?

"Veronica O'Farrell," she said, holding out her hand as if Tara had spoken the question out loud.

"Tara Meehan." Veronica O'Farrell's hand was ice-cold. She should have left the gloves on. She began inspecting the shop as if she'd been invited.

"I'm not open," Tara repeated.

"Obviously," Veronica said disapprovingly. She snapped her fingers at the man by the door, and for the first time Tara noticed he was carrying a small black satchel. He removed a folder and handed it to her without a word. "That's it, Bartley." She handed the folder to Tara, who felt she had no choice but to glance at it.

On the cover was the photo of a handsome man: chiseled jaw, a knowing smile, and brown eyes sulking beneath a tweed patchwork cap. He was a little too posed for Tara's liking. She preferred scruffy men. Speaking of scruffy men, Danny O'Donnell should be home from Scotland soon. He'd been on a sourcing expedition for eight days. *Pirating around* as he liked to say. Not that she was counting. She hadn't even had a chance to tell him about finding Nancy Halligan, or grill him about whether or not he'd left the flyer under her lion's-head door knocker. He was more than a friend, and less than a boyfriend, and he equally confused and thrilled her. *Focus.* She glanced back at the photograph. A name was scrawled above the handsome, brooding face: Eddie Oh!

"It's his artist name," Veronica said.

"Oh."

"Exactly."

Veronica's prolonged stare forced Tara to open the folder. It appeared to be an artist portfolio. She flipped through pages of abstract paintings and metal sculptures. His work had a quirky, wild abandon. Portraits with somewhat distorted faces and sculptures that looked like a cross between humans and dolls. She had to admit, she couldn't look away. "It's arresting work," she said, meaning every word of it. "But I'm not an art gallery." She held the portfolio out.

"You could be." Tara waited for Veronica to take it. Instead she waved her away like Tara was being a nuisance. "He's taking the art world by storm." Galway had a ton of art galleries. There was no way this woman didn't know that. Why pick her shop? Why pick *her*? Was this the vibe that Rose didn't like? Veronica swept the room as if looking for something in particular. "Ah. Here it is." She came to a stop below the framed newspaper article. "Renewals." She tapped it with a long, white fingernail. "This is why I'm here." Tara blinked as if that would clear the confusion from her head. It didn't. The woman continued to tap the article.

"I don't understand."

Veronica turned, and for the first time smiled. She'd had work done on her teeth, they were straight and blindingly white, something Tara didn't see as often in Ireland as she did in America. "Renewals," Veronica said again, this time her green eyes lighting up. "I read your story in the paper. I loved it." She clasped her hands together as if in prayer, and looked to the ceiling.

"Thank you."

Veronica's eyes landed on Tara and locked in. They looked like the eyes of a wild tiger—green with hints of yellow. Tara stared, wondering if they were colored contacts. "I'm renewing myself too." Veronica stuck her chin in the air as if posing for an invisible photographer.

"Okay." Definitely, colored contacts. Perhaps part of her renewal. Tara could get behind that. Renewing was good at any age.

"Don't you see? You inspired me." Veronica snapped her fingers again and once more Bartley dug into his satchel. If Tara were him she'd want to bite Veronica's fingers off by now. He held up what appeared to be a coin and tossed it to Veronica, who caught it while looking elsewhere. She rolled the coin through her fingers. "My one-year sobriety chip."

"Congratulations."

She waved her off again. "It's time I made amends. My sponsor thinks I'm ready." At this she turned to Bartley. "Speaking of that rebellious devil, has she called me back yet?"

"No, madam."

She sighed. "That woman. Call her again." She waved Bartley out, who followed her command with a phone in his hand and a hustle out the front door. "Where was I? Oh, right. Amends. I've chosen your shop at which to do it."

"Amends? Here?" Tara looked at a nearby Buddha sculpture as if expecting it to weigh in on the matter. It did not.

"I was an evil drunk. Wasn't I, Bartley?" Veronica scanned the room, mouth open as she realized he was nowhere to be seen.

"You sent him out to make a phone call," Tara pointed out.

"Right, so." Veronica blinked as if trying to remember. "My sponsor is being a bad girl."

Tara liked this sponsor already, but she really had no idea what to say about that. "People," Tara settled on. "Am I right?"

Veronica frowned, then cleared her throat and nodded. "First, she refuses to stay at the impeccable accommodations I secured, all expenses paid, of course, and then she won't answer my calls?"

"What can you do?" Tara gave an exaggerated shrug. She was going to have to start listening to Rose's predictions.

Veronica tilted her head as if it had been a true question. "What *can* I do?"

Tara shrugged. "Ask Bartley?" Was she really having this conversation?

Veronica nodded and looked a little bit relieved. She probably relied on Bartley for everything. "I assure you when Bartley returns he'll tell you I used to be quite evil."

"I have no doubt."

"There you have it. Straight from the butler's mouth." She cupped her hand over her mouth as if sharing a secret just with Tara. "He's not really a butler. He has a law degree."

Once again, Tara had no idea how to respond. "Good for him." That poor sucker, Tara doubted the younger him ever imagined using his life experience to work for a woman like Veronica.

Veronica wagged her finger at Tara as if she was in need of scolding. "Aren't you even a little bit intrigued? Wild heiress says sorry? Think of the publicity for your wee shop."

Wild heiress? She looked so refined it was hard to picture. But after a few seconds of feeling her intense gaze, Tara could see it. Somewhere behind those colored contacts was a history filled with mischief and pain. This woman had *stories.* "I'm flattered, but my wee shop still doesn't open for another ten days."

Veronica walked toward Tara, still fondling her sobriety chip. She threw it over her shoulder. It clinked to the floor. Bartley, who had just hurried back in and wasn't prepared for it to come sailing in his direction, immediately began scouring the floor until he found it, snatched it up, and placed it back in the satchel. "I'm sorry, ma'am, I was only able to reach Ms. Halligan's voicemail."

"Dreadful Nancy!" Veronica said, balling her fists. "When I find her, I'm going to kill her."

Chapter 4

Tara felt her blood run cold, which up until now she thought was just a cliché. "Did you say Nancy? Nancy Halligan?" Tara's voice was tinged with panic, even she could hear it. Tara hadn't meant to blurt that out. Now what was she going to do?

"Yes," Veronica said, taking a step forward. "Do you know Nancy?" She squinted at her. "Are you a friend of Bill?"

"Bill?"

"Yes. Are you in the program?"

"The program?"

"For heaven's sake, are you a recovering alcoholic?"

"No, no." In fact, Tara would die for a nip of whiskey right now, but she kept that to herself.

Veronica nodded. "I understand." She gave an exaggerated wink. "It's called Alcoholics *Anonymous* for a reason, is it not?"

"That's not it."

But Veronica didn't care. She moved on. Her heels clicked to the patio doors and she stood looking out. "She's probably dealing with someone's relapse. It couldn't be worse timing, she knows how important this step is to me." She turned and took a step toward Tara. *Tell her. Just tell her. How crazy is this? How could this be happening?* "I'm bringing a very special group together for my amends."

"I'm so sorry to be the one to tell you this." Tara cleared her throat. "A week ago, I was looking at an old house for sale in Connemara."

Veronica shook her head. "You're very rude."

"Pardon?" Everything was going wrong. Why, why, why didn't she listen to Rose and close the shop? She could be at the mill right now, drinking a cup of coffee and eating a scone as big as her head.

"We've just met," Veronica said, wagging her finger. "It's too soon to ask me to buy you a house."

Buy me a house? Was that even a thing? "Nancy Halligan passed away last week." Tara said it as fast as she could, like ripping off a Band-Aid. Or the strip of pink tape her mam used to plaster over her bangs in order to cut them. She always ended up looking like she had a bowl over her head instead of hair. Veronica just stared and blinked. *I'm the one who found her, by the way.* Tara couldn't bring herself to say that part. It sounded too fantastical. Veronica O'Farrell seemed frozen in time, not moving a muscle.

"Oh dear," Bartley said. "Oh dear." His voice was soft for such a big man. His bald head glowed from the light of the chandelier.

"That's ridiculous," Veronica said, coming back to

life. "Take that back." She made it sound as if Tara had power over life and death.

"She was found near an old stone farmhouse in Connemara. It looks as if she collapsed from the heat, but I don't know what they've ascertained yet." Tara had the feeling they were going to assume it was natural causes. Heatstroke. A heart attack. That wasn't sitting well with Tara. She liked all the pieces to fall in place. And there were definitely some missing. Why was she found with no wallet, or jewelry, or mobile phone? What did the guards make of that? Did someone else come across her body after she passed, and instead of calling the guards, he or she simply robbed her of her valuables? Did they run off knowing poor little Savage was out there as well? It was too horrible to imagine, but not out of the realm of possibility. Anything was possible when it came to humans.

Veronica let out a little cry, then lurched forward, as if to grab Tara. A piece of jewelry slipped from Veronica's silk scarf and clinked to the floor. When Veronica didn't make a move to fetch it, Tara found herself bending down and picking it up like she was Bartley 2.0. Minutes in her shop and the woman had Tara trained. But she forgot all about it when she held the object in her hand. It was an antique coat brooch. About three inches long, with a familiar colorful Celtic design. The Tara Brooch. This one looked antique and quite valuable. When she tried to hand it back to Veronica, the woman turned away.

"I cannot believe this." Veronica began to pace. "Why didn't anyone call me?"

"How did you learn of Nancy Halligan's passing?" Bartley asked. Veronica stopped pacing and waited for Tara to answer.

"I . . . I found her," Tara said.

"You found her?" Veronica asked. "How is that possible?"

"I was there to see the same stone house." *Because someone left me a flyer, and I thought it was a friend of mine.*

"And you say you've never met Nancy?"

"No. Never. I'm not in AA. I swear. Someone left me the flyer and a map, and so I decided to go."

"Someone left you a flyer and a map to find Nancy?" Veronica was in shock, and it wasn't helping her brain cells fire.

"No. The flyer was for an old stone house for sale." Tara threw out her arms. "Maybe Nancy saw a flyer for the house as well."

Veronica glanced at Bartley. "Madam?" he said.

"Did you know Nancy Halligan planned on seeing some old house in Connemara?"

"Of course not." His wide face flushed red. Tara wondered if it was anger or embarrassment.

"Tell me everything again," Veronica said, turning back to Tara. "From the beginning."

Tara cleared her throat and repeated the story, starting with the flyer. Veronica didn't lift an eyebrow at the mention of the pug, but she did shake her head a little. Tara figured she wasn't an animal lover. "I don't know how to get ahold of the state pathologist, but I believe she'd been deceased for a while before I found her."

"What is 'a while'?"

"At least a day."

Veronica sunk into a Queen Anne chair propped in the corner of the store. It was antique with navy upholstery trimmed in gold, and Tara hadn't planned on customers sitting on it, but now was not the time to ask someone to remain standing. "I cannot believe this."

"I'm so sorry," Tara said. "Here. I still have your Tara Brooch." Tara tried to hand it back. Veronica waved Tara away as if she wanted nothing more to do with it, which was odd, given its value. The most famous Tara Brooch was in the National Museum of Ireland and worth a fortune. Replicas were often made and sold, but this one looked genuine. Not that Tara was an expert. But the ornate metalwork was astounding. Tiny representations of dragons, and serpents, and heads. To Tara it looked like a crown in the middle of a circle, complete with a half-shield and a serpent's tail. Tiny bits of amber and green glass were woven into the seven-inch circumference. The three-inch pin was strong and sharp.

"Go ahead," Veronica said, pointing to Tara's camera on the counter. "Take a photograph. You'll never see one like it again."

"Thank you." It seemed like an odd thing at this moment, and Tara felt ashamed for wanting to take the photo, but salvaging antique items was her business, and she would love a photograph of this gorgeous pin. Tara moved to the counter, removed a piece of velvet from the case, and gently set down the brooch. She snapped several photos with her camera, then with her phone, before turning back to Veronica. "I have the name of the inn on Inishbofin Island where Nancy was staying. I believe her family has arrived. I'm not sure if they're still here. Would you like the phone number?" Tara had already called the inn and left a message that if any of the family was wondering, she had the pug. So far no one had called.

"I'll take that water now," Veronica said, snapping her fingers and holding out her hand. Tara reached into the tiny fridge she'd bought for the shop and handed her a bottle, then glanced at Bartley, who really looked like he could use some himself. She held out another bottle and he finally took it.

"Peace be with her," he said, crossing himself.

Veronica pointed to the counter. "Nancy loved that brooch. She made me promise she'd get it if I died first." Veronica placed her hands over her eyes for a moment as if saying a silent prayer, then placed them in her lap. "It's very rare." She held her hand out. "Unfortunately, it also rarely stays fastened."

Tara deposited the brooch onto Veronica's waiting palm. "Perhaps it's best kept somewhere safe."

Veronica went to refasten it, then stopped and held it back out to Tara. "Perhaps you'd like to try it on?"

"I couldn't."

"For Nancy," Veronica said. "She loved that brooch." Veronica approached and before Tara could protest again, she'd pinned it on her, just above her heart. "Now. You should take another photo."

Tara swiped her phone from the counter and took a selfie. She'd vowed to improve her presence on social media to promote her shop, and this would be a perfect opportunity. She'd have to emphasize that she didn't have it for sale. Hopefully that wouldn't backfire. She handed the brooch back, then quickly posted the pic with a hashtag: #KillerBrooch. "Are you interested in selling it?"

Veronica laughed, a sound that did not warm,

then shook her head as she took the brooch back and re-pinned it to her scarf. "You could sell everything in this tiny little store, then sell everything in that monster of a warehouse you're affiliated with, then rob all of Galway city, and still not have nearly what that brooch is worth." She grinned as she stroked her scarf. Bartley cleared his throat. "What is it?" Veronica asked without turning around.

Monster of a warehouse she was affiliated with? Veronica was speaking of Irish Revivals, her uncle's salvage mill near the bay. Veronica O'Farrell had certainly done her homework. It was a strange feeling knowing she'd been researched so thoroughly.

"The driver, madam. He is in need of the facilities."

Veronica rolled her eyes. "What is the point of having a young driver if he doesn't have a robust bladder?" She seemed content to let him sweat it out.

"Please," Tara said. "He can use the restroom." She pointed to the bathroom door blending into the corner behind the counter. "My tiny little store, and I insist."

Bartley talked into an earpiece and minutes later the lad rushed into the shop. He was indeed young, and handsome. His patchwork tweed cap caught her attention.

"Tank you, tank you, tank you," he said, tipping his cap and jiggling. Before she could even say hello he dashed to the bathroom.

Why did he look so familiar? Tara glanced at the portfolio on her counter. That was it. She stared at the patchwork tweed cap on the cover. Was it the same man? The build was the same, and so was the brown hair. Was she going to be forced to put one of his sculptures in her shop? "Eddie Oh is also your driver?"

Veronica's perfectly tweezed brows furled. "Pardon?" She lifted herself out of the Queen Anne chair. *Queen*. Another hit from psychic-Rose. Tara swiped the portfolio from the counter, pointed to the picture, and then the restroom. "Isn't that him?"

"You think my driver looks like Eddie?" Veronica threw her head back and cackled. It wasn't a laugh, it was truly a cackle. Bartley coughed. "What was that?" Veronica called back to the man.

"I'm laughing, madam."

"Anyone can hear that," Veronica said. "What on earth are you laughing at?"

"Andy," Bartley said. "He's not the creative type."

"Unless he's on a roundabout," Veronica quipped.

Tara was getting dizzy trying to follow them, and half wanting to pinch them to see if they were for real.

Andy emerged from the restroom and Tara held the brochure up to him. She immediately felt foolish. It was definitely not the same man. Andy appeared to be in his early thirties, at least a decade younger than the photo of the chiseled artist, and his eyes were blue whereas Eddie Oh had eyes so dark they were almost black. Tara shrugged and pointed. "From a distance they look alike. Especially with the cap."

Veronica eyed the cap on Andy's head as if it now offended her.

"She's right," Bartley said with a nod to the portfolio. "It's a younger picture of Eddie."

"I don't see any resemblance," Veronica said, her gaze ping-ponging between Eddie's photo and the man standing in front of her. Tara had a sinking feeling she'd just gotten the poor driver in trouble. "He looks more like old Bixby than he does Eddie, don't you think Bartley?"

Bartley squinted at Andy. "Quite right, madam."

Veronica turned to Tara with a smile. "He always says that."

"Eddie used to lift the cap off Bixby when he was tipping the bottle," Bartley said.

"Bixby?" Veronica said as if she was having trouble placing him.

"Your previous driver, madam. Martin Bixby."

"Right. The old man."

"He was in his sixties, madam."

Veronica blinked. Bartley's implication was clear. *She* was older than the man she was calling an old man. "Was he? He wasn't aging well then."

Andy cringed as if he'd suddenly seen himself thirty years from now, still driving Ms. O'Farrell around. If Tara were him, she would've run for the door.

"Eddie used to lift Bixby's cap?" Veronica was still stuck on the conversation.

"More than once," Bartley said.

"Always the life of the party, my Eddie."

Andy and Bartley exchanged a look that could only be interpreted as *Poor Bixby*.

Andy touched his cap. "It's part of me uniform."

"I am a firm believer in uniforms," Veronica said. "They're what hold society together. Delineate the roles."

If Andy was insulted to have his role clearly delineated, he didn't show it.

"Eddie once swiped the cap off his head while

Bixby was driving," Bartley said. "He nearly killed us all."

"Did he?" Veronica said. "That sounds like him." She smiled as if they were discussing a wonderful memory.

"Martin Bixby was not amused," Bartley clipped.

"Who?" Veronica scrunched her face.

"Your previous driver, madam. He was on staff for nearly thirty years." This time Tara detected a trace of irritation from the lawyer turned . . . whatever he was now.

Veronica snorted and glanced at Andy's cap. "And yet the uniform still looks good, don't you tink?"

Bartley opened and closed his mouth as if wrestling with the concept that he was allowed to think.

"I quite like it," Andy said, tipping the cap.

"What does that matter?" Veronica snapped.

Andy rocked back on his heels and stared at the chandelier. "Thank you for allowing me the use of the facilities," he said to Tara. He turned to Veronica but did not make eye contact. "I'll be in the vehicle." He exited nearly as quickly as he'd entered.

Veronica wasted no time in picking up where she left off. "This little group I'm gathering, there are seven of them, and I assure you they will spend money in this little shop."

Little group. Little shop. Tara was having big, bad feelings about this woman.

"Are you sure you want to continue with this," Bartley stammered, "given the circumstances?"

"Circumstances?" Veronica's eyebrow arched.

"Ms. Halligan's passing."

"Yes," Veronica said. "Nancy was the one who

wanted me to do this. Encouraged. Dare I say *prod-ded*. I have to keep going. It's the best way to honor her memory."

Bartley gave a stilted bow. "Of course, madam."

Veronica turned back to Tara. "I'm hosting the seven guests of honor and I insist we meet at your shop."

Insist. Tara resisted making a joke about the Seven Dwarfs. "When were you thinking of having them over?"

"Tomorrow evening."

"I'm sorry. That's not possible."

"Anything is possible." Veronica gestured grandly to the newspaper article. "Or was it all lies?"

"I have a grand-opening party planned in ten days." *If my permit arrives.* Why was it taking so long?

"I'm afraid that will be too late." Veronica clutched her hands to her chest. "Just like dear Nancy." Behind her, Bartley made a gurgling sound as if he was literally trying to hold his tongue back. Tara just wanted them gone.

"My uncle owns a salvage mill near the bay. Irish Revivals. He's always open to renting out space. Perhaps you should speak with him about hosting your event."

"Hosting," Veronica said, "is only part of my request."

"Oh?"

"I want you to source an item for each of my guests. Something that *suits* them. A physical representation of my apology." She smiled, which was not at all beguiling. "And of course, name your fee."

Tara had to admit, that did interest her. "Give me

the budget, and the timeline, and I'll work up a proposal."

"Budget. Proposal." Veronica waved her hand like they were made-up words. "You name it, I'll pay it."

That was an offer Tara was in no position to refuse. "I'm in."

Bartley's earpiece chirped. "Andy is double-parked, madam, and the guards are circling."

Veronica exhaled dramatically, and swept her scarf over her shoulder. The Tara Brooch stayed pinned. "I'll have Mimi send you the contract."

Tara had no idea who Mimi was. Another poor soul Veronica bossed around, most likely. "I need to know something about these guests—so I can pick out the right items."

"Before you die," Veronica murmured.

"What?" Did she really just say that?

The heiress threw a glance to the mantel where Tara had propped up the travel book. "Oh," Tara said. "It's not mine."

"Morbid," Veronica said, before gliding out the door. A thick folder materialized in Veronica's hands, then dropped to the floor. And this time, not even Bartley stooped to pick it up.

Chapter 5

❧

Tara stood outside the shop yet again, first staring up the street, then down at the folder Veronica O'Farrell had dropped to the floor instead of handing it to her. On the cover, CLIFDEN CASTLE was sprawled across the top in black marker. Below it, a typed list was taped:

Sheila Murphy	
John Murphy	Tenants/Unforeseen/ Common
Lainey Burke	Perspective/Makes one crazy
Mimi Griffin	Apologies/brooch
Eddie O'Farrell	His heart's desire
Cassidy Hughes	She wishes
Iona Kelly	Mend or Foe?

Were these the seven people Veronica had referred to? The cryptic little notes didn't sound very nice. Was she really trying to make amends?

Tara's stomach grumbled. It was way past her lunch hour. She grabbed her purse, locked up the shop, and took the folder to a nearby café at the end of the street. The rain had driven away any possibility of sitting outside. Inside, she found a small table by the window and placed the folder on top. A few servers, young college types, were cleaning up from what appeared to be the lunch rush. After placing an order for spicy avocado toast and a cappuccino, Tara opened the folder. The top sheet was dedicated to the first two names on the list: SHEILA AND JOHN MURPHY.

It included a photo of a smiling young couple, holding hands and grinning. Both with brown hair, Sheila's was long and wavy, John's cut short as if he was military. His smile looked pained, hers seemed natural. They were standing on lush manicured grounds with flowers sprouting in the background. CONFIDENTIAL was stamped at the top of the sheet, and typewritten notes from Veronica had been expanded:

I will be surprising this couple with a new flat. They are trying to adopt a child, but some people just aren't meant to be parents. Find a decorative item for their new home. John is controlling, so Sheila will be happy with anything that satisfies him. Do not get anything related to children as it is a trigger for her. I believe he likes boats so something nautical perhaps.

That was the end of it. How strange. It seemed Veronica intended on micromanaging every item Tara picked out. Not her favorite assignment, but Tara had dealt with "Veronicas" before. Every job not only required the skills necessary to perform its functions, but people skills were needed as well. Most people were miserable in their jobs because of the latter. *Other people.* It was one of the reasons Tara was looking forward to running her own shop. Should she have turned down this job? Was she taking a step backward? *Name your price.* She sighed and looked again at the notes for Sheila and John Murphy: *Tenants/Unforeseen/Common.*

What on earth did that mean? Tara would have to dig up one of her design notebooks she had stashed in her loft. She had an entire batch of colorful notebooks and she used them for every one of her interior design clients; she'd complete an entire book of sketches and notes before creating a larger vision board. Whereas many designers were using their iPads now, Tara preferred real paper and colored pencils, and swatches, and glue.

This was the part of the job she loved, had loved since she was a child, when all she needed to escape were sixty-four colored crayons and white paper. It was also one of the activities she'd enjoyed most with her toddler son, Thomas. His wonderful drawings. Sitting on the floor with her boy, surrounded by paper and crayons, had been the happiest days of her life.

Thomas died three years and four months ago when he was three years old. A terrible, terrible playground accident. Tara had been working that day. Her husband, Gabriel, had been five feet away. The jungle gym was too high, his little hand was too sweaty. The drop too sudden. Her ex-husband was a good man, had been a good father. Their five-year marriage simply couldn't bear the collective weight of their grief. They divorced less than a year after Thomas passed. They spoke a few times a year, checking in with each other, sharing memories of their son, as much as they could bear. Tara now had a Winnie-the-Pooh tattoo on her back along with the name Thomas. He was part of her skin (and soul) for the rest of her life.

She still wondered what he might have become. What kind of man he would have been. He would have been six-and-a-half years old. She found herself creating an image of him for every age he would have been. She didn't know if that was normal, or healthy, or unhealthy, but it hardly mattered. Nothing could stop her from imagining it. One day, when she could look at his drawings without crying, she intended on making a collage and hanging it as an art piece. That day had not yet come. She would not rush it.

She returned to Sheila and John's sheet and circled *Tenants/Unforeseen/Common*. She added a few question marks, then jotted down key words in the margins: *Young. Couple. New home. Romantic.* On the other side she added: *Controlling? Nautical? No child themes.* Perhaps she could find them an antique diving helmet. She wouldn't mind having one herself.

Some people just aren't meant to be parents.

What a thing to say. Did Veronica know something she wasn't telling? Was she afraid this controlling husband would be abusive? Was it based on pure conjecture, or fact? Did Veronica have children? If not, maybe she regretted it and her jealousy was seeping through. The more she thought about Veronica telling others not to have children, the angrier she grew. Tara turned to the next sheet in the folder:

ELAINE BURKE

The photo that followed was of two beautiful young women, dressed in shiny gowns. Arms looped around each other, sloppy grins on their faces. The beauty on the left had hair as black as Tara's, the other was a platinum blonde. The dark-haired one looked familiar. Tara leaned in, and that's when the dots connected. It was a much younger Veronica O'Farrell. "Wow." With those looks and money it was hardly a surprise that she exuded star power. Elaine Burke must be the other woman in the photo. She turned to Veronica's notes.

Lainey was my best friend until I stole the love of her life. She has no idea what a lucky break that was for her. I want something very personal as her gift. Something you would give a sister. Feminine but strong.

Stole the love of her life? This was like a soap opera. Tara turned to Elaine Burke's page. In the margins she wrote: *Stole love of her life?* and underlined it. Then added: *Recent photo?* Tara wanted to get her hands on one. Had it been forty-some years since Veronica had seen this so-called best friend? Was Elaine Burke still carrying a grudge?

"Here ya go." The waitress hovered over her with her plate.

"Sorry." Tara placed the pages back in the folder and set it out of the way. The girl set down the plate and Tara's cappuccino, eyeing the folder. "Thank you."

"No problem at all."

Tara dug into her avocado toast, marveling at how different each establishment served it. This one was top of the charts. The avocado was chopped along with hardboiled eggs and seasoned with sea salt and a bit of cayenne pepper, then laid on top of thick toasted bread, slathered with butter. Tiny bits of radish and cilantro topped it off. Simple yet so delicious, it was genius. Once again, Tara vowed to herself that she was going to start using her fantastic kitchen. She could see where cooking was an art just like interior designing. Taste, texture, and presentation. Just as the avocado toast used only a few ingredients, but the highest quality, Tara had the same approach to designing. A strong, simple palette of impeccable quality. Furniture by craftsmen. Materials that were not only luxurious but were durable, and livable. Interiors shouldn't feel like museums. They were supposed to be the place that welcomed you, and lifted your spirits. Just like this avocado toast.

But as much as she tried to make avocado toast at home, it was always lacking something. At least Galway had a plethora of restaurants that could pull it off in diverse ways. *Diversity*. Tara loved that word. And she loved the growing diversity of the City of the Tribes. As much as Tara loved the Irish, and she did, she was grateful that Galway drew people from all cultures, and the crowds weren't just a sea of shiny white faces (although, yes, there were plenty), but there were many other races and cultures to complete the gorgeous tapestry. There was color here. Tara saw it. And she loved it. Tara had been so lost in thought she was shocked when she looked down and saw an empty plate.

"You must have been starved, you poor ting," the young waitress said as she swiped up Tara's plate.

"My compliments to the chef," Tara said.

"Don't be saying that now, he can barely fit his big head in the door as it is."

"I heard that," a deep voice said from the kitchen. The waitress laughed, and made off with her plate. Tara finished her cappuccino and stared at the list of guests taped to the folder.

Supposedly all of these people had accepted Veronica's invitation. Whatever had gone down between them, it was nice they were willing to accept her apology in the first place. Everyone operating out of good faith. This was a job Tara could get behind. They had really good apple tarts here as well. She shoved her urge for dessert away and turned to the next guest in the folder:

MIMI GRIFFIN

This photo was of a heavyset middle-aged woman with curly hair the color of honey, big glasses, and a wide grin. She stood in front of a gorgeous fountain, in a lavender suit. Something about her screamed she was trying too hard, although Tara had no basis for the impression. She turned to the notes.

Mimi is my personal assistant. Years ago my Tara Brooch went missing. Mimi had been the last person in my room, and I accused her of stealing it. Later, I found the brooch in my garden, near the fountain. Accusing Mimi of

*being a thief took an emotional toll on her, and I am ready
to make amends. No, I am not giving her the Tara Brooch.
She'll be receiving a special surprise from me, but I would
like you to get her something that makes her feel worthy.*

What a tall order. Tara would love to make everyone feel worthy, but she highly doubted that came
from gifts. Maybe in Veronica's world it did. Another
tick mark for growing up with modest means.

Tara jotted a few notes on the inside of the folder,
then closed it. Time to move. She took her time
strolling back to the shop so she could soak in the
city. Music from buskers filled the air. A German
shepherd lay near an older man who was working a
puppet. Tourists huddled in groups in front of their
guides. Shops, restaurants, and pubs swelled with
customers. Cigarette smoke and laughter mingled in
the air. A common refrain around here was "Mind
your liver." Galway was a city of temptations. Speaking of temptations, she wished she had ordered the
apple tart. Maybe on the way home. She had just returned to her shop, took the pups out for a quick
break, and was just about to google Clifden Castle
when a knock sounded at her garden doors. Tara
whirled around to see Breanna Cunningham's round
face smiling in at her, hoisting two bags of crisps. Tara
returned the smile. Hound's big drooling face
popped up behind her. Like Breanna, he was a little
addict for potato chips. Tara was just about to look
for Savage when she spotted him tucked into Breanna's arm.

"Come in," Tara called.

Breanna swung open the door and danced in like
the Pied Piper. Savage was gazing at her like the dog
was in love. "Why didn't ya tell me what a gorgeous

little ting she is?" She was a clerk at the Garda Station in Galway and was becoming someone Tara could really call a friend. Her optimism was infectious and she was rarely in a bad mood. "Love your posting on Insta," she added.

"What?"

"Killer brooch? I want to see it." She set Savage down and held up the bags of crisps and jiggled them like they were bribes.

"Oh, that," Tara said. "It wasn't mine. It left with an heiress, and apparently I couldn't afford it even if I robbed all of Galway city."

Breanna snorted, a sound which always made Tara laugh. "My, my, my, you do have the life," Breanna said with a sigh.

"You're never going to believe this."

"Try me," Breanna said, leaning on the counter. "I'll believe most anything."

"The heiress—her name is Veronica O'Farrell—is sober and in AA—"

Breanna held up her hand and turned her face away as if she didn't even want to look at Tara. "I don't tink you're supposed to be telling me that, now."

Tara laughed, hoping Breanna was just teasing. "Only mentioning it because *she* did. It's the reason she's here. To make amends, and her sponsor—this is the part where you need to listen." Breanna was holding Savage up to her face; they were nose-to-nose. "Breanna?"

"Sorry, luv, she's just like a spoonful of medicine." Breanna kissed the pug on the head, then put her down. "Go on, so."

"Nancy Halligan was Veronica O'Farrell's sponsor.

Veronica is the reason Nancy was visiting Connemara in the first place."

Breanna opened and closed her mouth several times. "You're joking me."

"It's wild. Right?" Tara was starting to worry it was more than wild. But she couldn't bring herself to say it out loud. Was it a stretch to think the flyer, and finding Nancy's body, were orchestrated? If Nancy's death was ruled a heart attack, or a natural cause, then how could anything be orchestrated? It would mean that someone else came across Nancy's body and instead of reporting it, decided to leave a flyer on Tara's door, hoping she would make the trip and eventually find the body. Okay . . . that was totally ridiculous. She was so glad she didn't say that out loud. Was it a wild coincidence? Yes. But that's all it was.

But what about the book? *Places to See in Ireland Before You Die.* Getting it a week after she found Nancy. It wasn't sitting well with Tara. "What are the chances?" Breanna shrugged. "No. I'm really asking. What are the chances?"

"County Galway isn't exactly a tiny village, but we're still pretty small comparatively. And it happened, so I'm not sure what you're getting at." Breanna studied her. "What are you getting at?"

"She must have seen the same flyer," Tara said. "I just find it odd."

"Flyer?"

"The stone house for sale." Maybe Tara should stop into Heather Milton's realty shop. Heather had rented Tara this space. Tara could ask about the stone house, find out who had the listing.

Hound whined, reminding Breanna that yes, he would like another crisp. Savage went back to her spot near the fireplace and curled up into a ball.

Tara gazed at her. "The vet said she's healthy but all she does is sleep."

"She?"

"The pug."

"Right, so," Breanna said. "When I was a kid I thought all dogs were boys and all cats were girls." She threw her head back and spread her infectious laugh across the room once more.

"Don't let Hound have any more crisps," Tara said, just as one hovered above his big tongue. He snapped it up and gave her a *Take that* look before mooning at Breanna again.

"Mammy said no more," she said to Hound with a shrug.

"I'm not his mammy," Tara said. "I'm his human."

"I'm supposed to be on a diet meself, but I was kicked out of the overeaters group."

"What?" Tara said. "Why?"

"Because I'm honest, dat's why. The so-called leader of the group asked everyone what was their trigger food, like, what did they really crave, and I couldn't pick just one. I told her I loved it all. The breads, and crisps, and salty, and sweet, and chocolates, and apple tarts. She said—'Apple! Next time you're in SuperValu just imagine that you're craving an apple.' And I said—'Are you joking me? Who in their right mind craves an apple, like?' And the rest of the group agreed with me, I tink dat's what put her off. When I said there was no fecking way I could imagine meself craving an apple, she booted me out the door, so she did."

Apple tarts. Tara really should have ordered one. With ice cream. "I hear you."

Breanna crossed her arms and squinted, giving Tara the impression that a lecture was coming. "How is it you eat just as much as I do and you're just a stick of a thing, and I eat that and it goes straight to me arse?"

Tara laughed. "Your guess is as good as mine. I think I worry so much it burns off any extra calories."

"Black hair, blue eyes, and that figure," Breanna said, shaking her head. "It's not fair at all, like." She opened the chips and dug in, then tossed another to Hound.

"You can take him with you to the station," Tara said. "Let him fumigate you instead of me."

Breanna laughed. "Speaking of eating, should we go have a pint?" If Breanna was off at lunchtime, they often took sack lunches to the grassy area near the Spanish Arch, and stared at the river or made up the lives of the tourists passing by. If she was off at dinnertime, they'd find a pub and sit in the back and imagine the lives and secrets of the tourists and locals alike. In New York, most of Tara's outings had been business related. They'd talk swatches, not secrets. Tara was grateful to have Breanna in her life.

"I'll be honest. It's been a full day. I'm looking forward to bed." Tara's head was also full of the job she'd just accepted from Veronica. Amends gifts. She was itching to pick up where she left off. Veronica's folder of snarky notes. It was a little like reading a diary. Maybe she was just thrilled to be immersed in someone else's drama for a change. Waiting for her business permit was driving her mental. This would be a good distraction.

Breanna sidled over and noticed the top sheet from the folder.

"What's this?"

"The heiress dropped it." Tara ran her finger down the list. "Perhaps on purpose. I think these are the people she's hired me to find amends gifts for."

"You didn't tell me she hired you."

"I did. Just now."

Breanna tilted her head. "What's she the heiress of?"

Tara felt like such an idiot. "I didn't think to ask. I'll have to google her later."

Breanna whipped out her phone and tapped on the keyboard. "Sheep farming. Wool products."

"Really?" Tara had imagined something a little more glamorous. She'd bet money that Veronica had never shorn a sheep in her life. The image of Veronica, holding a shearer whilst standing in a ball gown over fluffy sheep, materialized in front of Tara.

Breanna was still staring at the folder. "Clifden Castle."

"Have you heard of it?"

" Course I have. It's a ruined manor house in Connemara. We used to go to Clifden when I was little. It's gorgeous." She gestured to Tara's laptop. "May I?"

"Have at it."

Breanna typed, then turned the screen in Tara's direction. On it were the remains of a gorgeous stone castle, set in the middle of a rolling green field, bursting with towers and turrets, so common in Gothic Revival, complete with a grand entryway marked by a family crest. Tara had yet to get over the jaw-dropping beauty of this land her mother had been lucky enough to call home. "What year was this built?"

Breanna squinted at the screen. "In 1818. John D'Arcy."

"Tell me more."

Breanna laughed and scanned the page. "He built up the town, lived in the castle with his family, died, left it to his son, and the son mismanaged it."

"Typical."

"Then the famine hit."

"Oh." Not so typical. "Awful."

Breanna nodded. "Then owner after owner, scandal after scandal, blah blah blah." Breanna was not one for history. "Until it became the property of the Clifden Cooperative, aka the farmers who owned the land around it. They sued a man who tried to buy it, claiming it was their land. They won. Since then the castle has been stripped of everything, including the roof, and it fell to ruins." Breanna looked up and grinned. "And the tourists keep coming."

"I don't blame them." Tara sighed. She would have loved to be in on a salvage like that. "It's still gorgeous."

"'Tis." Tara snapped a photo of the castle on the screen and added it to her social media postings with #StormTheCastle. Breanna's phone dinged, and she immediately brought up the posting. "I'll be the first to like ya."

"Thank you." Tara gestured to the travel book on her mantel. "Someone left this in my shop."

Breanna barely gave it a glance. "Brilliant."

"Kind of weird, don't you think?"

"How so?"

"I don't know who left it or how they got in. And . . ." She gestured to the title. "*Places to See in Ireland Before You Die.* Don't you find that a bit morbid?"

Breanna shrugged as her eyes swept the shop. "Did they take anything or just leave ya something?"

"I think they just left the book."

"You'd be laughed out of the station if you come in to report dat."

"I realize. It's just . . ." *I don't like all of these coincidences.*

"There are loads of places I want to see before I die, but not just in Ireland." Breanna put a finger to her lips. "Maybe I should write a book. *Things to Eat Before You Die* and you can bet there won't be a single page dedicated to fecking apples!"

She did it again, brightened the room with her rowdy humor. Tara packed up her laptop and belongings, and set to closing the shop. She eyed the book. She had to call Danny and find out if he left the flyer or the book. Then all of her worry would be for nothing. "I wonder if this is from a local bookshop?" Galway had at least five bookshops. It would be easy enough to visit them all. Tara began to thumb through it. She came to Connemara and, sure enough, Clifden Castle was listed. She showed it to Breanna.

"It's fate. You should go."

"Do you want to come?"

Breanna shook her head. "You see one ruined castle in a field full of cows and sheep, you've seen them all." She winked. "I would, but I'm on duty all week."

Tara laughed. "Got it." They headed out the door with the dogs in tow, and Tara made sure to check all the locks. The French doors had been finicky in the past and she meant to find sturdier locks. Had someone picked them and that's how they left the book on her counter? *Paranoia. Not your friend.* Still. It wouldn't hurt to improve the locks.

Before they parted, Tara had one more question for Breanna. She didn't like to use her connection with Breanna for information, but she was dying of curiosity. "Speaking of Nancy Halligan?" She let the rest dangle.

Breanna shook her head. "I shouldn't be talking out of school."

"I normally wouldn't ask but . . ."

"I know. You were there."

"Exactly."

"The state pathologist has declared the official cause of death a heat stroke. She had also taken sleeping pills, which were prescribed to her, but nothing close to an overdose."

"Sleeping pills? During the day? And what about her things?"

Breanna held her hand up. "The body is being released to the family. Right now the theory is that someone found her before you did and robbed her things off her."

"Evil."

"Isn't it? I wish the donkeys could talk."

"I don't like it. Why would she take sleeping pills during the day?"

"I don't know. To be honest with ya, I don't think they can tell exactly when she took the sleeping pills. I'm not a toxicology expert. Maybe she didn't sleep the night before; maybe she wanted to nap during the day."

"She was on a hike," Tara said. *Or an excursion. Or something.* She wasn't in bed.

Breanna shrugged. "Maybe she forgot she'd taken them or thought she was taking headache tablets, or maybe she started to feel ill that moment and took the wrong tablets. I'd only be guessing."

"How can they close the case with so many unanswered questions?"

"I think her family was adamant that they wanted to move on. They're already on their way back to Dublin with her remains. Cremated." Breanna shuddered and crossed herself.

"Cremated? Already?" Most Irish probably preferred traditional burials. Tara wanted to be cremated and have her ashes spread somewhere beautiful. But that kind of talk upset Breanna, so she kept it to herself.

Breanna nodded. "Probably the best choice. Considering she wasn't found right away." Breanna crossed herself again. Tara nodded. See? She was being paranoid. She and Nancy did not show up at the old stone house at the same time. Although if they had, maybe a quick call to 999 could have saved her. Sometimes a flyer was just a flyer, and Curly or Moe could have left that book in the shop. The lads were finished doing work for her, but she needed to find them and ask them if someone came in with the book while they were there. Hopefully Uncle Johnny would know how to get ahold of them. *This too shall pass.* She waved goodbye as Breanna ambled off in the opposite direction, and talked to her mam in her head as she and the pups ventured back to the mill, feasting her eyes on all the people streaming by in either direction—a pop of color, and noise, and life being lived. She stopped along the way to lose herself in the river, and then the bay; she stopped to watch fishermen haul in their boats; she stopped to watch a trio of Irish dancers make tourists clap; she stopped to delight in the angry red streaks cutting across the Irish sky; and if she stopped and asked a college kid to watch her pups for a quick second so she could pop in for apple tarts, it was a secret she planned on taking to the grave.

Chapter 6

The rectangular stone building with massive wooden doors was shrouded in the dark. Tara hadn't realized how late it was. The red sign reading IRISH RE-VIVALS was barely visible. Next to the mill, the small creek with a turning wheel gurgled. Tara found the sound comforting. She entered and locked the doors behind her, then headed directly up the staircase to her loft on the second floor. Uncle Johnny had a cottage nearby, and he and Rose switched between living in it and her caravan, depending on the weather. Tara had lived in that same cottage when she first arrived, but had now moved to the loft in the mill. She loved her dwellings. It was an open-concept floor-plan with concrete floors, brick walls, and a timber ceiling. Fifteen hundred square feet of freedom. The kitchen was done to the nines, gourmet style. The kitchen island was sourced with marble from the quarry in Connemara, white with streaks of their signature green. She vowed she was going to start cooking, and a stack of cookbooks backed her up on that, but the takeaway containers in the rubbish bin doubted her.

She wouldn't be able to touch an apartment like this in Manhattan, or any of the boroughs for that matter. She'd furnished it with many of the items from the mill, including a green woven rug from Donegal. Sometimes at night she stood just outside her loft, where a hallway overlooked the warehouse. She'd gaze at the objects below, and imagine where they came from, who had touched and loved them, what their lives might have been like. Tonight, she had other things to occupy her, so she kicked off her shoes, poured a finger of whiskey, and plopped onto her sleek yet soft sectional.

She reached into the bag at her feet and retrieved Veronica's folder, then dug out her design book, tape, and markers. She turned to the next page in the folder:

EDDIE O'FARRELL

She had seen this photo before—Eddie O'Farrell was Eddie Oh. The one with the tweed cap that he'd swiped off the head of Veronica's previous driver. Who was Eddie Oh to Veronica? Ex-husband? Had Veronica mentioned that? Tara couldn't remember. Her visit was a whirlwind. A second photo of a bride and groom kissing confirmed it. Eddie Oh was Veronica's ex-husband. No wonder she was trying to push his work on Tara. Her eyes fell to the notes.

Eddie is my second ex-husband.

Interesting. *Second* . . . still talking up the ex . . .

A brilliant artist. He hasn't created lately and I am de-termined to change that. I want to find a venue to throw him an exclusive art opening complete with publicity, and celebrities. See me on this one.

In the shop Veronica had said that Eddie Oh was taking the art world by storm. But that had been a lie. *He hasn't created lately . . .*

Veronica was certainly slippery with the truth.

Tara wondered how recent Eddie's photo was. He looked a good twenty years younger than Veronica. Not that there was anything wrong with that. How long had it been since he created a piece of art? Was Veronica still in love with him? She taped Eddie's sheet to her design book, jotted down a few notes, and moved on.

CASSIDY HUGHES

The photo accompanying this name was of a young blonde posing in front of a mansion, dressed to the nines. She was stunning.

My niece by marriage. Piece of work. Doesn't matter what you buy for her. I'm only trying to keep peace in the family. If you ask me, she's the one who should be apologizing. Anything designer will do. Personally, I'm sending her to rehab. Wish me luck.

Interesting. Sending her to rehab? Was that for real or sarcasm? Was Veronica jealous of the young beauty? What should this Cassidy be apologizing for? She did look a bit like a diva, and once again Tara reminded herself to keep an open mind. Her job was to find unique items for these guests. She reached the last name:

IONA KELLY

The photo was of a woman on a hike. She was tan, early forties, with short red hair. Athletic, no makeup.

I accidentally bumped into this woman years ago on a photo shoot. Literally. I knocked her over. She claimed to suffer an injury from the fall. I've been paying her medical bills. I've had it. I think she's faking it, and while at Ballynahinch Castle I will be keeping a very close eye on her. Buy her something hiking-related to throw her off. I can't have her suspecting she's being watched.

Tara realized her mouth was hanging open. What kind of amends were these? She quickly googled Ballynahinch Castle. It was a four-star hotel in Connemara. Very fancy. That must be where Veronica and her guests were staying. Had she invited the last guest as a ploy to spy on Iona Kelly? Maybe Tara didn't want to be a part of this after all. She closed the folder and her design book, finished her whiskey, then laid her head back, vowing she would get up soon to brush her teeth and get on her pajamas.

A jarring melody jabbed through her head. She opened her eyes as the tune rang through the air, made hollow by the concrete floors. She'd fallen asleep. She flailed to grab her cell phone dancing across the coffee table. PRIVATE CALLER. Probably a wrong number. A drunk. In New York it could have been a booty call. Here, she'd been too busy to court that kind of trouble. Unless you counted Danny O'Donnell, and not only was he away, but when he called his name came up as DANNY BOY, along with the theme song. Hardly anyone had her Irish cell phone number, and those that did wouldn't call from a blocked number. She sunk back into the sofa and let it ring.

With the morning came a stiff neck and a self-admonition for not making it into her pajamas or bed. Burning the candles at both ends, her mam would have said. She hit the shower and thought about making a green juice in her new blender, but put coffee on instead. She wished she had one of those ginormous blueberry scones to go with it. Once her coffee was ready, she poured it in a travel mug and headed out for her early morning walk with Hound and Savage. She loved the quiet of the city before it woke, the gentle lapping of the Galway Bay, boats bobbing at the shore. She picked up the pace until she was out of breath and broke a sweat. The dogs easily kept up. It wasn't until she returned, showered and dressed, fed the pups, and was looking for her phone that she remembered the strange call in the middle of the night. No wonder she was so tired. She lifted her cell off the coffee table and was surprised to find the caller had left a message. She put it on speaker and pushed play. A woman's distraught voice rang out.

"They're all liars! All of them! I'm going to expose them all!" Tara frowned, staring at the phone as if it were a person. The voice was somewhat familiar, but through the woman's hysteria it was hard to place. She played it again. Was it a wrong number? It was as she was going out the door that she recognized the voice. It was the heiress from yesterday. Veronica O'Farrell. Why had she called Tara? How had she gotten her number?

Tara's new business cards. They'd been sitting on the counter. Veronica must have snatched one when she wasn't looking. As she headed outside, she pushed the number and listened to it ring. There was a click as if someone had picked up.

"Hello? Hello?" Another click and a dial tone filled her ear. She tried once more, and it went straight to voicemail. She didn't leave a message. Perhaps Veronica had been drinking? And now was too embarrassed or hung over to admit it. She certainly sounded hysterical, and drink would explain it. She felt a squeeze of pity for the woman. It couldn't be easy to fall off the wagon.

Tara had just opened the door to her flat to go down to the mill when someone pounded on the main front door. She could see the wooden door jostling with each pound. It was too early for treasure hunters, although she'd quickly come to learn that treasure hunters didn't abide by the rules. She jogged down the rest of the steps. The massive wooden door didn't have a peephole. "Hello?" It did, however, have plenty of cracks, so she knew whoever was standing out there would be able to hear her.

"Tara? It's Breanna."

"Breanna." Tara started to undo the locks. Why had she sounded so formal—and something else. She sounded afraid. Tara was already tense by the time she worked the old door open. Breanna stood before her flanked by guards, one of whom was Sergeant Gable. They'd met when Tara first came to town, and discovered a man's body in her uncle's cottage.

"Hey," Breanna said, trying to sound casual.

"Hey," Tara replied.

"Hello, Miss Meehan," Detective Sergeant Gable said. A sense of dread flooded her. Was it Danny? Uncle Johnny? Nancy Halligan?

"Detective." Tara nodded. "What's wrong?"

Gable stepped up. "This is voluntary, but I'd like you to accompany me to a crime scene in Connemara."

That was the last thing she expected to hear. "Nancy Halligan?"

"No."

"A crime scene?" Tara's eyes flicked to Breanna, and if she wasn't mistaken she saw an apology in them. Or was it worry?

"Remember the woman you described in your shop the other day?" Breanna said. "The one with the brooch?"

Veronica's hysterical voice rose in her mind. *They're all liars! I'm going to expose them all!* "Yes. Veronica O'Farrell."

"We have a body out at Clifden Castle," Sergeant Gable said. "We'd like to know if it's the woman you encountered."

"Veronica?" Tara stared, dumbfounded. "Clifden Castle?" She looked at Breanna, hoping it was a joke. "Are you serious?"

Gable nodded. "As a heart attack." He cleared his throat as if just realizing the comment wasn't quite appropriate for the situation. "It's a bit unorthodox, but she's not a local, and the sooner we get an identification the better."

"I can't believe this." She lifted her phone. "She called me."

Gable stood at full attention. "When?"

"In the middle of the night." She held up her phone, which seemed to nearly always be in her hand these days, and opened her voicemail. "Just after midnight."

"What did she want?"

"I didn't pick up. I had no idea it was her calling."
She put the message on speaker and pushed play.
They all listened as Veronica wailed that they were all
liars and she was going to expose them all.

"What does that mean?" Gable frowned.

"I don't know. She sounds drunk. And she was one
year sober. I saw her sobriety chip." Tara gasped. "I
hate to say this—but I hope it wasn't because I broke
the news to her about Nancy Halligan's death."

"I heard about that," Sergeant Gable said. "That's
quite a strange coincidence."

"I hope it's not more than that," Tara said. She
glanced at Breanna.

"I've told him all about your concerns," Breanna
said. "The flyer, the book, and Veronica's visit. I'm sorry
I didn't take it seriously before. If I did, maybe . . ."

"Nonsense," Tara said. "None of us could have
known about Veronica." She hesitated. "You said
crime scene. Are you sure this isn't an accident or an
overdose?"

Gable nodded. "Veronica O'Farrell was murdered.
I think you should see for yourself."

That didn't make sense. Tara wasn't a guard.
"Why me?"

"Because you're our quickest link to identifying
her."

"Okay." Was that the only reason? "She was here to
make amends. I have her guest list."

"I'm going to want that as well, like," Gable said.

Tara swallowed and nodded. She had a million
questions, not to mention a million things to do, and
she didn't relish the prospect of visiting a crime
scene, but Sergeant Gable deemed it necessary and
she wasn't going to argue. "I'll grab Veronica's list

and my things." She called Uncle Johnny and woke him up. His grumpy demeanor faded as she filled him in on what was happening and he said he'd be at the mill to take care of the dogs. Tara picked up Veronica's list. She hadn't mentioned her design book to Gable. She didn't want to give it up. Would the list be enough for him? What about Veronica's additional notes? Why didn't Tara mention them? Darn it. She couldn't keep it from him. She had to turn over everything. But was there any harm in taking photos of every page so she could recreate it? Wouldn't it be a nice gesture to Veronica's memory to complete the job? All but spying on Iona Kelly, that is. As she snapped photos, thoughts jumped out at her:

Stole the love of her life

Some people aren't meant to be parents

A piece of work

Hasn't created

Accused her of stealing

Injured, might be faking it

This was no longer just an amends list. And everyone seemed to have a motive. These people thought they were coming here to accept a grand apology, and now it was looking like they were all going to be suspects in a murder inquiry.

Chapter 7

❧❦❧

Clifden Castle was a few miles outside of downtown Clifden, known as the capital of Connemara. This time, Tara's mood did not lift with the rising hills. She was finding it impossible to believe that the vivacious tornado of a woman who whirled into her shop the other day was gone. Just like that. Before Tara knew it, Sergeant Gable was parking in a car park across from a stone gateway, built in medieval style by the D'Arcy family with an arch and a tower. Blue-and-white guard tape was strung across the entry, and Gable lifted it, allowing them to duck under. "It's a bit of a rocky walk, and there's some muck from the rain," the detective said, glancing at Tara's hiking boots with approval. "Technically we could drive it, but I want us to take the walk. There were no fresh tracks from vehicles, so we believe our victim and her killer arrived on foot."

"All the way from Ballynahinch Castle?" Tara

asked. They'd passed the Ballynahinch Castle on their drive here; the fancy hotel was about twenty minutes away by car.

"Not necessarily. Although none of the cars in the car park belonged to her. Her driver said he was not aware she had left Ballynahinch Castle. We're assuming she got a ride here. But visitors are not allowed to drive up to the Clifden Castle."

"I don't know how anyone could," Tara said as she looked down at the narrow path, covered in rocks.

"The farmers manage to drive the path, given they own it. We could have brought a vehicle that could make the drive, and we probably will once we secure the scene. But for now, everyone is banned from driving it, including our farmers."

Tara wondered how long they had to walk before they reached the castle; she saw nothing but pastures. The path rose up a small hill and curved around. There, on a fencepost, was a white poster board, with CAST written on one line, LE beneath it, with a crude arrow. She was starting to wonder just what to expect of this castle, with such a crude sign, when she glanced across the dipping pasture, first gasping at the Clifden Bay in the distance, and then spotting the castle nestled into a valley below. Even from here, it was an impressive building, a proper castle, like something out of a fairy tale. The hill started downward, and a pair of standing stones loomed ahead of her, one on each side of the path, at least ten feet tall. Tara read that the D'Arcy family had the stones placed on the property. *Ancient gate markers.* They were incredibly cool, and Tara had to tamp down her excitement; they were not here to be wowed.

The dirt path turned to stones, and then mud as

they reached the final hill up to the castle. Once they plodded through, Detective Sergeant Gable pointed to a mat on the ground. More crime scene tape was blocking off the perimeter of the castle. Tara wiped her boots on the mat, and Gable handed her booties and gloves. The sun was out, but the temperature was in the low sixties. "It's stunning," Tara said. She meant every word of it.

Gable nodded and pointed to the bay. "That's Clifden Bay. They built the castle facing south in order to take advantage of the view."

"I don't blame them." The water sparkled in front of them. Tara could imagine herself standing in one of the castle's multiple towers, gazing out at the bay. There was a round tower, a square one, and an entry tower with a pair of turrets. It was truly stunning, even in its ruined state. It was impossible to take it in without imagining the people who used to live there, wondering what kind of lives they led. The people who lived here had been through turbulent times, there was no doubt. She read there was a graveyard to the North near the road for three of the Eyre children who died in the 1880s. There was something so haunting about deaths so young. It was right up there with murder.

Gable pointed to the field beyond the castle. "To the west is a farmyard with the remains of an old grain store, workers' cottages, stable, and cottages."

"My word." Tara wanted to see every inch of it.

"Unfortunately, you won't be seeing them today."

"I understand." She did. They were not here to sight see. She wished she had made this trek earlier.

Gable looked at her intently.

"Are you sure you can handle this?"

Tara swallowed, put on her booties and gloves, and nodded. He gave her a quick pat on the shoulder. "Don't touch anything, and follow behind me." He passed the front of the castle, walking along the side, heading directly to the back.

Tara found herself wishing she could peek in the doorways and openings they were passing, but was once again mindful they were not here on a sightseeing expedition. Along with its roof, the castle had long ago lost its floor and ceiling. Grass sprouted through pieces of old stone. They entered what looked like a courtyard in the back. The structure framed an L-shape around it with a main entrance straight ahead and smaller rooms laid out on the right. The detective pointed to the right. There, in a space just large enough for a twin bed and night table, with a tree growing into the stone wall, lay a woman's body. *Veronica's body.* She was on her back. Tara closed her eyes for a moment and took a deep breath before opening them again. She made herself look.

Veronica O'Farrell had a presence, even in death. She was in a navy tracksuit, perhaps out for an early stroll. *Just like Nancy Halligan.* Tracksuits were the popular outfit for power walks among Irish women. But what were the chances of this? First Nancy Halligan discovered lying in the grass in a tracksuit, and now Veronica O'Farrell? But there was a marked difference between this body and Nancy's, and Tara was having a hard time believing what she was seeing. Stones had been placed over her eyes, and mouth, and heart.

Red stones over her eyes, a green stone over her mouth, and a black stone on her heart.

"They're pieces of marble," Gable said quietly. Tara's hand flew to her mouth.

Sticking out of her heart, just next to the black marble, was something metal. Blood pooled around it. Tara inched forward and peered down. It was the Tara Brooch. And someone had plunged it into her heart. Tara stood, then fled to the middle of the courtyard. She stared at the grass, then the sky, trying to breathe. Sergeant Gable gave her a few minutes.

"Are you ready for a few questions?"

"Yes."

"Did you see stones on Nancy Halligan?"

"No. Nor was there a Tara Brooch stuck in her heart."

Gable nodded. "We think someone snuck up behind her and plunged it into her. Then staged the body."

"You mentioned Nancy. Do you think her death was also . . . murder?"

"We intended to re-examine her body. But she's already been cremated."

"Who requested the cremation?"

"We're checking on that now. Also waiting to speak with the state pathologist. Hopefully her records of the body before cremation are thorough." He took out a notebook. "I need you to take me through every detail of finding Nancy Halligan."

Tara took a deep breath and nodded. She began her story, starting from finding the flyer and making the drive to the house. She tried to remember everything. "I didn't see any other cars around. Only a small rowboat."

"Was anyone in it?"

"No. And it was down the hill."

She glanced at Veronica's body again, and said a silent prayer. She turned to Gable. "Isn't this the jurisdiction of the Clifden Guards?"

"We're joining forces on this one. I have more experience with murder inquiries."

"I can't believe this." Tara pointed to the stones. "Why did they do that?"

"A calling card. Or maybe a message. We're dealing with something strange, alright."

"She didn't deserve this."

"For the record. Is this the woman who came into your shop?" Gable's voice had softened; he could see she was distressed.

She nodded. "And that." She pointed to the brooch. "The Tara Brooch. She showed it to me. She suggested I try it on and take a picture of it. She said it fell off all the time." *She didn't just suggest it. She urged you to try it on and take a picture. And like an eager idiot, you did.* No wonder Gable brought her here. He wanted to see her reaction for himself. She was a suspect. Her fingerprints were on the murder weapon. How could this be happening? He didn't really think she was a killer, did he? Had she passed his test?

Gable jotted down a few notes, then turned to leave. "Come on." He hurried her out of the interior, and it wasn't until they were back in front of the ruined manor house that she realized she was shaking.

"The stones," she said. "Have you ever seen anything like that?"

He shook his head. "As I stated, they're pieces of marble. Possibly from the Connemara Marble Visitor Centre."

"Did Veronica have anything to do with marble?"

"We're very early in the investigation."

"Of course."

"As I said. I believe it's a message. Any ideas?"

"Me?" A nibble of worry turned into little bites. "Why would I have any ideas?"

He turned the screen of his smartphone to her. She was looking at the photo of herself holding the murder weapon with a big grin on her face. #Killer-Brooch.

Idiot, idiot, idiot.

Detective Gable swiped to the next screen on his phone. The photo of the manor house. #StormThe-Castle. Her hand flew up to her mouth once as she shook her head. Posting pictures of the murder weapon and the crime scene before the murder. It looked bad. Really, really bad. Even she could see that. Did the killer get the idea from her postings? The thought was a horrific one. "Veronica handed me the brooch. Actually, it slipped off her scarf and when I picked it up she said to try it on." Her mouth was dry. She swallowed. "That's when she told me how it slipped off all the time. She wanted me to take a picture with it on. For Nancy, she said. I guess Nancy loved the brooch. I don't know what else to tell you."

"Why don't you tell me again how it is that you discovered Nancy Halligan's body?"

Again? She'd already told him, and so had Breanna, but she knew this was part of his method. To see if Tara's story would change. "Someone left a flyer on the door to my shop. It was for the old stone farmhouse. It's up for sale."

"Are you in the market for an old stone farmhouse?"

"Who isn't," Tara blurted out.

"You're going to have to be more specific."

"I'm not actively in the market. But as part of my new position, I am interested in older homes. I thought Danny O'Donnell left me the flyer."

"Are you involved with Danny O'Donnell?"

Involved? That was kind of personal, wasn't it? You could say involved, couldn't you? She was aware that Danny might answer the question very differently. Did she really need to tell this detective that they were on-and-off lovers? If it were up to her they'd be more on than off. She'd love to see Gable posing this question to Danny O'Donnell. "It's complicated. He works for my uncle. But we've gone out socially. Yes." *And he hasn't called since he's been away.* Solve that mystery for me, Detective. She felt guilty for worrying about her petty problems at this moment and brought her mind back to focus. "He's been encouraging me to see new places. I haven't spoken with him to confirm it. I'm no longer sure it's him who left the flyer. I think it's the same person who left the book."

"The book?"

"It's back at my shop. I showed Breanna. I think it's better you see it for yourself."

"And how did Veronica come to be in your shop?"

"She said she saw an article written about me in the paper. She identified with the name of my shop. Renewals."

At least that's what she said. Could Veronica have known that Tara found Nancy's body? Was that the *real* reason Veronica came into her shop? Was she only pretending to be shocked by the news of Nancy's death? After all, she was having Iona Kelly watched.

What if she was doing the same to Tara? Did Veronica think Nancy's death was suspicious and Tara had something to do with it? It seemed outrageous, but Tara really didn't know what to think anymore.

"The list of guests I turned over have notes from Veronica. One woman—Iona Kelly—Veronica was suspicious of." Guilt thudded through her again. Was she actually tossing out names from Veronica's list in order to defend herself?

"Suspicious how?"

Tara filled him in on what she knew. Gable took notes. "I'll check it out. Anything else?"

"Her butler was with her. Bartley. I don't know if he's really a butler, but he was definitely in her employ somehow. She said he had a law degree. And her driver. Andy."

"We've spoken with him briefly. He said he was supposed to drive Veronica to the castle for a meeting here at half nine. He claims he has no idea why she was here early or how she arrived."

Tara made note of the word *claims*. She assumed it would be relatively easy to check whether or not the vehicle Andy was driving Veronica in left the hotel early that morning or not. But it wasn't her job to do his job, and she certainly didn't want to antagonize a guard, so she kept that to herself. "Her ex-husband is one of the guests as well. Eddie O'Farrell. He's an artist. At first I thought he was the reason why she came to my shop—to try and get me to carry his sculptures—" She was talking a mile a minute, hoping to convince him that she was being roped into this somehow. "You need to talk to Bartley, and Andy, and the seven people on that list. They're all involved." *Stop talking, Tara. What are you doing?*

"Involved in what exactly?"

There was that word again. *Involved.* It was starting to sound like a horrible word. "I don't know anything more than what I've already told you. But what if Veronica knew Nancy Halligan was dead? Maybe she was investigating. Everything else—hiring me—the artist portfolio—it could have been a ruse to question me."

"You think she suspected you of killing Nancy Halligan?"

"I think—like you—she wondered how I found the body. I don't know. I'm just trying to figure this out."

Gable ran his hand through his stubble. "Did Ms. O'Farrell mention anything else?"

"She talked mostly about the amends she was here to make. She said a lot of things."

"Did she mention any other locations?"

"Locations?" He seemed to know something and be driving toward it; she had no idea what. "You need to speak with Bartley. He is a big man who was dressed in black, carrying a satchel." Her hands were sweating. She *felt* like a criminal. She could suddenly understand how innocent people confessed. This was a panicky, squeezing feeling, and she wasn't even being railroaded or mistreated, but just the thought was churning up dreadful feelings. "I just can't believe it." Gable had taken her phone as well because of the voicemail. The call had come in just past midnight. "She was calling them all liars. Said she was going to expose them all. Something terrible must have happened after she left my shop yesterday." Had someone been listening when she made that rambling call? Did they take the threat personally?

"We'll certainly be looking into everything," Sergeant Gable said.

Tara pointed toward the crime scene. "It can't be a coincidence. Two older women lying dead in their tracksuits?"

Gable gestured to the exit. "Let's get you home."

Home. She barely knew where that was now. This had thrown her off-kilter. They were silent on the walk back to the car, which was a long way to be silent. She wished she had come here first as a tourist so she could simply marvel at the castle out in the middle of a pasture. With giant oval boulders marking the entry. The past so tantalizingly close, yet so far away. When they reached the car park, Breanna was standing off to the side with what appeared to be a forensic team. Breanna mainly handled clerical aspects at the Garda Station, and she was now organizing for this probe. That was good for her, a promotion of sorts. But it would mean there would be a distance between them until this case was solved. At least the body wouldn't be left there too long. Tara tried to make eye contact, but Breanna did not lift her head in her direction. It wasn't personal. She had a job to do. Tara hated how much she wanted her phone back in this moment. She had so many calls to make for her opening, but how could she be thinking about that now? Two women were dead. At least one murdered, maybe both, and she was freaking out about a phone?

Tara knew it was how the mind worked, how it was always trying to protect itself from this kind of horror, and it didn't make her a bad person. It was self-preservation. She had nothing to do with either death, and there was no need to feel guilty on top of frightened, and incredibly sad. Yes, the woman had been like a tornado, swirling into her shop. But Tara also liked her. Formidable, but a definite character. Trying to make amends. Unless she was lying . . .

She followed Gable to the car, her mind and stomach churning. He chatted away on the drive home about everyday things, and even though she knew he was doing it to calm her nerves, it barely penetrated the surface. The green fields, and cows, and sheep, and mountains, and water, all framed the background. How could evil things be happening with such savage beauty all around them? "Savage." She said it out loud.

"What?" Gable was on alert.

"Nancy's pug."

"What about it?"

"I don't know. If someone took her handbag, and phone—why not the pug?"

Gable nodded. "Maybe it ran away." *Yes. She hid. Somewhere in the old stone house. If Nancy Halligan was lured out there, and left in a vulnerable state to die, the pug knew who did it.* "Even if something untoward happened to Ms. Halligan, it's not like the pug is going to be tattling," Gable added.

"Is it too late to find fingerprints on her collar?"

"With you and everyone else passing around the wee ting? Yes, I'd say it's definitely too late."

Tara nodded. Poor thing. If only she could talk. What happened that morning? Why was someone after two older women in sobriety? "Maybe Savage bit or scratched someone."

"If we ever have a suspect with bites or scratches, I'll keep dat in mind."

She should keep her mouth shut. He didn't want help on the case. He wanted to eliminate her as a suspect. She needed to rein it in. It wasn't until the detective pulled up to the mill that she reminded him about the book.

"I'll wait here while you fetch it."

"Sorry. It's at my shop."

It took only minutes for him to drive there and double park in front of Renewals. Soon they were standing in her shop by the fireplace with Gable leafing through *Places to See in Ireland Before You Die.* "You think this has something to do with Ms. O'Farrell?"

"The timing is strange. I didn't leave the book here. Minutes later she arrives on—you asked about places—maybe there is a connection."

"You have no idea who left this?"

"None. When Veronica saw it—she commented on it—so I don't think it was her."

"What kind of comment?"

"Morbid." Tara shivered. "She said it was morbid."

"Who could have left it?"

Tara shook her head. "I've only had delivery people and . . ." *The lads who hung her chandelier.*

"And?"

She didn't want to drag them into this. "There were two young men who hung my chandelier."

"I'd like their names."

"Curly and Moe." Gable put his hands on his hips and gave her a withering look. *Shoot.* She held her hands up. "It's not me. That's what they told me. Uncle Johnny recommended them."

"I'll give Johnny a bell," Gable said. "Ask who the sarcastic lads were that he recommended to hang your chandelier." The description fit every Irishman Tara had ever met. "Was anyone else in the shop?"

"I've had deliveries. I can't attest to every single

one." Tara's reputation, having risen a little since the article was published, would probably slide again once word got out that the victim had visited her shop shortly before she was killed. Not to mention Tara's posting a picture of the murder weapon. Oh God. And the crime scene. How could any of this be happening? She was supposed to be opening her shop, basking in the joy. *Posed with marbles.* She shivered as she remembered Rose's warning. A bad vibe. A strange visitor. Indeed. Why didn't she listen to Rose? She should have closed the shop for the day.

It could have been Andy. Or Bartley. Were they trying to frame her? Was she marked as an easy scapegoat? *Stop it.* She didn't want anyone accusing her based on circumstantial evidence and she vowed not to do the same to anyone else. Veronica mentioned that the pin slipped off easily. She'd witnessed it herself. Maybe they could trace Veronica's steps after she left the shop. The murderer must have found it. It seemed highly unlikely Veronica would have pinned it to a tracksuit. Not something that precious. And what of the book? Could it be a coincidence? A book was a book. That's all. A book of lovely places to see in Ireland. *Before you die.*

"If this book is part of this—then doesn't that suggest this had been planned far in advance?"

Gable cocked an eyebrow, raked his eyes over the book, and went on to survey her shop without commenting. "Do you have a camera? Security systems?"

"They're being installed this week."

"A little late."

"I had no way of foreseeing any of this."

"Of course." He continued to stare at her. "Did you leave your flat at all last night?"

"No."

"Good. That's good."

"You're saying I'm a suspect."

"I'm afraid that's how an investigation works. I know the mill has a security camera, so if you don't mind we'll check those, and the coordinates of your mobile phone, and I'm sure we'll clear you in due time."

In due time. Which meant at her grand opening she would be a murder suspect. "If there's anything I can do, please let me know."

"When you talk about this . . ."

"I won't."

He shook his head with a sad smile. "When you talk about this, do not mention the marble pieces."

"Of course." It was information that only the killer and the guards knew. Unless . . .

"May I ask who discovered the body?"

"A young couple. Out for a morning stroll." From the tone of his voice she felt there was more to the story, but that was all he was offering. At least the body had been discovered quickly. Every second was of the essence. "Don't leave town," he said with a half smile and a tug on his garda cap.

Chapter 8

Tara had been forbidden to mention the marble stones to anyone, but that didn't mean she couldn't do a little research. There was no way she'd be able to focus on the shop now. She had been at a mobile shop first thing this morning and replaced her phone. It was charging. At least that was a bit of work squared away. She dug out a new design book, and was suddenly grateful for the cloud; her pictures would be stored on her laptop. It also meant if the guards went through her photos they would know she took pictures of Veronica's folder before turning it over—but she could explain how she thought it might be nice to continue Veronica's mission of finding gifts for her guests.

She bought coffee and a blueberry scone as big as her head, then settled back into the shop with her laptop and design book. She'd have to find a place to print out the photos of the guests, but for now she made pages for all of them and transferred Veronica's notes. Not as satisfying as her original book, but at least it was something. She turned back to her laptop and googled *Connemara marble.* Before she knew it she was lost in the history of Connemara and its two marble quarries. The oldest, Streamstown Marble Quarry, opened in 1822 and was located in Letternoosh, Clifden. The site went on to say that Stone Age men had worked the quarry some four thousand years ago, extracting marble for axes. How she'd love to see an item like that, but to do so she'd have to go to the National Museum of Ireland. She tucked it away for a future adventure.

The second quarry was the Cregg Marble Quarry in Letterfrack. This was the quarry that sourced white marble with a vein of light green. The same as her kitchen island. A surprising connection leapt out at her as she read through the history. It said the founder, Richard Martin, who also founded the Society for the Prevention of Cruelty to Animals, had placed marble from his quarry in his home—Ballynahinch Castle—with every second stone white and green.

Ballynahinch Castle. It was in Veronica's notes. She read further. *Baile na hinse.* "Household of the island." What strange connections. Marble. Ballynahinch. The four-star hotel Tara found mentioned in Veronica's notes. She assumed it's where Veronica and her guests were staying. Veronica didn't seem like the type to lose herself in history and pick a hotel based on those strange connections, but then again, Tara could hardly claim to know the woman. What she did know was that someone deliberately placed marble stones over Veronica's eyes, and mouth, and heart. The quarries were not open to the public, so where did the marble stones come from?

She quickly found the website for the Connemara marble factory. At the Connemara Marble Visitor Centre gift shop, they sold black marble, Irish jade—which was very rare—and red marble. The visitor center and shop sold mostly jewelry and smaller stones. The green marble was the rarest form in the world. Red was the color you would associate with a heart. The killer gave her a black one and red eyes. Hungover? Green for the mouth. A jealous mouth? Or were the stones meant to throw them off?

The killer had decorated her. Tara knew a thing or two about decorating. Designing. Staging. In some odd way, this killer was speaking Tara's language. But what was the message?

Tara turned once again to posts about Bally-nahinch Castle, the four-star luxury hotel. She recognized the grounds from the photo of Sheila and John Murphy as well as Mimi Griffin. They'd been taken recently, at their lodgings.

Realizing she wasn't going to solve the riddle of the stones this morning, Tara busied herself in the shop the rest of the afternoon. She took care of a wall that needed to be patched and painted, dusted and shined the counters, and made a call to confirm the caterers for the grand opening. If her permit did not come through, she would lose out on her deposit. *Keep the faith.* For lunch, she grabbed her now-charged mobile phone and dashed to the pub next door. She treated herself to their glorious seafood chowder, with a healthy slice of brown bread slathered with butter, and after the morning she'd had, a Guinness. Heavenly. She had just stepped onto the streets and was heading back to the shop when her new phone rang. "Hello?"

"How ya?"

A buoyancy filled her as Danny O'Donnell's low voice came across the line. He wasn't dependable. His moods changed like the weather. One minute she was convinced he was in love with her, and the next he would disappear for days on end. But right now, his voice was like a life raft in the ocean, and she was happy to cling to it. "You wouldn't believe me if I told you."

"You discovered another dead body." As Tara's mouth gaped open, Danny began to laugh. It came to an abrupt stop. "I was joking ya."

"The joke is on you."

"You can't be serious."

"A woman died from heatstroke near the old stone house for sale in Clifden."

"What old stone house for sale?"

Darn. Tara had hoped Danny would confess he'd put the flyer on her door. It would have made things so much easier. And less sinister. "It's a long story."

"Give me the short version for now."

"That's where I found the first body."

"Don't tell me there's a second, or I'm hanging up on ya."

"Her name is Veronica O'Farrell. She's an heiress. Who hired me. And was murdered the next day. I didn't discover the body. Sergeant Gable drove me out to it. Because she came to my shop the day before." Tara let it all come out in a rush.

Silence filled the phone. Then. "Jaysus. I'm coming home. I'll be at the mill by six."

It took longer than she wanted to get ready for Danny because she wanted to look effortlessly good, which Tara decided took much longer than looking blatantly good. She wore a navy shirt that made her black hair shine and sky-blue eyes pop. She applied a bit more mascara than usual and a touch of gloss. Jeans were all she usually wore, but she picked her most flattering pair, and topped it off with her black leather shoes that had a bit of a heel. But instead of the romantic hello she'd been expecting, her view of the scruffy, handsome Irishman who sent her heart pattering and pulse beating was countered by Uncle Johnny lumbering in behind him.

"What's this about another body?" Johnny scratched his mountainous beard.

"We might as well get comfortable," Tara said. She felt the heat of someone's gaze and looked up to see Danny watching her. She blushed, and mentally high-fived herself for choosing the navy top. If only they had a bit of time alone, but that would have to wait. She grabbed a cup of coffee for herself as Johnny held up a bottle of Powers whiskey and they convened in the middle of the expansive warehouse where Tara had used some of the antique furniture to set up a makeshift living room. At first Johnny had grumbled about it, but not only was it popular with customers, he was a frequent visitor as well. As he poured himself a round, Tara filled them in on the happenings.

"Veronica O'Farrell," Danny said, thumbing through his mobile phone.

"Have you heard of her?" Tara directed the question to both of them.

Johnny shook his head. "An heiress," he said, as if their luck had finally changed. "My kind of customer."

"Here she is," Danny said. He turned his phone to show a glamour shot of Veronica. She was standing in front of a mansion in a red ball gown. She may have died too soon, but she certainly seemed to live it up while she was here, and Tara was somewhat comforted by that. Then again, it seemed a portion of Veronica's life had been spent in an alcoholic blur. Yin and yang, light and dark to every life.

"That's her."

"What was the family fortune in?" Johnny asked.

"Sheep farming," Danny said. "Then wool products. Jumpers, scarves, blankets. Looks like her late husband was wealthy as well."

Terrance Hughes. The first husband. Tara hadn't looked into him yet. "She said she'd arranged an all-expense-paid holiday for her guests, then one of them did this."

"In Clifden?" Johnny asked.

"She just said Connemara, but I think they're staying at the Ballynahinch Castle."

Danny got to his feet. "Who's up for a drive through Connemara?"

"Us? Now?" Part of Tara had been hoping she and Danny could catch up. But he was right, she'd never be able to concentrate on anything but this case.

"Not now," Johnny said. "First thing in the morning. That's when the fly-fishing will start, and it's a perfect excuse for us to be nosing around."

"Don't you have to be a guest to do that?" Tara asked.

Johnny shrugged. "You have to *pretend* to be a guest to do it."

Danny grinned. "Who would begrudge a couple of Irishmen fly-fishing on a Sunday?"

Tara frowned. "I'm surprised you two want to nose around. I thought you'd try and talk me out of it."

Johnny waved her off. "Gable was sniffing around asking for camera footage. That means you're a suspect. If you have a bead on suspects, and you're going to nose around anyway—"

"Which we both know you will," Danny interjected.

"—then we're going with you," Uncle Johnny finished.

"Perfect," Tara said. "Uncle Johnny, I need another favor."

"What's the story?"

"I need you to speak with the lads you hired to hang my chandelier. Curly and Moe."

Uncle Johnny chuckled. "Did they mess up?"

"I think they let someone into my shop. Either that or one of them left a book."

He arched an eyebrow. "A book?"

"*Places to See in Ireland Before You Die.*"

"I'll track them down."

"Thank you."

Uncle Johnny and Danny exchanged a look. They were now fully engaged in protector mode. She felt a lump in her throat. These men. Uncle Johnny was family. Danny was—well—whatever he was. More than a friend. Less than a partner. They'd figure it out eventually. But right now, they had her back. It meant something. She bit her cheek so she wouldn't cry. "First thing in the morning."

"Off to see me Rose," Uncle Johnny said with a salute.

Danny stood, and Tara waited to see if he would propose dinner, or a drink, or a walk. "How was your trip?"

He nodded. "I made out alright. There was an old chapel that had some beautiful sconces, iron gates, the like. I'll be loading them in this week."

"Should we unload now?"

He shook his head. "A few lads are going to do it in the morning."

She thought of her empty refrigerator. She'd been too busy to think about shopping, or cooking. "Should we grab a bite to eat?"

He hesitated. "I'd like that." He reached for her hand and held it for a moment. A spark zipped through her. He dropped her hand. "But if we're heading off in the morning, I'd better get a few things sorted."

Like what? She knew so little about his life. She'd never even been to his place. What kind of relationship was this? "No worries."

His gaze traveled up and down her. "You look nice."

"Thanks." Her heart thudded in her chest. "You too."

He winked, and was gone.

* * *

The drive to Ballynahinch Castle was just as stunning as the first time Tara had driven through Connemara, especially with the gorgeous sunrise they'd witnessed, but their minds were elsewhere.

"Imagine, she puts you up at a fancy castle and you murder her," Danny said with a shake of his head.

Tara stared at him. "So if she put them up at a rundown motel?"

He thought it through then laughed. "Right, so. Dat's a fair point, now. I guess neither is a justification for murder. But to go all out, like, and have that happen to you." He shook his head. Tara shivered, thinking of how Veronica had been laid out. *Decorated.* He had no idea. She'd kept her promise to Sergeant Gable; she wouldn't breathe a word of the marble stones.

The entrance to Ballynahinch Castle was just ahead. Tara's nerves danced as they pulled up the long drive. Lush trees and hedges abounded, promising something spectacular at the end. Tara had googled the four-star castle and couldn't wait to see it for herself. Seven hundred luxurious acres. Woods, a river, and walking paths, topped off by the Twelve Bens mountains. It had its own salmon fishery and walled garden where vegetables were grown and used by the renowned chefs. They drove so long Tara was wondering if there really was a castle, but at last it loomed ahead. The three-story country house was stunning. A stately and magnificent structure that was, at the same time, cozy and welcoming. Set in the middle of all the gorgeous scenery of Connemara in one unforgettable setting. *Paradise.* They weren't even out of the vehicle and Tara never wanted to leave. At the edge of the castle, the Ballynahinch River shimmered. Danny whistled.

"We're here for fly-fishing," Danny said as they parked. "You do . . . whatever it is you do . . ."

"I'm here to scope out the castle for a future event," Tara said, hoping the declaration sounded believable.

"Have at it." Johnny gave her a look. "Just don't book any future events."

Luxury described every nook and cranny of the grounds. Manicured pastures, a river, woods, water fountains, and lush flowers abounded. She could only imagine the money and man-hours it took to keep it looking this fantastic. Veronica had obviously gone to great expense for this get-together. And one of the guests had betrayed her.

Breanna had informed her that the guests were all told to stay in town for the next few days, and further instructed to remain on the grounds today until they could all be interviewed. It was a pleasantly cool day, and so far there was no sign of rain or punishing heat. Tara scoped out an outdoor patio that was both shaded if the sun deemed it worthy to peek out, (or one needed shelter from the rain), but open to the elements. And the bar and restaurant were close at hand, so it was the perfect spot to stake out ground and run into some of their suspects.

It didn't take long for a waiter to arrive, and she was suddenly hungry. Tara ordered a cappuccino, eggs and toast, and made herself comfy at a bistro table in the middle of the patio.

It took an hour before she saw a young couple dart out and huddle at the edge of the patio. It was easy to recognize them from the photo Veronica supplied. Sheila and John Murphy. Tara was sitting too far away from them to hear their conversation, but from their bowed heads and the cigarette smoke pluming above them, she got the feeling it was anything but relaxed. As a New Yorker, Tara wasn't the type to intrude on other people. New Yorkers went out of their way to avoid contact, losing themselves in the daily throng of strangers. This time she had no choice but to intrude. Someone had dragged her into this drama, someone had already murdered two women, and she would feel less safe if she sat around doing nothing. She removed the postcard for her grand opening from her purse, plastered a smile on her face, and approached the couple.

"Where do you tink she stashed it?" she heard Sheila wail. John caught a glimpse of Tara and whispered something into his wife's ear. Sheila's head whipped around and soon the pair of them were peering at Tara.

"Sorry to bother you," Tara chirped when she drew closer. "If you're in the area for a while, you might want to come into Galway city and enjoy my shop." Tara held out a business card as they gaped at her. She didn't blame them. Galway city wasn't exactly next door.

"We're leaving as soon as possible," John Murphy said.

"No, thank you," Sheila said, turning her back. Her brunette hair was longer than in the pictures, down past her shoulder blades, and wavy.

"Worth a shot," Tara said, slipping the calling card back into her purse. "I need to do something to keep my spirits up after that poor woman's death."

"Wait," Sheila said, her brown eyes back on Tara. "Did you know her?" She had such a wholesome look, the pretty girl next door. But anxiety seeped out of her. That was natural, of course; murder had a way of spooking everyone.

But something else occurred to Tara. Sergeant Gable said that a young couple found the body. Was is Sheila and John? If so, they also knew about the marble stones. That would explain the stress etched into Sheila's face. Had they kept it to themselves, or did everyone know by now?

Tara turned. "As a matter of fact, she came into my shop the day before."

Sheila gasped, and threw a look to her husband, whose jaw clenched.

"May I see?" John held his hand out for a business card. Tara handed it to him and gave him a moment to look it over, while she looked him over. He had the good looks that often accompanied youth, and from his muscular arms she suspected he was at the gym at least six days a week. His hair was cropped closely to his head, a buzz cut. He was handsome, but she'd yet to see him smile, so there was a rough edge to him that Tara found off-putting. In her notes Veronica had said something about him being controlling. *Some people just aren't meant to be parents.* Was Veronica talking about him, imagining he would be too strict? Because Sheila, despite her anxiety, seemed like a sweet woman. Then again, maybe her anxiety was like a constant dark cloud over her head. Regardless, it really wasn't Veronica's place to decide who should have children.

"That makes you one of the last people to see her alive," Sheila said, interrupting Tara's thoughts.

"Really?" Tara said. "I gathered all of you saw her here Friday night?"

The pair looked away immediately, gazing in opposite directions. "We went to bed early," Sheila finally said. "So we could get up for our morning walk."

Morning walk. "Oh? Where did you walk?"

John lifted his dark eyes and stared past Tara. "We found her." His voice choked up.

"It was awful," Sheila added.

"That's terrible." Tara pulled out an empty chair and sat. She gestured for them to join her. Sheila sat first, and then John with a sigh.

Sheila folded her arms across her chest. "I just want the image to go away."

Did she mean the stones covering Veronica's face or something else? "Was it just a coincidence?"

John cocked his eyebrow. "Coincidence?"

"That you found the body?"

"What else would it be?" He was extremely defensive.

"Sorry. But something made Veronica go to Clifden Castle that early in the morning. Then something made the two of you go as well. Just wondering. What was that something?"

John folded his arms across his chest. "We were all supposed to meet at the castle grounds at half nine."

"Why is that?"

John's eyes narrowed as he considered Tara.

"She wanted a group photo," Sheila piped in. "And supposedly since she's been sober she's a 'morning person.'" Sheila used air quotes and rolled her eyes.

"But you were there early?" Tara wanted to keep asking questions while she had them talking.

"We decided it would be a great place to watch the sunrise," Sheila said.

"And by *we* she means *her*," John added, giving his wife a nudge. Tara was happy to see the moment of affection pass between them.

"We had no idea she'd be there," Sheila said. "Let alone . . ." She shook her head as if trying to dislodge the image of Veronica. "Who would do such a thing?"

"That's what we're all wondering," Tara said. "Do either of you have any theories?"

"Why would we?" John snapped.

Sheila rubbed his back. "Don't be such a porcupine, luv." She gave Tara a half smile. "It's been quite the morning." She looked over her shoulder, and then back. "As a matter of fact, I think it has to be someone in our group who killed her."

"Sheila," John said. From his tone, he didn't want his wife talking.

"When did you last see her alive?" Tara held her breath, hoping she wouldn't come across like she was a detective. John was coiled and ready to spring, but Sheila was itching to talk.

"I'm going to get another drink," he said, hoisting up an empty glass.

"This early?" Sheila could dish it out as well as her husband.

"The minute there's a murder, it's time to drink." He

walked away without asking either of them if they'd like one. Sheila watched him leave, then turned back to Tara.

"We last saw her alive Friday just before dinner."

"Minutes ago you claimed you didn't see her."

Sheila frowned. "We don't know you."

"True," Tara said.

"Do you want to hear the truth or not?" Her hackles were up.

"I do."

"She stormed past us in the lobby, red-faced and steaming."

"Was she alone?"

"That bodyguard of hers was lurking behind her, but otherwise she was alone."

"Bodyguard? Do you mean Bartley?"

Sheila scrunched her face. "The big bald yoke." *That would be Bartley.* "I tried to talk to her and I swear to God she hissed at me."

That made sense in light of the voicemail Tara had received. "Any idea why she was so angry?"

Sheila shook her head. "I'm just glad it wasn't us."

How can you be so sure? Tara simply nodded. "Do you think she'd been drinking?"

Sheila chewed on her bottom lip. "I suspected. But she's been sober for a year!"

"Relapse is part of recovery."

"Someone must have upset her terribly."

"You mentioned your group. Is there anyone in particular you suspect?"

"John's right," Sheila said, pushing back from the table. "Me mouth never stops running. I have no idea who killed her. From here on out, I vow not to gossip." She stood up.

Tara reluctantly stood too, as it became obvious that Sheila wanted her to go. "She told me she was making amends."

"Supposedly." Sheila folded her arms and looked away as if she was locking some kind of secret pain inside.

"Did she treat you badly in the past?"

Sheila snorted. "She evicted us at the lowest point in our lives." She looked at Tara. "Is it gossiping if I'm talking about myself?"

"No. It's sharing."

"Sharing with a complete stranger. I do need to get a grip." She gave a pained smile. They hadn't mentioned the marble stones to Tara. Did that mean they'd kept the secret?

"Of course. I didn't mean to pry." *Darn.* Tara reminded herself it was none of her business. She wished there was an easy way to bring up the comment she'd overheard—*I wonder where she stashed it.* Were they talking about Veronica? Stashed what? Sheila, without saying goodbye, headed off. Evicted at the lowest point in their lives. There was a story there. Question was—was it bad enough that they'd take matters into their own hands? Was it something that led to murder?

"Wait," Tara said, catching up with Sheila. She turned, and waited, impatience stamped across her face.

"How did you get to the castle?" It wasn't close enough to walk from Ballynahinch Castle. The drive up to the castle alone would be considered a hike. And Tara remembered Gable mentioning Andy. How he was waiting that morning to take Veronica to the castle, but she set out earlier and he had no idea how she got there.

"We drove."

"Oh."

"Why?"

"I heard there was a driver to take everyone places."

Sheila laughed. "Veronica has a driver. But John prefers to have autonomy. We drove here from Dublin." Did they drive Veronica to the castle that morning? Then kill her, and pretend to discover the body?

"Do most of the guests have their own car?"

Sheila frowned. "I know a few of them came by bus. But I couldn't really tell you. Why?"

"Just curious. I've only just learned to drive myself, so I guess it's always on my mind." Even though it was partly true, Tara realized how ridiculous it sounded, and now Sheila was peering at her as if she was trying to imprint her image for a later recall.

"I wouldn't go around asking too many questions," Sheila said. "The grounds are probably crawling with undercover guards." And with that she walked away.

Crawling with undercover guards. Sheila was definitely paranoid. Perhaps that's why they didn't spill much. Tara should have found a place to eavesdrop instead of approaching them. They'd been in a heated discussion when she approached. *Where do you think she stashed it*? Had they been talking about Veronica? What were they looking for? Did it have anything to do with her murder? Undercover or not, Tara had a feeling that the guards were not going to have an easy time with this group.

Chapter 9

Tara was walking around the front of the grounds, wondering if she could just plant herself in the lobby of the hotel without arousing suspicion, when a black SUV eased up the drive and parked to the side. Andy emerged as the valet hurried up to park it. His hat looked even more smooshed than it did the other day. Was he sleeping in the vehicle? Tara planted herself in his path, and at first he didn't even look up. "Hello."

He finally saw her. He frowned. "I know you." He was having trouble placing her.

"You came into my shop and used the restroom the other day."

He snapped his fingers. "Was that only yesterday?"

"I'm afraid so. Terrible, terrible news."

"How did you find out?" He removed a pack of cigarettes from his pocket, and stuck one in his mouth without lighting it.

She hesitated. She didn't want to go into her friendship with Breanna or any of the other reasons the guards thought of her when they discovered Veronica's body. She was here to get information, not give it. "It's kind of a long story."

Andy took off his hat and slapped it against his leg, then brought it up and tried plumping it up with his hands. "Aren't they all?"

"I would say so."

"It's a terrible, terrible shock." He took the cigarette out of his mouth. "I don't suppose you smoke?"

"No."

"I'll wait then." He stuck it back in the pack.

"Thank you." He was used to pleasing others. "Did you drive Ms. O'Farrell to the Clifden Castle that Friday morning?" Sergeant Gable had already told her that Andy had told him he did not. But Tara wanted to hear it for herself. People lied to the guards all the time, especially during murder investigations.

He looked up at her, bleary-eyed. "Me?"

"You are her driver."

"Right, right." He shook his head. "After we left your shop, we had a few more stops, then arrived here. She gave me the rest of the night off. I was supposed to drive her to the castle at nine in the mornin' sharp."

That gelled with what Sergeant Gable said, that they were all to meet at the grounds by half past nine. "Do you think she walked from here to the castle?"

"Not a chance. That's quite a walk, even if you are in it for the power."

"The power?"

He pumped his arms. "Power walking."

"Oh. Was she in the habit of power walking?" She was dressed in a track suit. Had he seen her that morning? Is that why he mentioned power walking? She hoped the guards hadn't allowed anyone else to see the body.

"I'm only messing. I don't know how she slipped past me. I was in the SUV early meself. With the newspaper and coffee. I was parked out front. But I suppose she could have slipped by me. She must have."

"Could another in the group have driven her?" *Sheila and John Murphy?*

"Anything is possible." He sighed. "I don't understand why she wouldn't have asked me. It's what I'm here for."

"Maybe she wanted you to have your rest."

"Not to be rude, but it never struck me she'd be concerned about such a ting."

He was right. She wouldn't. What had she been up to that she didn't want even her driver to know about? "Did you see any taxis pull in, or other cars go out?"

"No. But I wasn't always watching. I had me alarm set on my phone for eight. If she left before then I was probably snoozing in the SUV." He gestured toward the parking lot where a couple of valets were directing guests where to park. "You can ask them. They saw me."

Had Veronica asked the concierge to call her a taxi? Tara wondered if the front desk would be willing to speak with her. Probably not. Hopefully the guards were on it. "Remember the portfolio she brought me yesterday of the artist?"

"Eddie Oh?"

Tara nodded. "I didn't realize he's her ex-husband."

"I've heard the rumors. Never met the man meself."

This was news. "Isn't he here?"

"Never even bothered to show up. I'd say he'll regret it." He placed his cap back on his head. "I heard a few tongues wagging that they thought the two of them were rekindling their relationship. Looks like he'll be in for a shock." He started walking. "Unless he's the one who killed her," he said, lighting his cigarette as he walked away.

"Do you have any reason to think he did?" she called after him. He either didn't hear her, or ignored her.

Tara planted herself in the lobby, and wandered in and out of a few of the cozy sitting rooms adorned with fat leather sofas and crackling fires, but if any of the folks she encountered were Veronica's guests, she had no way of knowing. They'd all agreed to spend four hours here, and the time had passed. What had she been thinking? She wasn't a detective, and it had been awkward questioning Sheila and John, and even Andy. They didn't have to answer her questions. She needed to step away. The guards would find the murderer, and now that the client was deceased, and payment had never been exchanged, she could assume she was no longer going to be sourcing gifts for the guests. This had been a waste of time. She headed outside to wait for Danny and Uncle Johnny.

Danny and Johnny chattered about fly-fishing the entire drive back to Galway city. At least it hadn't been a waste for them. They didn't catch anything, yet still seemed to thoroughly enjoy themselves. Tara felt drained. Despite her decision to clear her mind of all this murder business, her mind kept circling back to it anyway. Veronica had risen early, and made her way to the castle without using her driver. What about Bartley? Where was he? She should have asked Andy. Bartley seemed to know everything Veronica did. An image of Veronica entering the ruins of the manor house materialized before Tara. Then what? Gable posited that her killer had snuck up from behind and plunged the brooch into her heart. Did he have evidence to support this? Did Veronica even know who her killer was? Or had someone entered with her? Someone she trusted. Had Veronica dropped the brooch at the hotel the night before? Or was she wearing the brooch that morning? On a track suit? Once again, Tara highly doubted it.

If Veronica had gone to Clifden Castle alone— how had someone gotten that close without Veronica turning around? Was she listening to music and had earbuds in? Veronica didn't look like the earbud type of woman. The guards would check all of this out, ask all the questions she was asking, and find the answers. She had a life and a shop to open. "You've been awfully quiet," Uncle Johnny said as they neared Galway city. "Did you learn anything useful?"

"I met a few of the guests," Tara said. "Including the young couple who found her. But they didn't say much."

"What's the end goal here?" Danny asked.

"There isn't one," Tara said. "I'm going to stay out of it."

"I think that's for the best," Uncle Johnny said.

"Agree," Danny chimed in. "But it was nice to do some fly-fishing." When Johnny pulled up to the mill, Danny immediately headed for his truck.

"You're not staying?" She hoped she didn't sound desperate.

"Can't," he said. "Things to do." He tossed the fishing poles in the cab of his truck.

"You didn't catch anything," she observed. It wasn't like he had fish to clean.

"You're a cruel woman, Miss America," he said, then drove off as she laughed.

She nearly collided with Uncle Johnny when she turned around. "What's the story with you and Romeo?"

She sighed. "I haven't a clue."

Johnny squinted. "Maybe Rose could read your cards."

She shivered. That was the last thing she needed. "Maybe." She headed up to the flat, where she crashed on the sofa and fell asleep in front of the telly.

Monday, she woke refreshed, and determined to get back into the groove. She walked along the bay with Hound and Savage, checked her mail (with fingers crossed) for her permit (nada), checked in on the store, sent a few emails, stopped into her favorite pub for lunch, and when that was done curled up on the patio of the salvage mill with a good book. She was in bed early and back at the shop first thing Tuesday morning. There was something comforting about settling into a routine. The shop would be good for her. As an interior designer she was used to being on the go, always entering someone else's home. It would be nice to have her own for a change. So why was she so antsy? That worried her. A shop was a commitment. Would she grow bored of it? Nonsense. She was antsy because they weren't open yet. Once the shop was filled with customers, it would be a different story.

She'd been there two hours when a rap came at her front door. She opened it to find a short, fifty-something round woman in a light blue pantsuit, a cream blouse, and matching blue heels. Her tight blond curls were pulled back in a clip that reminded Tara of ones she'd worn as a teenager. Her makeup had been liberally applied.

"I'm sorry, I'm not open for another week," Tara said as déjà vu washed over her.

The woman stuck out her hand. "I'm Mimi Griffin, personal assistant to Veronica O'Farrell." She blinked rapidly and squeezed Tara's hand hard before dropping it. "*Was* her personal assistant. Or still am. Even though she's no longer here." Her cheeks flushed pink.

"Yes. I'm so sorry." Now she recognized her. In the photo she'd been wearing a lavender suit. This was the assistant Veronica had accused of stealing. She seemed sweet. It was hard to picture this woman with sticky fingers.

"May I come in?" Mimi hoisted her cream-colored handbag and moved past Tara without waiting for the answer. She entered the space with an approving glance, then plunked her handbag down on the counter before diving into it and removing a notebook. "I know this may seem odd, but I worked as Veronica's assistant for over twenty-five years, a quarter of a century, don't you know, and now we're all supposed to wait around for the guards to question us, and I had prepared to work all week, and I just can't sit back with me feet propped up and a straw in me mouth when someone among us killed Ms. O'Farrell and dat's when I thought, you know what, I'm still being paid to work, and I'm going to work. Now." She opened her notebook, flipped past several filled pages, ran her finger down the last page. "Here. It says that Friday she was coming into your shop to see if she could book it for her amends, and she hired you to source items for her guests. Is that correct?"

Tara stared at her for a moment. She reminded Tara of herself, with all her notebooks and zest for work. "Yes. I'm assuming you spoke with her after?"

"I was her right arm." She offered a little smile.

"Would you like tea or coffee?" Tara asked. The shop didn't have a kitchen, but Tara had set up a small table for both a kettle and coffee. There were some little luxuries one could not live without.

"No, thank you." She gazed at the kettle.

"Please," Tara said. "Let me make you a cup."

"Just a small one, please." Tara switched the kettle on, and prepared a cup of tea. Then she pulled out a box of digestives as Mimi continued to chatter. *Digestives.* The most unappetizing name for cookies Tara had ever heard. One of those little cultural differences that made Tara smile. Sometimes they called them biscuits, which was slightly better. She arranged the cookies on a plate and set them on the counter. The only seats were on the back patio, but a cold wind was whipping through. If Mimi minded having her tea and cookies while standing, she gave no indication of it. "I'd like to say I knew Roni better than most. And I'd like you to continue the job she hired you for."

Tara had just poured the water into her cup and nearly scalded herself. "Pardon?"

"I'm in charge of the budget, so you don't have to worry about being paid. Have you decided on your fee?"

Tara set milk and sugar on the counter and gestured for Mimi to make up her tea. Tara sipped hers as she watched, then shoved a cookie into her mouth, mostly to give her time to answer. "I worked up a proposal." She hesitated. "It feels awkward to be billing Veronica's estate."

"Veronica would be thrilled you're going to finish the job." Mimi handed Tara a card. "Email me the invoice and I'll cut you a check straightaway."

This was it. Once Tara took that check, she'd be tied to this group until they left. She hesitated. The architectural salvage business was fickle. Starting your own business was a risk. Most small business owners needed enough to keep afloat for at least a year before seeing a profit. Tara couldn't afford to turn down this job. "I'll email it as soon as we're finished."

Mimi nodded, then held her cup of tea and saucer, took a sip, and set them back on the counter. "What were you doing at the castle on Saturday?"

The question took Tara by surprise and she started coughing. Mimi stepped up and pounded her on the back. She had strength in her round body. "Sorry," Tara finally said. "I guess I was just curious. I'd like to get to know the guests so I can pick out the right items."

"I think I have a solution. We have an open room at the Ballynahinch Castle. It was supposed to be for Veronica's sponsor but she never showed up. If she had—maybe Veronica would still be alive."

"Oh?" Tara stepped forward. Did Mimi know that Nancy Halligan was dead? "Why do you say that?"

Mimi blinked. "I don't know. I guess it sounds silly. But something set Veronica off Friday evening, and my guess is that it had something to do with that woman not showing up."

It sounded as if Veronica did not tell anyone the news about Nancy's death. Why not? it also meant that Bartley and Andy followed her lead—or her order—not to mention it. Most people were compelled to share such news. Mimi claimed she was Veronica's right arm. There had to be something to this. "I am afraid I have bad news where Nancy Halligan is concerned. I assumed you knew."

Mimi began to blink rapidly. "Knew what?"

"She passed away about a week ago."

Mimi gasped. "How do you know?"

Tara had hoped she wouldn't ask. "It's an odd coincidence but . . . I found her. In Connemara last Saturday near the remains of an old stone house. The pathologist said she died of a heart attack brought on by the heat."

Mimi placed her hand on her heart. "That heat was deadly. I knew it. I can't believe it." She began to pace. "Do you think Roni heard the news? Was that why she was so upset Friday evening?"

"I'm afraid I was the one to break the news."

Mimi kept her hand over her heart. "And here I was thinking what a selfish woman Nancy Halligan was. How could I?"

"You didn't know." Tara moved closer. "You've mentioned several times how upset Veronica was on Friday. Can you tell me what you observed?"

Mimi packed her notebooks and turned to Tara. "I don't know yet if we will be reading her will, or her wishes—even I don't know what they are, I'm waiting to see what Bartley, her solicitor, has to say—but I thought it would be fitting if we still gathered here to receive her last words, and gifts to the chosen seven. How long will it take you to find the gifts?"

Had she not heard Tara's question, or was she avoiding it? "How long are you here?"

Mimi cast her gaze downward. "Seven days." She was clasping the handle of her handbag so tight Tara could see the tension in her knuckles.

Seven people, seven days. "I need at least a day or two to meet everyone, and then another two days to find the right items." There were several estate sales coming up that would be perfect, and she'd read that Clifden had an array of shops including an antique shop.

"Perfect," Mimi said. "We'll give out the amends gifts six days from now. And will you take Nancy's room?"

"Yes. I will take the room." Mimi was avoiding the question about Friday night. Tara was a stranger. She needed to get closer to all of the guests. Maybe then they'd talk to her. Besides, Ballynahinch Castle was something out of a dream. "But I'm afraid I won't be able to accommodate the shop for the amends, given that I'm waiting for a permit to officially open. I told Veronica all of this on Friday."

"I see. Veronica did not indicate to me that you

turned her down. That meant she still intended on getting her way."

"I suggested she use our larger salvage mill by the bay. Perhaps you would like to see it."

"I have the time," Mimi said, looking relieved to be moving on. "Shall we have a look now?"

Chapter 10

On the walk to the mill, they passed Andy snoozing in the car at the curb. Mimi snorted. "Veronica drove her previous driver to an early grave. Pun intended. This new one is always asleep at the wheel. But he's young. Veronica always likes her men young."

"Like Eddie O'Farrell?"

"How do you know about Eddie?"

"She brought me his portfolio."

Mimi made a tsk-tsk sound. "Heart of gold, dat woman. Always looking after strays."

Strays. That was a telling description of Eddie. Then again, *heart of gold* wasn't an accurate description of Veronica. "Wasn't she making amends because she *didn't* have a heart of gold?" *Didn't she accuse you of stealing the very brooch that was used to murder her?*

"That was in the past. She was a changed woman. 'Tis a pity she didn't live long enough to prove it."

Mimi took in the crowds as they crossed over toward the Spanish Arch, then made a right at the river to the promenade. "I must say I prefer Dublin," she said, holding her purse close as if a college student, street performer, or tourist were keen to snatch it away.

"I love it here, but I'm eager to explore more of Ireland," Tara said. It was true. Although now that she had decided to open her shop, she'd be doing less traveling than if she were sourcing items for the mill. They walked a bit before Tara directed the conversation back to the case. "Do you know everyone on Veronica's amends list?"

"Of course. I helped her put together the list. Although I tried to talk her out of putting me on it."

From the look on Mimi's face Tara guessed she didn't try very hard. Tara very much doubted that Mimi had seen Veronica's notes after each guest's name. "Do you have any idea who might have wanted to harm her?"

Mimi's face turned so red it was almost purple. "I don't have the faintest idea!" It came out as a yell, but soon was swallowed up by the noise of the city. Mimi picked up her pace, as if she was trying to outrun Tara's questions.

Tara was dying to ask Mimi about Veronica accusing her of stealing the Tara Brooch, and wasn't it ironic that it's what killed her in the end, but the guards hadn't released that information to the public. Then again, it wouldn't surprise Tara if John and Sheila had opened their mouths. Imagine, Mimi killing Veronica with the very brooch she was accused of stealing. That would definitely send a message. Just like the stones. They were key. Figuring out what the stones meant. Tara turned her attention back to details she could discuss. "Sheila Murphy said she saw Veronica on Friday afternoon—or early evening—and that Veronica seemed angry. Possibly even . . . drunk. Do you have any idea why that might be?"

Mimi came to an abrupt stop. "Drunk?"

"It's possible she relapsed."

Mimi blinked rapidly. For a moment, she looked like a robot whose wiring had suddenly malfunctioned. "I think people often misunderstood Veronica. She was probably just busy, or heaven forbid she didn't stop to listen to Sheila complain about her room again." Mimi took a deep breath and began walking again. Tara had to jog to catch up.

"Was something wrong with Sheila and John's room?"

"Absolutely nothing. Four-poster bed, a lounging sofa, windows overlooking the river and the mountains. They should be ashamed of themselves. Have you seen the rooms in that castle?"

"Not yet." But she was already imagining herself looking out at the river.

"Exquisite. But did that stop the Murphys from complaining? No." Mimi shook her head in disgust. "They've never seen a room so nice and they know it."

Tara tucked that tidbit away for later. "Then you're not aware that Veronica was upset on Friday evening?"

Mimi stopped again and fixed her eyes on Tara. "What are you doing?"

"Pardon?"

"You sound like a detective."

"I'm sorry. I know. I'm just horrified by what's happened. I guess I'm trying to figure it out."

Mimi took Tara's hands and squeezed them. Really, really, hard. "Put your energy into choosing the gifts."

"Of course." *One of the gifts might be for a killer.*

"Sheila and John Murphy are no experts on Veronica's moods."

"But you are?"

Mimi dropped Tara's hands as they started their journey again, then kept her gaze on the water. Tara was relieved when they finally reached the salvage mill. "I love it already," Mimi said as Tara opened the doors. "It's massive."

"Yes," Tara said. "And there's an intimate seating arrangement in the middle of the room, and a lovely patio out back." They were small touches, but Tara was proud of them nonetheless.

Mimi clasped her hands as a broad smile transformed her face. "This will be the perfect place for her little group to get together, listen to her amends, and pay their respects."

Tara couldn't agree more. She was dying to meet everyone in person. Especially after reading all of Veronica's cryptic little notes. Speaking of notes . . . Tara had a feeling a lot of the answers could be found in Mimi Griffin's notebooks. They seemed quite extensive. She wondered if there was any way to get a peek at them. Tara hoped to question her a little more after the tour. If anyone knew what Veronica's additional notes meant, it would be Mimi Griffin. If Danny could read her mind he'd probably accuse her of being addicted to the drama. He'd tease her. And then he would lecture her. And then he would start laughing again. He was irritating like that. But still somewhat adorable. For someone so irritating.

After the tour of the mill, where Mimi happily fondled the architectural wares, Mimi's mobile phone dinged. "The driver is here," she said. "At least this one is punctual." She said her goodbyes and headed to the front of the mill where the luxury SUV was waiting. Andy might snooze on his time off, but he was Johnny-on-the-spot when called. Even after Veronica was gone. Maybe he should have been on her amends list. You could tell a lot about a person from the way they treated employees. Veronica probably hadn't changed at all. And one of her guests knew it. Tara headed for the back patio, where she hoped she could clear her head.

She was nearly asleep in her patio chair when Danny O'Donnell appeared. "I'm off to Ballynahinch Castle," he said. "Johnny left a fishing rod behind."

Tara scrambled to her feet. Yes! Now that she'd been offered a room she was anxious to pack a bag and check in. "I'll join you. I just need to pop into my loft first and pack a bag."

"A bag?" He arched an eyebrow. "I'm just picking up a rod."

Did he think she was propositioning him? He should be so lucky. The worst bit is, he seemed poised to reject the phantom offer. "I've been offered a room at the castle. The job to source gifts for all the guests is still on." She'd already checked in with Uncle Johnny and he agreed to watch Hound. Breanna had already picked up Savage.

Danny shook his head with a wry smile. "I knew it. You want to be involved."

"I want to earn money. For myself, the shop, the mill."

"Can't argue with that."

"And since I have a room to relax in—might as well have dinner at the castle, don't you think?" She'd seen photos of the dining room, complete with a carving station and waiters pouring champagne as guests looked out at the jaw-dropping scenery.

Danny grinned, finally getting on board. "It would be rude not to."

Tara couldn't get over her room. It was just as Mimi described. Luxury. The view, the four-poster bed, the outdoor patio. The tiny bottles of shampoo, and conditioner, and lotion, and bath gel in the decadent bathroom were enough to make her swoon. Why did she have to be here under such sad circumstances? She wanted to lounge around all day in a bathrobe and read a good book, then go to dinner, then have a walk, then start the cycle all over again. It had been booked for Nancy Halligan, which made Tara feel guilty. What if Veronica had discovered something sinister or knew who might have harmed Nancy?

It was possible, but not plausible. There hadn't been much time. *They're all liars! I'm going to expose them all.* It sounded less as if it had to with Nancy and more like one of her guests was upsetting Veronica personally. Even so . . . the two women were linked. In life, and now in death. Tara could see why someone would have it out for Veronica—but why Nancy? Then again, Tara didn't know anything about her. She was going to have to do some research.

Once she finished soaking up the room, she planted herself in the lobby. The leather sofas and crackling fireplaces were growing on her. Danny was out there somewhere in search of his fishing rod. *Spare the rod, spoil the . . . fish?* Sometimes odd things crept into her mind to keep her entertained. But soon she didn't need it. A redheaded woman traipsed through the lobby with gear piled on her back. It only took a second for Tara to recognize her. Iona Kelly. The one Veronica had supposedly injured. The one Veronica had intended on spying on. On her heels, Mimi Griffin tried to keep pace, holding her notebook aloft.

"But you were gone all day and we're all supposed to be available for the guards," Mimi called as she struggled to keep up with the woman.

"I was on a day hike. I had me phone. Nature remedies everything. I'm hiking every day, if you want to join me." Mimi, who had a bit extra around the middle, blushed. Iona started walking again, and that's when Tara noticed the limp. She was favoring her right side. She was in shorts and hiking boots, and her left leg had a bandage around the knee. She looked in fantastic shape despite the injury. "We're having dinner tonight in the castle, as a group. Will you be joining us?"

Iona Kelly sighed, then shrugged. "I suppose."

"Two hours. Don't be late, Iona."

Two hours until dinner. They certainly were late diners. Would Tara be able to convince Danny to hang around for another two hours? And then what? Hide near their table and hope they heard something good? She watched as Iona disappeared down a hall. The castle did not have elevators, so it looked as if Iona had been given a room on the ground floor. Tara hesitated for a few seconds and then followed her.

Tara's heart pounded. Iona was at the end of the hall. She'd already spotted Tara. She was a terrible stalker. *Introduce yourself already before it's too late and you're officially a creeper.*

"Can I help you?" she called out as Tara was trying to figure out her next move. Tara smiled, hoping she looked completely innocent. "Are you Iona Kelly?"

"Guilty," Iona said.

Tara had no choice but to approach. Up close, Iona's pale face was friendly but guarded. "I've been dying to see the Connemara National Park. Is that where you went hiking?" Iona cocked her head. "Sorry. I overheard you speaking with Mimi Griffin."

"*You're* part of our group? An American?"

From her tone, that wasn't a good thing. "No. I met Veronica the other day. It's a long story. Such a terrible tragedy." Iona chewed on her lip. "I'm Tara Meehan." Iona nodded. She didn't offer anything else or expound on her day of hiking. Tara really did want to see the Connemara National Park. "It must be hard to hike with an injury." Tara held her breath. It could be considered a rude statement.

"You just have to know how to work with it," Iona said. "I took it easy." She put the key in her door and opened it. "What's the story?"

"Veronica came into my shop the day before she was murdered and hired me to find amends gifts for everyone on her list. Including you." Iona tossed her bag into the room, then turned as if waiting to hear more. "I work for a salvage company that sources architectural items."

"Is that what you're really doing here?" Iona released the gear from her back.

"No. I'm trying to find out who killed her." There was something about this woman that made Tara think that blunt honesty would be the best policy. Iona gestured for Tara to enter the room. She stood awkwardly inside as Iona brought her gear into the room and began turning on lights.

"Have you met everyone in the group?" Iona called out.

Tara ventured into the main room. It was lovely. A four-poster bed, a small seating area, and windows looking out at the mountains and river. The color palette was creams and grays with touches of gold. Tara would call the room Sophisticated Antique. Perfect for a castle. She would have loved decorating it herself. "I've only met a few of Veronica's guests so far."

Iona ran her hand through her hair. It was such a vibrant shade of red it was hard not to stare at it. "Do you think one of us killed her?"

"I think it's a good possibility."

"Me too." Iona sunk onto the bed.

"Anyone in particular?"

"Help yourself to the minibar, it's all on Veronica," Iona said. She stood and stretched. "I'm going to hop in the shower."

Tara thought she'd feel awkward partaking of someone else's minibar while they were in the shower, especially when it was being paid for by a dead woman, but a few sips into her sparkling water and she was feeling fine about it. A little something stronger was tempting, but just the fact that Veronica had arranged all of this as a celebration of being sober made her pause. Tara was grateful she could enjoy a few drinks without going overboard, but she could also leave them alone for a few days out of respect to Veronica's memory. Besides, it would help her keep a clear head, which was always a good idea when there was a killer in the mix. Maybe even in the shower . . .

Iona emerged dressed in sweatpants and a long woolly jumper, shaking her head out like a wet dog. Tara wanted to verify that she was still limping, but she didn't want to seem as if she was staring at her just out of the shower, so she wasn't able to tell. "There's nothing like a hot shower after a long hike." She headed for the minibar and mixed herself a drink, then plopped down across from Tara. "I met Veronica five years ago on a hike. I'm a member of TMHC."

"TMHC?"

"The Mountain Hikers Club. Or as we like to say— THC with a mountain." She stopped to laugh at her own joke.

"I can't picture Veronica O'Farrell on a hike."

Iona swung her leg, and grinned. "You're not wrong there. She was on a photo shoot three years ago. Us hikers got in the middle of it."

"Uh-oh."

"She was a holy terror when she was drinking." Iona shivered.

"She was drunk on a photo shoot?"

Iona laughed. "It would only have been a story if

she *wasn't* drunk on a photo shoot. You're lucky you didn't know her back then." Iona stopped the story, staring openly at Tara. "Where are you from?"

"New York City."

"All that concrete. I could never."

Tara believed her. The woman looked like she belonged in nature. "But I've relocated to Galway. My mother is from here."

"I'm a Dublin girl, but I love hiking all of Ireland."

Most of the guests, Veronica included, were from the Dublin area. Why had Veronica chosen Connemara for the reunion? Perhaps she'd simply wanted a change of scenery. Still, it was like a piece of thread dangling from a tapestry and Tara didn't like hanging threads. "I'm jealous."

"Jealous?" Iona swirled her drink as she waited for Tara to elaborate.

"I walk a lot. But I'd love to go on longer hikes."

"You should. You're in good shape."

"Thank you."

Iona clunked her drink on the table between them and leaned forward, her elbows planted on her thighs. "Listen. I forgave Veronica a long time ago. It was an accident."

"What happened?"

Iona raised an eyebrow. "I assumed you knew."

"No."

She sighed. "Just as Veronica's photo shoot was wrapping up, she passed me, and stumbled. I was standing too close to the edge. I rolled down the hill—which is actually a mountain."

"Awful."

Iona shrugged. "I knew how to roll with it. But I still busted up my knee. Too many large, sharp rocks on the way down. But Veronica manned up. She's been paying my rehab bills for the past three years. I didn't expect anything more."

If Iona had any suspicion that Veronica brought her here to spy on her, she was doing a good job hiding it. Tara wondered just how much these rehab bills had added up to. Was Iona faking it? Tara had to be careful; she didn't want to overstep. "How well do you know the other guests?"

Iona finished her drink, set it on the coffee table, then stared at it as if she missed it. "Are you asking me who I think killed her?"

"If you suspect someone, yes."

Iona nodded. "Have you met Cassidy Hughes?"

"No." But she'd read about her. The stunning young blonde.

"Veronica's niece."

Tara waited for Iona to say more. She did not. "Any particular reason why you suspect her?"

Iona inched closer to Tara. "This stays between us."

"Absolutely." *Maybe*.

"I saw her and Veronica arguing Friday evening."

Bingo. Friday evening. She had Tara's full attention now. "What did they say? Where were they?"

A knock on the door interrupted them. "Room service," Iona said, getting up to answer it. She opened the door and a young steward rolled in a gleaming silver cart covered with plates. Iona turned to Tara. "I'm sorry. I'd like to eat alone." The steward nodded, then left. "I meant you," Iona added when Tara didn't make a move for the door. Why had she clammed up so suddenly?

"I thought you were meeting them downstairs for dinner?"

Iona waved the question away. "I lied. I'm starving, and not in the mood to be around those people." She kept the door open and gestured for Tara to leave.

"I did want to hear about the argument." It wasn't in Tara's nature not to oblige with social cues, but she couldn't leave it hanging.

"Argument?"

Tara had the feeling that Iona regretted mentioning it. And now she was trying to take it back. "Between Veronica and her niece."

Iona shrugged. "I'm sure it was nothing. Family squabbles."

"I see." Tara had no choice but to leave. "Enjoy your dinner."

Iona closed the door in Tara's face. Despite the rude ending, it hadn't been a waste. One, she'd learned Veronica and Cassidy had been arguing Friday night. And two . . . Tara stood for a second, replaying Iona's walk to the door in her mind. Unless she was going crazy, when Iona answered the door for room service, there hadn't been a whiff of a limp.

Chapter 11

A wild-eyed man shoved his way past Tara as she emerged from the hall. His blazing eyes locked with hers. He saluted, then winked as he headed for a stairwell. The scent of whiskey lingered in the air even after he'd disappeared.

"Eddie Oh." Tara whipped around to see Danny standing behind her. He pointed. "That was Eddie Oh."

"Oh," Tara said, not intending the pun. "The ex-husband?"

"What?" He sounded bewildered and exasperated. "No. The *artist*."

"Oh."

"Would you stop saying that?"

"That was Veronica O'Farrell's ex-husband."

"You're joking me."

Tara shook her head. "The moment we met she shoved his portfolio at me." Danny just looked at her. "I take it you're a fan?"

"His sculptures are groundbreaking," Danny said, the excitement ringing through his voice. "Part innovation, part old-school recycling, part performance art." Tara had never seen the fanboy side of Danny and she wasn't sure she liked it. "I wonder which room he's in."

"From the looks and smell of him, he's been on a bender," Tara said.

"I believe he's only just found out about Veronica's death." Interesting. Danny was keen to defend Eddie. He also avoided the word *murder*. She didn't blame him. Murder was a horrible word. But that's what this was. She motioned for Danny to follow her outside. The evening was cooling off. The heat wave had passed and there were rumors of storms on the way.

"If he's just arrived," Tara said, "I wonder where he's been?" *Creating an alibi? Pretending he wasn't even here when she was murdered?*

"Most likely working. He's always working."

Tara shook her head. "Veronica said he hasn't created in years."

"Years?" Danny looked devastated.

"Where did you first see his art?"

"The annual art festival in Galway. People come from all over the world."

Tara knew all about the art festival and was looking forward to experiencing it. She filled Danny in on her run-in with Iona.

"Maimed for life because of Veronica," Danny mused. "I'd say that's a strong motive for murder."

"And if she's not maimed for life—because I'm pretty sure I saw her walk without a limp—then she's been milking Veronica for money."

"Pretty sure that isn't enough to call her out."

"I'm not about to call anyone out. I'm just say-ing—What if she's faking the injury and Veronica found out?"

Danny shifted, looking uncomfortable with the discussion. "Bad news if that's the case."

"Right? Veronica specifically said in writing that she had eyes on Iona." Tara began to pace. She wasn't going to call Iona out to her face, or in front of the other suspects, but she was going to have to say some-thing to Sergeant Gable. He wasn't going to like that she was involving herself with them. She was pretty sure she was in for a lecture. "Iona also told me that she heard Cassidy and Veronica arguing Friday night."

"Who's Cassidy?"

"Sorry. Veronica's niece." Tara hesitated, leaving out that she was a young, hot blonde. Danny was part hound dog, after all.

"You have inserted yourself pretty quickly, haven't you?"

"It's my job."

Danny didn't get a chance to reply; from behind them a high-pitched scream rang out. They whirled around. Mimi barreled past them. "He's here?" Mimi practically threw herself on the check-in desk, bel-lowing at the startled clerk sitting behind it. Tara and Danny edged in behind her. "Call his room and get Eddie Oh down here now." Tara didn't hear what the clerk responded. "I don't care! Tell him the castle is on fire and he'd better get his behind down here if he doesn't want to burn!"

"Drama," Danny said. Just then, Sheila and John Murphy entered. As the entrance doors flew open,

Tara caught a glimpse of Andy and Bartley standing by the SUV. Andy was smoking, Bartley was on his mobile phone, pacing as he talked. Tara wouldn't mind having a chat with Bartley. He had to know something about the events of Friday evening, not to mention how and why Veronica decided to go to Clifden Castle hours earlier than she had originally planned. But before she could make her way to them, a blond bombshell appeared in a red dress. *Cassidy Hughes*. Tara didn't have to look at Danny to know his mouth was hanging open. Cassidy Hughes took her time, and scanned the lobby, as if the twentysomething expected all eyes to be on her. And to be fair, they were. And to be honest, Tara really wished they weren't. She could only imagine how upstaged Veronica had felt by her femme fatale niece. *Green marble for jealousy?*

"There you are," Mimi said, hurrying toward the young woman.

"I told you I would be here," Cassidy said. "Have you called the funeral home? I want to see my aunt."

"The guards won't allow that yet," Tara said without thinking.

Cassidy Hughes slowly turned to Tara and she took a moment to rake her gaze over her, as if conducting an on-the-spot inspection. It was difficult to discern her eye color; her pupils were so big they looked black. The phrase *devil in the red dress* flashed through Tara's mind. "Who are you?"

Mimi grabbed the woman's arm and began hauling her off. "Never mind her. We need to talk. All of us."

Tara's hands clenched into fists at her side. Mimi was the one who insisted Tara continue with the job. The one who offered her the room at the castle. Now she was treating her like a nobody. Even Veronica had given her more respect. Something had wound Mimi Griffin into this state and Tara wanted to know what it was. She felt Danny's breath in her ear. "Making friends already."

Tara shoved Danny slightly in front of her. For once his hound-dogging might come in handy. "Find out what's going on."

"How am I supposed to do that?"

"Flirt."

He gave her a side-eye. Then looked across the room where Cassidy Hughes was posing, hair cascading down her back, hip jutted out, and extremely fake eyelashes that seemed to be doing the blinking for her. Danny grinned. "If I must."

Tara resisted the urge to kick him. She found a giant potted tree and edged behind it. Not that Cassidy was paying any attention to little old Tara. Did she think Tara was old? Twentysomethings definitely thought thirtysomethings were old. She moved a leaf away from her mouth, and focused.

It only took moments of Danny O'Donnell standing in front of Cassidy Hughes for the woman's laughter to peal across the lobby. Tara felt a stab of jealousy on multiple fronts. The obvious, of course, that the man who made her adrenaline fire anytime he gave her a lingering look, was now flirting with this gorgeous creature. But more so, Cassidy's genuine laughter within seconds of meeting him was a sudden reminder that she was an outsider. The Irish, she'd noted, laughed more than she did.

She'd experienced it time and time again when something someone said elicited a smile from her, but belly laughs from them. Tara wished she was the same. Was there something wrong with her? How could she be more like them? Even in the midst of a murder, there was mirth. And Danny O'Donnell took to flirting like a duck to water. And despite being the one who asked him to flirt, Tara was imagining tarring and feathering him.

"Cassidy Hughes," Danny said proudly when he returned from his assignment.

"I know her name," Tara said, hoping she didn't sound jealous but knowing she did. They were in the dining room, enjoying the dinner buffet, but all their suspects had dashed off somewhere secret.

"She's Veronica's niece," Danny continued. "But not by blood."

"Terrance Hughes," Tara said. "The first husband." She'd learned a thing or three from Mimi Griffin and Google. Terrance Hughes had been some kind of media mogul. He and Veronica had been quite the power couple.

"Correct." He hummed as he ate, which was both adorable and irritating. The full buffet and a carving station was a sight to behold: lamb, turkey, roast beef, ham, and potatoes made three ways to Sunday, wild salmon, presumably from the river they could see from the windows, and carrots and parsnips, and bacon and cabbage, and shepherd's pie, and seafood chowder, and potato and leek soup, and brown bread, and soda bread, and Tara hadn't even looked at the dessert table yet, but it seemed Danny had a sample of everything and was very much communing with his plate. Tara was so worked up she could barely eat her bacon and cabbage.

"Anything else?"

"I think she works in fashion. Or at least that's what her Instagram followers think." He took a second to look up. "I'm one of them now."

"One of what?" Tara snapped.

"Her followers." He hid his grin in his plate. He was definitely enjoying this. Tara wished she hadn't made that silent vow to not drink in honor of Veronica, because she really wanted a whiskey right now. And not a shot. Entire bottles. And if she finished them, she could clunk Danny over the head with the empties. Instead, she focused on their suspects.

Cassidy Hughes. Iona Kelly. Eddie Oh. Sheila and John Murphy. Mimi Griffin. Six of the seven Veronica had gathered. Tara thought over the list. There was one still missing. Elaine Burke. Lainey. The best friend. Veronica said she'd stolen the love of her life. Was she talking about her first husband, Terrance Hughes, the mogul? Did Veronica *steal* him away from Elaine Burke? Why hadn't Elaine arrived?

"Need me to flirt with anyone else?" Danny asked with a hopeful edge to his voice. "I'm happy to oblige."

The dining room was beginning to fill up, but there wasn't a hint of any of their suspects. Weren't they supposed to meet for dinner? Had their plans changed? Tara pulled out her cell phone as Danny left the table and returned with, of all things, an apple tart topped with a generous scoop of vanilla ice cream. Tara contemplated grabbing a spoon, but they hadn't reached the eating-off-each-other's-plates stage of their relationship yet. And from the way Danny ate, she had the feeling they never would. "Yes. Elaine Burke's room, please."

"You're calling the lobby of this hotel from the restaurant?" He raised his eyebrow as she lifted a finger to her lips.

"I see. Have you heard from her? Oh. Yes. I understand." She hung up. "They won't give me additional information."

"Shocker."

"But Elaine Burke hasn't shown up. I wonder if the guards are following up on that."

Danny jabbed a fork in her direction. "If a guard walked into your shop one day and suddenly decided to run it, would you let him?"

"What?"

"Answer the question." She eyed the last few bites of his apple tart. He did not offer her any.

"Why would a guard show up and want to run my shop?"

Danny pinned her with a look. "Now isn't that an excellent question?"

"Fine. I'm too involved. Is that what you're trying to say?"

"Look, I get it. This woman sweeps into your shop with compliments, and big plans, then suddenly her life is snuffed out. It's drama. And you thrive on it."

"I do not." She hesitated. "She *hired* me. And Mimi Griffin insisted I complete the job. This is business." Danny had part of it right. A woman's life had been snuffed out. It wasn't right. And like it or not, Tara had been dragged into this. She was simply trying to find her way out.

Danny finished the apple tart and wagged his finger at her. She wanted to bite it. "Business is your shop is opening—technically, as an employee of the salvage company, may I be so bold as to say 'our' shop is opening in less than a week—and instead of focusing on it, you're here hiding behind plotted plants and worried about people you've never even met!"

"Don't be ridiculous." Tara glanced toward the lobby. She didn't realize Danny had seen her hiding behind the plant while he flirted. Was she that obvious? Were they all laughing at her? "I know I'm getting a little worked up. But Veronica was such a vibrant force. She brings this group together to give them a free trip and make amends, and this is how one of them repays her?" The waiter arrived with coffee and hot water. Danny took tea, while Tara took coffee. What did it matter? She couldn't imagine herself getting to sleep tonight anyway. Several cups of caffeine a day keeps killers away! "And there's more."

Danny sipped his tea, then clinked it down. "More?"

"It can't be coincidence that I found Nancy Halligan's body." She reached into her purse and pulled out the flyer for the old stone house. "Someone left this under my door knocker at the shop."

"Knocker," Danny said, chuckling.

"Get over it, frat boy. This is serious."

Danny studied the flyer. "What about it?"

"Because of this flyer, that I thought was from you, I went to that old stone house, and found Nancy's body!"

"Are you saying it's my fault?"

Were they really doing this? Fighting in the upscale restaurant of the Ballynahinch Castle? "No. I'm saying I was *lured* there. Maybe by the killer." She held her breath. She'd finally spoken her biggest fear out loud. It sounded outlandish. Part of her knew that. It was also true. Part of her knew that. She wondered how many parts of her existed and would they ever be able to get along?

Danny pondered this. "First, didn't the guards say she died of a heart attack?"

"Yes. But why didn't she have water? Or a phone? Or anything on her?"

"What are you thinking?"

"I think someone brought her there, then somehow left her in a vulnerable position so she couldn't go for help."

Danny jostled the flyer. "The same person who left this under your door knocker?"

"Yes." Was he finally taking her seriously? She hoped so. She didn't want to be alone in her paranoia. She also didn't want to be right. But he wasn't talking her out of her crazy theories, he was considering them.

"Why? None of these people even know you."

"True. But Veronica had already decided to hire me. Because of the article written about me, and the name of the shop. Renewals. She was renewing her life and thought I'd be a perfect fit."

"I'm still not following."

"What if the killer knew Veronica planned on hiring me? Knew she had the article. Decided to get me more involved. *Wanted* me to find Nancy's body." There was a time she wondered if that someone was Veronica. But now that Veronica was gone, Tara was no longer sure that made sense.

"Why?"

"I don't know!"

Danny put his hands up. "Lower your voice."

She wanted to snap back, but he was right. People were listening. The walls were probably listening. A killer could be listening. She lowered her voice. "And then there's the book."

"What book?"

Had she really not told him any of this? *Places to See in Ireland Before You Die.* Someone left it in my shop."

"That's it," Danny said. "We're out of here." He stood and looked around. "Do we have the check yet?"

Tara stood. "The meals are already paid for. By Veronica."

Danny shut his eyes for a moment to absorb that. They exited quickly, and Tara had that guilty feeling like they were doing a dine and dash. They stood in the lobby, the air thick between them. Tara placed her hand on his arm.

"The guards are questioning me too. Clearing my name is good for *our* shop."

He moved his arm away from her touch. "You're a terrible liar."

"What?"

"I happen to know the guards have already seen the security tape from the mill. You entered at six p.m. and there's no sign of you until the guards knock on your door the next morning. We handed over the tape. Your alibi is clear."

"Good." *Shoot.* What excuse was she going to use now? It was hard to explain, but she couldn't drop this. She just couldn't. The fact that someone was drawing her into this morbid game made her even more determined to find out who it was and stop him or her.

"Let's get out of here. You can get back to focusing on the shop, and we never have to come here again."

"What do you have against castles?" Tara tried to keep her voice light and flirtatious. She didn't want Danny browned off with her.

"The draft," Danny said with a straight face. "It's a little chilly in here."

"My room is paid for, and I've been hired to source gifts for all of them. I'm staying."

"You'll be staying alone then. I prefer the comforts of home."

A home which he had never invited her to experience. And here he was letting her know in a jovial way that he wasn't going to spend a romantic night with her in a four-star castle. What was his deal? Should she just decide, here and now, for herself, that she and Danny O'Donnell were friends and business partners, and never, ever anything else? No matter how handsome and charming he was. No matter how lonely she was? No matter how much he made all her cylinders fire? "Fine," she said. "I'll walk you out."

"Aren't you a gentleman," Danny said. They were silent as they headed out to his car. The weather had taken the same turn as their relationship, cold and biting. Tara was trying to figure out what she could say to repair some of the damage when two figures hurried past them. She recognized the wild black-haired man, who had at least showered and instead of whiskey she caught the scent of cologne. Eddie Oh. Next to him was an older woman trying to keep pace with him.

"Was that Eddie?" Danny stopped in his tracks, his eyes glued to the pair.

"Yes."

"Who is he with?"

"I was wondering the same thing." *Who is over-involved now?* "You want to follow him, don't you?" Tara kept her voice light.

"We're here," Danny said, giving her a sheepish look. "Might as well make it an all-nighter."

Chapter 12

Eddie and the mysterious woman slid into a taxi that was waiting to pick them up.

Danny looked dejected as he glanced at his truck. "What's up?" Tara said. "Let's follow them."

"I'm nearly out of petrol. Believe me, you don't want to get stranded in the dark out here."

Tara spotted Andy, standing by his SUV, orange embers from his cigarette pulsing in the night. She grabbed Danny's arm and ran toward him.

"What are you doing?" Danny said.

"Tara," Andy said as they neared. "How ya." He stubbed out his cigarette.

"Grand," she said. "Listen. I wanted to ask Eddie Oh a question—you know I'm trying to figure out everyone's gifts and he's a bit of a mystery—and then he just took off . . ."

Andy followed her gaze to the taxi that was winding out of the grounds.

"Not a bother," he said, holding open the door to the SUV. Tara slid in but Danny hesitated.

"Who is this guy?"

"Sorry," Tara said. "This is Veronica's driver. Andy, I'd like you to meet Danny O'Donnell."

The two men sized each other up. Andy tipped his cap. Tara got in the back as Danny stood outside. "Are you coming?"

"Isn't it going to be obvious we're following them?" Danny asked.

"No need to follow closely," Andy said, as he started the SUV. "I know where they're headed."

On the way over, Andy was happy to fill them in. The woman was the last guest on Veronica's list: Elaine Burke. She'd been waylaid at her home in Kinsale. Andy had just picked her up at the bus station.

"She's not a suspect then," Tara said.

"Unless she's lying," Andy replied. "She was definitely at the bus station in Galway. But I didn't actually see her get off a bus."

Galway was far enough away that if the woman was trying to cover her tracks she was extremely diabolical. Then again, the flyer and the book hinted of a killer that was exactly that. "Any reason to suspect she's lying?" Andy had the unique position of getting to know all of the guests. Taxi drivers heard and saw everything. It had to be the same for chauffeurs. People often forgot the driver was there, let their guards down. He was probably a wealth of information.

"No. Just stating a fact."

"Veronica mentioned that she once stole the love of Elaine's life. Was she talking about Terrance Hughes?"

Andy's eyes flicked to hers through the rearview

mirror, then to Danny, who was looking out the window, pretending not to listen. "I've only heard rumors."

"Such as?"

"Elaine used to be in love with Terrance Hughes, alright. They were engaged when Veronica swooped in."

"Ouch."

"I'd say," Andy said. "It's especially salacious when you factor in Cassidy Hughes."

"Cassidy?" Danny piped up. "She seems lovely."

Tara imagined her elbow driving into his side.

"Easy on the eyes, alright," Andy said. "She also accused Veronica of murdering her uncle."

"What?" Tara and Danny said at the same time.

"I didn't work for Veronica then," Andy said. "I heard it from Bartley."

Bartley. Tara definitely needed to speak with him. "Why did she think Veronica killed him?"

"Forgive me, I'm gossiping without all the facts. I don't know if there was any particular reason, other than a rich man dies and the new wife inherits everything. Veronica in turn accused Cassidy of being a pill-popper. I'm guessing there's always been animosity between the two."

"What was the official cause of Terrance's death?"

Andy met her gaze in the rearview mirror. "I'm sorry, I don't know that either."

"No worries. Just curious." *She was definitely going to find out.* Tara thought back to Veronica's short note after Elaine's name. *Perspective. Makes one crazy.* Was she calling Elaine crazy? Did Elaine believe Cassidy's accusation? Who wouldn't go a little nuts if a best friend stole the love of her life? *Not to mention if Veronica ended up murdering him.* Tara had to be careful not to go down the rabbit hole of rumors. If Terrance Hughes had died under suspicious circumstances, surely there had been a thorough investigation. Especially given his wealth and stature. Cassidy Hughes was becoming more interesting by the minute. Tara's mental list of people to follow up on was growing.

They entered the downtown area of Clifden dotted with shops, and restaurants, and hotels, and pubs, all built up and down hills. With the mountains, and a church steeple rising in the background, it was a striking sight. Common of other Irish towns, the façades of the restaurants and shops were painted in cheerful blues, yellows, and pinks, a battle against the gray skies, and the colors were winning. Andy pulled over and pointed to the end of the street where a yellow taxi was just pulling away. "I believe they went into the pub at dat corner. They have a great trad session this evening, and Eddie is a fan." Andy definitely knew a lot about their suspects. He was smart and observant. If Tara were a guard, she'd be employing him as a spy.

Spy. The word stuck in her throat. Had Veronica asked Andy to spy on Iona? Had he discovered that Iona was faking her injury and did he report that to Veronica before she died? Tara would have to find a way of asking him, without offending him. She couldn't afford to alienate him or set off his radar.

"Thank you," Tara said.

"How did you know?" Danny asked.

"Pardon?" Andy seemed startled.

Ahead, Eddie and Elaine could be seen standing in front of a popular pub. "That they'd be coming here?"

"I brought him here last night," Andy said.

Tara froze halfway out the door of the vehicle when she registered what he just said. "I thought he just arrived?"

Andy lowered his head. "Never mind. I said nothing."

Eddie hadn't just arrived. He'd been here. Andy didn't want to tattle. Was he a fan like Danny? Tara tried to give Andy ten euro, but he refused to take it. "I'm still on the payroll," he said, handing her a calling card. "Call or text if you want a ride back to the castle." He nodded at Danny. "And I'll get your car filled with petrol in the meantime."

"I couldn't ask you to do that."

"You didn't. I'm offering."

"You have to let me pay you."

"Sort me out later."

Tara was just about to follow up on the bombshell that Eddie Oh had arrived earlier than he claimed when Andy saluted and drove away. Tara didn't have a choice. She was going to have to follow up on this, and if Andy wouldn't answer her questions, she would have to take it to Sergeant Gable. These guests couldn't afford to lie, especially about alibis, when the stakes were so high.

A sense of uneasiness washed over Tara as his SUV faded into the distance. "How did he know I needed petrol?" Danny asked.

"He's always listening," Tara said. "Which makes him a valuable asset."

"Or puts him squarely in danger," Danny mused.

Tara hadn't thought of that. He was young, and strong. But that didn't mean he wasn't vulnerable. She hoped he had enough sense to watch his back.

* * *

The pub was small, and cozy, and packed. Shiny dark wood covered every surface: the bar, the walls, the tables, the built-in benches. Candles adorned the tabletops, their flames dancing. Tara was surprised to see candles without glass covers, and resisted the urge to yell *Fire hazard!* and blow them all out. The Irish didn't seem worried. Maybe there was something wrong with her that made it impossible for her to loosen up and relax. Maybe she was a good interior designer because it gave her always-worrying mind something to focus on. Colors, and textures, and patterns. She would never decorate with candles without a protective glass cover. Especially in a public place like this where everyone was crammed into a tiny room, sleeves hanging innocently, squeezing past people to get a seat.

"What's your deal?" Danny whispered in her ear. It made her shiver. "Do you want to be left alone with a candle?"

Tara elbowed Danny in the side. He laughed. The trad players were bunched up in the back booth, instruments out and warming up. Danny grabbed Tara's hand and pulled her to the bench along the wall, where there didn't appear to be any seats. But one grin from Danny O'Donnell and people parted on both sides, allowing them to sardine in. The feel of his body pressed tightly against hers hit her like a drug. "Going for a pint," Danny said. "What's your pleasure?"

You. Don't move. "Just a Coke."

"Did you give up the drink?" Danny sounded slightly horrified.

"Out of respect for Veronica," Tara said. "It's temporary."

He gazed at her for a while, then nodded. Danny went up to the bar and returned with a pint and a Coke. Tara allowed herself a moment to imagine they were on a date. The candlelight didn't help, nor did the fact that he was sitting so close. She scanned the crowd as they sipped.

"I feel like we're voyeurs," Tara said. She'd yet to spot Eddie and Elaine. Had they slipped into another pub?

"We have drinks in front of us," Danny said, lifting his. "That makes us patrons."

That's when Tara spotted them. Eddie and Elaine were on the opposite side of the pub in a two-seater. They were sitting close to a wall splashed with their shadows. Eddie leaned in and spoke to her, and Elaine's gaze never left his face. His voice rose above the din; he was telling a story. Tara couldn't take her eyes off them. "They look cozy."

Danny nodded. "Indeed."

"I mean, I know there's quite an age difference."

"He was married to Veronica. I think maybe older women are his type." Danny's grin said that he approved. "Do you think they're knocking boots?"

Tara stared at the odd couple as she contemplated his question. Elaine Burke was still a very beautiful woman. Her figure was trim, and the blond hair that flowed in the picture Veronica had supplied of the two of them in their glamour days was colored to keep the same vibrancy, and cut in sleek layers. She was way too dressed up for this pub, a designer dress that was probably made in Italy. Like Veronica, Elaine Burke held a presence that seemed to openly defy people to claim she was anything other than still viable. And Eddie Oh was definitely glued to her. "Doesn't it look . . . possible?"

Danny cocked his head. "She's a Helen Mirren type. Definitely still doable."

"Honestly!" Tara smacked his thigh. Danny laughed.

"No disrespect, Miss America, but when a woman is hot, she's hot, no matter her age."

"Too bad Dr. Seuss is gone, sounds like a title for his next book."

"Huh?"

"*When A Woman Is Hot She Is Hot No Matter Her Age.*" He just stared at her. "*I will date if she's December and I am May, I will date her anyway.*" This time Tara laughed and Danny did not.

"First you're jealous of Cassidy, now this stunning older woman?"

"I'm not jealous. Go for it, cowboy. And while you're at it, ask if she murdered her best friend."

"I think they're knocking boots. Should we put money on it?"

"For real?" Danny, she'd learned, liked to bet. On anything. And no matter what the bet, she was usually on the losing end of it.

"For real, Miss America."

Tara bit her lip. She hated losing. And she wasn't confident the pair of them were dating, just flirting. "No. I do not want to."

"Afraid I'll win?"

"Do you have to turn everything into a contest?"

"You do not like to lose, do you?"

"I don't want to turn our investigation into a betting game." *She so did not like to lose.* Who did?

"*Our* investigation, is it?"

"Why do you always pick the weirdest times to flirt with me?"

"Is that what you think I'm doing?"

"Can we get back to them?"

"Excuse me," a deep male voice interrupted. Startled, Tara looked up to find Eddie and Elaine standing in front of them. The entire bench was watching. Tara was so stunned to find them there, that she couldn't speak.

"How ya," Danny said easily.

Eddie ignored Danny and jabbed his finger at Tara. "Are you Tara Meehan?"

"Yes," she said, wondering if she should pretend not to know who he was.

"I told you," Elaine said. "Thank goodness."

"Please," Eddie said, gesturing to their table across the room. "Join us."

Chapter 13

It felt so odd following Eddie and Elaine to their table. Eddie grabbed a couple of stray chairs and crammed them into their two-seater. Given the crowd, Tara wondered if he was stealing previously occupied seats. So much for a successful stakeout; the targets had not only made them, they were now inviting them over, gaining the upper hand. Danny was right. She was out of her element. Danny didn't seem fazed at all by the reversal. His eyes were dancing, probably from keeping his fanboy all bottled in. Eddie leaned in. He reeked of whiskey. "Is it true? Veronica came to see you at your shop?"

"Renewals," Elaine said. For a woman who had just arrived she was certainly in the know.

"I didn't get your name," Tara said. She was debating whether or not to admit that she knew very well who she was, and decided to feign innocence.

"I'm Elaine Burke. I was Veronica's best friend."

"We know *your* name," Danny said, directing the statement to Eddie, and sticking his hand out. "I'm a big fan."

Eddie's head cocked back, and he gave Danny about two seconds before turning to Tara. "Tell us everything about the day Veronica came into your shop." Danny's hand flopped back by his side, and Tara felt a twinge of pity for him. Seconds after meeting his idol and he was already let down.

"I've told the cops everything I know," Tara found herself saying like a suspect in a movie.

Eddie placed his hand on his chest. "Have you ever been married?"

She tensed, not wanting this man she'd barely met to inquire into her personal life. One she was trying to heal from, but the wounds were vulnerable and needed some boundaries. Danny shifted beside her; he knew all about her previous marriage to Gabriel, how it dissolved after Thomas died. Three years was all she had with Thomas. Three years. She guarded those memories like a mother bear. Her son wasn't open for discussion unless she initiated it, not with this man, not with anyone.

"What are you trying to ask her?" Danny said. He'd switched to protection mode and Tara was grateful for it. She felt his hand wrap around hers and squeeze. She bit back tears. He had her back when it counted the most.

"I wasn't trying to pry," Eddie said, finally reading the room, and sitting back in his chair. "It's just. When you're divorced, people assume you aren't grieving. But I am. I couldn't have loved Veronica more. And the guards aren't talking. I need to know what she said, is there anything that might have . . ."

"Given me a clue as to who did this?" Tara said.

Eddie swallowed and nodded. Tara saw her own grief reflected in his face. He had loved her. And he seemed bent on getting answers. *Unless he's lying . . .*

"I'm sorry. I swear to you there's nothing she said that will help us find her killer. But I'd be happy to tell you about her visit to my shop. I get why you want to know."

"Tank you."

She filled them in on her first meeting with the heiress, making a point to emphasize Veronica's devotion to Eddie's art. He listened intently, nodding, shaking his head when he learned she'd given Tara his portfolio. He laughed when she recounted Bartley's story of Eddie swiping the cap from Veronica's driver.

"Good old Bixby," Eddie said. "He was such an old fuss I couldn't help meself." He turned to Elaine. "Whatever happened to him?"

Her face looked pinched. "He passed away."

"He did? When?"

"I think we're getting off topic," Elaine said softly. "He was in his early sixties. Life took him way too young."

Eddie whistled and rubbed his face. "He was a good old sport." He shrugged and turned back to Tara. "Veronica still believed in me. Even though I haven't created in a long time."

"I hope that changes soon," Danny said.

"Did she mention me?" Elaine Burke asked, her voice filled with desperation.

"Your name was on her amends list," Tara said. "But I never got the chance to speak with her about it."

"I see." Elaine looked down at the table.

"But in her notes she mentioned you were her best friend, and she used your nickname. Lainey." Tara felt a squeeze of pity for Elaine; her sadness was palpable.

When Elaine looked up, for a second Tara saw the young girl from the picture. "I was her best friend once. That was a long time ago." Pain swam in her eyes. Was she thinking of Terrance, the love of her life? Or did she fixate on Veronica's betrayal?

"I hope it's some comfort she intended to make amends," Tara said. "And I believed she was sincere."

Elaine grasped her drink. "In her drinking days she was either in love with you or out to get you. Usually both. Male, female, related, stranger. It didn't matter. I suppose recovery has been good for her. *Was* good for her," she corrected. "Her sponsor must be a remarkable woman." She looked to Eddie as if wanting him to pitch in.

"Of course," Eddie said, waving it away. "There was no need for apologies. That woman doesn't remember half the things she did."

That woman. So much for all the love he claimed to feel for his ex-wife. "Speaking of her sponsor," Tara said. "Did either of you know Nancy Halligan?"

"Is that her name?" Elaine said. "I've yet to meet her."

"None of us knew the 'new' Veronica," Eddie said. "But I'm guessing the old one was a lot more fun." He finished the rest of his pint in one long swallow as if drinking for the both of them.

"Then you haven't heard the news," Tara said, treading lightly. Their faces turned toward her expectantly. "Nancy Halligan passed away one week before Veronica. A heart attack."

Elaine gasped. "My word. How awful."

Eddie stared off into the distance. "One week before Veronica?"

"Yes," Tara said. *I found her. And I think Veronica's killer led me to her.* Was it one of the two sitting before her? She looked at Elaine. "Veronica must have driven you crazy."

"Me?" Elaine said. "Why do you tink dat?"

Perspective. Makes one crazy. "Oh, just in general. It must have been difficult."

"It's her niece and her first husband she drove crazy. She drove her husband to the grave and don't tell me that pill habit of Cassie's has nothing to do with Roni, because it certainly does."

Drove her husband to the grave. The best friend had claws. And Elaine had certainly not forgotten. Did that mean she truly suspected Veronica of killing Terrance Hughes, or was it just an expression?

"Is her niece the pretty young blonde?" Danny asked. He knew the answer, but Tara was grateful he was willing to help keep them talking as well.

"Yes," Elaine said, her lips pursed. "Cassidy Hughes is a little addict and a manipulator."

"And easy on the eyes," Eddie added with a conspiratorial wink to Danny.

"When a woman is hot she is hot no matter her age," Danny said with a straight face while his foot nudged hers under the table.

Eddie frowned, then laughed and lifted his pint, staring at it as if surprised to find it drained.

"You mentioned something about Cassidy and pills," Tara said, hoping to bring this table back to order.

Elaine arched an eyebrow in disapproval, then

smoothed her hand across the table. "I'll say no more."

Danny turned the attention back to Eddie. "Are you working on any art projects at the moment?"

"Nothing the world will get to see," Eddie said. "Veronica was my muse." It was the utterings of a man drunk on Guinness and nostalgia. Even so, there was something *scripted* about it. Danny might be fooled, but Tara didn't believe his act for a second. *Nothing the world would get to see . . .* What did that mean? The marbles that covered Veronica flashed in her mind yet again. She had been posed. Decorated. If Eddie was the killer, was that his calling card? Did he turn her into a sculpture?

"He'll create until he dies," Lainey said. "He did not choose to be an artist, he is an artist, it's a part of him like blood, and breathing." Eddie lifted his head for a second as if her words were the sun and he was basking in it. Then he swiped his empty pint glass and clumsily stumbled up from the table and toward the bar. Handsome and brooding and a whole world of trouble. Some women couldn't get enough of that. Tara glanced at Danny.

"We'd better be going." Tara pushed back her chair and stood. If Eddie had murdered Veronica, then staged her like one of his sculptures, she couldn't sit this close to him. She felt a clawing need to flee.

"Really?" Danny said.

"I'm not feeling well. I need to go."

"We should be off too," Elaine said, glancing at Eddie, who had elbowed his way to the front of the bar. "Luckily that SUV can fit the entire group."

"Looks like he's staying," Tara said, pointing at

Eddie. "But I really have to go." She headed for the door.

"Where's the fire?" Eddie had snuck up from behind her. He lurched and knocked over a chair.

"Steady now," the publican yelled out. A book fell out of Eddie's pocket and thudded to the floor. Tara bent down to retrieve it. *Places to See in Ireland Before You Die.* She gasped and dropped it again.

Eddie swiped it up and glared. "What on earth is the matter with ya?"

"That book. Where did you get it?"

"We all have one," Lainey said, as she and Danny caught up. "From Veronica." The publican, a tall man with an impressive glare, showed up behind them. "Why don't you move this outside. Our musicians deserve a bit of respect."

Danny helped hustle them out the door. Outside, the wind was biting, but Tara could hardly feel it. *The book was from Veronica?* Veronica acted like she'd never seen the book. Called it morbid. Had that been some kind of game?

Elaine stepped up to Tara, who was trying not to hyperventilate. "Why do you look as if you've seen a ghost?"

Tara swallowed. "Someone left a copy of that book for me in the shop."

Elaine arched an eyebrow. "Must have been her then." She let out a soft laugh. "I guess we weren't so special after all."

"She acted as if she'd never seen the book before," Tara said. "She called it morbid."

"Roni liked games," Elaine said. "I guess even sobriety hadn't changed that."

Tara leaned forward. "How do you know it was from Veronica? Was there a note from her? Did she tell you she sent it?"

For a moment, Eddie and Elaine froze. Elaine shook her head. "I don't think so. Come to think of it, mine was sitting at me front door. But I'd just received the invitation from Veronica. So I assumed . . ." She looked to Eddie. He took a few staggering steps.

"What?"

"Where did you find your book?" Elaine asked.

"My book?"

Elaine grabbed the book from his hands and shoved it in his face. "This one."

He took a step back and nearly fell. Danny held him up. "From Roni," he said, waving his hand.

"We'll ask him when he's sober," Tara said. "We also have to talk to the others."

"I don't like this development," Elaine said.

Neither did Tara. An SUV slid up to the pub and Andy stepped out. "Are we ready to go home?"

"You waited for us?" Tara said.

He smiled. "It's a lot livelier around here than back at the castle."

Eddie pointed to Andy's cap. "It's Bixby's cap," he said. "He's wearing Bixby's cap."

"For heaven's sake, just get in," Elaine said, shoving Eddie in the back.

"What are you saying about the book?" Eddie said, refusing to get in the vehicle. He pointed at Tara. "What is she saying about the book?"

"She's saying it might not have been Roni who left us that book," Elaine said before Tara could answer. "Now get in."

Eddie crawled into the very back and the rest of them filed in after. Andy pulled away from the curb, his eyes watching the drama in the rearview mirror.

"If Roni didn't leave us da book, den who did?" Eddie mumbled. "Who left us the book?" A moment of awkward silence filled the space.

"The killer," Elaine said at last. Her voice was soft but clear. "She's saying it could have been left by the killer."

Chapter 14

The next morning, Elaine helped gather all the guests onto a private spot on the grounds of the castle. Nearby the river gurgled. There was a bite to the air, and the wind whipped around them as the threat of rain hung overhead. Many showed up with their books, all with similar stories of finding it in their path and assuming it was from Veronica. "I assure you," Bartley said, his tall frame looming over them, "if Veronica was behind that book I would have been the one distributing it. I did not."

"She could have asked someone else," Eddie scoffed. Tara wondered if there was a history between those two, or was Eddie just surly with everyone? Temperamental artist? "Did you get a book?"

Bartley folded his arms. "No, sir. I did not."

"Who else doesn't have a book?" Mimi said. "He could be the killer."

"Are you calling me a killer, madam?" Bartley's

voice remained professional. "I've worked for the O'Farrell family for forty years. I assure you if I was a murderer, I wouldn't have waited this long."

Tara thought he had a good point. On the other hand, didn't everyone have a breaking point? Just like alcoholics needed to reach bottom before getting help? Maybe it took him forty years to reach his. Or maybe he felt left out. He wasn't on Veronica's amends list. Tara found it hard to believe that he'd been treated well the past forty years.

"You're always around her," Cassidy said. "How could she have snuck out that morning without your knowledge?"

Tara was surprised to hear Cassidy ask the very question she'd been dying to. She held her breath as she waited for Bartley to answer.

"She didn't alert me or her driver," Bartley said. "I was her employee, not her servant."

"She called you her butler," Cassidy said.

"She had a robust sense of humor," Bartley answered without a hint of humor.

"Where were you when she was killed?" Cassidy continued.

"In my room. Having a well-needed rest. Where were you? That is, if you can remember."

"Why wouldn't I remember?" Cassidy put her hands on her shapely hips.

"It can be hard to recall things through a fog," Bartley said.

"I could very well inherit the estate," Cassidy said. "My first order of business will be cutting the dead weight from the staff."

"I could have retired years ago," Bartley said. "I'm only here out of loyalty."

"Enough," Mimi Griffin said. "There's no need for squabbling."

"I agree," Iona said. She lifted her book. "This sounds like a threat. How do we know one of us isn't next?"

"I want to go home," Sheila said.

"So do I," John added. "Is it legal for them to keep us here? Will they arrest us if we try to leave?"

"We're all suspects," Tara said. "I can't speak for the legalities, but I don't think it will look good if you leave."

"Who cares what looks good," Sheila said. "One of you is a killer."

"We'll be safer if we stick together," Mimi said. "Don't go anywhere alone, and if someone tries to get you alone, report it immediately."

"Spy on each other?" Iona said. "Is that what you're suggesting?"

"Of course not." Tara replied. "Look out for each other. We aren't safe until we know who did this."

"What's this *we* business?" John interjected. He glared at Tara. "You don't have to stay at this castle surrounded by a killer."

"Yet she chooses to," Iona said. "Maybe she's the killer."

The group turned as one to wait for Tara to defend herself. The weight of everyone's gaze was visceral. "I was hired to do a job." There was a mob mentality at work here and she didn't like it.

"What was the job exactly?" John asked.

"It involved doing something nice for all of you." In New York Tara had been in high demand as a designer. She'd reached the fortunate position where she could choose the places she wanted to design, and was always welcomed with open arms. It was jarring to be treated as an outsider, let alone a killer.

"I think Iona might be on to something," Sheila said, turning on Tara and pointing. "She's the one who posted the murder weapon hours before poor Veronica was found dead." Sheila brought up her phone and showed them the tweet. #Killerbrooch. Tara had since taken it down, so Sheila must have done a screen capture. Why would she do that?

A gasp ran through the patio as one by one the guests looked at her. "Total coincidence," Tara said. She pointed at Bartley. "Ask him." Bartley looked at his shoes. Apparently, he didn't want to back her up. Was he just trying to throw suspicion off himself? "Where's Andy?" Tara asked. "He was there too." She looked around, but the young driver wasn't in sight.

"I don't understand," Elaine said. "Why did you do something so vulgar?" She stared at Tara.

"I posted that *before* she died," Tara said. "She encouraged me to take a picture of her brooch. It was a piece of art."

"Hardly a piece of art," Eddie said, as if the comment was an insult to his work. He glanced at Cassidy. "Where's your copy of the book?"

"I didn't bring that stupid book with me," Cassidy said, crossing her arms. "Why do I need to visit me own country for, like?"

"Because it's filled with magic and wonder?" Iona said, a lecturing tone obvious in her voice.

"Traipsing around in the muck and the rain?" Cassidy shook her head. "Pop culture is more my ting."

"Did anyone's book come with writing, or something slipped inside . . . anything?" Tara asked. One by one they looked at each other and shook their heads. A few rifled through their books. All books had been delivered to either their home or place of work, not mailed. "We're going to have to tell the guards." She took a breath. "In the meantime, I'd like to write down where everyone received the book, and anything else they can remember."

"Does that include me?"

The smell of cigarette smoke hit Tara. She turned to find Andy, who had just exited through the patio doors. "Did you get a book too?"

He reached into his inside jacket pocket and pulled it out.

"Where did you find it?" Mimi asked before Tara could.

"On the passenger seat of me car. I thought maybe someone else left it behind."

Why hadn't he mentioned it earlier? Tara flashed back to Veronica being in her store. By the time Veronica noticed her book, Andy had already exited. She was going to have to be careful, it was so easy to suspect everyone else, and she didn't like it when it was being done to her.

"What does any of this mean?" Sheila asked. John put his arm around her and pulled her close.

"It means the killer is playing a game," Mimi said. "And Veronica may have been the first on his or her list. But what if she's not the last?"

Chapter 15

Tara was eager to return to her loft the following day. She needed a sense of assurance that only the comfort of home could bring. This business with the travel books had unnerved her. It suggested a far more sinister plot. For some reason an impulsive kill was less threatening. A regular human being overwhelmed in the moment. After all, the brooch wasn't a weapon the killer had brought to the scene . . .

An enigma for sure. Why draw up an elaborate plan of revenge, yet leave the murder weapon to a whim? Veronica had mentioned how the Tara Brooch was always slipping off. And it appeared she was in quite the state Friday night. Had it slipped off in the castle or on the grounds? Did the murderer change his or her mind about the weapon *after* discovering the brooch? Or was the book from Veronica, was all of this *her* premeditated plot, and was the murder still an impulsive act? These were all the questions that had kept Tara up the night before. She hoped if she went back to her loft, and her bed, she could get some much needed sleep. She was also eager to get some of her thoughts down on paper, get back to her comfort zone of creating.

The minute she entered her loft, Tara felt herself relax. People often had the impression that interior design was superfluous. Nice for those who could afford it, but at the end of the day of little importance. But now, walking into her home, her safe place, she was reminded that her work was about so much more than that. It was about lowering stress, feeling cradled at home. Wherever home was. And one didn't have to spend a ton of money to do it. A bit of paint, de-cluttering, and a mason jar of wildflowers could do the trick.

Tara still needed to add original pieces of artwork to her loft, which brought her mind back to Eddie. After Danny had made such a fuss over him, she'd looked through the catalogue Veronica had left with her, and there was something compelling about his sculptures. She could see having a piece of his work in her loft if she could afford it. She wanted to be extra careful with her savings, and she'd spent a good bit of it on the shop. But *he* didn't know she couldn't afford it. It might be a good way to get closer to him. Enough worrying about it while standing still, she needed her morning walk with the dogs. Breanna had been stopping by the mill to take care of them, along with Uncle Johnny, but Tara knew neither of them were early risers. She left a note on the door of the mill just in case they stopped by, dressed, and headed for the door with Hound and

Savage at her heels. She gave Hound a pat on the head, thrilled as ever for her enthusiastic walking buddy. Savage was too low to the ground to pet, nor did she seem to want to do anything but explore. Hound only protested the walk if it was raining too hard, and today was only a light mist. Tara welcomed it, as if the rain might wash away some of her worries, bring everything back to a clean slate. Hound kept pace beside her, sniffing everything in sight as Savage double-timed it to keep up, her tiny body vibrating with excitement. They walked until Tara felt the clouds from her mind clear, and her heart pump with blood. Back home she showered, dressed, and headed down to the mill. Johnny was in his office drinking a large mug of tea, feet up on his desk. *Nice life.*

"How ya," he called when she stepped in the doorway. He lifted his feet off and plopped them on the floor. "Get this. They did it for a tenner."

She had no idea what he was talking about. "Who did what for a tenner?"

"The lads who installed your chandelier. They forgot to lock the doors when they were working in the shop. A boy came in with a gift. Said it was for you. Left it on the counter. Gave them a tenner."

A tenner. Ten euro. To leave the book. *Some gift.* Tara picked a pile of books off one of his chairs, set them on the ground and sat across from him. She was never going to get Johnny to be organized, his mess was his comfort zone. "When you say boy?"

Johnny shook his head. "A grown lad."

"Don't leave me in suspense. Who was it?"

"They were up on a ladder and said they didn't get a good look at him."

"Nothing? Approximate age? Was he wearing a cap?"

"One of them said he was wearing a cap, the other said he wasn't, and the two of them went back and forth until I needed me headache tablets."

Typical. "Thanks anyway," she said. "I can't believe I'm embroiled in another murder inquiry. If only I hadn't taken a selfie with that brooch."

He lifted an eyebrow. "The Tara Brooch you're on about, is it?"

"Indeed." *Killer brooch.*

"It's too bad. What a find that would have been."

She nearly laughed. Johnny meant no harm. He was too eager for antiques to think through his statement. "I think it's probably a little more too bad that it was used to stab someone through the heart."

"Well, there's dat." He waved his hand as if to shoo the thought away.

"Do you have much knowledge about marble?" She couldn't help but be haunted by the marble stones placed over Veronica's face. "I'm thinking of getting a few pieces for the shop." She felt guilty lying, but she'd promised the guards to keep the marble stones under wrap.

Johnny nodded. "Tourists eat it up, but the Connemara Marble Visitor Centre has the market on dat."

"Really?"

"Yes, besides bigger orders that the quarry gets in, they make trinkets for tourists and sell it at the visitor center."

"What kind of marble?"

"Mostly a green marble rare to these parts. But all kinds. Red, black, white."

"Sounds interesting. Maybe I'll have to pay them a visit."

He jabbed a finger at her. "It's your shop you should be visiting first, and no more of this Sherlocking."

She laughed; the Irish always surprised her with their quick wit. "Got it," she said. "Although it's the city you should be wagging your finger at for dragging their feet on my permit." *Sherlocking*. He was right. She did need to get back to her shop. "I'm heading there now."

He grinned and saluted. "My work here is done then." He thumped his feet back on the desk and put his mug where his mouth was.

It was while she was on the way to the shop that she decided to pop into the bookshop. It was a long shot, but if there was even the slightest possibility that *Places to See in Ireland Before You Die* had been purchased in Galway, it was worth the trip. She ducked in, scoured the shelves where there were plenty of travel books, but not that exact one. She headed to the clerk and asked after it.

He typed something into his computer. "I can have it for ya in about ten days."

"No, sorry, I already have it, I just wondered if anyone else has come in lately. Perhaps they bought multiple copies?"

He tilted his head at her. "What do ya tink we do here, snoop on all our customers and report their buying activity to any yoke who walks in?"

She bit her lip. She was kinda hoping they did.

"We had one copy." The voice came from a young woman shelving books. The clerk shook his head at her, then went back to whatever he was doing. Tara moved in closer.

"Is there any chance you knew who you sold it to?"

She shook her head. "He was wearing a cap, that's all I can remember. Like he was a chauffeur."

Andy? "Was he young?" The clerk shrugged, then shook her head. Of course. When you're a baby like she was, you think everyone is old. "Did he look like a wild-eyed artist, or was he a younger guy who smelled like cigarette smoke?"

"I'm sorry I said anything. He had a cap. That's all I know."

It was probably Andy, he was the one who had been in Galway. Then again, that didn't mean Eddie couldn't have come here. Eddie seemed the type to gravitate toward the city. But the only time Tara had mixed up the two was when she saw Eddie in the same cap in his artist picture. In person, she'd never seen Eddie wearing a cap. Andy claimed he found his book on the passenger seat. Had he purchased it instead? Why the lie? The girl was starting to move away from Tara; she had one more shot. "When did he come in?"

She sighed, rolled her eyes, but Tara could see she was mulling it over. "Thursday afternoon." *The day before Veronica came into her shop. Did this matter?*

"You're sure?"

She nodded. "I was trying to close and he was my last customer. I wanted to hurry him along, which is why all I know is he was just some lad in a cap who bought a book." She stepped closer. "Why? Who is he?"

Shoot. The last thing Tara needed was to start gossip. "It's not a big deal. Thank you."

"Why? I said nothing."

Tara shrugged. "You tried."

The girl shrugged back. She was going to have shoulder problems later in life if she kept that up.

Tara headed for the door. "If you think of anything else, I own Renewals on Quay Street."

"The place the dead woman visited?"

Great. The girl didn't know much, but she knew that. Tara shook her head. "I've only had live visitors so far," she said as she headed out the door.

The rest of the afternoon Tara threw herself into work. When her mailbox didn't house her business permit, she called the city, only to get a spiel about how they were backed up with permits and she would get it when she got it. She secretly wondered if it was because she was an American and they somehow knew that and were just trying to torture her. She entered inventory and prices on an Excel database that would allow for easy purchasing via an iPad. She was tempted to email everyone who had confirmed their attendance to her grand opening, just to make sure the recent murder hadn't scared anyone away, but in the end she decided that would draw too much attention to it. No one had canceled, she wasn't cursed, this was happening. She supposed it was very Irish of her to find a way to worry even when things were going well. It made sense on an evolutionary level. Worrying meant you were on-the-ready for challenges to come. That is, if worrying led to strategy. Most of the time, it didn't. Just played in a loop in her head all day long. Same as her mam. No wonder she was always so wrecked when she came home at the end of a day.

To cheer herself up, Tara feasted on the items in her shop. The stone sculptures. The chandelier. A collection of antique fire pokers. A coin collection. An old advertising poster for Guinness that she secretly wanted no one to buy so she raised the price to an unreasonable sum. A few select pieces of jewelry. No brooches. She'd never sell those now. She turned to her list and decided to jot down notes for gift possibilities:

Sheila and John Murphy: a piece of decor for their home. Something attractive, yet functional.

Tara glanced at her own notes: an antique diving helmet. If she could find one, that would be a great gift for the pair. She'd love to have one herself.

Iona Kelly: something outdoorsy. A painting of nature, or a sculpture made out of driftwood.

Mimi Griffin: She thought Mimi would prefer some sort of organizer, but of course there were no architectural items in that vein. Unless she found her an old-fashioned library card cabinet, but she didn't even know if she could find those in Ireland or the UK. Still, she loved the idea.

Eddie Oh: He didn't seem the type to like anyone else's work but his own. Maybe something to do with drink. An old whiskey barrel to use as a coffee table, or if he wanted he could turn that into an art project. She'd have to schedule delivery, as he wouldn't want to be dragging it around.

Elaine Burke: What do you get someone's ex-best friend after stealing the love of her life?

Something dainty and nostalgic? A music box?

Cassidy Hughes: Tara could see her in a vintage movie-star type dress. Irish Revivals didn't source any vintage clothing, but Tara certainly could. Some-thing with a hat and shoes and a matching handbag.

Just jotting down her ideas made her feel better. Now she could start looking. It had been several days since she'd driven her Jeep. She'd tried to drive every other day so that her fears couldn't creep back in. She hadn't gone on enough architectural shopping excursions, namely because Johnny and Danny loved it too much to make room for her. But this assignment was all hers. She'd start on it right after lunch with Breanna. It would be good to make use of herself, before she went stir-crazy waiting for the shop to open or looking over her shoulder for a killer.

Chapter 16

By lunchtime Breanna had sent a message that she wouldn't be able to meet. She'd probably been advised to avoid Tara until the case was over. That made sense, but Tara felt a pang of emptiness. She bought seafood chowder at her favorite restaurant and brought it back to her shop. The skies had opened up and it was lashing rain. She imagined lugging her newfound objects in and out of the sopping mess and decided to go on her shopping excursion another day. Downtown Clifden had an antique shop; she'd start there the next time she headed for Connemara. In the meantime, she remembered the two people who weren't in the immediate group, whom she needed to learn a little bit more about: Nancy Halligan and Terrance Hughes. She'd start with the latter; there was likely to be more information on the media mogul.

As soon as she typed his name into the search engine and hit enter, a picture came up of a gorgeous young couple at a wedding complete with a splashy headline: HEIRESS MARRIES MOGUL. Veronica was barely recognizable. She had a youthful wild-eyed grin. Even from the picture you could tell her much older husband was a bore. His lips were pursed in disapproval, hands clenched in front of him. Is that why after the divorce she went for Eddie—the opposite of her first husband?

There was more: MOGUL MARRIED TO HEIRESS DIES AT 74

She scanned the article; he died of natural causes. *Then again, that's what they said about Nancy Halligan.* Nancy probably did die of heatstroke, but that didn't mean someone didn't lure her out there and leave her vulnerable. She was about to close out the search when she noticed another mention, and a short arti-cle:

CASSIDY HUGHES DECLARES MOGUL'S DEATH FOUL PLAY

Cassidy Hughes, the niece of media outlet owner Terrance Hughes, insists her uncle did not die naturally of a heart at-tack. "Take a look at the Black Widow," Cassidy said. "That viper at the end of a bottle killed me uncle."

The rumor was true, there it was in black and white. Why on earth would Veronica make amends to Cassidy after she'd accused her of being a murderer? *A viper at the end of a bottle.* Her notes made it clear that she was adding Cassidy to the list grudgingly, but given their past animosity, Tara was still surprised. One thing was obvious: Cassidy had been eager to stir the pot. So why accept the invite? She needed to get to know these people better. Could Bartley shed more light on this story?

Bartley. What a funny man. He was hard to read. He rarely showed any emotion, even after Veronica's death. Was he just a consummate employee, or was he busy keeping something close to his chest?

Tara strolled the streets, taking in the sights and sounds. It was necessary to get away from the shop, and get her mind off work, and murder. She was passing a pub when she heard a familiar voice. "Hey." She turned to find Andy leaning against the wall smoking a cigarette. It took her a minute to place him; he wasn't wearing his cap. His hair was thick, but slicked back on his head.

"Oh. Hello."

He stubbed the cigarette out and gave her a nod. "I had to get away from that lot back at the castle."

"I'm sure."

"Join me for a pint?"

She hesitated. She still wasn't drinking, and wondered if he would give her a hard time about it. But he'd been driving her around when he didn't have to, and she could try and suss out whether or not he was in the bookstore the other day buying *Places to See in Ireland Before You Die.* "Why not."

"Dat's the spirit."

The pub was fairly quiet, the locals, or "old stock," were around, enjoying the lull before the happy hour crowd.

Andy didn't make a fuss when she told him she was abstaining from alcohol for a bit to honor Veronica's memory. It seemed he was more interested in the company than having a day-drinking buddy, which was a good sign.

"I have a strange question," Tara said when the small talk was out of the way.

"I'll probably give ya a strange answer then," he replied.

"Did I see you in a Galway bookstore the other day? The one near my shop?"

He stared at her, blinking. He chewed his bottom lip. Then nodded. "You caught me." He raised an eyebrow. "Were you there?"

"I came in as you were leaving," Tara said. She hated lying, but the alternative, that she was asking around about him, would sound much worse.

"I'm a sucker for bookshops."

"Big reader?"

"Comes with the territory."

"It does?"

"Of course. All that time waiting. Reading is a fringe benefit. I get that from me father."

"What do you like to read?"

"Most anything."

"It's an adorable bookstore. I love supporting the locals. Did you buy anything?" She hated how rehearsed it sounded. Would he get suspicious?

"I always buy something," he said. "I like to support the locals too." He dug into his pocket and pulled out a paperback. It was a Western. "My father loved these. I started on them after he died. Makes me feel closer to him."

"I love that." *Was that all he bought?* The clerk didn't mention the guy she spotted buying anything else. Then again her memory wasn't the best. Every other man in Galway probably had a similar cap. It wasn't out of the realm of possibility that someone else bought that book. "What are you going to do when this is all over?"

"How do you mean?"

"Are you going to try to find a job as someone else's driver?"

"Me?" He sounded startled, then laughed. "No. It was only a filler job. I'm going to Trinity College in the winter."

"That's wonderful."

"Tank you. Me father was a working man. It was his dream that I'd go to university." He lifted his pint up. "To his memory. I'm a bit late to honoring his wishes, but better late than never."

Tara toasted him with her Coke. "I agree. What will you study?"

He shrugged. "History is a passion of mine. But I don't know where I'll take it, career wise." He grinned. "You seem to have figured it all out."

Tara nodded. "You have to make a lot of sacrifices when you work for yourself. But I wouldn't have it any other way."

"I admire that."

His smile was easy, his pint almost finished. It was now or never. "Where did you guys go that day after you left my shop?"

"We stopped at a realtor shop here in Galway, and an art gallery in Clifden."

Realty shop. That was news. Was it Heather Milton's? Did it have something to do with a new lease for Sheila and John Murphy? "What did Veronica want with a realtor in Galway?"

Andy shrugged. "Had us stay in the car. She was only in the shop for about twenty minutes."

"Did Bartley go in with her?"

Andy shook his head. "He stayed behind too. She definitely didn't share everything with him."

"What is your take on this little group?"

"I've only been her driver for a year. Never knew her during her drinking days, tanks be to God, but I've heard things, of course."

"Oh? Like what?"

"She was a mean drunk, I tell you dat."

"I hope this doesn't sound like I'm gossiping but—did Veronica relapse that Friday night?"

Andy's eyebrow raised. "What makes you tink dat?"

She noted he didn't answer her question. "I heard a rumor." She wasn't going to tell anyone that Veronica called her. It was too risky.

Andy appeared to be thinking about it. "I didn't see her after we got back to the castle. But some of the other lads working the car park said something about her, alright. Something about her being back on the sauce. To tell you the truth, I didn't think anything of it. They talk a lot of shite. Pardon my language."

"Were you in your room?"

"My room?" He laughed. "I didn't get a room at Ballynahinch."

"You didn't?"

Andy shook his head. "She did book me a room at the Clifden Station House Hotel. But it was too far away, so I ended up staying in the SUV." He held up his hand as if to stop her from talking. "I wanted to. Those seats are as soft as any bed. And the staff let me sneak in for showers and changes."

"That was nice of them."

He shrugged. "I threw them a few bob. We look out for each other."

Tara finished her Coke and didn't want another one. She still had no idea if Andy had bought that book. But what did it really mean? Maybe he was just curious to see why everyone else had a copy. Was he investigating Veronica's murder on the sly? "I'd better get back to the store."

He nodded. "I'll walk you."

As they headed for the shop he bounced by her side, whistling. Tara was replaying their conversation. Andy said they went two places after they left her shop. She'd forgotten to ask about the second. "The art gallery in Clifden," Tara said. "Was that about Eddie?"

"The artist," Andy said, using air quotes. "Why on earth would she be apologizing to him? A no-good hanger-on, after her money. Making his 'art.' He's the one who cheated on *her*."

"Cheated on her? With whom?"

He shrugged. "Shouldn't have said a word. Who am I? Just the driver. This isn't *Downton* fecking *Abbey*, where I'll end up marrying into the family and rising in stature."

Tara laughed. "Who would you marry? Cassidy?" Andy's face flamed red. Tara felt a little guilty about cornering him. Why wouldn't he be attracted to Cassidy? "I'm surprised you watch *Downton Abbey*," she said to lighten the mood. They'd reached Tara's shop.

"I'm full of surprises," he said with a wink. "If you ever want to learn more, the seats in the SUV fold back nicely."

* * *

The realty shop, Galway Properties, was on Tara's way home. She stopped to look at the flyers in the windows, wondering what prompted Veronica to stop in. She was peering at an advertisement for a one-bedroom flat when the owner, Heather Milton, exited the shop. As usual she looked impeccable in a tan suit, her red hair piled on top of her head. "What now?" Heather said, stopping when she spotted Tara. "Not happy at the mill? Or is it the shop?" Tara had rented the shop from Heather, so she guessed the woman was half teasing.

"Very happy," Tara said. "Just window browsing."

"How is the shop?"

"It's coming along nicely. Just waiting for my permit."

Heather groaned. "Dat's the worst part of opening a business here. Permits. Waiting on the city. Nightmare." She shuddered.

Tara wholeheartedly agreed. "Will I see you at the opening?"

"Of course. There could be loads of potential clients there." *Of course.* Heather winked, adjusted her satchel, and headed off.

"Wait."

Heather stopped, but looked like a runner waiting to zoom off. "What is it? I have an appointment."

"I heard Veronica O'Farrell came to see you."

Heather regarded her carefully. "What are you doing?"

"What do you mean?"

"People here are finally starting to accept you."

"That's great."

"Then knock it off. It's none of your business whether or not Ms. O'Farrell came to see me."

"I thought you'd rather tell me than the guards."

"You thought wrong." Heather whirled on her heels and clacked away, leaving Tara feeling foolish. The feeling was soon replaced by curiosity. What was Heather hiding? Why had Veronica come to see her? The one piece of the puzzle Tara had was that Veronica was looking into housing for John and Sheila Murphy. Tara assumed that housing would be in Dublin, where they currently lived. Was it possible that Veronica planned on getting them housing elsewhere, forcing them to decide whether to move? And if so, had the couple learned that their "gift" came with life-changing strings? Sheila's desperate voice came back to her: *Where do you think she stashed it?*

Mimi Griffin said something about Sheila and John complaining about their room. Tara needed to know more about that. Was it actually the hotel room they were complaining about, or had Mimi just assumed? Was it information she heard *directly*, or had she eavesdropped on them and jumped to her own conclusions? Tara headed home, the questions tumbling in her mind as she walked.

Rose's caravan was parked in its usual spot by the bay. For a second Tara was tempted to go in and say hello. But Rose would insist on reading her cards. And Tara couldn't take any more dire warnings. What was the one from a few days ago? *Don't let your light shine?* Despite being her uncle's lover, Tara still felt as if Rose was a complete mystery to her. Tara passed the caravan and made her way back to the salvage mill. Danny was outside rinsing dust off iron gates, then polishing them with a rag. Danny turned off the spray, then pointed the nozzle at Tara with a devious look in his eyes.

"Try it," she said. "You'll be sorry."

"Maybe," he said. "But not for the first twenty seconds." He grinned; she shook her head. It had been a while since he'd flirted so openly with her. *Maddening.*

"I'm thinking of checking out an art gallery in Clifden," she said.

"Of course you are." He dropped the hose. "I'll get me keys."

Chapter 17

Three art galleries could be found in downtown Clifden, interspersed between pubs, and restaurants, and shops. It would be easy to walk to all three, and they began with the one closest to their starting point. It looked small from the outside, but inside they discovered a series of small rooms, their walls filled top to bottom with colorful oil paintings. Many depicted the stunning scenery of Connemara, another featured household items: a row of colorful wellies, a dining room table decorated for a feast, umbrellas. Tara wished they had more leisure time; she loved getting lost in the paintings. The back room contained sculptures, but unlike the wild creations Tara had seen in Eddie's portfolio, these were of jackrabbits, dogs, foxes. An older woman watched them walk through with a nod. Tara felt this was not the gallery Veronica had sought out, but if she was wrong, she'd have to return.

The second gallery was closed. Dark blinds covered the doors. The sign listed the opening hours, and they were well within them. "It looks like it's been closed for a while," Danny said.

"Let's hope the third time's the charm," Tara replied. On the way, they passed shops with touristy items, bakeries, pubs, and gift shops. They also passed the antique shop that Tara wanted to hit later. It appeared to be two long rooms, and just spying an old-fashioned telephone, lamp, and typewriter in the window made her itch to go inside. Danny stopped as well. "I prefer going to the source," Danny said. "Getting me hands dirty." By the source he meant chapels, estate sales, old barns. Tara would love that too. But it would be much easier to buy gifts for their guests here, at least knock a few off the list. They reached the final art gallery. The façade was painted a vibrant red, and inside canvases took center stage on faded brick walls. Many were of local scenery, and Tara and Danny took a few minutes to breathe them in. Galway Bay, and Galway city, and the Connemara mountains, and Kylemore Abbey. One of her favorites was simply sheep crossing in front of a tractor waiting to make its way down the road. She didn't see any sculptures, or work that was similar to the art in Eddie's portfolio. She approached the desk, where a clerk was absorbed in his computer screen. Piles of papers surrounded him. It didn't take long to spot the portfolio for Eddie Oh amidst the pile. It was just like the portfolio that Veronica had left with her.

"May I help you?" The clerk had stopped looking at his screen and was peering at Tara through glasses that had slid halfway down his nose.

"Yes." She pointed at the portfolio. "Veronica O'Farrell also came to see me that Friday and drop off Eddie's portfolio."

He stared at her. "Okay." He was on guard.

"She also hired me to do some work for her, and I was wondering if you could tell me about her visit."

He swiped up the portfolio. "She stopped in. Gave me this, said I had to convince him to have a show here." He laughed. "Convince. As if it's my job not only to showcase an artist but convince them?" He shook his head as he leafed through the portfolio. "This work is all a decade old. It has a certain appeal, I'll give you dat." He gestured to the paintings. "I mostly show oils. But she was a very convincing woman and so I called him. He's never called me back."

"I've met him recently. He said he doesn't create anymore."

"That's what I would have told her. But she never came back." He shook his head. "A murder. Right here in Connemara. At the end of tourist season."

Tara nodded, knowing the last bit wasn't at all important; murder was murder regardless of tourists, although she supposed a murder in a small place like Clifden could impact business. "Did she come in alone?"

He rubbed his chin. "No. There was a fella with her. Big guy."

"Bald? Dressed in black?"

"Dat's the one."

Bartley. Seems he rarely stayed in the car. "Thanks." She pulled out the travel book. "Did anyone ever leave a copy of this in your gallery?"

He squinted at the book. "No." He straightened up. "Are we in there?"

"I don't think so."

"Terrible book then, tis."

She slipped it back into her bag. "Is there anything else you can tell me about the visit?"

He shook his head. "Sorry."

"Thanks." She set her card on top of the counter and started to walk away.

"Except I did let her driver in to use the jax." *Jax.* The Irish word for bathroom.

She stopped. Turned. "Oh?"

"Poor lad, it was the big guy in black who had to ask for him. She seemed inclined to let him wait it out."

What in the world? Either Veronica kept him driving all the time without restroom breaks, or there was something else going on. Some kind of choreographed act? What on earth for?

"Tara?" Danny stood in front of her. "What is it?"

The art gallery owner was watching her. She tilted her head down and lowered her voice. "Let's walk and talk."

They stopped at a bakery. Tara desperately needed sugar and caffeine. She got an apple tart and coffee. Danny copied her. They sat in the back so they could talk. It was the best apple tart Tara had ever tasted. Amazingly soft and flaky crust, sweet, thick apples, just the right amount of sweet. She indulged in it for a few minutes before filling Danny in on the strange coincidence of Andy needing to use the restroom, and Bartley asking for him. Scratch *coincidence.* It was exactly the same. It was choreographed. But why?

"Two choices," Danny said. "The man consumes a

lot of liquids while driving and has a tiny bladder, or as you theorized, it's some kind of deliberate act. A distraction?"

"To what end?"

"That's the mystery."

Did Veronica use the distraction to plant the book? Whatever for? "What?" Danny said. "You've got a really strange look on your face."

She filled Danny in on the crazy thoughts in her head. "What if . . . Veronica planned this? All of this?"

Danny lifted an eyebrow. "Planned her own murder?"

"Isn't it possible?"

"Why?"

"Maybe she was already dying. Some kind of terminal disease. And she wanted to get revenge? And what better revenge than making them all murder suspects?"

Danny eyed the plate where her apple tart once sat. "I'm starting to worry that was laced with something."

"I know. I know. It's crazy." Talk about morbid. "You're right. Veronica's too selfish to sacrifice herself, even for revenge."

Danny arched an eyebrow. "If not staging your own murder is selfish, I'd say we all are."

"True." Tara was talking crazy. But it was part of her process. When designing, it was good to let your mind spool, to go too far. Most people were so protected by their boundaries that the only way to break open was to barrel right through them. Then you could pull back. "Let's say the distraction was all about leaving me the book, no matter the reason."

"Okay," Danny said.

"The art gallery owner didn't get a book."

"He said he didn't get a book?"

She sighed. It was nearly impossible to figure out a case when you had to factor in the sad truth that absolutely everyone could be lying. And why wouldn't they lie to her? She wasn't a guard. "Let's say he's telling the truth and he didn't get a book. Why all the bathroom antics?"

"You could ask the driver or Bartley."

She intended to. They cleaned up their table and stood outside. She removed Andy's card from her pocket. "I was at a pub with Andy yesterday."

"Doing some day drinking, Miss America?"

He sounded jealous. Good. She shoved him gently. "No, I wasn't doing some day drinking, I had a Coke."

"Why are you hanging around these people?"

"I thought I saw him in a bookstore in Galway. I was wondering if he would fess up."

"Did he?"

"Yes. And no."

Danny sighed. "I'm going to need more than dat."

"He admitted to being in the bookstore, but he claimed he just bought a Western."

"A Western?"

"In honor of his dad." She hesitated. "But I think he bought a second book he forgot to mention."

"*Places to See in Ireland Before You Die,*" Danny said.

"Yep."

"What do you make of dat?"

"Truthfully? I think he wanted to know what the fuss was about."

"Then why didn't he 'fess up,' as you put it?"

"Either he didn't think it was any of my business,

or he doesn't want me knowing that he's also looking into the case."

"You're saying the driver is playing amateur detective?"

"He is around all the suspects. And he's basically invisible as the driver. I bet he's heard all sorts of things."

"Good thing you learned to drive here. Maybe you'll get better at it and take his place."

"Ha, ha." She gave him another shove; he pretended to stumble, then grabbed Tara and pulled her into him.

"Do me a favor," Danny said, his voice low. "Meet with these yokes all you want. Just don't do it alone. It's not safe."

"You might be right," Tara said.

Danny rocked back on his heels. The wind was picking up, their hair began whipping around them. "Me, right? Be still me heart," he said with a laugh.

"Look at this." Tara removed her smartphone and brought up the article on Terrance Hughes. She handed it to Danny. He read through it, his lips moving silently as he read, which wasn't adorable at all. He finished reading and whistled.

"So Cassidy did accuse Veronica of being a murderer. What do you make of it?"

"It's confusing. Veronica does not seem like the type of woman to forgive *that.*"

"Maybe she didn't." Danny paused to watch a pretty girl stroll by. Tara resisted the urge to kick him in the shin.

"Meaning?"

"She's making amends. Maybe she went off the deep end with Cassidy after this accusation—did something to her—and *that's* what she's trying to make up for." Danny stopped. "I wonder if Veronica is responsible for Cassidy's pill addiction."

Tara stopped. "Cassidy is responsible for her pill addiction. If she is addicted to pills. So far it's all just gossip."

"But if Veronica did get her addicted—that would be evil."

"I just don't think a person can blame anyone else for his or her addictions."

"Touché." Were they arguing? It seemed as if they always ended up in an argument. Partly because Danny just liked to argue. She'd had a mellow relationship with Gabriel. Practical. Loving, but she had to admit, it was not passionate. Danny made her toes curl at times. Her heart beat faster at the sight of him. She equally wanted to pummel him. It was maddening. And she was slightly addicted.

"The more I learn about these people, the less I want to be around them," Danny said.

"You don't have to be."

"I do if I want to keep you safe."

"I'm perfectly capable of keeping myself safe." There were other things he could do for her, but at the moment they wouldn't be doing any of them.

They were almost to Danny's car, ready to call it a day, when the door to a nearby restaurant swung open and Sheila Murphy flew out, tears streaming down her face. John Murphy emerged next, jaw set, sunglasses hiding his eyes. Sheila raced down the footpath, but John didn't follow. Instead, he stood near the door to the restaurant and pulled out his cell phone as if he prepared to wait out whatever this tantrum was. Lovers' quarrel. Sheila stopped in front of a pub a few doors down, leaned against the stone façade, and pulled out a pack of cigarettes.

Tara nudged Danny. "That's Sheila and John Murphy. They're two of the seven guests. Veronica was their landlady years ago and evicted them."

Danny glanced between husband and wife. "Because they argue a lot?"

"I don't know the reason. But they've never seen you. Don't you feel like saying hello to a stranger?"

Danny followed her gaze to Sheila, still smoking outside the pub. He sighed. "First Cassidy, now this one. Are you pimping me out, Miss America?"

"A pimp for information." He gave her the side-eye. "What can I say? You have a talent."

Before Tara could ask again, Danny was striding over to Sheila, a grin on his face. For a second Tara wondered if this was a bad idea. John seemed like the jealous type. Tara put her sunglasses on and wandered to the shop next to the pub, hoping to eavesdrop. Danny had no problem warming Sheila up; she was mid-complaint when Tara reached the shop.

"—horrible woman! But that was five years ago. We've moved on. Literally and figuratively. We told the guards, we had no reason to kill her. Now that woman that she maimed for life—*she* has a reason to kill her."

"Maimed for life?"

Iona, Tara thought from her hidey-spot.

"She's a hiker. Veronica tripped her once, caused her to snap a ligament or something. All I know is she's still paying her medical bills. I heard her arguing with Veronica the day before she died."

This was news. Maybe Veronica did argue with

every single one of them Friday night. *They're all liars! I'm going to expose them all!*

"—hollering at each other until Iona broke down in sobs. You should see this woman. More of a lad, if you ask me. I can only imagine what it took to bring her to tears. I tried to ask her if she was alright and she told me to mind me own bleeping business. How's that for rude?"

"Sounds terribly rude to me," Danny agreed. He turned up the charm, a thousand-watt smile. Sheila's cheeks grew rosy. Tara glanced at John. He was still buried in his phone and had yet to notice Danny chatting up his wife.

"Veronica stole from us yet again."

Stole from them? *Where do you think she stashed it?* Tara listened for more, wishing she could hurry Sheila along. *Stole what?*

"Sheila!" John Murphy had caught on. He now stood in front of her, fists clenched at his side. "Let's go. Now." She stubbed her cigarette out and hurried after her husband, who was already walking away. "Keep your big mouth shut," Tara heard him say. *Lovely.*

"Thanks anyway," Tara said when Danny returned.

"He's a bully." Danny watched as John and Sheila disappeared in the distance.

"I think they're looking for something that Veronica had." She described the other conversation she'd overheard.

"*Stashed it,*" Danny mused.

"Wonder what *it* is."

Danny shrugged. "Iona is the bird you followed to her room, is she not?"

"Yes. She's the bird I followed to her room. The hiker. THC with a Mountain."

Danny's forehead crinkled in confusion. "What?"

"Never mind."

"So where shall I take you, m'lady?"

"Back to the castle, m'lord." Danny laughed. "Wanna join me?"

"I don't see why not," he said with a lingering look that made Tara's heart pick up the pace.

"Speaking of THC," she said. "Tomorrow I'd like to get stones."

"Stoned?" Danny sounded on board but surprised.

"Stones," Tara said. "As in marble." The marble stones placed on Veronica's face were the killer's calling card. A visit to the Connemara marble factory was long overdue.

"Good idea," Danny said. "Because you've definitely lost your marbles."

Chapter 18

After what Tara had to admit was a tick-mark night for keeping Danny as a romantic partner (okay maybe *two* tick marks), and a full Irish breakfast, and another trip back to the room (three times is the charm), they arrived at the Connemara marble factory just as a jovial employee was finishing his presentation. They slipped in as he spoke.

"Connemara marble can be found in the floors of the Galway Cathedral, Westminster Cathedral, London's General Post Office, and the Oxford University Natural History Museum. America has used it in many churches, cathedrals, and even the Senate Chamber and Senate Post Office of the State Capitol Building in Harrisburg, Pennsylvania. I hope you've enjoyed the tour, and please do visit our gift shop where you can take home a piece of our precious Connemara marble."

The crowd applauded and soon they moved into the gift shop. Tara quickly spotted the same marble stones that she'd seen on Veronica. The purchase price for five stones would have been around forty euro. Easy enough to pay that in cash and it would have been the smart thing to do. The guards must have checked it out already. Had they shown photos of all the suspects to the gift-shop employees? Danny snuck up behind her. "What are we really doing here?"

She sighed. "I can't tell you everything, but I was curious about something, and I have part of an answer."

"A woman of mystery," he said. Danny could be sarcastic, even caustic at times, but he was a kind, smart man. He knew Tara would tell him if she could.

"Indeed." They shared a rare public kiss, nothing that would draw any alarm from passersby.

As they were leaving, she caught a glimpse of a book parked near the register. *Places to See in Ireland Before You Die.* She stopped in her tracks. "You've got to be kidding me."

Danny followed her gaze. "That book is certainly making the rounds."

There was already another customer in the middle of a transaction. "Is that your book?" Tara said lightly, hoping the employee was able to multitask. The twentysomething lad looked up at her, then back at his customer and finished the transaction.

"I'm waiting for the owner to come back for it," he said with a grin. "See if I can get a date."

"Oh?"

"She's me future wife."

"Like the niece of an heiress would want you," another clerk joked. The lad shot him a look.

Cassidy Hughes.

"The plot thickens," Danny said.

"Indeed." Tara was slightly stunned. Cassidy Hughes had been in the gift shop, where she'd left her copy of the book. Had she also bought marble stones? Two black ones, a red one, and a green one? "I know her," Tara said. "I bet she bought out the store . . ." The clerk didn't reply. "I'm staying at the same hotel." Tara hoisted the book. "I can give this back to her."

The clerk shook his head, but the manager intervened. "We'd appreciate it." He put the book in a store gift bag and handed it to her.

Tara flipped through the book on her way out. A note written on the title page caught her eye: *Forgiveness is a virtue. You have none.*

A note in the book! The note was printed in black ink, and block letters. When everyone gathered on the grounds of the castle, they swore up and down there were no markings in the books. Of course. Why should they tell Tara anything? She wasn't a detective. She was going to have to report this to the guards. Would they think she was being nosy? Whether they did or not, she couldn't worry about it. This was bigger than her. This was about justice for Veronica. She placed the book back in the bag, wondering if anyone else had notes written in theirs. Who was she kidding? They probably *all* had notes. Maybe they were all waiting for someone else to come forward and admit they had a note and that the note hadn't been so nice. It brought back the question—was it Veronica who dropped the books off to everyone, or someone else?

Would the guards be able to verify whether or not this was Veronica's handwriting? If it wasn't hers—it was the killer's. It looked as if someone was trying to write in a very plain way. An effort to disguise his or her handwriting? Tara needed a sample of Veronica's handwriting.

"I don't know about you, but I want a pint," Danny said.

"Lead the way." A pint sounded good. She'd had her day of abstinence, and hopefully that would be enough to honor Veronica's memory. She wasn't eager to go back to the castle; she needed to mull over her next steps. As they rolled into town, they caught sight of the mountains covered in a layer of shimmering mist. Joy surged through Tara. How was it Yeats described Connemara? *The savage heart of beauty.* Tara concurred.

Like homing pigeons, they returned to the pub they'd visited earlier in Clifden. "Look who's here." Tara followed Danny's gaze. Eddie was planted on a stool, and from the way he was rocking himself, he'd been there a while.

Here we go again.

Tara was torn. She'd really wanted a break from it all. But when people were oiled up, that's when sometimes they let things spill. And, given that Eddie Oh was oiled up in the early afternoon, she had a feeling he had things to spill. They'd probably drown in it.

"Let's find somewhere else," Danny said. Apparently, he was in no mood for a swim.

Tara was debating how to break it to Danny that she wanted to stay when Eddie did it for her. "Hey!" Eddie had spotted them and was off his stool, stumbling toward them. "Hey, Miss America."

Danny leaned in. "Thought that was my special line for ya."

"Not my fault," she whispered back. Danny was staring at her hand. She was wondering why when she remembered she was carrying the gift bag from Connemara Marble Visitor Centre.

"It's true," Eddie said, swaying, and trying to point at her bag. "Someone put *marble stones* on her face?"

"What?" Danny said.

His outburst startled Tara. She shushed him. Eddie grabbed her shoulders, nearly shaking her. "I need to know."

"Hands off." Danny stepped in, forcing Eddie to drop his hands. Danny leaned in. "What's he on about. Marble stones on her face?"

How did Eddie find out? It wasn't her. She hadn't said a word to anyone. "I don't know what you're talking about," Tara lied. She'd promised she wouldn't say a word. The guards were going to have to know about this too. Eddie stepped back and gave Danny the once-over. Then his gaze slid to Tara as a lascivious grin took over his face. "You two are knocking boots," he said, laughing delightedly. "Good on you, lads."

"Enough," Tara said as Eddie stumbled in front of them and leaned against the wall, blocking their exit. He started to bang his head against it.

"I loved her. I *loved* her."

She sighed. He'd be of no use to them in this shape. "Why don't you let us take you back to the castle."

"Great," Danny muttered under his breath.

"Castle!" he said, throwing up his hands. "She put us up in a castle. Because that's who Veronica was. Who did this. Who?" He whirled on Tara as if expecting her to provide the answer.

"It's painful to lose someone you love. Especially if you screwed up." Tara wasn't proud of herself, antagonizing a drunk man who seemed to be grieving, but she had to know—if he wasn't the killer—how did he know she had the marble stones on her? Were Sheila and John blabbing?

He glared at her. "Screwed up. Me?"

"Never mind." Her tone very much conveyed there was something to mind.

"Not a chance. What do you mean?"

"I didn't mean." She hesitated. "I heard you cheated on her. I'm not judging."

He leaned in with a look that could only be interpreted as menacing. "Cheated on whom?"

"Veronica," Tara said. She wanted to move back, away from his breath, but held her ground.

"Me? Cheat on *her*?" To her surprise, he stepped back and howled with laughter. It took him a moment to stop and compose himself. His face then morphed into one of sadness. "She cheated on me. That's why we divorced." He whirled around, and stumbled out onto the sidewalk. Tara and Danny followed.

"Is that why she wanted to make amends?" she said. "Because she cheated on you?"

He shrugged, then began lurching up the footpath. "Doubt it. She was a sexually free woman. No apologies necessary."

"You just said you divorced her over it."

He waved his hand. "That was my problem. I was too weak to take it. So jealous." He stopped, balled his hand into a fist and banged his forehead. "I should have let her be free. Like a little randy bird."

Danny cleared his throat, struggling not to laugh. "Then why was she making amends?"

"My career," he said. "After I left her . . . she sabotaged it." He tottered up to the window of a shop selling touristy trinkets, and stared at them through the glass.

"We should get you back to the castle," Danny said, taking his arm. "Doesn't that sound nice?"

Eddie brightened. "We could go fishing!"

"Sure!" Danny said. He threw a look to Tara and shook his head. The three of them managed to get to Danny's truck with Eddie wobbling between them. Tara wished Andy was here to take her home; she hated the thought of being squeezed in with drunk Eddie.

"I want to know about the marble," he said once they started driving. "Black for the heart was it? Green for the eyes? Red mouth?"

He didn't have it quite right. Or he was pretending not to have it quite right. Given his state of intoxication, Tara had to lean toward the former. But the fact that he knew was startling. John and Sheila. They had to be running their big mouths. Or just Sheila. Was that why John was telling her to keep her mouth shut? "I'm afraid I'm not involved in that aspect of the case."

Danny gave her the side-eye; he was going to grill her about the marble stones the minute he got the chance. Especially since she'd been so inquisitive about them at the factory. She would have to tell Danny and pray *he'd* keep his mouth shut. Trying to keep a secret was a losing battle.

"It's some kind of code. Message," Eddie rambled. He snapped his fingers. "That assistant. That woman. Mimi."

"Mimi Griffin?" Tara couldn't help but engage.

"Dat's the one." Eddie's head bobbed up and down. "She's the type who speaks in codes. Bet she has it written down in one of those notebooks of hers."

It was an interesting observation, even for a man as trashed as Eddie. "It's really not a good idea to point fingers," Tara said. Danny gave her another furtive glance, and when he looked away there was a definite smirk on his face. Yes, she was being a bit of a hypocrite. But there was no danger of her confronting any of the guests about her suspicions. Eddie, on the other hand, was a walking stick of dynamite.

"I'll show you. The answer has to be in those notebooks of hers. Just wait until I get me hands on them."

"That would be a big mistake," Tara said. "The guards are watching all of you."

He mumbled something to himself, then put his head back on the seat. Seconds later he was snoring.

"Marble stones on her?" Danny asked.

Tara sighed. "What I'm about to tell you cannot leave this truck."

Andy was in his usual smoking spot, to the side of the castle. He offered to help maneuver Eddie to his room. Between himself and Danny, they managed to stumble him along through the lobby, although he drew quite the attention as guests were congregating for dinner. Eddie was half awake and his mouth was running. As they passed a hotel employee, Tara caught the tail end of his conversation.

"The guards are finished with the room. Her solicitor has been given permission to retrieve the rest of her personal things. It's slated for a full cleaning tomorrow morning."

Veronica's room . . .

"Sheila and John Murphy," Eddie yelled out ahead. Tara glanced up to see the bewildered expression on Sheila's face, but John appeared disgusted with Eddie's intoxication. He made a face, but kept walking. Eddie whirled on them, and pointed. "I was there when they got their eviction notice. The missus was hauled away in an ambulance."

"Sheila was hauled away in an ambulance?" Tara asked.

"Dat's what I said," Eddie replied.

The pair stopped walking. Sheila let out a cry. They turned around to face Eddie. "Shut your mouth," John said, stepping in front of his wife.

"He's drunk," Andy said, holding out his hand.

"I don't care," John Murphy said, squaring off. "If he doesn't shut it, I'll shut it for him."

"No," Danny said. "You won't." All three men tensed, as they regarded each other.

"Don't," Sheila said, coming up behind John. "For me."

John glared at Eddie, who surprisingly kept his

mouth shut, his chin lowering. John allowed Sheila to drag him away. "What floor is he on?" Tara asked.

"Tree," Johnny said.

Top floor. *Great.* Danny and Andy groaned in unison as they headed for the stairs.

Ambulance? Sheila? Was there any truth to that? Tara felt a presence behind her and swiveled her head. There stood Mimi Griffin and Elaine Burke, hands over their mouths like a pair of horrified bookends as Eddie stopped at the bottom of the stairs and started mumbling again.

"He's had a bit too much," Tara explained.

"A bit? I can smell the alcohol coming off him," Mimi said, her head shaking with disapproval.

"And don't trust Cassidy, that little pill-popper," Eddie said. "She accused my Roni of killing Terrance just so she could have the family fortune." *For the love of God, get him up to his room.* They managed to coax him up a few steps, which didn't stop his mouth from running. "Not to mention that man-hating hiker. She's faking that injury!"

Finally, they made progress up and away. Tara didn't want to be with Eddie anymore, especially taking the stairs up to the third floor, but she also didn't want to miss a word. "Nancy. Why did she have to die?" Eddie's head lolled over to Andy as the two men struggled to keep Eddie marching on.

"She was a good woman, wasn't she?"

"I'm sure she was," Andy said.

"You know she was!" Eddie said as if Andy had started a fight with him.

"Of course," Andy said. "Of course she was."

Eddie calmed down. "She didn't deserve to die." His head bobbed back, snoring away.

"I didn't realize Eddie knew Nancy," Tara said. She was going to have to ask him about her when he was sober.

"I think he's been in and out of the rooms," Andy said.

The rooms. He meant AA. "Oh." Tara's heart squeezed with compassion. Eddie knew he had a drinking problem. Veronica, and her sponsor Nancy, had probably tried to help him. Now both of these women who may have championed him into sobriety were gone. She hoped when this was over, Eddie would go back to those rooms and get sober. Surprisingly, Eddie seemed to run out of steam. He fell quiet and they climbed to the third floor with only the sounds of labored breathing. When they reached the door to his room it took several attempts to find his card key. It was tucked into the back pocket of his trousers. When it became apparent that Eddie was in no shape to do it himself, Danny was forced to fetch them.

"You owe me one," Danny said, handing her the keys. "Or twelve."

As soon as they opened the door, Andy saluted. "I'll leave you here."

"Thank you," Danny said.

"Yes, thank you," Tara said.

Andy nodded, and made his exit. Together, they moved in and deposited Eddie on the bed. "Roni. Roni."

"Go to sleep," Tara said.

He lifted his head and stared at the adjoining door. "That was her room."

Startled, Tara stared at the door. It was unlocked and standing open. The other door was shut. But that didn't mean it was locked. And Eddie had just admitted (intentionally or not) that even though he hadn't officially checked in until after Veronica's death, he was definitely here. Otherwise how could he possibly know it was Veronica's room? And if it was . . . how could Tara *not* go in?

Chapter 19

Tara approached the door on tiptoe, as if that made any sense at all.

"Hey," Danny said, making her jump. "Whatcha doing?"

Tara stopped and pointed to the door. "Did you hear him? It could lead to Veronica's room."

"I heard." Danny stared at the door. "You can't go in there."

"I overheard housekeeping downstairs. The guards are finished with it. Bartley will be collecting her things."

"What's your plan here?"

Handwriting sample? Tara shrugged. "Just have a quick look."

"That doesn't sound prudent."

"Prudent? Since when do you think things like that, let alone say them?"

"If you're going to have a quick look, you should at least wear a pair of gloves."

"Good point." She continued to stare at the door. "It might be locked." She held up a finger, then hurried to the bathroom and came out with a hand towel. Tara wrapped the towel around the handle and pushed. The door opened. Danny and Tara exchanged a look. "Gloves?" Danny asked.

Tara lifted the towel. "If I have to touch anything I'll use this."

"Be quick."

"You're not coming?"

Danny shook his head. "I'll wait in the hall. If anyone comes, I'll whistle."

"Didn't know you could whistle."

"There's a lot of things you don't know about me." He glanced at Eddie, still snoring. "Hurry up."

"Sure." He didn't want to be in Veronica's hotel room. *Morbid*, Tara imagined Veronica saying in her ear, along with a laugh. She was losing it. Danny tucked into the hall as Tara stepped into the room.

A Chanel luggage bag lay open on a bench at the foot of the four-poster bed. A few gowns hung in the closet. At the base at least a dozen heels were standing in a row, including a pair covered in gold jewels. Tara had no idea what she was doing here. She peeked into the wastebasket by the desk. Empty. There was no handbag; Tara assumed the guards had it. She glanced at the notepad and pen by the telephone. Nothing was written on it, not even an imprint of a previous note she could suss out by shading over it with pencil. Veronica hadn't been a note-taker, she'd been a finger-snapper.

She glanced at the adjoining door, still ajar. Had

Veronica requested that Eddie's room adjoin hers? She must have. With such easy access to her room, if Eddie was the killer, wouldn't he have found a subtler way of doing it? Then again, subtle didn't seem his style. As an artist he was experimental to say the least. And on that early morning she was killed, Eddie hadn't checked into the hotel yet. But that didn't mean he wasn't here . . .

Tara ducked into the bathroom. Red marks were slashed across the mirror. Blood? Her heart began to thud against her rib cage. BAR was written with a slash mark—an interrupted T? *Bartley?* A tube of smooshed red lipstick lay on the counter, its lid on the floor. Who wrote this and what made them stop so suddenly? Was it Veronica? Spelling out who she was going to meet at Clifden Castle that morning? The hotel clerk mentioned the guards had processed the room. That meant they knew about this. Tara took a picture with her phone. Shimmering gold on the counter caught her eye; a sparkly makeup bag. The wastebasket was empty in here as well, solidifying Tara's theory that the guards had taken the rubbish. Strange, how the things we threw away in life were important clues in death. Tara heard a swish, and a click. It came from the room. *Someone else was in here.* Adrenaline coursed through her as she stilled. She listened for a whistle. Nothing. She tiptoed back into the room, heading for the adjoining door. It was closed. She had purposely left it open.

Could a breeze have shut it? She glanced at the windows. The curtains were drawn on the right side, but partly open on the left. The windows were shut. Had both curtains been drawn when she came in?

Yes. There was more light now. Someone had been

in here. Where were they now? If they'd escaped to
the hall, wouldn't she have heard an exclamation
from Danny?

If the person wasn't in the hall, that meant he or
she was in Eddie Oh's room. Was Eddie in danger?
Maybe the guards *hadn't* seen the writing on the mirror. Maybe it was fresh. Maybe it was Tara who interrupted the message . . .

Bartley was the one being sent to pack up Veronica's things. Was someone trying to scare him? Or tip
him off that he or she knew he was a killer?

Tara cracked open the door to the hall. Danny was
leaning against the wall. "Anything?"

She put her finger to her lips and stepped out,
quietly closing the door.

"Where's the hand towel?" he asked. She'd left it
in the bathroom. It didn't matter now. She pointed
to Eddie's room.

"Someone's in there."

"What? How?"

She grabbed him and pulled him farther down
the hall to a dark recess, where she told him everything in a panicked whisper. "We have to go in. Make
sure Eddie's okay."

"How? We no longer have the key and you just
shut Veronica's door."

A creak sounded; a door was opening somewhere
on the floor. They flattened themselves against the
wall. "What are you two doing?"

The deep male voice came from behind them.
They whirled around to see Bartley looming over
them. He was wearing thick black gloves and carrying matching duffel bags. A swooshing sound came
from the opposite direction. A figure dressed in a

long black coat with a pile of clothing draped over his or her head and a pillowcase filled to the brim, bolted down the hall. He or she disappeared into the stairwell, the door slamming behind him or her.

"Are those Veronica's dresses?" Bartley said. He started down the hall.

"Wait," Tara said. "I need the key to Veronica's room." Bartley hesitated, clearly wanting to sprint down the hall. "We have to check on Eddie."

"What is going on?" Bartley repeated.

"Should I run after him?" Danny said.

Or her. Tara shook her head. "Eddie comes first." She raced to the room with Danny right behind her, and Bartley shouting in the rear.

"What on earth is happening?"

Tara held her hand out and Bartley reluctantly handed her the key. She entered Veronica's room, then opened the adjoining door. Eddie was on the bed, on his back, snoring. "Thank heavens." Tara hadn't realized how much terror she was holding inside until she let it all out in a big breath. "He's breathing."

She returned to the hall, closed his door, and slumped with relief against the wall.

Bartley pointed down the hall. "Who and what was that?"

"Someone stealing from Veronica's room," Tara said. Maybe Veronica shouldn't have been making amends at all. "I interrupted them." *And I think they tried to throw shade at you . . .*

Bartley would notice the writing on the mirror. Should Tara mention it? Should she wait and see if *he* reported it to the guards? What would it mean if he wiped it clean and said nothing?

"I'm here to collect her things," Bartley said. "We must report this at once."

"I know." Tara handed back the key. Bartley hurried over to Veronica's door and opened it. Tara followed him in. The gowns were missing from the closet. The shoes were gone. The Chanel luggage bag must have been too hard to swipe for it was still at the foot of the bed. "We know it's a woman then," Bartley said.

"No," Tara said. "We don't." *It probably was.* But it wasn't good to jump to conclusions. Danny poked his head in.

"Everything okay?"

"No," Bartley said. "One of you had better start talking."

"We were hauling Eddie up to his bed," Tara said. "He was drunk."

"How did that . . . thing . . . get into Veronica's room?"

"Eddie has an adjoining room and the door was unlocked."

"But Eddie's room was locked," Danny said. "And presumably Veronica's. Did someone else have a key or do you think they followed in behind us?"

It was an eerie thought. "Wouldn't we have noticed?"

"We were focused on hauling his drunken arse, so no, I don't think we would have."

"They must have been quick," Tara said. *Nerves of steel. Nerves to steal.*

"And very quiet," Danny added.

Bartley dipped his hand into his pocket and retrieved his mobile phone. "Should I call the hotel manager first?"

"Probably a good place to start," Tara said. "They can direct you to the detective or guards who've been handling the hotel."

Bartley paced the hall as he placed the call, then when he was finished returned and wiped his brow with his gloves. "We should knock on every guest's door and conduct an inspection until we find our thief."

Tara finally had her chance to speak with the one man who might have the answers she needed. "Can you fill me in on everything that happened with Veronica after you left my shop that day?"

The hallway was dim. Shadows fell across Bartley's broad face. He did not look like a friendly man. "Why would I do that?"

"I'm just trying to piece it all together."

"I've already spoken with the detective. I think it's best if I leave it at that." Bartley returned to the edge of Veronica's room, hovering. Was he just avoiding Tara's questions? Should she leave him alone to see how he reacted to the writing on the mirror?

"Veronica called me," Tara said. "That night."

Bartley's body did not move but he turned his head. "What?"

Danny touched Tara's elbow. "Careful," he whispered. Tara had told him about the writing on the mirror. Danny didn't want her to antagonize a killer. But the manager was on his way up, and presumably the guards had been called. If anyone knew all of Veronica's secrets, it was this man. And her news about the phone call seemed to interest him.

"I didn't answer," Tara continued. "It was after midnight, and I didn't recognize the number." If she had answered, would Veronica still be alive?

Bartley looked up as if he was trying to snatch a memory from the ceiling. He slowly turned to face Tara. "We ran a few errands after we left your shop and we were back at the castle before seven p.m. She gave me the night off," he said. "Along with Andy."

Andy had given the same account, although he'd been more specific about the errands. "What kind of mood was she in?"

Bartley's gaze now turned to the carpeted hall. "She was tired. We all were. That's all I can recall."

"She wasn't angry?"

Bartley shook his head. "Not at all."

"Then what?"

"I retired to my room and didn't come out until eight a.m. We were to meet in front of the castle at nine a.m. sharp. I waited with the rest of the group. We all thought Veronica slept in. You know the rest."

"When you gathered to leave for the castle, did you see all of the guests present?"

Bartley shook his head. "Sheila and John Murphy were nowhere in sight. Neither was Eddie—he hadn't arrived yet." *At least that's what Eddie wanted everyone to think.* Tara kept this to herself; she had no proof. Bartley frowned as he tried to recall that morning. "Elaine hadn't arrived yet either." A worrisome look clouded his face.

"Andy picked Elaine up at a bus station in Galway," Tara said. *Although he made a point of saying he didn't actually see her get off a bus.* But Galway city was far enough away from Ballynahinch Castle that if her late arrival was a ruse to concoct an alibi, it was a pretty good one. Then again, this killer was not ordinary. They were playing an elaborate game. And maybe having a good alibi was all part of their grand scheme.

"Everyone else was present. Cassidy was late. She looked like something the cat dragged in." He stopped again. "I thought she was hungover. But what if her wild look was because she had just plunged that brooch into Veronica's heart?"

Tara had never heard him so emotive. "Does Cassidy have her own car here?"

"I don't know. I can only hope the guards have talked to the valets. If anyone left, or if a taxi pulled up, they would know."

"What about you?"

Bartley straightened. "What about me?"

"You didn't come out of your room at all Friday evening?"

"I did not. I showered. Dined in my room, read a book, watched television. I was knackered."

"Did you hear anything?"

"My room is tucked away. I fell asleep with the television on. What is it you think I would have heard?"

"Veronica. Arguing with some of her guests."

Bartley shook his head.

"You knew Veronica better than anyone. You know all of her guests." Tara stepped forward. "Is there anyone you're suspicious of?"

"Yes," Bartley said. Danny and Tara stilled.

"Who?" Tara said, wanting him to spit it out.

He pinned her with his eyes. "You," he said. "I'm suspicious of you."

Chapter 20

"You sleeping here tonight?" Danny asked, after Bartley shut Veronica's door in their faces.

"No," she said. "I want to go back to the mill." And she did. She missed Hound. And Savage. And her loft. And Galway city. She didn't need a castle. Or suspects pointing the finger at *her*. Bartley couldn't really suspect her, could he? And who had been the person hiding in Veronica's room, writing Bartley's name on the mirror and stealing Veronica's clothes? Was it the killer or just an opportunistic thief? Would the guards conduct room-to-room inspections? It was all swimming in her head and she needed the comfort of home. And she secretly hoped Danny would stay over. They were quiet on the drive back. Danny put the radio on, and they each retreated into their own thoughts, buffered by the mountains shrouded in darkness on either side of them. It had been quite a busy day. Tara nodded off and by the time she woke, Danny was pulling up to the mill.

He didn't park in his usual spot; instead he left the engine running, waiting for her to get out. "You want to come in?" She hated that she felt timid even asking it—no, she hated that she had to ask. "Sit by the fire with a drink?"

"After that shower of savages?" he said with a dry laugh. "I'm beat."

"Me too." *We could just sleep, you know.* She got out of the car and gave a half wave.

"Get a good night's sleep."

"You too." She already knew she would not.

Hound and Savage were welcome sights. They were in the mill but eagerly followed her up to the loft, where she gave them kisses, and hugs, and treats. Hound took his usual spot by the fire, but Savage curled up on her lap as she lounged on the sofa while clutching a warm mug of tea. The beverage was winning her over from coffee, especially before bed. She'd meant to get her mind off the *shower of savages*, as Danny put it, but she found herself ruminating on the case. Were the guards following up on Nancy Halligan? Was her case now considered a homicide? Was it possible that the killer thought Nancy Halligan was Veronica? They were similar in height and weight, and both had white hair and wore tracksuits. But Nancy was taken to that location. Wait a minute. Could the rowboat have been Nancy's? Did the guards see it? Tara didn't know she was at a possible murder scene at the time, so she hadn't scoured the scene. Should she go back? Maybe clues had been missed. Especially if the guards weren't treating her death as suspicious. Her to-do list was filling up. Buy gifts, go back to the old stone house, then perhaps a visit to Inishbofin Island was in order. And of course, there was her shop to keep her busy. Maybe tomorrow would be the day that her permit would be in the mail.

Tara was at Renewals before the sun rose the next morning. She immersed herself in ordering flowers and champagne for her grand opening. It was just the distraction she needed. The mail usually arrived in the late afternoon. She had hope that today would be permit day. Three hours flew by, and she was startled to hear a knock at the door. She opened it to find Grace Quinn on the doorstep. Grace ran the nearby Bay Inn. As usual her white hair was pulled into a tight bun. Tara had stayed at the inn when she first came to town. Which was how she knew the basket of scones in Grace's hand was probably not the friendly gesture she wanted her to believe. Grace was here for gossip.

"Mrs. Quinn, what a lovely surprise."

She silently smacked her lips. "I've told you to call me Grace." She thrust the basket at Tara and stepped around her to enter the shop. "I see it's coming along." Grace surveyed the shop with pursed lips.

"The grand opening is next week. I trust you got your invitation?"

"I'm glad it wasn't one of those e-vites. Although I suppose you are killing trees sending out all of those paper cards, are you not?"

Tara sighed. There wasn't enough Guinness in Ireland to make this woman pleasant. "Well, it's a good thing I'm only going to have one grand opening then." She suddenly found herself trying to imagine Grace as a little girl and the image that came to her was an exact replica only with plumper, rosier skin. It made her slightly sad for younger Grace. What, or who had made her so cranky?

Grace stood under the article that had drawn Veronica to her shop. She wagged her finger at it. "You had a second chance, now you've gone and wrapped yourself up in another murder!"

She imagined if she had Xanax she would be popping one now and she felt a tug of pity for Cassidy. *There but for the grace of God go I.* "It's hardly anything I've done," Tara said.

"Murder just follows you around, does it? Like a little black cloud."

"A most unfortunate coincidence, I assure you."

"Then why are you staying out at Ballynahinch Castle?"

Tara sighed. What doesn't this woman know? "I'm working."

Grace pursed her lips. "Right, so."

"Thank you so much for stopping by." Tara smiled her sweetest smile.

Grace studied her for a moment and turned to go. "I wonder what your mother would tink." The door slammed behind her. It wasn't until Tara went to lock the door behind her that she saw a package sitting in front of the door. Bigger than a breadbox, she thought, lifting it. It was light. She wasn't expecting any more orders. She brought it in, scrambling to figure out what it could be. Had she forgotten anything? She set the package on the counter, then grabbed a pair of scissors and sliced through the tape. She opened it to a pile of sharp, silver pins. It took her a second to realize they were Tara Brooches like the ones they sold at the Connemara Marble Visitor Centre. There must have been fifty of them. A piece of paper was folded on top.

#KILLERBROOCHES

Tara gasped and dropped the box. Who had done this? It could be anyone, the rumor mill was churning. But who would actually spend this kind of money on a prank? Was this the killer? Sending a message? She reached for her mobile, her fingers shaking as she dialed the Garda Station.

Sergeant Gable stood in Tara's shop, staring at the box of brooches and scratching his head. "I can't recall the last time I was summoned because someone left them a gift."

"A gift?" She almost spit out her coffee. "With a note like that?"

"That's exactly what you posted on social media."

"*Before* Veronica was murdered. Had I posted it *after* she was murdered, that would make me a psychopath."

"You're saying a psychopath is after ya?"

She nudged the box. "What if this is from the killer?"

He shrugged, then picked it up. "We'll see what we can find." He didn't sound eager to look into it.

"Why did you make it known that Veronica was stabbed with a Tara Brooch?"

Gable set his gaze on her. "Pardon?"

"You haven't disclosed the marble stones found on Veronica, but you let everyone know she was stabbed with her Tara Brooch. You could have just said she was stabbed."

"I won't have you questioning my methods."

"You put a target on my back."

"That was not my intention."

Tara pointed to the box. "That is a threat. And I don't get the feeling you're taking it seriously."

"If you feel so threatened, why are you throwing yourself in the middle of it?"

"Because I was hired to do a job."

"Does that job include a visit to the Connemara Marble Visitor Centre?"

The lightbulb went on. He was livid. In his mind she was butting in, acting like she could do his job better than he could. She couldn't afford to alienate the guards. "Eddie Oh knows about the marble stones on Veronica's face. I just wanted to see if that's where they were purchased." She was twisting the truth, given she'd learned that from Eddie *after* her visit, but she wanted Gable on her side.

From the look he was giving her, it wasn't working anyway. "What do you mean, Eddie Oh knows?"

"He was drunk last night. He babbled on about it. He had the order wrong—the colors—but he knew marbles had been placed over her eyes, mouth, and heart."

"Who did he hear it from?"

"Not me. I assure you."

"Yet you're just telling me about this now?"

"It just happened, I haven't had the chance." *And*

look at the reaction when I do call you. She kept that part to herself. She was already on thin ice.

"Security cameras? Alarm?"

"Not yet." He was right. She could hardly claim to be worried about a threat if she didn't have basic protections set up. "I'll see to it today." He headed toward the door with the box. "I didn't want this, you know." She wished she didn't care, wished Grace's words hadn't affected her, but she loathed the thought that people in this city might think she was to blame for these murders. She wanted to go about her business, open her shop, stroll along Galway Bay with Hound. Wasn't she doing her duty as a human being by honoring the wishes of a dying woman even if it was inconvenient? Even if it damaged her reputation?

Sergeant Gable didn't answer her. He must not have heard her. If she told herself often enough she might start to believe it. He did at least commit to checking into the purchase of the brooches, so that was progress.

She stopped him just as he was about to exit the shop. "I heard you searched Veronica's room at the Ballynahinch Hotel."

"What business is that of yours?"

"Did you know Eddie has an adjoining room?" Two could play the game of ignoring each other's questions. He arched his eyebrow then shifted his gaze. She took that as a no.

"Was there writing on the mirror in her hotel bathroom?"

Gable slammed the box down. "Pardon?" Tara filled him in on the recent events. He began to pace. Maybe now he would take her seriously.

"Stay away from the suspects for now. I need to

have a think on this." Gable picked up the box and once more headed for the door.

"What about Nancy Halligan?"

"What about her?"

"Is her case now considered a murder?"

Gable shifted uncomfortably. "We turned over a few stones, but the state pathologist was firm. She died of heat complications."

"She wore the same tracksuit as Veronica. She had no water, no personal belongings."

"It's possible someone discovered the body before you, and took those items."

"Or it's possible someone lured her out there and left her in a vulnerable state."

"Similar tracksuits aren't going to reopen a case." He tipped his hat and headed for the exit.

"Iona Kelly has been accused by Eddie of faking her injury. He's also suggested Cassidy Hughes is a pill-popper. Cassidy also once accused Veronica of murdering her late uncle—Terrance Hughes. Mimi Griffin has kept meticulous notebooks working for Veronica the last twenty years, Sheila and John Murphy were evicted—"

He groaned. "What are you doing?"

"I'm telling you things you probably don't know. Precisely because I've been in the thick of things. Do you want to catch a killer or not?"

He lifted the box. "I'm going to follow up on these. You concentrate on opening your wee shop, and if you were smart you'd simply give the money back for the job and stay away from that lot." He gave her a nod and was out the door. After he left, Tara couldn't concentrate on a thing. Gable told her to stay away from the suspects. Was that an actual order? He couldn't prevent her from doing her job. But her job didn't require her to interact with them. In fact, once she bought the gifts for the seven, she was done. She could, and would walk away. The sooner she bought them the better. She would go to the antique store in Clifden. But first she needed guidance. Even if it was of the unconventional kind.

Chapter 21

Rose promptly answered Tara's knock on the door. "Don't let your light shine," she blurted out as she stared at Tara.

Dark clouds overhead capped Rose's cryptic warning. "What does that mean?"

Rose shook her head. "I wish I knew. It's meant for you."

"Well, it better not be about my grand opening, because that's happening."

Rose scrunched her face. "When?"

"If I get the permit in time, the opening is three days from now. And in the meantime, I have to hit up a thrift store in Clifden."

Rose nodded. "Is this about the seven guests of Veronica O'Farrell?"

Tara stepped forward. "Yes. Did you get a premonition?"

"No." Rose lifted her mobile phone. "I got a text message from Johnny."

Tara laughed. It felt good. "Do you want to come? It's a bit of a drive, but the scenery is stunning."

"No. But come in," Rose said, gesturing to the caravan. "I'd better read your cards first."

"Just a quick read," Tara said. Rose's caravan was small but neat. The only decorations were an African violet by the kitchen sink area. They sat in the built-in two-seater next to it. Rose carefully lifted her cards out of a silk scarf and handed them to Tara to shuffle and divide into three piles. Rose liked doing Celtic Cross readings, but they could take a long time.

"How about just a past, present, future read?"

Rose turned over three cards, one at a time, and studied them. "An opportunity. A reversal. And a hidden meaning." Her head popped up. "Family," she said. "I see family involvement."

"I wonder if the antique shop is the opportunity, or the grand opening?" Tara mused. "The seven could be a family of sorts. Or Cassidy Hughes. Or Eddie."

"I need to see more." Rose flipped out another card. The tip of her tongue poked out the corner of her mouth. "I see activity around your shop."

"That sounds like good news. Maybe my permit will come today."

Rose laid out yet another card. "There's something in front of you. Some kind of understanding. You just haven't figured it out. You're struggling to figure it out." Tara didn't move, or blink, or scratch her head. Was this about the marble stones? Rose leaned in. "You know, don't you? What the cards are telling you?"

"Not exactly."

"You know enough."

"Is it a warning?"

"A caution. Go forward. But be careful."

"Thank you." It didn't quite help, but it was nice of Rose to try. She stood up. "Thanks for trying."

Rose smiled. "That'll be forty euro."

A few minutes into the antique shop and Tara found a music box. It had dark wood and elegant carvings on the lid. When she lifted it, a jaunty reel began to play.

" 'Cooley's Reel,' " the clerk said. "She's a beauty."

"She is." This was the perfect gift for Elaine. "Do you happen to have an antique diving helmet?"

The clerk tipped his head up. "Not in the shop. But I know a fella. I can make a call."

"I'd be very interested." Tara continued through the shop while the clerk made a phone call. Minutes later he called out to her.

"I can get you an antique diving helmet It's in good shape, but it's quite dear."

"I have room in my budget." Excitement thrummed through her. Two gifts down.

The clerk nodded. "Before you leave make sure to jot down your digits. I'll give you a bell when the helmet arrives."

Tara nodded, then headed for the back of the store where vintage dresses hung on a clothes rack. Was Cassidy too young to appreciate vintage? It was hip in New York, but perhaps not here. Clothing was always a risky purchase, especially if you didn't have a person's exact measurements. On the counter near the dresses, Tara spied an emerald and diamond tiara. The jewels were costume, of course, but Tara thought it was perfect for Cassidy. She would go with her gut and get it. Two down—three if the diving helmet came through. Next, she saw a wooden chest of small drawers, like something an old-fashioned chemist or apothecary would use. Perfect for Mimi. It was related to organization, but not a notebook. She was on a roll. Eddie and Iona were the only two left. A walking staff would be perfect for Iona, and she just happened to be standing in front of a nice bin of them. And she was just about to give up on Eddie for the day when she saw an old whiskey barrel in the corner. As long as she could arrange shipping to wherever Eddie wanted it delivered, it made a nice little table. She headed for the counter. "If you can arrange for shipment to my salvage mill in Galway, including the diving helmet, I'm going to buy a nice little haul."

The clerk flashed a wide grin. "Let's get you sorted."

"How went the hunt?"

Tara stood in the doorway of Uncle Johnny's office. He was somewhere behind the mound of papers and books cluttering his desk, steam from a mug of tea rising above it, as if there were a little village nestled in there, townsfolk warming themselves by a fire.

"Mission accomplished. The antique store in Clifden will be delivering the items here in a few days, and all our guests will gather to receive them." At which time Veronica's amends would be read. Then

Tara would be able to walk away and focus on her shop.

"The shop already called. Said Veronica's driver will drop off the items," Uncle Johnny said. "I'll be sure to be here to receive them."

"Typical," Tara said. Now that Veronica was gone, she'd noticed Bartley was making sure to keep Andy busy. "But thank you. I appreciate the help."

"And I appreciate the business," Johnny said. "Just make sure nobody ends up dead." He grinned. "At least not until after I collect the rent for the space."

She shook her head. "Too soon."

He laughed, then shrugged. The group was probably going stir-crazy at the castle, as gorgeous as it was. "I'll spread the news and let you know soon when the group is going to arrive."

"You're family," Johnny said with a wave of his hand. "It's going to cost you." She started to leave. "Hang on." Uncle Johnny tossed her an envelope. It was from the city. It was also open.

"Is it?"

He grinned. "Your shop can open in five days."

Her grand opening would have to be slightly delayed. But it was thrilling news. "Do you always open my mail?"

"Only when I'm over there fixing French doors and putting up security cameras."

"Thank you."

"You're welcome."

"But seriously. Don't open my mail."

"Should I take back the locks and the cameras?"

"No."

"Then I'd leave it at a thank-you if I were you."

"Thank you."

"You're welcome."

But seriously, never open my mail again. This time she kept it to herself, and went to frame her business permit.

The guests entered the mill, excitement obvious in their voices as they took in the cavernous space filled with treasures. The gifts had arrived from the antique shop in Clifden that morning, packed in crates and waiting to be opened. Tara was eager to hand them out. She even purchased a new satchel for Bartley, and a cap for Andy. But first, everyone wanted to have a nose around the mill, and Tara couldn't blame them. It was fascinating to see all of them in a new environment.

"Don't hover over them," Johnny said, sneaking up on her. She let out a little yelp. He laughed. "The gifts are in the storeroom; why don't you get those ready while they shop?"

"They're not shopping, they're browsing."

"Today's browser is tomorrow's buyer." Johnny wagged his finger at her. "Don't forget that when in you're in your own shop."

"Touché." She did need to pull her acquisitions out of the crates, make sure they were presentable.

"I'll keep an eye on this lot," Uncle Johnny said. "Let you know if any one of them do anything killer-like."

Tara laughed. Then, in a rare display of public affection, she kissed Uncle Johnny on the cheek before heading into the storage room where packed crates awaited her. She grabbed a pry bar and opened the first crate. The items were packed in straw. She brushed it out of the way and lifted out the tiara. She wished she knew its history; the stories embedded in the costume jewels. Who had worn it and where and when? What drama had they witnessed? What lavish events had they attended? Next, she took out the music box and set it aside. She'd wind it in a minute to make sure it played. The whiskey barrel was already set up in the middle of the loft where the guests would gather, along with Mimi's organizing drawers. Iona's walking stick leaned against the wall. It was dark wood and the top had a gorgeous crown carved into it. Iona could call herself the queen of The Mountain Hikers Club.

Tara turned to the next crate, wedged it open, and lifted out the antique diving helmet. It was gorgeous. A nice bronze one, and heavy to boot. The clerk had been right, the price was a little dear, but this was for two of them, not just one. Would Veronica announce their new flat in her amends speech? Mimi Griffin, who had the amends list in her possession, would be reading it soon, and Tara was eager to hear them.

Tara turned to the old music box and cranked it. But instead of the smooth rendition of "Cooley's Reel" that she'd heard in the store, the notes began to clink out in a disjointed manner. Just her luck— the Frankenstein of music boxes. Maybe it just needed to warm up. She continued to crank it and although it definitely wasn't "Cooley's Reel," it began to play a distinct melody. Tara didn't recognize the tune. She kept cranking it, not caring what the tune was, hoping the music box would soon smooth out. She got so lost in what she was doing, it took a while to realize she was being watched. She turned to find several folks in the doorway. Uncle Johnny, Danny, Rose, Andy. And the rest were heading toward the storage room like she was the Pied Piper. She stopped cranking.

"Keep playing," Danny said. "I've almost got it."

" 'The Old Woman from Wexford,' " Johnny said.

"I was just trying to get it to smooth out," Tara said. "It sounds a bit off-key."

Danny stepped forward and peered at the mechanisms. "That's because someone doctored it to play the song."

"Do you all know it?" she asked, feeling left out. Heads began to nod.

"It's a famous Irish ballad," Andy said. " 'The Old Woman from Wexford.' "

So they'd said. They were making her anxious. "How does it go?" Tara waited for one of them to start belting it out. Instead, they began to exchange glances. The rest of the guests had caught up by now, and every one of them had some version of a horrified expression on his or her face. She stared at them as they stared at the music box. Tara realized she was back to cranking it. She stopped. She was missing something. Had they never heard a music box before? "What?"

"That song is what," Elaine said. "Is it some kind of joke?"

No, it's your gift. Or at least it was. "It's supposed to play 'Cooley's Reel.' It didn't sound like this in the shop. I don't know what this song is." She took in their faces again. "But you guys obviously recognize it."

"You could say that again," Danny said.

"What? You're scaring me." And they were. The vibes were definitely bad in here, and this time she didn't need Rose to tell her. "What's with the song?"

"There are many variations," Uncle Johnny said.

"It's about a woman who tries to murder her blind husband," Rose blurted out.

"So she can be with her lover," Elaine added.

Iona stepped up. "But he tricks her."

"Tricks her," Tara repeated.

Cassidy pushed her way to the front of the crowd. "And just as the old woman goes to push her poor husband into the sea, he steps aside, and she tumbles to her death instead."

Chapter 22

They all stared at the music box as if it were deadly in and of itself. "I had no idea," Tara said. "I swear it played 'Cooley's Reel' in the antique shop."

"It's a message from the killer," Cassidy said.

Like the books, and the box of brand-new Tara Brooches. This killer loved sending messages.

"It can't be a coincidence," Elaine said. "Someone is messing with us." Heads swiveled as they all accused each other with their eyes.

"Uncle Terry fits the description of the husband in the song," Cassidy said. "I told you Veronica murdered him."

"Terrance wasn't blind," Elaine said.

"It's a *metaphor*," Cassidy snipped.

"That's nonsense," Elaine said. "Veronica didn't murder Terrance. If I thought she did—believe me, I wouldn't have rested until she was brought to justice." Her face flushed, and in that second, Tara saw the history. Elaine had indeed once been in love with Terrance. "He had a heart attack, and we all know how much he loved going to the chipper."

"A song about a wife who tries to murder her husband?" Cassidy stomped her foot, which until then Tara only thought was an expression, apart from toddlers. "Don't tell me that's a coincidence!"

"We know all about your accusations," Mimi said, turning to Cassidy. "Which is why we're all shocked Veronica invited you here in the first place. How do we know you didn't tinker with that music box?"

"So I could out myself as a killer?" Cassidy said. "Don't be daft."

"It doesn't make sense," Elaine said. "In the song the woman tries to murder her husband but *fails*." She shuddered. "And believe me, Terrance is no longer alive."

"He definitely is not," Cassidy said, with a nearly identical shudder.

"Maybe the killer couldn't find an *exact* song, but it has to be a message," Eddie said.

Cassidy turned on him. "A message. A *living* husband. Like you."

"We have to stop being so literal," Eddie said.

"You can count me out," Iona said. "I've never even heard of the song."

"We need to call the guards," Tara said. She wished she hadn't touched it. Could they get fingerprints off it?

"Is this mine?" Mimi said, gravitating toward the wooden organizer.

"I meant to officially give them out," Tara said.

"But yes." Tara pointed out the rest of the gifts; it was too late to put the genie back in the bottle, so she'd might as well get it over with.

"I love it," Iona said, hoisting her walking stick. Andy and Bartley seemed touched by their gifts too.

"It can't just be the music box that was messed with," Eddie said. "Everyone examine your gift, take it apart, see if it contains any clues." Eddie upended his whiskey barrel to see if there was anything inside. "I need to rip this open."

"Please," Tara said. "No one needs to rip anything open. I'm sure they're all fine."

"I don't want that thing," Elaine said, backing away from the music box. "It's not fine."

John walked around the diving helmet. "It's creepy," Sheila said.

This was a disaster. One by one the remaining guests examined their gifts as if they were ticking. Nothing else seemed to be altered, but a sense of unease remained, and all enthusiasm about the gifts evaporated. Disaster.

Uncle Johnny turned to Tara. "Were the crates sealed shut?"

"They were," Tara said, with a nod to the pry bar. Then she wished she hadn't pointed it out. All a killer would have to do is sneak up on someone from behind with a weapon like that . . .

"Someone could have pried it open and glued it shut again," Danny said.

"Who all had access to this room?"

Danny glanced at Andy.

"It's okay," Andy said. "I helped him carry the crates in."

"We didn't linger though," Danny said.

"I moved a few crates in," Bartley said. "But you're assuming the music box was tinkered with after it arrived here?"

"If it's a message from the killer, I'm afraid so."

"Here's a version of the song." Danny pressed play on his smartphone as the eerie little ballad sang out quite cheerfully.

"That's creepy," Cassidy said.

"I think it's time for an official group meeting," Elaine said. "Now."

Bartley stood in the middle of the salvage mill, the group arranged on the sofas and chairs around him. Iona perched on the arm instead of a seat, Cassidy lounged with sunglasses on as if she were on a beach in Spain, Eddie paced alongside a wall of decorative door knockers, John and Sheila huddled on the sofa, clinging to each other, Mimi was already jotting notes in her notebook, perched on a fold-out chair, and Elaine was the only one looking somewhat relaxed, sitting back, her legs crossed, her hands folded over her knee. Andy was immersed in his mobile phone by the door, as if at-the-ready if anyone needed a ride. But when he lifted his eyes, they were rimmed in red. It was hard to imagine he had shed a tear over Veronica; it was more likely he was suffering a hangover. She hoped no one asked for a ride until he was in better shape.

Bartley grabbed the paper the amends were written on and cleared his throat.

"Wait," Mimi said. "You can't just grab my papers. I'm responsible for them."

"This is taking too long," Bartley said.

"I thought they were out of order. Have you been going through my things?"

"Don't be ridiculous," Bartley said. "How and when would I have done that?"

"I swear someone has been pawing through them." Mimi's eyes darted around the room.

"Get on with it," Cassidy said. His eyes flashed but he quickly bowed his head, and when he lifted them again the hint of aggression was well masked. "Veronica had prepared her amends. I don't know if it's appropriate to go through with them after everything that's happened." He scanned the room as if trying to detect a murderer amongst them.

"Always the loyal henchman," Cassidy said. "I wonder why you didn't share such concerns when my uncle was murdered."

"Your uncle died of natural causes." His anger was back twofold. When he didn't begin to read from Veronica's prepared sheets, Elaine was off the sofa and after three strides whipped them out of his hands.

"She was my best friend, I'll do it."

"If she was your best friend, why didn't you go walking with her that morning?" The jab came from Eddie. His body had stopped pacing but his eyes had not. Whereas Andy looked as if he needed the hair of the dog, Eddie looked jittery and wound tight.

"Because she left me a nasty voicemail Friday," Elaine said. "There. Are you happy?"

"What voicemail?" Tara asked.

Elaine sighed, and reached into her handbag. She brought out her mobile phone and pushed play. Veronica's voice filled the mill:

"Is it you? Did you kill Nancy? Maybe you killed

Terrance. Maybe you've been out to get me all this time. He didn't love you. He loved me. Get over it." She was drunk, that was obvious. Yelling, babbling, slurring. "One of you killed Nancy. Who is it? Who is it?" The message cut off.

"I was flabbergasted," Elaine said. "A year of sobriety down the drain."

"Why didn't you tell us about this before?" Bartley demanded.

"I told the guards. It's all ridiculous anyway."

A picture was emerging. Friday at Tara's shop Veronica learned that Nancy was dead. By that evening, she'd relapsed. And convinced herself that Nancy was murdered. Or had someone else convinced her? Tara hated that she was the one who broke the news to Veronica.

"You've been hiding this from us," Eddie said, pointing at Elaine. "What else are you hiding?"

Elaine calmly scanned him from head to toe. "I never knew what she saw in you."

"How dare you."

Elaine laughed. How had she developed that Teflon exterior? Tara wore her emotions way too close to her sleeve; she was fascinated by Elaine's composure. Elaine turned back to the paper and started to read aloud. " 'Subtly announce that I won the Woman of the Year award and appear humble as I blush.' " She blinked in confusion, as did the rest of the room. Uncle Johnny was the first to throw his head back and laugh. At first the startled guests swiveled to gawp at him, and then Rose joined the laughter. Soon everyone was laughing.

"That's so Veronica," Mimi said, wiping a tear from her eye. "I'll miss that chutzpah."

Elaine tried to shush the laughter, holding up the paper. "*Hold for applause* is underlined." The laughter was back, this time a chorus that was infectious. Tara wasn't quite sure when it turned to tears, but before she knew it, Elaine was sobbing.

"She didn't invite me to go walking with her," she gasped. "Or I would have."

"Wait," Tara said. "I thought you hadn't arrived yet."

Heads began swiveling again, looking at each other, then Tara as if she was the unwanted guest.

"I made arrangements at another hotel first," Elaine said.

"Another *castle*," Mimi said. It was obvious she disapproved.

"I didn't trust what Veronica was up to," Elaine admitted. "But I spoke with her that Friday and I was convinced she was truly making amends."

Mimi began flipping through a notebook. "Then why were you not only at Ballynahinch Castle that Saturday, before checking in, but there so early?"

Elaine's tears shut off like a faucet as she began to blink. "Pardon?"

"You were standing on the back patio at half five in the morning."

Eddie edged forward, trying to peer over Mimi's shoulders. "Are you spying on us?"

"I was hired to do a job. You should try it sometime."

Was that who Veronica was referring to when she said Iona was being watched? Or had she asked every guest to spy on another? Every second Tara was convinced that Veronica was on the up-and-up, something happened to make her doubt it.

"Veronica hired you to spy on us?" Eddie wouldn't relent.

Mimi fussed with the corner of her notebook, bending it. She was probably one of those people who shredded cocktail napkins. "She simply wanted to know what everyone was up to. I'm sure it was just so she knew you had a good time."

"Bullhorns," Cassidy called from her lounge chair. "Spying is right."

"I wasn't up at half five, let alone at Ballynahinch Castle," Elaine insisted. "You scratch that out."

"Personally, I only want juicy gossip about me in that notebook," Cassidy said. "I want people to gasp when they read it!"

"What else does your notebook say?" Eddie insisted. "Who else was up early the morning she died?"

Iona jumped off the arm of the chair. "I thought you were supposed to turn those notebooks over to the guards."

John stood up, yanking Sheila with him. "Are you going to read Veronica's amends or not?"

"I made a copy for the guards," Mimi said. "They never said they had to have my originals."

"Convenient," Eddie said. "Who's been spying on *you*?"

"For the last time, I'm not a spy." Mimi gave a sly smile as if she wished she were.

"We're leaving," John said.

"We can't," Sheila said. She turned to Elaine. "Please. Read the amends." Desperation rang from her voice. *Where do you think she stashed it?* What were they looking for? Was Sheila the person Tara saw running away from Veronica's hotel room, draped in her clothing?

"What are you so worried about?" Cassidy said, peeling her sunglasses down to the bridge of her nose to gaze at Eddie. The two shared a long look.

"Why are you always wearing sunglasses?" Iona said. "Even indoors."

"Because I'm very sensitive to light," Cassidy said.

"It's Ireland," Iona said. "I don't buy that for a second."

"I'm a recognizable figure," Cassidy said. "You wouldn't know what that's like."

"I think everyone should sit down," Bartley said, glancing from Iona to Eddie, to John and Sheila. "Out of respect."

"You're standing as well," Iona pointed out. "So are they." Her hand swept the back where Johnny, Rose, Tara, and Andy stood. Tara couldn't believe she was being publicly shamed for standing. By arguably the most athletic in the group. They were getting off topic.

"I think we should focus on the reason Veronica brought you together," Tara said. "I saw her the day before she died. She was a total stranger, I grant that, but she shared her story with me. She seemed sincere in wanting to make amends. I think that's worth listening to, don't you?"

Slowly, heads turned, scanning first Tara and then each other.

When no one protested, Mimi jotted something down in her notebook, then waved to Elaine. "Go on, so."

Elaine took her place once more in the center. "I'd better start over. I'll paraphrase. Even after winning Woman of the Year—"

"Who awarded her dat?" Cassidy's nostrils flared as she interrupted. Elaine looked at her sheet.

"It doesn't say."

"The city," Mimi said, flipping through a notebook. "Some committee. Which she chairs." Murmurs went through the group. Mimi shut the notebook. "I think it's wonderful. "

"You would," Cassidy said.

Mimi shook her finger at the young woman. "Doesn't it feel better to be gracious? Her success doesn't impede your own."

Cassidy sprung from her chair and took off her sunglasses. "Woman of the Year. For what? Throwing poor people out of their homes?" She pointed to John and Sheila, who seemed to cower on the sofa. "Berating her niece in public? Accusing her assistant of being a thief? Castrating her ex-husband?" Her eyes flicked to Eddie.

"I assure you," he said, "it's all in working order." He grinned at her.

Bartley cleared his throat. "Leave the past in the past. Veronica was attempting to make amends. And one of you was too heartless and cruel to give her that chance." He bowed his head. "Evil."

Sheila Murphy stood. John grabbed her hand as if to pull her down, but she yanked it away. "Evil is when you tell your landlady you're pregnant, only for her to throw us out, *and* keep our deposit. I don't care *what* the doctors say. I know she's the reason I miscarried five years ago." Gasps and murmurs went around the room. Mimi and Elaine hurried over and began rubbing her arm. *So that's why an ambulance was called*, Tara thought. What a traumatic day that must have been for the young couple.

"You poor ting," Mimi cooed as she continued to stroke Sheila's arm.

Sheila pulled away. "It's common. However . . . I'm convinced that stress played a role. And that stress was named Veronica."

John buried his head in his hands. "Don't talk about that in public."

Despite her husband's pleading, a look of determination was planted on Sheila's face. "I've kept silent for the past five years. Does it look like it's helped?" Tears streamed down her face. "I've never been able to get pregnant since."

Tara's heart squeezed. She knew the pain of losing a child. She struggled with herself not to compare, not to judge, just to listen. Pain was pain. And Sheila was right. Bottling things up could be destructive. Eat away at you. Cause you to misdirect the rage into something . . . evil. Was Sheila confessing? Was that why her husband was trying to quiet her down?

Uncle Johnny stepped up. His face looked pained as he tried to smile. "Who wants a nice cup of tea?"

"I need something stronger." Cassidy dug in her purse. "Where is it?" Her voice raised to a shriek. Someone stole my prescription bottle!" She looked around expectantly, but was met with open stares.

"You should go for a hike," Iona said. "Literally."

"If we're not going to read this, I'm going to sit down." Elaine stalked over to a chair and slid into it.

Mimi stood, stormed over to Elaine and grabbed the sheet. "I'll read it. I want to see if she's apologized for accusing me of being a thief."

Elaine suddenly sat up straight. "I remember that," she said. "Wait. Wasn't it her antique brooch she accused you of stealing?"

"The Tara Brooch," Eddie said, outrage in his voice. "You're the killer!"

A pink hue crawled up the side of Mimi's face. She looked as if she wanted to turn back time and swallow her words. "I did not steal that brooch and I certainly am no killer."

If Mimi was the one Tara saw fleeing Veronica's room, then she was lying about not being a thief. Could she be lying about not being a killer, as well?

Cassidy snapped her fingers. "Elaine is *right*. It was the brooch."

"The same brooch that was plunged through her heart," Eddie said.

"That's nothing to do with me!" Mimi said. "It was proven I never stole it in the first place. Remember?"

Elaine shook her head. "No."

"She found it! In her garden, by her fountain. Why do you tink she's making amends to me?"

"I didn't think about it at all," Elaine said.

"Typical," Mimi said under her breath.

"Who's to say you didn't steal it and then put it back?" Cassidy posed. "Seeing as how you know exactly where she kept it."

"I was her assistant," Mimi said. "It was my job to know."

"Enough!" Bartley raised his voice, startling all of them. "If you don't want to hear her apologies, maybe you'd like to hear what she planned on compensating you with. Is that it?" He nodded to John and Sheila. "A flat for the young couple, an art gallery opening for Eddie, a rehab program for Cassidy—"

"I will not go to rehab!" Cassidy put her sunglasses back on. "Unless it's attended by celebrities."

"Who cares about a flat," Sheila said. "Does it say anything about a *letter*?"

"A letter?" Tara asked.

Sheila nodded. "A recommendation letter. For adoption. She said she had connections."

So that's what they were looking for. Was there ever a recommendation letter? Tara approached Mimi and gently took the sheet out of her hands. She started to read out loud. " 'To my best friend, Lainey. I am sorry you lost the love of your life . . .' " Tara stopped as she stared at the page.

"Yes?" Elaine said. "Don't stop now. What else?"

Tara couldn't believe what she was seeing. The words floated in front of her.

To my best friend, Lainey. I'm sorry you lost the love of your life you ungrateful cow.

Chapter 23

Tara shifted her weight from one foot to the other as she wrestled with the words in front of her. "Bartley was right. Let's skip to the compensation." It had all been a ruse. Veronica hadn't come here to make amends. She'd come here to shame them once again. When had it happened? Veronica's original words were scratched out, the new version written on top. This must have been around the same time Veronica left Tara the message about all of them betraying her. What had she found out? Was it possible someone else had written this? The killer?

Wait. The handwriting. Tara peered closer. She would need the book for comparison, but it did not look like the handwriting that was in Cassidy's book. *Forgiveness is a virtue. You have none . . .*

"Is this Veronica's handwriting?" Tara showed it to Mimi.

Mimi's eyes widened as she took in the words. "Yes."

"Are you sure?"

"Quite sure."

That meant someone else had written the words in the book. Someone else had handed out the books. *The killer.*

"What does it say?" Elaine persisted.

"Someone scratched out Veronica's original apology," Tara said.

"I just told you it's Veronica's handwriting," Mimi said. "I have no doubt." Before Tara could stop her, she snatched the papers out of her hand. " 'To my best friend Lainey, I'm sorry you lost your husband you ungrateful cow.' "

Elaine grabbed the sheet out of Mimi's hands. "How dare she! I did love Terrance. And she knew very well what she was doing when she swept in that night in her little black dress and literally pulled him away from me. She was only ever after his money."

"Was she drunk when she wrote that?" Eddie asked. "Did she fall off the wagon?"

"Then threw us under it," John said. "I think I've had quite enough." He stood, bringing Sheila with him. "Let's go home."

"I think she did relapse Friday night," Tara said. "Do any of you know anything about that?"

"We're leaving," John repeated.

"We can't go anywhere until the guards say so," Iona said.

"Let them arrest me," John said. "They can't hold us here against our will."

"Is there really a flat?" Sheila's voice was a hopeful whisper.

"A flat in Galway," John said.

"Galway?" Sheila said. "We live in Dublin."

Tara stepped forward. "How did you know about the flat in Galway?"

"He was stalking her," Andy said. "I knew I saw you in Galway!"

"You did?" Tara asked. "Why didn't you say anything?"

Andy looked horrified. "It's me job to keep me mouth shut. And I thought it was him but I wasn't sure."

"Not only were you stalking her, you were the ones to find the body," Eddie said. The crowd moved in on John and Sheila.

"Neither of us would ever kill her," Sheila said. "All we want is a child."

"Then why did Veronica have this?" Mimi whipped a newspaper article from her stack of folders and held it out for everyone to see:

NEWLY SOBER HEIRESS PLAYS STORK

The guests moved in, trying to read the article.

"It's just a stupid interview I did back home. A local newspaper," Sheila said. "I don't know how she got her hands on it. Someone was trying to turn her against us."

Sheila did not seem surprised that Mimi had the article. Tara turned to her. "You knew about this?"

Sheila nodded, tears pooling in her eyes. "That's

what she confronted us with Friday evening. Shoved the article in our face. Accused us of setting her up."

"She was drunk," John said. "My wife was excited when she talked to the reporter. We knew there was no guarantee of getting a child. We didn't think Veronica had that kind of power."

"What else did she say?" Tara knew they were holding onto something.

John stepped up. "She said the same thing we just heard on Elaine's voicemail. That someone murdered Nancy. And she was going to find out who." He shook his head. "I thought it was all the ramblings of a relapsing alcoholic. But then when we found Veronica the next morning . . . there are things you don't know . . . I wouldn't ever think of doing something like that!" Repulsion was written all over John's face. He was talking about the marble stones, yet not coming out and saying it. Still honoring the wishes of the guards.

"I think it's time you tell everyone about the stones," Eddie said.

Or maybe they hadn't honored the guards wishes at all. "Stop." Tara made sure her voice could be heard. "You can't say anything more. The guards need that kept confidential."

"What stones?" Bartley asked.

"Nothing," Eddie said. "The castle was full of stones."

"Was she stoned to death?" Bartley continued. "I thought it was the brooch that killed her."

Stoned to death. That was an interesting thought. Were the stones some kind of metaphor?

"Let's just say we're dealing with a very sick killer," Eddie said.

"Or very creative," John added with a long look at Eddie. "It's like she was turned into a living sculpture."

Sheila cleared her throat. "Not living," she said. John's face turned bright pink.

"Enough!" Elaine said. "Veronica is doing this, making us turn on each other. Her games all started with this stupid book!" She waved a copy of *Places to See in Ireland Before You Die*. Then tossed it down on the coffee table. The book landed and fell open. A red X stared up from the corner of the page.

"What is that?" Mimi lunged after the book, then turned it so the group could see.

"X marks the spot," Bartley said. "This wasn't part of her plan. Veronica never said a word to me about this."

"She always did like her secrets," Cassidy said with a glance at Eddie.

"Bartley's right," Mimi said. "This wasn't in her amends."

Andy cleared his throat. Everyone turned to him. "I don't want to overstep, but she did say something to me."

"Out with it," Mimi demanded.

"On our drive from Tara's shop to Ballynahinch, she said . . . 'Let the games begin.' "

Once more heads swiveled around. "I didn't hear her say that," Bartley said.

"You had already exited the vehicle sir," Andy said.

Bartley rubbed his jawline, then nodded. "As I recall she remained in the vehicle for quite some time."

Andy nodded. "She was very upset about her friend's death. I was happy to listen."

"It's no wonder I didn't see the X before," Elaine said, bringing the conversation back to the book. "Did she really think we were going to actually read the entire book? Who has that kind of time?"

"Has anyone else noticed a red X in their book?" Tara asked. One by one, the guests shook their heads.

"This page is about the Connemara National Park," Mimi exclaimed. "Maybe we're supposed to find our 'amends' at our location."

"Why would I get the park?" Elaine said. "Shouldn't that be for Iona?"

"Who else has their book?" Tara asked.

"I have mine right here." Iona held hers up.

"Go on, see if you have a red X."

Iona began turning pages. Soon she let out a little gasp. "Connemara Stables." She turned the book to face the group. "At least it sounds outdoorsy."

"We all need to find our copies," Cassidy said. "Check for a red X."

"I have your copy," Tara said.

Cassidy whirled around. "What?"

"You left it—" She stopped, realizing if she said the location, Eddie and John would accuse her of being a killer. "Behind. You left it behind. It's in my hotel room." Tara wished she would have thumbed through it more carefully; even she missed the red X. Cassidy frowned but kept her mouth shut. It made Tara wonder if Cassidy remembered exactly where she left the book. Which would also mean she knew why the marbles had a murderous connotation. Was she the killer?

Nobody else had their book with them. Everyone wanted to go back to the castle to retrieve them.

"X marks the spot," Bartley said. "Very *Treasure Island* of her."

"We need to figure out why on earth she distributed this ridiculous book in the first place," Eddie said.

Tara was sure by now that it wasn't Veronica, but she had to keep this mum too.

"I know why." The statement came from Andy. "She got the idea from me."

Tara wasn't expecting that. Had she jumped to the wrong conclusion? "You?"

He stepped forward from the shadows. "Me da used to have a First Edition of dat book." His eyes teared up. He cleared his throat. "When he retired it was his dream to travel all of Ireland. I told her all about it."

Tara stepped forward. "Did you buy your own copy in Galway? At the bookshop where you bought the Western?"

Andy's face turned red. He nodded. "I did."

"Why?" Tara probed.

"Because I was taken aback when I learned she'd given everyone the book. I never even knew she was listening when I told her the story about me da. It was never meant to be sinister."

"Why didn't you say anything before?" Tara couldn't help but ask.

He shifted awkwardly. "The guards asked me not to."

"And yet you're telling us now," Bartley said.

"I see the way you're all pointing fingers at each other. I don't know why she decided to use the book, but I'm not going to take the brunt of it."

"Calm down," Bartley said. "Every valet in the Ballynahinch Castle saw you sleeping in the SUV the morning of the murder. If that's not a solid alibi, I don't know what is."

"Why on earth would you be sleeping in the SUV when you had a perfectly good hotel room?" Mimi sounded personally affronted.

"I was worried I'd oversleep. The valets promised to wake me an hour before Veronica wanted to leave." He didn't mention that Veronica had booked him at a different hotel. Was it pride?

"Let's say we all find a red X in our books," Eddie said. "Then what?"

"We go to the location and see if we can find our true amends," Mimi said.

Elaine shook her finger at Mimi. "She called me an ungrateful cow. You call that a true amends?"

"That was a last-minute change," Mimi said. "She was obviously drunk. But the true amends had been made much earlier. Before she was murdered."

Heads swiveled as they silently checked in to see what each other thought of the idea. "You may have a point," Elaine said.

Iona raised her hand. "I'm in."

"We aren't guards," John said. "This isn't a game. There's a killer among us."

"We all go together," Iona said. "To each location. All of us or none of us."

"No," John said. "We're going home."

"We can start with the closest and easiest location," Iona said. "If there's nothing there, we stop."

"Count us out," John said.

Sheila touched his hand. "Even if it means we lose our recommendation? Maybe even a flat?"

He sighed. She whispered in his ear. His shoulders relaxed. "Fine. One location. Just to see."

Was that why Veronica was killed? *Had she distributed amends at certain places, and was about to take them back?* Had the killer killed to stop her? Did anyone have Clifden Castle listed as their spot?

"That's settled then," Mimi said. "Everyone go back to the hotel and look at your books. Email me the location she's marked with an X. I'll check to see which is the closest. Gather in the lobby at nine a.m. sharp tomorrow morning and we'll head off."

That officially ended the afternoon. The guests filed out, leaving Tara feeling drained. She needed her sofa and a show on telly to binge watch. She turned to head up to her loft. Danny and Uncle Johnny blocked her at the stairs.

"What?"

"You gave them their gifts. You have your permit. You're done, right?" Uncle Johnny said.

"Yes," Tara said. "But my things are still in the room at the castle. I have to pick them up."

"I'll do it," Danny said.

Shoot. She wanted to see who else had a red X in their book. "Not necessary. I'll go in the morning, gather my things, say goodbye, and be done." She smiled, and squeezed past them, knowing full well that if the suspects were all going to one of the locations in the book, there was no way she was going to miss that. Whoever messed with that music box was messing with *her*. What she didn't mention to Uncle Johnny or Danny, was that deep down she knew. She could pretend to be done with the group, but the killer was not done with her. Until he or she was caught, she'd be safer sticking with the group.

Chapter 24

❧⨯❧

The next morning, under a gray sky, the group stood in front of Ballynahinch Castle, grasping copies of their books. Each of the seven indeed had a red X. Tara's book did not, neither did Andy's. "We won't have to go far," Mimi said. "The first stop is right here at this castle." They had agreed to order the locations by proximity.

"Whose location is it?" From her tone it sounded as if Cassidy wasn't a morning person.

"Mine, as a matter of fact," Mimi said.

Heads swiveled as everyone regarded each other. "What now?" This from Elaine.

"Quite honestly, I don't know," Mimi said. "All we have to go on is the passage in the book." She cleared her throat. "I've summarized the main points. The finest luxury. Seven hundred acres. Heart of Connemara—"

"We're supposed to search seven hundred acres?" The squeak came from Sheila.

"I'm all for it," Iona said.

"Some other words to describe the location: Authentic. Unpretentious." Mimi paused to blink, as if hoping someone would compliment her further. "They mention the salmon fishery, and of course the Twelve Bens mountains in the background. Four-star luxury."

"This is a waste of time." John was in the same surly mood as yesterday.

"I agree," Cassidy said. "We have no idea what we're supposed to do."

"We could take a walk," Iona said. "Honestly, just forty-five minutes a day would improve everyone's attitude."

"Look how well it worked out for Veronica," Cassidy quipped.

Iona gasped. "That's a wretched thing to say."

Cassidy's bottom lip jutted out. "It's not my fault she went wandering around by herself at all hours of the morning. Who does that?"

"Focus on the task at hand," Elaine said. "And we can all be done with each other for the day."

Eddie threw his arms out. "Me head is pounding and I need a nap. What do you want us to do?"

"We have to figure out why Veronica picked this location for Mimi," Elaine said.

"We know it's not because she thought Mimi was four-star luxury," Cassidy said.

Anger swelled in Tara as Mimi's eyes filled with tears. Cassidy was a bully. "Why?" Mimi said. "Because I'm not thin and blonde and twentysomething?"

"You were her assistant," Cassidy said. "Don't blame me for her prejudices."

"You take a ton of notes," Tara said to Mimi, hoping to counterbalance the digs. "Very well organized."

"Tank you."

"The grounds are well organized," Iona said. "Could that be the connection?" It was true, the grounds of the castle were impeccably laid out. The guests looked around hopelessly, as if the manicured bushes, flowers, or fields would speak to them.

"She accused you of stealing her brooch," Elaine said. "Take us through that day."

Mimi licked her lips. "I don't remember."

"I remember bits of it," Elaine said. "I remember Roni calling me and saying her antique brooch was gone and she was going to—" Elaine suddenly stopped.

John edged forward. "Going to what?"

"Going to kill whoever took it." She swallowed. "It was just an expression."

"It doesn't matter anyway," Mimi said. "She found it three days later."

"Where did she find it?" Tara couldn't help but ask.

"It had fallen in her garden, near her fountain," Elaine said.

Of course she had a fountain, she was an heiress. It was hard to fathom having that kind of life. Just a few days in this castle and Tara didn't quite like how quickly you could get used to luxury.

"Why are we all standing around?" Elaine urged. "There's a fountain here, in the middle of the gardens. We need to go there."

"My word," Mimi said. "You're right."

"Let's make this quick," John said, starting them off for the gardens.

As the rest of them stood back and watched, Mimi moved around the circular fountain as if the answers lay in the murky bottom.

"For the sake of all that's holy, you're making me dizzy," Cassidy said, turning away.

"Maybe she wanted you to make a wish," Elaine said.

"A wish." Mimi stopped. She placed her index finger on her chin and stared out at the lush grounds.

"Does that trigger something?" Elaine studied her intently, as if she could pull it out of her with her mind.

Mimi looked away. "I'd only just be guessing."

"Sure, what else do we have at this point? Guess away, so," Sheila said. She snuck up behind Mimi as if she was contemplating pushing her in.

"I used to say—'I wish I had more time.' "

"Time to do what?" Cassidy said. "Fill more notebooks that nobody is ever going to read?"

"Hush." Elaine bit into Cassidy, and for the first time, Tara saw the young woman shrink back.

"Time," Iona said, pointing to a flat rock in the distance. "A sun clock."

Mimi hurried over and lifted the giant rock. She grunted as she bent over to lift it. A folded piece of paper in a small plastic bag lay underneath. "There's something here." Sweat poured down her full face as she picked it up. The guests gathered around her as she removed the notecard from the plastic baggie. On the front it read:

CONGRATULATIONS
AMENDS TO MIMI

She opened it:

A jeweler in Connemara has your gift. May you sparkle!

"Sparkle," Mimi said as her blue eyes did just that. "Can I get a lift to town?" She raised her head and searched for Andy. A few feet away, smoking a cigarette, he nodded in acknowledgment.

"The car is ready whenever you are."

"How many jewelers are in Connemara?"

"I'd say she picked the one closest to the clue," Mimi said. "I'm going to the computer to look it up."

"Found it," Cassidy said, holding up her phone. Mimi looked disappointed that she didn't get to research.

"The shop won't be open this early, like," Elaine said. "Let's take a breather and meet here at half eleven. We might as well all see this through."

"Make it half twelve," Eddie said. "I don't want to miss the lunch buffet."

Mimi clutched the note to her chest. "She really didn't have to do this."

She didn't. Because if the voicemail was to be believed, in the end, she changed her mind. Or tried to. Something went on that evening. Yet none of them had elaborated on it. At least not to Tara. Had they all formed some kind of alliance? If so, it was only a matter of time before the bonds started to break.

It was a quarter to one in the afternoon when they all huddled around the jeweler. He clasped his hands. "I'm so thrilled. I wondered what I was to do if no one came in to claim it." He handed Mimi a black velvet box. She lifted the lid with trembling hands. A diamond watch sparkled from the box. Mimi gasped.

"It's too dear."

"It's already paid for," the jeweler said, not denying its value. "I've got papers to go with it." He hesitated. "And this." He handed her another note. It was typed.

I can't make up for lost time, so please accept this token instead

Amends, Veronica

Tara tried not to laugh. She couldn't bring herself to say *I'm sorry*, so she'd simply said *amends*.

"I forgive you, Veronica O'Farrell," Mimi said, wiping away tears as she held the box and note.

"This is all very confusing," Bartley said.

Tara edged forward. "What is it?"

"I knew about the watch. But she planned on handing it to Mimi. In your shop."

"Maybe she changed her mind when I said she couldn't use the shop."

"In a matter of hours? Impossible. Even if she had the idea, she didn't have the time to arrange it."

"It just means she didn't tell you about it," Elaine said.

"Impossible."

"You didn't know about the book either."

Bartley folded his arms and frowned.

"When did Veronica purchase this?" Elaine stepped up to the jeweler, the intensity obvious in her voice.

"It was all done online," the jeweler said. "A month ago."

"You never actually spoke with her?"

"I did not."

"Did she pay by credit card?"

"I won't be having this discussion unless the guards come to me with an order." He hesitated. "But I assure you it was all in order."

"Did she tell you that one of us would be coming in to pick it up?"

He shook his head. "No. She was supposed to pick it up."

Mimi was still staring at the watch. "I've never owned anything so lovely."

"Wait," Cassidy said. "How do we know she didn't booby-trap it? Shouldn't we make sure it's not ticking or the like?"

Mimi huffed. "Of course it's ticking, you eejit—it's a watch!"

Cassidy shrugged. "It's your funeral."

Sheila jumped up and down and grabbed John's hand. "I wonder what's in store for the rest of us."

"We need to stop this nonsense and call the guards," Bartley said. "This is not how it was meant to go down."

"But she did buy Mimi the watch?" Elaine asked.

Bartley sighed. Then nodded. "Yes. I know what each guest is to receive. That part is legitimate."

"Then what does it matter?" Elaine wasn't getting it. But Tara was.

"The killer could be manipulating this process. Trying to lure us into unsafe territory."

"Not to mention it's unseemly," Bartley said. "Going around collecting your gifts when the poor woman was murdered by one of you."

"Please," the clerk said. "Would you mind discussing this outside?"

The group obliged, and were soon standing on the footpath. The sun was peeking through the clouds on one side of the street, and it was raining on the other.

"We need to collect all the prizes," Iona said. "But we should let a neutral party hold on to them until we know who the killer is."

"We could give them to charity," Eddie said.

"Charity!" The shriek came from Sheila. "After what she put us through? Do what you want, but don't try to force it on the rest of us."

"I never got anything on my anniversaries," Mimi said, caressing her wrist. "I worked for dat woman for twenty-plus years. I'd say I'm the charity, alright, and I've earned this watch."

"That's right," John said, sticking out his chest. "We're taking ours as well, like."

"What if she kidnapped a child for ye? Will ye be taking dat?" Eddie said.

Sheila gasped, and Cassidy rolled her eyes and glared at Mimi as she held the watch up to catch the light. "If you're the killer, I hope you're ashamed of yourself right now," Cassidy said.

"Not a bit," Mimi said. She flashed a grin.

"You're all fools," Bartley said. "I'm calling the guards."

"They can't stop us," Iona said. "What law are we breaking?"

"Who can we trust to keep the gifts?" Elaine's voice sounded strained and worried.

Slowly, gazes shifted to Tara. "We do have a safe in the mill," she said. "And the building is under security monitoring."

What was she doing? No wonder Danny was browned off with her. Bartley was the one talking sense. Someone was manipulating Veronica's amends. What was it about her that couldn't let go?

"Let's all agree," Elaine said. "Tara will keep the gifts we find, in the safe until the killer is caught."

Tell them no. Tell them you're done.

Mimi held the watch to her chest as if whoever wanted it was going to have to take it by force.

"What if the killer is never caught?" Cassidy said. The thought seemed to excite her.

"Then we'll claim our possessions when the guards tell us we're free to go," Elaine said.

Mimi glanced at Tara. "Do you promise you'll keep our items safe?"

No. Tell her no. "Of course," Tara said as Elaine peeled the diamond watch from Mimi's clutches. "Of course I'll keep them safe." She took a deep breath. "But Bartley is right. We should let the guards accompany us to the rest of the locations. It isn't safe."

They simply stared at her. She sighed. They weren't children. Tara fell back as the rest of the guests began to stroll up the street, conferring with each other about their next move. Tara would warn the guards what they were up to; that's all she could do. She would tell them about the writing in Cassidy's book. How it didn't seem to match Veronica's handwriting, and she would tell them about Bartley's suspicion that someone knew Veronica's amends plans but was manipulating them to fit the locations in the book. Luring the guests to different locations. To what end? Were they truly dealing with a psychopath? Mimi had her diamond watch. She wasn't dead. The clerk basically confirmed that it was Veronica who paid for the watch, and Bartley confirmed that he knew Mimi was getting the watch. How was that a diabolical plan? What did the location matter?

Maybe Tara had the wrong end of the stick. Maybe the killer murdered Veronica because she'd changed her mind about the amends. Something set her off that Friday evening. She screamed she was going to expose them all. She changed her amends notes to nasty barbs. Did she also let it slip that they were no longer going to get their prizes? Maybe this was some kind of warped Peter Pan game the killer was playing. A shiver ran up her spine. The killer was someone who would have been furious when they found out Veronica had changed her mind and was taking it all back. Someone who would kill to keep his or her gift. Who had the most valuable amends?

Sheila and John. A flat. That recommendation letter. A child. It hardly seemed plausible that Mimi would have murdered Veronica over a diamond watch. Yet people had killed for less. Cassidy definitely wouldn't have killed over rehab, if that's truly what Veronica left her.

If Tara's theory was right, then the guests *did* have to collect their amends. It was the only way to see if anyone else had one they would kill to keep . . . If not—then Tara's money was on Sheila and John.

Andy said he'd told Veronica about the book. She believed him. But he was making the leap that it was Veronica who then bought the book. What if someone else had been listening? Andy wasn't the only one with big ears. Had someone else heard his story about the book? Bartley? Mimi? Eddie? Someone who was always around? If it was Bartley, he was doing a good job pretending to warn them off. But

Tara knew despite the warnings that the guests would be determined to seek out their winnings regardless of the danger. It was like winning the lottery and not collecting the money. Whatever was going on here, Tara was in way over her head. The guards would have to handle it from there. If someone else got killed chasing this game-playing killer, and Tara willingly participated in leading them into danger, she'd never forgive herself. That's it. She was done. And it wasn't as if she didn't have better things to do. She had the grandest of openings to attend.

Chapter 25

The day had finally come, the official grand opening of Renewals. Tara smoothed down her little black dress and practiced walking across the room. It had been so long since she'd worn high heels. She might be in for pain by the end of the evening, but she welcomed it. She touched her emerald earrings that had belonged to her mam, rubbing them for good luck. She'd gone to the hair salon for a wash and style, and now her black hair was straightened and shining. Extra mascara made her blue eyes pop. This was her night and her mood was soaring. This is what she needed to break away from the group. Just having Mimi's diamond watch in the safe back at the mill was like an irritant she couldn't soothe. This is where she belonged, in her shop, opening the doors for the first time, welcoming in the city. *Céad míle fáilte*—a hundred thousand welcomes, indeed.

Colorful bouquets adorned countertops; white lights had been set up on the patio, sparkling into the fountain and setting the Buddha statues next to it aglow; and bottles of champagne were lined up and ready to be popped. In the center of the room sat the largest bouquet Tara had ever seen. It was waiting at the door to her shop when she arrived with a note:

Best of luck with your grand opening. Veronica would have been thrilled.

Who sent them? Another mystery. One Tara didn't have time to figure out. At seven on the dot the grandfather clock in the corner (sourced from a Scottish castle) chimed, and Tara officially opened the doors to Renewals. Uncle Johnny swept in with Rose on his arm. Next came a grinning Breanna with Savage tucked into her arm.

"Thrilled to see you both," Tara said as she hugged her friend, careful not to suffocate Savage.

"I'm getting attached," Breanna admitted. "The station is in love with her. I've been sneaking her in in a wee purse."

"I'd say we have ourselves a new dog." Tara was perfectly happy sharing custody, and Savage did look content in Breanna's arms. Tara hoped Nancy Halligan was smiling down on them. She knew her mam was, and wee Thomas too. She found comfort in imagining her loved ones around her. A steady flow of people entered the shop, dressed up, smiling, chatting, partaking of champagne and appetizers, and exclaiming over Tara's careful selection of architectural wares. Since this was a celebration, Tara was not going to entertain any orders this evening; instead, she'd let people salivate over the items they wished to buy.

They were an hour into the celebrations when Veronica's group strolled in. *Please, no.* What on earth were they doing there? To their credit, they had all dressed up. It was so jarring to see them in dresses and suits, for a second Tara couldn't speak and she simply stared at them.

"Surprise," Mimi Griffin said, tottering in. Tara glanced down at Mimi's feet. Gold heels stared back at her. Veronica's shoes. The ones Tara had spotted in the closet of Veronica's hotel room right before they were stolen. And sadly, it wasn't a surprise. Tara felt her jaw clench. This was supposed to be *her* night. Did Mimi really think no one would notice? She'd have to deal with this later.

"Are we not welcome here?" Eddie said, straightening his bow tie. "You seemed to accept the invitation to the castle without hesitation."

Touché.

"I don't suppose you have my watch here?" Mimi said, batting her eyelashes. "I wouldn't mind giving it a little squeeze."

"No," Tara said, trying not to stare at Mimi's stolen heels. "I do not."

"Oh." Mimi bit her lip.

"You took a photo," Cassidy said. "Just stare at that some more."

"It's not the same thing."

"Mingle, enjoy yourselves," Tara said. She turned to find someone else, anyone else, to chat with.

"I need to speak with ya." The tug on Tara's sleeve

came from Mimi. She was so close Tara could feel her breath on her neck. It was the worst possible moment. The caterers wanted to be paid, a child was playing with the Viking helmet Uncle Johnny had given her, and a drunk lady was getting dangerously close to spilling her glass of champagne in the patio fountain. Tara held her finger up. "I'll be right with you."

"It's urgent," Mimi said. "I don't know who else to trust."

A very dramatic statement on what was supposed to be her special night. Had Mimi seen her staring at her gold heels and now she wanted to spin a story? "I'll be right back."

"Could we go somewhere a little more private?"

Had Mimi not heard Tara ask for a minute? A waiter went by with a tray of champagne. Tara grabbed two glasses and handed one to Mimi. "Have a glass of champagne."

"It was in my notebook all this time, the key to solving the murder—"

"I recognize those shoes," Tara said. "You stole them." Mimi chewed on her lip. "Why did you start to write Bartley on the mirror?"

Mimi shook her head. "His finances. He may have been skimming from Veronica."

"May have been?"

"There's more. Something I read in my notes. It was all right there in front of me."

"What?"

"Remember I said someone had been messing with my notes?"

"Yes."

"I thought it wasn't possible. I always carried them with me." She shook her head. "How could I be so stupid?"

"I don't understand." Just then Mimi's phone dinged. "Tell me," Tara urged. But Mimi's face was now buried in the screen of her mobile phone. "Mimi?"

Mimi's head popped up. "There's something in your vase." Panic rang from her voice.

"My vase?" Mimi was staring at the flowers that someone had left on Tara's doorstep. Tara had placed them on a pedestal table underneath the chandelier.

Mimi held up a finger as she raced over to them. Tara watched, first in confusion, then horror as Mimi began pulling flowers out, one by one, tossing them to the floor. *Was she on something?*

"What are you doing?" Tara started over. The kid wearing her Viking helmet darted in front of her, blocking her path. It was too heavy for his small head and was slipping over his eyes. "Hey, there," Tara said, crouching down. "You'll bang into something if you can't see." She gently lifted the helmet off his head.

He wailed. "Mine!" He grabbed for the helmet.

"Sorry, I told him to put it back." Tara turned to see his young mother, the stress evident on her face. The little boy was crying now, and screaming for the helmet. Tara felt the beginning of a migraine pulsing at her temple. Behind them, Mimi Griffin was a crazed woman. Sweat poured down her face as she continued ripping flowers from the vase. Tara needed to deal with Mimi, but she couldn't think with this little boy screaming his head off. Tara put the Viking helmet on her head and made a silly face. Way to ruin an expensive blow-out, but it did the trick. The boy stopped screaming, grinned, and pointed at Tara. "You look silly."

She crossed her eyes and stuck out her tongue. He laughed. The mother flashed her a *thank you* and dragged him away by the elbow. By the time the stressed-out mother and aspiring Viking had cleared the path, nearly all the gorgeous flowers were strewn all over the bamboo floor. Water dripped from the table. Mimi's head hovered over the tall crystal vase as if she was thinking of diving into it. *Is she on something?* "Mimi!" She either didn't hear Tara or didn't care. She stuffed her hand into the vase and swirled it in the water. From up above, the chandelier began to vibrate as if picking up on her distress.

"What in the world?" Just as Tara reached Mimi, a loud groan sounded from the ceiling. Tara's head snapped up. Cracks formed before her eyes, as another groan rang out. The chandelier slipped down an inch. Tara jumped. "Run," Tara said. "Run." A terrible thing to yell in a small, crowded space, but panic was doing the talking. A screech rang out this time as the chandelier dropped again.

"Watch out!" Danny yelled. Mimi wasn't moving. Tara grabbed her. Danny grabbed Tara. Everyone pulled as the loudest groan of them all rang out and a blur of medieval iron and crystal soared down. Mimi, neck craned up, was rooted to the spot. She resisted Tara's attempt to pull her away. Tara was forced to drop Mimi's arm and dart out of the way. She heard a clink, and felt a whack to the side of her helmet as a piece of the chandelier slammed into her. The blow sent Tara to the ground. The Viking helmet flew off. Mimi, the table, and the vase, were soon buried in a jumble on the ground. Screams rang out from every corner of the shop as a stampede formed for the front and back doors. Men raced toward Mimi, and she heard someone shouting they were calling 999. Tara wanted to sit up, but Danny was by her side begging her not to move. She touched her head. "I'm okay." The Viking helmet saved her life.

Even as her eyes took in the horrific scene, her mind was scrambling to prove this was not happening. Mimi's body was deathly still, and the chandelier completely covered her face. "Is she okay?" Tara asked, over and over. Danny did not answer. Men finally lifted the chandelier off Mimi and a figure bent over her, as if to do CPR. His head popped up, and he shook it. *No. No, no, no.* Guests gathered around, watching from the perimeter and through the patio doors. Was this Tara's fault—had she hired the wrong lads to hang it, was it too heavy to begin with? With Danny's help, she sat up, and then stood. "The guards are on their way," she heard a man say. Danny eased Tara into her Queen Anne chair. Tears poured down her face. "Mimi," was all she could say.

"You did everything you could," Danny said. "I saw you."

"Why wouldn't she move?"

Danny rubbed her shoulder. "Shock," he said. "She froze."

What in the world was she doing in that spot? Why was she throwing flowers out of the vase? And how on earth had that chandelier come down?

Chapter 26

Tara had been thinking of nothing but Rose's warning since Mimi's death. *Don't let your light shine.* Not once had she thought of her chandelier. Not once. But even if she had—there was no way of predicting what was going to happen, no indication that it wasn't secure. Tara had barely left her sofa since the incident. Mimi had been trying to tell her something. What was it? Whatever she'd learned, something from her notebooks, it had proved deadly. She told the guards everything, but had they listened? Really listened?

Uncle Johnny did his best to cheer her up. He was constantly bringing her a mug of tea and chatting with her. "This is where you're meant to be, luv. Not some small shop in town. You belong in this mill. You can accompany Danny on salvages. I'm getting too old to travel, but a treasure hunter is what you'll be and it's a fine way to make a living, if I do say so me-self."

"I'm not upset about the shop," she said. Not com-pared to a woman losing her life there before it even opened. She'd never be able to work there now. Not that anyone would come if she tried. The grapevine had been swift, and the verdict was that the shop (and some said Tara herself) was a bit of bad luck. She was out an entire year's worth of rent. But that wasn't where her focus was, except fleetingly. She'd been going over and over it, wondering if it was her fault. Could she have prevented it somehow? Mimi had been so eager to speak with Tara until her phone dinged. That's when she scurried over to the vase. What was the connection? Why on earth had she been yanking flowers out of the vase like a mad woman?

Mimi's text might hold the answer to that. But when the guards evacuated the guests, they'd searched every inch of the shop, but the phone was gone. Tara told the guards what Mimi said—how it sounded as if she'd found something in her notebook that she'd wanted to speak with Tara about, something that pointed to the killer. The guards were crawling over the crime scene now and additional guards had been dispatched to Mimi's room at the castle to see if they could find her additional notebooks. Tara had this clawing feeling that they'd be gone just like the mo-bile phone. This had been no accident. Someone had rigged the chandelier to fall, then lured Mimi over to it with a text.

Nothing had been found amongst the pieces of broken glass, and petals, and stems. It had been a ruse so that she'd be standing under the chandelier before it was let loose. The guards had collected the rest of the burner phones Veronica had given her guests. They ordered them to stop looking for their amends and turn over the list of locations marked in the books, along with the books. A second murder had spooked them, and everyone was on high alert. Tara was worried the guests weren't going to oblige with all the requests, especially when it came to scouting out their amends. Was someone picking off the guests, one by one? It was a terrifying thought.

How had someone rigged her chandelier? There was a vacant room above the shop. Tara was allowed to use it for storage and had planned on doing so in the future, but for now, she'd never even set foot up there. Someone must have gained access. She wished she could accompany the guards up to the space. *Stop it.* Tara was in over her head. There was nothing she could do. She would do what they'd wanted her to do all along. She would keep out of it and pray they found the killer.

Three mornings passed since the incident and Tara was just looking forward to her walk with Hound. Uncle Johnny was right, the mill was where she belonged. She could go on trips around Ireland, and Scotland, and Wales to source architectural items. What was she thinking—sticking herself in a shop? Maybe she'd return to her interior design roots as a side gig.

Detective Sergeant Gable was standing by Galway Bay, holding a cup of coffee. She stopped. He nodded to her. He didn't drink coffee, but he knew she did. She approached, her stomach knotted with dread of being scolded. "I'm going to stay out of it, I swear,"

she said. "I haven't spoken to a single one of them
since the incident." *Just say it. The murder.* Sergeant
Gable thrust the coffee at her. She stared at it, determined to refuse, but then the heavenly aroma over-
powered her and she took it. *Well played.* "Thanks."

"I need you to listen to me," Sergeant Gable
began.

Tara held her hand up. "No need for a lecture. I
promise you. I am out of it. I was wrong to stay involved with them in the first place. I got carried
away—although I dare say someone targeted me.
First leaving the advertisement for the old stone
house, then leaving the book in my shop, the box of
brooches, and maybe even planting that article in
front of Veronica so she would think to come to me."
That hadn't hit her until now. How diabolical. Who
was this killer? "But that's no excuse. And even though
I didn't invite them to my opening—I assure you, I
did not—I'm convinced someone tampered with the
chandelier."

"I believe you."

"I've placed a call to the lads who originally hung
it for me—" Tara stopped as his words finally registered. "You believe me?"

"Yes. I believe you. Every word."

"Oh." She hadn't expected that. "Thank you." She
swallowed. "Do you think . . . there's anything I
could have done to prevent this?" Her heart thudded
in her chest as she awaited his answer.

"No. I don't. If it hadn't been in your shop I believe Mimi Griffin would have been murdered somewhere else."

"Oh." A nagging child inside her wanted to ask,

Then why was she murdered in my shop? But this was a horrible time for self-pity.

"We need your help."

"Anything."

"We need you to go back to the castle, and continue visiting the places marked in the book, and report everything back to us."

Maybe not everything. Tara nearly spit out the coffee, and instead began to choke on it. He patted her on the back. His kind eyes stayed on her until she stopped coughing.

"But you've forbidden them to continue searching for the amends."

"That's why we need you."

"Need me to do what, exactly?"

"We've convinced the group to stay on three more days. Once they leave, I'd say the chances of catching our killer are close to zero. Three days. That's all we have to solve this murder. You're close to them. We need you on the inside."

"I can't." She shook her head, wishing she'd never gone for a walk. This is why sometimes staying in your room was the best option. These people who insisted fresh air was good for you didn't know what they were talking about. She was out. In her mind she was completely free of the murders.

Although she knew she'd never stop thinking about them. If the killer wasn't caught, it would be something that would haunt her for the rest of her life.

"The music box," she said. "We could follow up on that."

"I've got guards working on that. I need you with the suspects."

She sighed. Danny was going to go mental over the news. And this time not in a good way. "Alright."

"I'm sorry about your shop." He cleared his throat. "But I think public opinion will change once we catch the murderer. Maybe you could even have a new start there."

She shook her head. "You think that's what's bothering me? My shop? A woman died."

"It wasn't your fault. We've checked the room above. Someone loosened the chandelier and carved out a peephole. They lured Mimi to that spot and let the chandelier plummet."

"Evil." She shuddered.

"Yes. And if we don't catch him, he'll strike again."

Or her, Tara thought, but they weren't here to discuss pronouns. "What exactly do you want me to do?"

They began to stroll along the bay.

"We all know they're going to continue their little treasure hunt despite our warnings. We're going to give you a phone you can use to text me directly. Anything odd, out of place, out of the ordinary— changes in behavior—anything. You text me." It was dangerous. What if the guests found out she was spying on them? "Unless you're not up for it, and if that's the case, I completely understand."

"I can do it." She could. But *should* she?

"We can compensate you as a researcher, or associate."

"I won't accept payment." She owed this to Veronica. And Nancy. And Mimi.

"You can't breathe a word of this to anyone. Not even your uncle. Everyone must think it's your decision alone to join the ranks again."

"What about Danny?" This was going to cost her

with him, big-time. But was there any real relationship to lose in the first place? Did she really want to be with a man whose moods changed faster than the skies over Galway Bay?

"Especially not that hothead." Sergeant Gable took out a cigarette and turned against the wind to light it.

"Aren't you putting me squarely in danger?"

"We'll have a guard tailing you. And we have another man on the inside. Veronica's driver."

"Andy?"

Gable nodded. "He'll be driving you everywhere so you'll never be alone."

"You've cleared him as a suspect?"

Gable nodded again. "Besides every single valet telling us that they saw him in his vehicle during the time frame of the murder, we've also captured his image on camera. He was sleeping in the SUV, just like he said."

"He'll know I'm a plant?"

"Yes. If either of you text me, we'll be there. Don't allow any of them to lure you to any spot, or get you alone."

That was easier said than done. "If they're still following the order based on proximity to the castle, then Connemara Stables is next. I believe Iona will search for her amends there."

Iona had a bum leg. Or claimed to. What happened to horses when they broke their leg? Was that why the location was chosen for Iona? She hated the thought. She hated herself for thinking it. But they were dealing with someone sick.

"There's one more thing you should know."

"Yes?"

"We'll be reopening Nancy Halligan's case."

"Finally."

Sergeant Gable crossed himself, then patted Tara on the shoulder, and Hound on the head. "If it gets to be too much, we'll cut you loose."

"I can handle it."

He nodded, then headed off, leaving her staring out at the glistening, ever-changing bay.

Danny was waiting for her at the mill, tossing his truck keys into the air and catching them. "Are you ready, Miss America?"

Did he know? No, that was impossible. Unless he was stalking her. Which wasn't his style. Sometimes she wished it was. "Ready?"

"For our first salvage adventure. An old cathedral. It's about a two-hour drive. We leave in twenty minutes."

An old cathedral. The freedom of a salvage. Hours alone with Danny. It sounded amazing. She really wanted to go. "I can't."

"Of course you can." He eyed her. "Why can't you?"

She shifted. "I have to go back to Ballynahinch. There are a few loose ends."

"You're joking me."

"Just a few things I have to take care of."

"Such as?"

"There are a few days left on my stay at the castle. How can I turn that down?" Sergeant Gable had paid for her stay at the castle. She was to spend the next three days there.

"Absolutely not," Danny said. "Get your things, we're going on a salvage."

"I can't."

"Tara Meehan." He had never used her full name like that, not with that tone anyway.

"Three more days. That's it."

"Do you have a death wish? Is that it?"

"I promise you. I do not."

"Give me one good reason." He held up a finger. "Just one."

"I can get close to them," she said honestly. "They trust me."

He shook his head. "We just watched a woman die. *You* almost died."

"That's why I have to see this through."

"Stop saying you have to do this. I'm telling you. You don't." Gone was Danny's stoic demeanor. There was a stubbornness behind his words, as usual, but this time she detected something else. Fear. This was Danny's version of pleading with her.

"I understand where you're coming from. I hope you can understand why I have to see this through." He shook his head, frustration oozing out of him. "Believe me. I'm going to take precautions."

"What precautions?"

She shook her head. "That's all I can say."

They locked eyes. "If you do this, we're done."

The words hung between them. There were so many things she wanted to say. Mostly—*There's a we?* But now was not the time. Danny turned and she watched as he got in his truck. She stayed until the taillights disappeared in the mist.

Uncle Johnny followed her to the luxury SUV that was idling outside the mill. Andy lifted his hand in a wave, then exited the vehicle, his eyes mirroring the worry Tara felt inside.

"I forbid you to leave," Uncle Johnny said as Tara handed her luggage to Andy.

"You can't forbid me," Tara said. "And it's only three days."

"Or it's forever," Uncle Johnny said. "This is madness."

Tara ran to him and ambushed him with a hug. She stood back, her hands gripping his arms. "I promise you. I'll be okay. Please. I'm already fighting with Danny. I can't lose you too."

His face softened. "These are the times you remind me of your mam."

Tears welled in her eyes. "That's the nicest thing you've ever said to me." She kissed him on the cheek, and ran to the SUV before she could change her mind.

Chapter 27

The riding stables were nestled in the valley of a rolling pasture, with trails leading out along the glistening bay. The weather was cool, but no sign of rain, and there was a crisp feeling of fall in the air. Fall was Tara's favorite season, and she'd been warned there wasn't much of it in Ireland, but today proved them wrong. Somewhere close by someone was burning peat, adding the perfect touch of tart and sweetness to the air. Majestic horses of all colors were lined up, saddled in rich leather, and waiting for their arrival. The instructor was a perky black woman in her sixties, wearing riding boots and a fantastic cowboy hat. Her long silver hair was pulled back in a braid that ran down to her leather belt. "I'm Tina O'Neill, your guide for the day," she said. "Along with the horses." Tara liked her immediately, and not just because she was American. She had a million questions for her, wondering how long she'd lived in Ireland, if she liked it here, and how long she'd been riding horses, but there was no time for chitchat.

The group approached the horses, and Tina began pairing them up. Tara's horse was regal and white. Tara was in love. Iona, who stood beside the largest horse in the pack, so black he was almost blue, stroked his nose. "I told Veronica that as a girl I used to love riding," Iona said. "I can't believe she remembered."

"Mimi got a diamond watch," Elaine said. She was the only one not standing by her horse. She'd barely moved from the SUV. Andy, fiddling with an unlit cigarette, watched her with amusement.

"She's taking her watch to the grave," Cassidy said. The rest of the group quieted her with disapproving looks. The guards actually had the watch; Tara had turned it over after the murder.

"Maybe Veronica bought you a horse," Eddie said.

Iona tilted her head and stared at her horse, as if sizing him up for a lifetime commitment.

"I don't see why we *all* have to ride," Sheila said.

"Nobody has to ride," Tina said. "But these horses are all reliable and will do the work for you. All you have to do is let them."

"I'm stoked," Iona said. "But if you don't want to ride, don't ride."

"Let's do it," John said, surprising Tara with his enthusiasm. "I could use a change of pace."

At Tina's urging, they began mounting their horses. Tara felt a thrill as she swung her leg over and landed in the saddle. Her mother used to take her to stables in upstate New York in the fall. She hadn't ridden since she was a teenager, and her heart swelled with the memories of trotting by trees bursting with color as the smell of campfires and apples filled the air.

"I'm going to sit this one out," Elaine said, plopping down on a bale of hay by the barn.

"As will I," Bartley said, pulling up the bale next to her.

As they started down the path, one horse following the other, Tara relished the feel of the wind through her hair as the horses picked up speed near the bay. She was the last horse in line, which didn't bother her a bit. She loved listening to the sound of their collective hooves beating out a steady rhythm. Driving by the mountains and the water had been awe-inspiring, but now, riding along them, Tara felt as if she wasn't just looking at the scenery, she was a part of it. She'd almost forgotten she was here to suss out a killer. An hour flew by, and before Tara knew it, they were taking the path back to the stables. She knew one thing for sure. She was definitely going to do this again. For once the group was in harmony. Tara was so lost in the joy of the ride that she didn't notice Iona had stopped to wait for her, until their horses were side-by-side.

"Hey," Tara said. "Everything okay?"

"Fine," Iona said. "But I think there's something I should confess."

"Oh?"

"You seem to have the confidence of the guards."

"Not really." Did Iona know Tara was reporting back to them? She thought she'd been subtle.

"That Friday night," Iona said. "Veronica did approach me. She asked for my medical records."

"I see."

"No. You don't. She already had them. All of them.

I've sent her every scrap of paper from every doctor's appointment."

"Okay."

"Mimi had them."

"Why are you telling me this now?"

"I'm worried. Remember Mimi thought someone was going through her papers?"

"Yes."

"What if . . . someone's messed with my paperwork? Removed them. Or changed them?"

"If that's the case, your doctor's will have the originals."

Iona's face lit up. "Of course." She slapped a hand over her head. "I can't believe I didn't think of that." She grinned. "I'm in the clear." She squeezed her horse twice. "Giddyap." She took off without another word. Tara let her mind clear once more as she relaxed into the ride.

They had just turned to go home when John Murphy pulled up alongside Eddie's brown mare, reached over, and grabbed Eddie by the collar. The instructor, who was way ahead with Sheila and Iona, had her back to the ruckus. What on earth was he doing? It appeared as if he was trying to yank Eddie off the horse. The saddle slipped to the right, along with Eddie.

"Hey!" Tara yelled. She squeezed her legs around her horse and it obediently sped up. "Hands off." Her voice was all but lost in the wind. John Murphy didn't even throw a glance in her direction. The two men wrestled as their horses started to buck and whinny. Didn't John realize Tara had a clear view of the assault? She wasn't the only one to pick up speed; they were galloping now, hanging on to each other as their horses tried to flee. They were barreling down the path so quickly that if the instructor didn't cop on, she would be ambushed from behind. Tara's repeated yells were swallowed up. She was now riding parallel to the men, but had no idea how to slow down their horses.

"Easy, easy," she yelled, not knowing what else to do.

"Other side," John yelled. "You can try to pull him up."

"What are you doing?"

"His saddle has a burr underneath it. I was only trying to help."

Eddie lifted his head to lock eyes with Tara, sweat poured down his face. "Help."

Tara maneuvered her horse to the other side, and Eddie extended his arm. This was probably a bad idea, like letting a drowning victim pull you down with them. Instead, she squeezed her horse with her legs, reached over and grabbed the reins of Eddie's horse. "We're all going to slow down together," she yelled at John. "You got it?"

John nodded. She still had no idea if he was trying to pull something or genuinely trying to help Eddie, but all that mattered was stopping the horses before one or all of them were thrown to the ground. She took the reins of her horse in one hand and Eddie's in the other, as she pulled back. "Whoa," she said with as much authority as she could muster. It took two more tries before the horses slowed, jerking Eddie back slightly. She pulled them once more. "Whoa." The horses stopped. Eddie continued to slide off; his head was nearly to the ground, the saddle halfway off. Eddie's horse looked as if she wanted to rear back and knock him off the saddle. Eddie's arm flailed as he tried to grab onto Tara and then her horse to keep himself from hitting the ground. Sweat poured down her face as she tried to keep her horse calm while Eddie clung to her.

Finally, Tina looped back, instructing John and Tara to a safer distance where they could dismount. The instructor was already off her horse, helping Eddie slide safely to the ground, saddle and all. He sat on the ground for a moment, then suddenly stood, stumbled, and lunged toward John, cursing and screaming.

"I *saved* you," John said. "The saddle was slipping, I could see the horse was in pain."

Tina cut through their noise with a reprimand. "My horses deserve calm voices," she said. After a quick examination of the horse, and a carrot to calm him down, she turned to the two men. "He's fine."

"I swear I saw something like a burr, the saddle was slipping, I only tried to keep him upright," John stuttered.

"You tried to kill me!" Eddie shouted.

"Are you joking me? I save your life and this is the tanks I get?"

"The two of you will walk my horses back, and if you raise your voices again, you're going to have to deal with me." Her voice was calm, and a smile never left her face. "If you respect my horses, they'll respect you. As will I."

"Yes, of course," Eddie said.

"I'm sorry," John said.

Tara wished Tina O'Neill would follow them home. She'd never seen John and Eddie so compliant, and it was a joy to behold. Something buzzed and danced in her pocket, making her jump. Her phone. She lifted it out. *Private Caller.* The guards. She'd forgotten to check in with them. A few hours on the job and she was already blowing it. She had a feeling she was going to have a lot of explaining to do.

It took a ton of convincing to prevent the guards from coming out to the stables to document the incident. Tara knew if they did, the group would never trust her again. She had to push back on Detective Gable, explaining she was trying to do as he asked, but he was going to have to trust her. After everyone had returned safely to the barn, Tina O'Neill presented Iona a lifetime membership to an exclusive riding academy, where Iona could ride all over Ireland, take all the lessons she wanted, and stay at nearby resorts.

Iona's face was flushed with happiness. "This is perfect," she said. "This has already healed me more than Veronica will ever know."

"You don't get the prize yet," Elaine reminded her. "It still has to be turned over to Tara."

"You can't put a membership in a safe," Iona said.

Elaine blushed, then crossed her arms over her chest. "You won't be able to use the membership until you're cleared." She turned to Tina O'Neill. "Is that clear?"

Tina didn't even blink. "I know you're not talking to me with that tone."

"Sorry," Elaine said. "But we're all under a strict gag order."

"Sounds about right to me," Tina said, flicking her gaze over the group. "Watch me. I'm going to show you how to remove the saddle, and then I'll expect you to do the same. And don't forget to thank that beautiful creature that let you ride on its back." Someday, Tara was going to come back and get to know this woman. Tina demonstrated the saddle removal, and then stood back to see if they could manage it for themselves.

"You can't even let me enjoy this for a minute, can you?" Iona said under her breath to Elaine as they all began the process of removing the saddle.

Elaine folded her arms. "I don't think anybody should be enjoying anything when there have been two murders."

Three, Tara thought. *Counting Nancy Halligan. And they're all connected. They must be.* While the thought was on her mind, Tara texted the guards. **We need to find out which one of our suspects knew Nancy Halligan.**

Tara gave Tina O'Neill the card to Irish Revivals before they left. "I really enjoyed that. Thank you."

Tina smiled and nodded. "You're quite welcome."

"I hope to come back sometime. But in the meantime, if you're ever in Galway city, I'd love to share transplant stories."

"Transplant stories." Tina examined the card, then stuck it in her pocket. "That'll require alcohol."

Tara laughed. "That can be arranged."

Andy, who was often chatty on the rides, quickly sensed the tension in the vehicle, and for once the drive back was silent. Tara met Andy's gaze in the rearview mirror. He arched an eyebrow. She made a tell-you-later face. He nodded. He would be a good person to ask about Nancy Halligan. And Bartley. He sat in the passenger seat, and Tara stared at the back of his head as she mulled him over. He was always lurking about. His was the name Mimi had written on the mirror. Tara had tried to ask her why—but Mimi seemed to have directed the conversation back to her notebooks. Was that about Bartley? If anyone had secrets, Tara had a feeling it was that mountain of a man.

When they reached Ballynahinch Castle, the guests fled from the SUV and disappeared into the hotel. Andy leaned against the car and lit a cigarette as Tara filled him in on the bewildering tussle between John and Eddie.

"He claims he saw something under the saddle but the instructor found nothing."

"What did it look like to you?"

Tara sighed. "By the time I saw it, it looked as if John was trying to drag Eddie off the horse."

"Want me to keep an eye on him?"

Tara gave a low laugh.

"What?"

"You've already been doing that," Tara said. "Keeping an eye on all of them."

His face reddened and then he laughed. "I am in the perfect position to observe them."

"Well? What are your major observations so far?"

He frowned. "Quite honestly, I can make a case for each one of them being guilty. On the flip side, I could also argue their innocence."

"What about Bartley?"

"Bartley?" The surprise was evident in his voice.

"He's as steady as they get." Andy seemed prickly. Did he think she was going after loyal employees? Was he worried she would target him next?

"I just don't know very much about him," Tara said. "He's a mystery to me."

"He's a man of few words, I'll give you dat. But he's no killer. I bet he wants to find out who it is more than any of us."

It was a full-throated defense, and Tara decided to drop the subject of Bartley for now. "I believe Veronica relapsed that Friday evening, yet no one is talking about it."

Andy hung his head. "You're not wrong."

"What do you know?"

He put out his cigarette. "It's my fault."

This was news. "How so?"

"I had a bottle of Powers in the glove compartment of the vehicle. The anniversary of me father's death is coming up. It's how I celebrate, with a toast to the old man with his favorite whiskey. I didn't know Veronica would even think about opening the glove compartment or I wouldn't have . . ." He let the sentence drop. "I checked for it that Friday evening, when it was clear I wouldn't be driving anymore. Just to have a wee nip. The bottle was gone."

"Are you sure it was her?" He was surrounded by valets. Anyone could have taken the whiskey bottle.

"Did I see her take it?" He shook his head. "No, I did not. But I heard the guards talking when they came to the hotel. Said an empty bottle of Powers—empty, mind you, and it was a full big bottle—was found in her room."

Tara nodded. Veronica was definitely soused on that voicemail. She'd ask Gable if it was true they found the bottle in her room. "Do you have any idea what—or who—upset her so much that evening?"

He sighed. "I'd only be guessing."

"It's better than nothing."

Andy looked around, then leaned in and lowered his voice. "I think she caught Eddie and Cassidy knocking boots."

This was news. "Eddie and Cassidy?" Did he mean Elaine?

Andy nodded.

"Eddie—her ex-husband, and Cassidy—her niece?"

Another nod.

"My God." That would have definitely set Veronica O'Farrell ablaze. It was a shocking piece of news, yet somehow it fit. It would have had to be something quite shattering. Especially if Veronica had still been in love with Eddie. Which Tara suspected she was. For all she knew, Eddie was the real reason for all of these amends. But instead, he beds her niece. The young bombshell. The *current* addict. Who once accused Veronica of being a murderer. Yes, Tara could see that setting Veronica off, making her relapse. A downward spiral leading to her letting her guard down . . .

"And no matter what Ms. O'Farrell said, she was not over Eddie. Not by a long shot. To see him with the younger niece of her first husband? I think it did her head in." Andy had read her mind.

"Do you think it was a one-night stand or are they actually an item?" Tara asked, still trying to wrap her head around the revelation and what it could mean.

"I saw them shifting in the hallway Friday night. Just before the doors closed."

"Shifting?"

"Sorry. Forgot you are a Yank. *Kissing.*"

That was slightly less scandalous than her interpretation, but it was still a shock. If Veronica had seen Eddie and Cassidy kissing Friday evening in the hallway—that was potentially explosive. "So just to be clear. You did not tell Veronica what you saw?"

"Are you mental? I know what happens to the messenger." He winced as he realized it was a poor choice of words considering what happened to Veronica. "That's the last I saw or heard anything. But I heard several of the guests say that they saw Veronica after that. She was langered." *Drunk as a skunk.*

"Did you tell the guards?"

He nodded. "And they asked me to keep it to meself."

Tara nodded. They had a habit of doing that. "Don't worry. I won't say a thing."

Andy hung his head. "Maybe I should have done more. Maybe I should have checked on her."

"You couldn't have known. None of us could. Where was Bartley at this time?"

"I don't know. I didn't realize there would be any need to pay attention."

"I've been wondering why he worked for her. What made him stick around?"

Andy shrugged. "I guess it's true. People are more comfortable with the devil they know."

. . . *more comfortable with the devil they know.* It was starting to look like Veronica O'Farrell knew a lot of them.

Chapter 28

Tara received a text from Andy early the next morning:

Bartley headed into Clifden
You're taking him?
Wanted joe maxi instead of me

Joe maxi meant a taxi cab. That was interesting. Downtown Clifden was relatively small. Bartley was a tall, imposing figure. If he wanted privacy, he picked the wrong town. Andy agreed to drop Tara off close enough to downtown that she could walk, but far enough away that Bartley wouldn't spot the SUV.

"Are you sure you want to be following him, like?" Andy said, drumming his fingers on the steering wheel. "He could be dangerous."

"I'll keep my distance," Tara said.

"Do you want me to circle back here at a certain time?"

"Not at all. Who knows, I may get lost in shops myself. I'll get a cab home."

He nodded. "Text if you get in trouble."

"Will do." She hesitated.

"Change your mind?"

"No. Remember that day you came into my shop because you had to use the jax?"

He stared straight ahead. "I do."

"When I was in the art gallery in Clifden, the curator told me a very similar tale. It made me think the entire scenario had been scripted."

He made eye contact with her and she saw a flicker of admiration. "It was."

Even though she'd known it, it was still jarring to hear him say. "Why?"

"Veronica's little test."

"Meaning if I didn't insist you come in to use the restroom?"

"Then you weren't worthy."

"Does that mean she had backups chosen if we failed the test?"

Andy tilted his head. "I never thought of that. I don't know."

"Probably not important. I was just curious."

"I'm sorry."

"Don't be. Everyone did Veronica's bidding." She was a manipulator and a game player. *And someone got sick of it.* "Thanks for the ride." She hopped out of the SUV. There was something she held back. She was going to plan a trip to Inishbofin Island. But maybe it was something she should do alone. She had to take a ferry to the island. Under better circumstances that sounded fun. These were not better circumstances. But before Inishbofin, maybe she should go back to the old stone house. Were there any clues they missed? Was that little rowboat still there?

These were the questions swimming around her head when she entered town, suddenly feeling slightly foolish. What was she supposed to do now? Yes, it was a small enough downtown and Bartley was a tall man, always wearing black like a hitman, easy enough to spot. But he could be anywhere. She'd have to keep her expectations low, have a stroll, and practice her surprised look in case she ran into him. Maybe he simply wanted to get away from everyone and enjoy the adorable boutiques, but something told her that wasn't the case.

She passed storefronts, and pubs, and shops, soaking in the adorable downtown. She passed the gallery where she'd stopped in with Danny, the antique shop where she bought their (unappreciated) gifts, the restaurant where Sheila and John had been fighting, the pub where she'd first encountered Eddie Oh and Elaine. Eddie Oh.

Was Eddie having an affair with Cassidy? Or had the two of them paired up to drive Veronica mental? Maybe Tara should have a chat with Elaine about the subject, see if she had any inkling of a love affair. After all, love was a motive for murder.

Tara was just contemplating lunch when she looked up and saw Bartley. Mobile phone stuck to his ear, he paced in front of a shop, gesturing wildly. Even from across the street she could see the tension in his body, and from the way his mouth was moving, it was obvious he was giving out to someone. He then shoved the phone into his pocket and slipped inside the shop. Tara edged closer without crossing the street. It was hard to tell what kind of a shop it was from the outside, but as she moved closer it appeared to be equivalent to a pawn shop. She waited. He emerged ten minutes later. He wasn't carrying anything. How odd. A taxi pulled up in front of him, he got in, and sped away. Tara hurried across the street and entered the shop.

A bell dinged as Tara entered the cluttered shop. Cigar smoke lingered in the air. Behind the counter an older male was absorbed in a newspaper while a younger man hunched by a shelf, adjusting the product. "What can I do ya for?" the older man asked without looking up.

Darn. She hadn't figured out a sly way to ask about Bartley yet. "My uncle was just in here," she said.

He glanced up. Then frowned. "Your uncle?"

She laughed. "I was raised in America."

"I can tell." He went back to his paper.

"I was hoping you'd be willing to help me with a little surprise."

"I doubt it."

She glanced around the shop. There were the usual items. Jewelry. Trinkets. Books. Clothes. She could smell dust. Whenever they salvaged items, they cleaned them up before putting them on the floor of the mill. Yes, they would leave the rust, or patina, on certain objects as they added an extra beauty to how the object had aged, but that was a far cry from leaving it dirty. She couldn't picture Bartley in this shop. What on earth was he doing here? "I have to buy something for his birthday and he's just impossible to please."

"You don't say."

"I was hoping that you could tell me what it was that interested him in here—if he bought anything, that is."

"He wasn't buying for himself."

"Oh." Now she really wanted to know. Who was he buying for in here? What in the world was it? "I'm not surprised. He's a giver."

"You don't say."

What were the chances she found the one Irish shopkeeper who wasn't a talker. "Thank you." She turned and headed out.

"He already did."

She stopped at the door. *He already did.* He'd come here to thank the shopkeeper? Or ask him not to talk? What would have drawn him to this shop in the first place? "Do you ever repair items?" *Or damage them . . .*

He lowered his newspaper slightly. "Aye."

"Like music boxes."

The clerk grinned for the first time, showing gaps in his bottom front teeth. "Could ya even recognize the old tune?"

"Who wouldn't recognize 'The Old Woman from Wexford'?"

He grinned. "Sounded close enough, did it?"

"Everyone got the message." The music box had been tampered with before it was brought to the mill. Which meant Bartley had seen her purchase it. Had he been following her? She exited the shop, leaned against the wall and exhaled. If Bartley had altered the music box, her next question was—why? Was he pointing a finger at Elaine? Elaine had once been in love with Terrance. Was Bartley trying to tell her that Veronica had murdered him? Had Cassidy been right all along? Or was Bartley sending another kind of message? A threat? What had Mimi realized from her notebooks? She said something about his finances, didn't she? Had he been stealing money from Veronica's estate all these years? Was Bartley their killer?

She was starving and lunch was next on the agenda before she fainted. But first she texted Sergeant Gable, told him the name of the shop, and filled him in on what she'd learned. He responded:

Good work. The music box is actual evidence we can use.

Don't return to the shop. We'll take it from here.

She felt a flush of pride for being praised, but also noticed he couldn't help but tell her not to return to the shop. As if she was trying to take over. Tara felt a pang of loneliness and wished she could call Danny. He hadn't called her since their fight. It wasn't fair that the guards were asking her to keep those closest to her in the dark. Then again, she also didn't want to place those she loved in danger. *He doesn't want you in danger either, that's why he's angry.*

She entered a pub, sat at the counter, and ordered seafood chowder with brown bread and a pint of Guinness. She wanted to get her mind off the case, and for a few seconds she did let herself enjoy the seafood chowder, and brown bread. But like a boomerang, her thoughts returned.

Bartley had worked for Veronica the longest. Why would he wait all these years to murder her? What if, instead, he was trying to suss out the culprit himself? Playing detective. She suspected the same of Andy. And Mimi. Look how that turned out.

Why did Bartley *return* to the shop? It couldn't have been just to thank the man who tinkered with the music box. Was he checking to make sure no one else from the group had been in to ask about it? If so, she prayed he was satisfied and wouldn't go a third time. She certainly couldn't march back in and ask the shopkeeper, especially since the guards would be paying him a visit. She hoped they'd go in subtly, but she couldn't very well text Gable and tell him how to do his job.

"You're the American who's involved in the murder probe." Tara's hand froze with her spoon halfway to her mouth. The female voice came from behind her. She turned to see a woman her own age with flowing red hair, and a scrubbed look, no makeup, but freckles and inquisitive blue eyes.

"Accidentally involved," Tara said. There was no use denying it.

The woman took the stool next to Tara. "I need your help."

"My help?"

The woman swallowed. "I'm Alexis. I don't tink I introduced myself when we spoke on the phone."

"On the phone?"

"I'm an innkeeper on Inishbofin Island."

It was the last thing Tara expected her to say. "Yes," she said. "Nancy Halligan was staying with you when . . ."

Alexis nodded. "I'm sorry to ambush you. I was actually on my way to Ballynahinch Castle to see if I could find you—and here you are."

"Does the family want Savage back?"

"Savage?"

"Nancy's pug. She's being well taken care of. But if

you know someone in the family who wants her . . ."
Please, please no.

Alexis shook her head. "I'm glad she's being looked after."

"I've been meaning to come see you too," Tara said. "Have the guards been to see you?"

"Only to ask some basic questions. I've been waiting for someone to give me some answers, or pick up her things. I'm *still* waiting."

"Why did you come to see me?"

"You found Nancy."

"Yes."

"Did you see her backpack?"

Tara shook her head. "No."

"I told the guards she had a backpack. They've never followed up."

"They keep things close to their chest. What did it look like? What was in it?"

"It was black. She had water and sandwiches."

"How do you know?"

"I made the sandwiches. I saw the bottle of water. We spoke about the heat before she left."

"Why was she going for a hike in that weather?"

Alexis glanced to her right and left, then leaned in and lowered her voice. "I think she was meeting a man."

"Why did you think that?"

"She said nothing about going to Connemara. Then the night before she gets a phone call. I wasn't trying to eavesdrop."

"But?"

She sighed. "It's a small inn and she was in my back garden. I heard her say, 'Calm down. Where can we meet?'"

"Why do you think it was a man?"

"I made sure I was up early the next morning. I kind of ambushed her as she left. I teased. I said, looks like someone has a hot date. She just shook her head and laughed that her dog was the only hot date she had lined up." She paused. "But she blushed."

"Hot date? In a tracksuit?"

Alexis blinked. Her mouth opened several times but nothing came out but a little squeak. Then she shrugged. "She put on lipstick. And perfume."

"To go hiking?"

"Exactly."

"I think you need to speak with the guards again." Tara didn't want this woman knowing that she was working with them. She jotted down Sergeant Gable's number. "Here. Call him directly. Or Breanna Cunningham." She wrote down Breanna's number as well. "I promise they'll take you serious this time."

"Thank you."

"Did you call the police when she didn't return that morning?"

Alexis hunched over. "No. Besides, it was normal for Nancy to wander for days."

"Wait. Are you saying that's not the first time she'd stayed with you?"

"Heavens, no. Nancy has been coming to Inishbofin for years. I can't claim she was a dear friend. But she was a wonderful client. Kept to herself. That's why she loved Inishbofin. I never pried." Alexis's voice grew husky, and she took a minute to collect herself. "Everyone on the island knew Nancy. I'm sure you already know this."

"No," Tara said.

Alexis shrugged. "I think I told the guards Nancy

was a regular. I kept waiting to be interviewed. No one ever came. Maybe I should have contacted them. But I swear. She never indicated that anything was wrong. Not once."

"It's a terrible shock. You can't blame yourself. But you should contact the guards and tell them absolutely everything you just told me." If Nancy was planning on meeting someone, it meant it hadn't been a matter of mistaken identity. They did not confuse Nancy and Veronica. Which meant they wanted them both dead.

The question was why. Tara had to return to the stone house. Was there a backpack stashed somewhere nearby?

"Look," Alexis said, sweat forming on her brow. "I heard her tell the person on the phone to calm down."

"Yes, I heard you," Tara said slowly. Alexis nodded, chewing on her lip. Tara knew there was more.

"I heard a name, but I don't know what it means."

"What was the name?"

"Eddie."

A tingle went up her spine. "You heard her say Eddie?"

The woman swallowed, then nodded. " 'Calm down, Eddie. Where can we meet?' "

Chapter 29

Tara had planned on going back to Galway so she could speak with Sergeant Gable about the latest Nancy revelation, and remind him she wanted to look at Mimi's notebooks. If he wanted her help he was going to have to give her some leeway. She was on her way to the room to grab a few things when Andy stopped her at the entrance to the castle.

"I've just been asked to take the group to Connemara National Park in the morning."

"Oh." Either the group was getting antsy and wanted to hike, or Gable was right. They were still going after the amends. "Can I join?"

"I was expecting you would."

"Whose amends are they chasing?"

"Elaine Burke's."

Tara texted Gable the change of plans. She suddenly had a free evening in front of her. She hurried inside, eager to get to the room, where there was a paperback book on her nightstand and a bathrobe with her name on it.

The Connemara National Park had a visitor center with a small museum and gift shop on the top floor, and a café and sitting room on the lower level. From there you could exit onto the hiking paths, following three trails of varying difficulties. The most difficult path up to Diamond Hill, a distance of 3.7 kilometers, was marked in red. Yellow was the easiest. Most of the group decided to go with blue, the middle-child hike. Iona was the lone soul determined to take the longest hike. Gable let Tara know that one of his men would be at Connemara National Park, blending in with the other hikers, and Tara had a feeling this is when they would find out whether or not she was faking her injury.

The day had started with a cover of gray, but now the sun was peeking through the mountains, making it sunny and misty at the same time. The first part of the walk they saw cows, and sheep, and deer. Elaine was the last in the group, and when they reached the first hill, she balked.

"Why is the Connemara National Park my location for amends? Shouldn't this be Iona's?"

"Injury my arse," Cassidy said, pointing to Iona's back in the distance. "Look at her go."

"Perhaps we should inform the guards," Bartley said. "Whoever inherits the estate may want to discontinue her payments."

"Whoever?" Cassidy said. "I'm her only family."

"Did you ever find your pills?" Elaine asked.

"No." Cassidy pouted. "But turns out they were

just my sleeping pills. Why? Do you know who stole them?"

"I don't know a ting," Elaine said as they started uphill. "But why didn't you report it to the guards?"

"Because after two murders I hardly doubt they care about a little pill swipe. It was probably one of the housekeepers. Or the driver."

"Andy?" Tara said, her anger starting to simmer.

"He drove me to the chemist," Cassidy said. "I could have dropped them in the vehicle."

"That doesn't make him a thief," Tara said.

"He's responsible for cleaning it out, isn't he?" Cassidy argued.

Of course somebody like Cassidy would blame the hardworking staff. It was blood-boiling.

"I can't hike!" Elaine said, stopping halfway up the hill. "She's just doing this to embarrass me." As hills went, it was pretty modest. Tara vowed to keep herself in shape. It would feel terrible not to be able to climb this.

"Could this have anything to do with the day Veronica met Iona?" Tara asked.

Elaine gawped at her. "How could it?"

"I don't know. Were you supposed to accompany her that day?"

Elaine scrunched her face. "I don't remember. It doesn't ring a bell, but it was so long ago. I wish we had Mimi's notebooks."

Another thorn in Tara's side. She texted Gable once more:

I keep asking about Mimi's notebooks. Need to see them. Please respond.

The hike took them an hour, mainly because Elaine had to stop often and complain. The view from the top of the blue hike was stunning. Rolling mountains, trees with shining red leaves, and the bay shimmering in the distance. Tara took a moment to breathe, and soak it in. By the time they returned to the visitor center, Iona was there arguing with a strange man.

"She had the longest hike and she beat us?" Cassidy said. "Definitely faking that injury."

"I saw you filming me!" Iona screamed at the strange man.

"Just the scenery," he said. *Gable's man.*

"I demand you erase any footage of me."

"Certainly." He started to walk away.

"I want to see you do it!"

He shook his head, and kept walking.

"We saw you too," Cassidy said. "There was no sign of a limp."

Iona whirled around, her face red with fury. Or from exertion. Or both. "Mind your own business."

Cassidy stepped forward, jabbing her finger at Iona. "How much money have you been taking from Veronica for a fake injury?"

"It wasn't fake. I'm healing, that's all. And I've worked very hard to get here."

"You shouldn't be taking any more money."

"For your information my lawyers have already agreed on an end date. All of my progress records were being shared with her. She *knew* I was healing. There are only three months left of payments, and that was her idea, not mine."

Everyone turned to Bartley to see if he could verify this. "I do know she was receiving Iona's records. I did not read them. I'm sure they exist within Veronica's belongings."

"I can't wait to get away from you people," Iona said, then strode inside.

Tara texted Gable an update, including Iona's claims that Veronica had her progress records and the end date to the payments. He replied right away:

Good work. Come to the station. Mimi's notebooks will be made available.

Finally. They stood in the outdoor courtyard. "Do you think my amends are here?" Elaine asked. She looked to the group for answers. None were given.

"Maybe they're not all obvious," Sheila said.

Elaine sank onto a nearby bench. "That's not helpful at all."

Tara lifted her eyes to the sky. It looked like rain. "I don't know what else we can do today. But we can always come back."

"I don't need anything. An apology is enough."

"She never really apologized though, did she?" Cassidy pointed out.

"You can have my riding classes if you wish," Iona offered.

"She didn't even ride the first time," Cassidy said. "Can we give her Mimi's watch?" A gasp went through the crowd. "What? It's not like she's going to need it."

"It's fine," Elaine said. Andy entered the courtyard.

"There's something under the bench," he said, pointing to where Elaine was perched.

"If you mean my fat arse, I don't find that funny," she said.

Andy laughed. "No, ma'am. Looks like an envelope."

She bent over sideways, then upon seeing he was correct, reached under. Everyone moved in.

Elaine. You were a good friend. Galway Properties has your amends. You always said you wanted to retire in Connemara. There's an old stone house I think you'd like, plus a budget to rehab it. Can't wait to be invited over for tea and biscuits. Let's renew our friendship in our golden years. XOXO Roni

Tara gasped. Heads snapped toward her.

"What is it?" Elaine said.

Should she tell them?

"That's where Nancy Halligan died," Bartley said.

"My word," Elaine said. "I don't understand."

"A house?" Cassidy said. "Iona gets riding lessons, Mimi got a watch, and you get a house?"

"She stole my entire life," Elaine said, clutching the envelope and standing up to Cassidy. "I was supposed to marry your uncle. And you know it." Cassidy fell silent, twirling a strand of her long blond hair. "Besides, Veronica's new best friend died at the house? I'm not sure I even want it."

"It's not really a house," Tara said. "It would need to be completely rebuilt. But it's a gorgeous piece of property." Tara wouldn't mind living there herself.

Elaine headed toward the exit. "I want to go home."

After everyone else piled into the SUV, Tara hung back.

"You okay, there?" Andy asked.

"I'm going to stay. Clear my head."

He held eye contact, then nodded. "It's an interesting development." He gave her another nod, then pulled away. Tara stared until the SUV was out of sight. She began to pace. Veronica knew all about the old stone house. Was that why she visited Galway

Properties? It had to be. Not for Sheila and John. For Elaine.

Tara tried to remember her first meeting with Veronica. Did Tara tell Veronica where she'd found Nancy Halligan?

She didn't remember exactly, but she didn't think so. She'd said something about an old stone house, but that didn't mean Veronica connected it to the house she was buying for Nancy. Was that what Veronica found out later that evening? *Where* Nancy died? And what conclusions did she draw? That someone she'd invited to make amends had lured her sponsor to that stone house? The same one she was thinking of buying? Did Veronica realize right then that someone in her circle was a psychopath?

She recalled Alexis and her recollection of Nancy's phone call. *Calm down, Eddie.*

Had Eddie learned that Elaine was getting the old stone house? Did *he* call Nancy and lure her out there? Even if that was true, the lingering and most perplexing question remained the same one Tara had been asking herself over and over and over. Why?

Chapter 30

The room at the Garda Station was small and smelled like microwave popcorn and stale coffee. Twenty-five notebooks were piled in front of Tara. This had been a mistake. Tara slid the first one off the pile just to get an idea of the kinds of things Mimi wrote down. She turned to a page in the first notebook.

Everyone's walking on eggshells around the Dragon Lady today. She was screaming at her driver. Then again, the poor old man is hard of hearing.

That must have been the driver before Andy.

Eddie Oh came to see Veronica today. He's quite charming. Trouble.

The beginning of the affair. The next page had a newspaper article, but it was torn out. Only three words remained:

Died by Suicide

What? Who? Barely anything of the article was left,

except the date. Two years ago, in June. The notebook was older and the article was shoved inside. Mimi had been snooping into something. Correction. Into *someone*. Had a suicide two years ago sparked a murder now? Tara would have to ask a few heads about it. She stood up to stretch and yawn. She was going to fall asleep in this stuffy room. If they'd let her take them home, she could try and digest them a little at a time. She picked up the next notebook.

Bartley startled me today. What is his job anyway? If he's only her solicitor, then why is he always lurking about?

Tara skimmed through, looking for anything interesting.

Veronica accused me of stealing her Tara Brooch! Ah, this was the start of the amends she'd later make to Mimi.

I swear I didn't take it. Why accuse me? Anyone could have picked it up, it was always slipping off her. Now everyone is giving me the side-eye. I can't work in this hostile environment.

Tara was already getting antsy. She continued to flip:

I was crying so hard Veronica had her driver take me home.

Tara reached for the most recent notebook.

Veronica insists Eddie is working on a new sculpture. Something groundbreaking.

Tara felt a zip of adrenaline course through her. Was this true? *Groundbreaking.* Could this be a morbid reference to burying Veronica? Tara thought it through. *She was staged. Posed. Like a sculpture.* If Andy saw Eddie and Cassidy kissing in the hallway that evening, then why weren't they coming forward?

Wouldn't they be each other's alibi? She could see them wanting to protect the dirty little secret but not when murder was the accusation.

I heard Veronica on the phone this morning. She was freaking out about her bank accounts. I distinctly heard her mention Bartley's name. Maybe the rumors are true. Maybe he has been skimming all these years.

That was the last entry. Friday morning. Twenty-four hours later and Veronica would be dead. And a week after that so would Mimi.

"Anything good?" Sergeant Gable poked his head into the room.

Tara pointed out the items that had drawn her attention. Gable jotted them down. "Did you find out anything about the music box?" Tara held her breath, wondering if he would answer.

He nodded. "We spoke to the owner of the shop. Bartley was there to show him a photo."

"A photo?"

Sergeant Gable nodded. "Eddie is the one who brought the music box into the shop to have it doctored." He must have seen Tara purchasing it. Or watched her as she left the store, then entered and found out she'd bought the music box. Eddie had a lot of fans around here. If he asked the clerk to let him have the music box, it would have been easy to convince the clerk that his intentions were good.

"My God." The sculpture. The music box. The affair with Cassidy. The way Veronica's body was posed. And the innkeeper overhearing Nancy on the phone: *Calm down, Eddie . . .* "Are you bringing him in?"

"We will be. Checking on CCTV cameras now, and we have another guard tailing him."

"Did you ever find out how someone got into my shop and hid upstairs to rig the chandelier?"

"Heather Milton."

Tara wasn't expecting that. "What?"

"She said someone came into her shop that morning claiming to be the caterers. Said you were supposed to let them in, and if she didn't the caviar was going to go to waste."

"I didn't have caviar."

"We think it was the killer."

"I don't suppose she was able to identify him?"

"She said the man was literally hiding behind a huge stack of boxes."

"She let them in my shop?"

"Worse than that."

"What?"

He sighed. "She was in a hurry to get to an appointment. They swore up and down they would just drop the boxes off and return the key."

"She didn't."

"I'm afraid so. The key was returned several hours later. We checked with a key shop. Sure enough, a male came in to make a copy."

"Let me guess. They didn't get a good look either."

"Correct. We combed through CCTV footage. Whoever he is, he made sure not to look at the cameras. We only see a coat and his cap."

"If Eddie did have that music box tweaked—and he and Cassidy are sleeping together—"

"Wait. What's this?"

Shoot. She thought she'd told him. Or texted him.

Hadn't she? "Andy saw them kissing in the castle Friday evening."

"I thought he hadn't checked in yet."

"Exactly. If they're each other's alibis, why haven't they come forward?"

"Excellent question."

"Do you mind if we take a walk? I need fresh air."

Gable nodded and they headed out. Tara took a moment to breathe. The weather had taken a turn; there was a crisp, fall feel to the air.

"You seem to be turning something over," Gable said. "You'd make a good detective."

Tara laughed. "It's oddly similar to design."

"How so?"

"It's a pattern. I'm trying to work it out."

"Why don't you try working it out aloud?"

"Eddie rigged the music box to play 'The Old Woman From Wexford.' Cassidy is the one that accused Veronica of killing her husband. The song has the same theme—only the husband tricks the wife and—"

"I'm familiar with the song, Ms. Meehan."

"Well, given that her first husband is dead and therefore not a suspect . . ."

"Go on."

"Do you think Cassidy thought Veronica planned on killing Eddie?"

"Why on earth would she kill an ex-husband?"

"I worded that wrong." They started to walk. The musicians and tourists were out. Music and chatter and laughter poured from every corner. Cigarette smoke curled into the air. "What if Cassidy was winding Eddie up?"

"You're thinking Cassidy is in on this?"

"You tell me. Did she buy the marble stones?"

Gable didn't answer directly. "That's not enough proof."

She did buy the marble stones. "Have you checked into Bartley's finances?"

"We're trying to get a court order. By the time it's approved, this lot will be long gone."

"He's always around. And he's been with her a very long time." Someone had been planning this for a very long time. "Why wasn't he on her amends list?"

"Perhaps she treated him differently than the others."

"Does that seem likely?"

"Have you seen the man? He's a hulk. I wouldn't mess with him and I'm a guard."

Tara laughed again. She stopped short. Just ahead, a man was standing outside a pub, looking out toward the bay. Danny.

"Go on, so," Gable said. He touched Tara's shoulder. "Your work with me is done. I rescind the gag order."

By the time she reached the pub, Danny was no longer outside. She found him bent over a pool table, and it wasn't a bad view. She wasn't paying attention to his shot, but from the grin on his face when he stood and turned, it found its pocket. His grin disappeared as their eyes locked. "Give me a minute," he said to his pool partner. He set his stick down and approached. "I see you're alive."

"And well."

"Good to know."

"I was asked to help out on the case. He didn't

want anyone knowing, including you and Uncle Johnny, and I'm sorry about that."

Danny frowned. "Sergeant Gable?"

"Yes. They needed an in. Time was running out."

"Was?" Danny arched an eyebrow. "Did they catch him?"

"They're narrowing in on a suspect. They said I was done."

Danny looked at her for a long time. "Are you? Done?"

"No," she said, stepping up. "I'm not done. Not with this case, and not with you." It was the most brazen thing she'd ever said to him. "Are you?"

He looked at her for a long time. "I'm not involved with this case."

"You know what I mean."

"No," he said. "I'm not walking away."

"Good. I have a few things I want to check out."

"Are you asking me to come with you?"

"Yes. I'm asking you to come with me."

"Will you tell me everything you know?"

"Yes. I will." She owed him that. And she didn't want to do this alone.

"Where are we going?"

"Not necessarily in order—the realty shop, Ballynahinch Castle, Clifden art gallery, the old stone house, and Inishbofin Island."

Danny whistled, then let out a low laugh that made her feel like doing somersaults. "Let me rephrase that. Is there anywhere we aren't going?"

Chapter 31

Heather Milton was not thrilled to see Tara, but she did soften at Danny's handsome face. She let them enter and asked if they wanted coffee or tea.

"The old stone house," Tara said. She'd found a copy of the flyer and produced it. "Did Veronica purchase it?"

"I've already told the guards."

"Please," Danny said. "It's important."

Heather gestured for them to sit down. "It's still available. If you're in the market."

"But . . ." *Didn't Veronica purchase it for Elaine?*

"She died in the middle of the negotiation."

"I see."

Heather sighed. "I went to the first property visit with her."

This was news. "You did?"

Heather nodded. "Of course. You've seen that old ruin. It's only worth the land if you ask me." Tara disagreed. She'd keep the old stone and use it to re-build. "Veronica's driver took us. Her bodyguard and that sponsor woman was with her."

"Bartley and Nancy?"

Heather's eyes were wide. She swallowed and nodded.

"Why didn't you come forward when I found her body there?"

"I did." She folded her arms. "To the guards."

"Oh. Good."

"I've seen you with Sergeant Gable." Sweat beaded on Heather's forehead. Something was bothering her. "Do you have his ear?"

"She does," Danny said. "Go on."

Heather swallowed. "I didn't think it was important at the time, it's probably not."

Tara was literally on the edge of her seat. She wanted to shake Heather to make the words tumble out faster. "Go on."

"Veronica started a fire."

"A fire?"

Heather waved her hand. "Just a little one. She burned something out there. We all smelled like peat when we came back."

"What on earth did she burn?"

She shrugged. "I didn't pry. They all seemed to know. Except me and the driver."

"How do you know?"

"Because she and Nancy, and the bodyguard, watched it burn. Then they shook hands."

Calm down, Eddie. Tara didn't know how that fit the pattern. But somehow, it was key to solving this.

* * *

Danny and Tara stood outside as a cold wind whipped around him. "We have a few options," Tara said.

"Tell the guards immediately, or check out the old stone house first," Danny said.

"Exactly."

Danny took his truck keys from his pocket and began to toss them in the air. Tara laughed as they headed for the property.

"Just a quick look and we won't touch a thing."

"I can see why you like it," Danny said as the old stone house came into view.

"Who said I like it?"

"Your eyes," Danny said. "They danced every time Heather Milton mentioned it."

They reached the structure and stepped in. "Can you believe Heather would tear it down?"

"She doesn't have the eye for preservation that you do," he said. "Before we start looking for clues, tell me what you would do with this structure, Miss Interior Designer." Tara filled him on her imaginings: the dark wood floors, the wall of windows, the open kitchen, the roaring fireplace. Danny's inner builder came out as he added specifics to her ideas, and before they knew it they were standing in a completed house, overlooking the bay, drinking coffee, while Tara read the newspaper and Danny fiddled with something under the sink. It was the first time they'd flirted about such a future together. They fell silent at the same time, stretching out the daydream.

"Let's look for clues," Tara said, pulling out two pairs of gloves and handing one to Danny.

The fire pit was opposite where Tara had found Nancy's body. Whatever they had burned was long gone. "I was hoping for a scrap of paper, something," Tara admitted.

"Was Nancy Halligan on her official amends list?"

"No."

"So why was she here?"

"Nancy was her sponsor. Perhaps she was just here for moral support. Amends were a big step for Veronica."

Danny nodded. "And Bartley was involved because?"

"I think he handles Veronica's finances."

"And there were rumors he was skimming?"

"Just from Mimi's notebook. If the innkeeper is to be believed, it was Eddie who lured Nancy out here."

"Show me where you found her."

Tara led him to the other side of the house. She pointed to the area. "There." She looked out to the bay. The rowboat was gone. "If Eddie lured her out here—how did he subdue her?"

"Subdue her?"

"Let's say he picked her up at the ferry and drove her out here. Fine. Why didn't she just walk somewhere for help? Why stay right here? She wasn't tied up . . ." Tara gasped.

"What?"

"Cassidy's sleeping pills."

"I'm lost."

"Cassidy said her sleeping pills were missing."

"Did they do a toxicology report on Nancy?"

Tara shook her head. "I don't think so. Her death was at first considered heat stroke. It wasn't until

Veronica's body was found that murder was suspected. By then Nancy had been cremated."

"If Cassidy was in cahoots with Eddie, why would she announce that her pills had been stolen?"

"To give herself cover."

"When there was no suspicion of pills in Nancy's system and no way to prove it?"

"That is a good point." Tara began to pace. "Either she's innocent and her pills were stolen—by Eddie—or . . ."

"Or?"

"She blamed Andy for stealing the pills, and the marble stones. She was either hoping he'd work as a scapegoat or . . ." Tara's head snapped up. "Or she's worried about evidence that hasn't yet been discovered."

Danny nodded. "I guess we know what we're looking for now."

They started at the base of the hill where Tara had seen the rowboat. They searched in one section at a time as cows, and sheep, and a donkey looked on with general curiosity that waned the longer they were there. They searched all the way up the hill, and in every corner of what remained of the old stone house. The skies opened up and it began to rain. "We should go," Danny said. "We won't be good to anyone if we get sick."

He was right. They started back toward the car. If Nancy had a backpack with her, and Tara had just killed her, what would she do with it? *Take it with me.* But the pill bottle might have dropped. On the way back to the car, Tara stopped and looked at the ground. "This is where we need to search. All the way back to the car."

They started scouring in sections again, forced to bend down closer to the ground as the rain came in. They were soaked, and nearly to the road when Danny yelped.

"Found something."

Tara hurried up. It was a white bottle covered in dirt. Danny wiped it off with his gloved hand, just enough to see the name, and Tara huddled closer. "Sleeping tablets," he said. Tara looked at the name, holding her breath.

Cassidy Hughes

Chapter 32

Things moved quickly after the guards took the prescription bottle as evidence. Detective Gable gave her a heads-up that the guards would be retaining Eddie and Cassidy but letting the other guests leave. He needed her help to keep the group together before they could arrest the pair. Bartley's finances had checked out; there was no evidence he'd been skimming from Veronica. He said they were burning a list of Veronica's regrets at that fire pit, an idea of Nancy's to help Veronica let go of the past. Iona's story about her medical care coming to an end had checked out, and Sheila and John had indeed received a recommendation letter when they went to their location in the book. Along with marriage counseling, apparently, an offer Tara hoped the couple would take advantage of.

The book. Tara didn't know how that fit into Eddie and Cassidy's scheme, or the tracksuits, and she hoped she would find out. She also didn't know what Mimi had discovered in one of her notebooks that set off her radar. It was frustrating, all these hanging threads. But Tara had a feeling that once they brought the pair in, one or both would start spilling. As Danny pulled into the long road leading to Ballynahinch Castle, Savage started to bark excitedly. Tara wanted to see if Savage would have a reaction to Eddie. It would help convince Tara that he was the killer. She couldn't shake the feeling that the guards had it wrong. Maybe she was too close to the suspects. She felt a twinge of sadness. She was actually going to miss this motley crew, and was definitely going to miss the castle. She was touched they wanted her at their goodbye celebration. She wasn't looking forward to the guards interrupting the goodbyes to bring Eddie and Cassidy to the station, but staging this goodbye was the only way they could guarantee the pair wouldn't run.

The patio had been decorated with white lights, a portable bar was set up, and waiters were winding through the guests with appetizers. The group was surprisingly engaged with each other, laughing and more relaxed than Tara had ever seen them. After all, they all believed they were going home. Andy and Bartley were part of the mix, and for the first time both of them were in their casual clothes as opposed to the driver's uniform or Bartley's stuffy suits.

Savage was happy to be passed from person to person. Tara was chatting with Iona when the wind picked up, prompting Eddie to put on his tweed cap. Savage, who was nestled in Iona's arms, went mental, scratching to be let down and yelping. Iona let out a scream of surprise and immediately set Savage free.

The dog barreled for Eddie, snarling and snapping at his heels before turning and tearing off across the lawn.

"What was that?" Eddie said, as everyone turned to stare.

"You always did have a way with the women," Elaine said, lifting a martini.

"I'll get her," Danny said, taking off after Savage. Tara stared at Eddie. Did Savage suddenly remember him? Had the poor pup witnessed the murder? Was Eddie wearing that cap at the time?

From the shadows, guards stepped into the celebration. "Eddie O'Farrell and Cassidy Hughes," they announced.

"Yes?" Eddie turned.

"Who wants to know?" Cassidy quipped. The guards asked to see them in private, and after a few awkward laughs, Eddie downed his shot. "Am I under arrest because that little savage didn't like me?"

The guards separated them from the group, as they read them the charge and their rights. Their attempt not to make a scene was moot when Cassidy began raging. She could probably be heard inside every room in the castle. Threats, calls for solicitors, and name-calling poured out of her. The remaining guests huddled together listening to every word.

"Why are you arresting me?" Cassidy screamed. "You just arrested him."

Eddie howled with drunken laughter. "They think we're in on it together."

"If I was going to kill her I would have done it a long time ago," Cassidy screamed. "Do you know what my amends was? Rehab! And now you're not going to let me go? I need help, not prison!"

Eddie pointed. "Don't say a word. Ask for a solicitor—not one word!"

"Is this about the box of brooches?" Cassidy asked.

"What?" Tara was on high alert.

"I left them for you as a joke," Cassidy said. "I thought you could make a killing selling them."

"It wasn't funny," Tara said.

Cassidy shrugged. "Americans are so uptight. Who gets arrested for giving someone a gift?"

"You certainly aren't doing us any favors here," Eddie said, throwing a warning look to Cassidy.

"This is unfathomable," Cassidy screamed. "Bartley! Tell these idiots to release me."

"I'm afraid I cannot represent you," Bartley said, the glee obvious in his voice. "You'll have to find another solicitor."

"Eddie did this all on his own," Cassidy screamed. "He's probably the one who got Veronica all riled up Friday evening."

"I wasn't even here," Eddie said. "I didn't check in until after my Veronica was murdered."

"Then why did she accost me Friday evening? Accuse me of shifting you in the elevator?"

Eddie threw his arms open. "Did you shift me in the elevator?"

"Of course not!"

"Then what's your point?"

Cassidy folded her arms. "Maybe you were here Friday evening. Maybe told her you kissed me. Maybe you told her you were in love with me."

"My word. That's a lot of maybes." Eddie shook his head. "You're not helping either of us."

Tara waited for Cassidy to admit that Eddie was here. With her. She did not. Strange. Weren't they each other's alibi? What did it mean if they're weren't having an affair?

"How do we know you weren't sleeping together?" Elaine said. "Maybe the two of you are in this together."

"Have you seen me?" Cassidy screamed. "Why would I sleep with an aging alcoholic—a washed up artist?"

"You little pill-popper," Eddie said as the pair was dragged to separate guard cars. "Stop screaming nonsense or you're going to get us convicted."

Tara sighed. They weren't even off the property and they were already turning on each other. It probably wouldn't be long until one or both spilled out the unvarnished truth.

"Unfathomable," Elaine said, echoing Cassidy's earlier word. "I had no idea her vocabulary was that advanced." The group fell into transfixed silence as the guard cars pulled away.

"Eddie and Cassidy?" Sheila said. "They killed Roni? Both of them?"

Everyone slowly turned to Tara as Danny returned to the patio with Savage in his arms. "The guards have found evidence that implicates them," Tara said. Sergeant Gable had authorized her to say that and nothing more. It wouldn't be until much later that they would learn about their affair, Eddie's proclamation of creating groundbreaking new sculptures, Cassidy's sleeping pills found at the first murder scene, and the proof that she'd purchased the marble stones found on Veronica. And Tara herself didn't know if Veronica's will held additional evidence, such as Cassidy inheriting the bulk of the estate. They would probably need a confession to prosecute. It was all circumstantial as far as she could see.

"I told Veronica that man was trouble," Elaine said. "If only she would have listened to me."

"To Veronica," Iona said, holding up her glass.

"To Veronica," the remainder of the group echoed.

"I must say, that's a relief," Bartley said, wiping his brow. "I'm a good saver, and my healthy bank account nearly got me accused of murder."

"We should all keep in touch," Sheila said.

"We certainly want to hear when you adopt a child," Elaine said. "I know it will happen for you."

Sheila beamed, but John looked stiff and uncomfortable. Tara had a feeling the pair still had a tough road in front of them, and secretly hoped they wouldn't adopt a child until he was completely on board. Children deserved mature and happy parents. If life had turned out differently and she and Gabriel had passed away, she couldn't imagine little Thomas being raised by Sheila and John. But she could see him happy with Uncle Johnny and Rose; as odd as the pair was, they were good people. They were family. The sun was just starting to set when they said their final goodbyes and headed for Danny's truck.

"Sad to leave the castle?" Danny asked.

"No," Tara said. "I like the mill." She meant it. It was home.

Danny put his arm around her. "Are you going to tell me what's been occupying that big brain of yours?"

Tara laughed. "Is my brain big?"

Danny grinned. "It's the perfect size. But right now it seems to be on overdrive."

She hesitated. It was hard to put this feeling into words, and she didn't quite trust it. She wasn't a guard. "I had a client once, back in New York. He hired me to decorate his one-bedroom."

"Okay."

"No expense spared. And I understood his style. But we argued over this one sofa."

"Ugly, was it?"

Tara laughed. "No. It was a beautiful sofa. Sleek. Modern. But it was too big for his space. It just didn't fit."

"I see."

"But he insisted. So I was forced to place this enormous sofa in this tiny space and decorate around it. I did the job. I got paid. But I wasn't happy. Because no matter what he said, that sofa didn't fit."

"You don't think Eddie and Cassidy fit?"

Tara shook her head. "I can see all the pieces that *do* fit. On the surface it looks as if the guards have nailed it. But there are missing pieces. And I can't explain it, but I can't stop thinking about that sofa. I obsessed over it. And I have the same feeling now."

Before Danny could reply, a truck careened up the drive, dirt and gravel spitting from its tires. A man in a baseball cap and a flannel shirt stuck his head out the window and called to Tara. "How ya."

"What now?" Danny said under his breath.

"I saw you with the guards at the castle," he said.

"Okay," Tara said. She had no idea who this man was.

"I own a farm near Clifden Castle. Me sheep dog found something. I didn't touch it. Would you mind coming to have a look at it?"

"You just missed the guards," Danny said. "We can call 999."

The farmer shook his head. "Me neighbors will kill me if I get a flood of guards out to us again for nothing. Would you just have a look? And if you tink it's something, then I'll call in the cavalry."

"Yes," Tara said. "We'll have a look."

"Tara," Danny said.

"We won't touch anything," Tara said.

"I can drive." They didn't realize Andy was nearby until he spoke.

"You can hop in with me," the farmer said.

Danny sighed. "So close, and yet so far."

"Thanks, Andy," Tara said. "But I think you're officially off duty."

He nodded. "I suppose I am."

Tara and Danny headed for the farmer's truck. "Call the guards if we don't come back," Danny called out.

Chapter 33

There was a haunting beauty to the Clifden Castle as the setting sun set it aglow. The farmer pulled his truck to the back, and then led them down a path to another set of ruined stone buildings. It appeared to be an old carriage house, or stables. The sheepdog ran ahead of them, all muscle and energy.

The farmer stopped and pointed into an open space within a portion of the crumbling structure where weeds choked the dirt floor. "Looks like women's clothing. I promise ye it wasn't there last time I was here."

Tara followed his finger until she saw fabric poking out of a backpack. It was purple and white. Tara gasped. "I think it's Nancy Halligan's." She turned to the farmer. "When was the last time you were here?"

"About a week before the murder."

"You say your dog found it?" Danny said.

The farmer nodded and pointed again. "Seems it was buried, he dug it up, see?"

Indeed they could see. They inched closer. Stuffed underneath the first blouse was a second one. It appeared to be lightweight, designer. Like something Veronica would wear. Beneath it, the edge of a bag could be seen. Tara had a feeling it contained Nancy Halligan's belongings. Everything she brought with her to the stone cottage when she arrived to meet Eddie. She couldn't touch the items in case it was evidence. But what did it mean? Did Eddie get her to take sleeping pills and wait until she fell asleep? Then left her, or worse yet, dragged her out into the blazing sun, taking her water, and belongings? Tara thought back to Veronica's tracksuit. Identical to Nancy's tracksuit. It seemed odd that Nancy would wear a tracksuit in that heat. Hadn't Alexis made a funny face when Tara mentioned Nancy's tracksuit? If she hadn't worn it that day, then why didn't Alexis just say so?

"What are you thinking?" Danny said.

"What if—the killer dressed them?"

"Eddie?" Danny said. "Part of his sculptures?"

"Maybe." It seemed like such an unartistic choice, if that was the case.

"You're still thinking about that sofa, aren't you?"

She nodded and turned to the farmer. "You did the right thing by not touching it. But I'm afraid we have to call the guards."

Why tracksuits? And the stones? Art was subjective, but the artist usually knew his or her own meaning. What meaning did stones and tracksuits hold for Eddie? If it was him, would he ever tell them? She turned to Danny. "I almost forgot how much you like Eddie."

"I'm losing interest as we speak," Danny said solemnly. They were silent on the way back to Bally-nahinch, each lost in thought. Once the farmer dropped them off at the hotel, Danny held open the door to his truck, and Tara was about to step in when her phone rang. She glanced at the screen. *Alexis*. "Interesting."

"What?"

Tara held up a finger and answered. "Thank goodness I reached you," Alexis said.

"Is everything alright?" Tara was going to ask her about Nancy's tracksuit, but first she needed to find out why Alexis was calling her.

Danny mimed banging his head into his truck. Tara shook her head and smiled.

"I just discovered some of Nancy's things still in her room. Including some kind of prescription bottle for Savage."

"Oh," Tara said. "What's the prescription for?"

"I haven't a clue. Sorry, I guess it doesn't matter, as long as she seems healthy."

"I'd still like to know." She glanced at the cab where Savage was curled into a sleeping ball. "What else is there?"

"Clothing, and some personal papers. I've called the family, but they haven't returned my call. Should I just box it up?"

Tara hesitated. Inishbofin Island was a forty-minute ferry ride from Clifden. If she went all the way back to Galway, she'd never have a look at whatever these items were. What if something in there was the missing piece? Could Tara really just walk away?

"The last ferry of the day leaves in twenty minutes," Alexis said, as if reading Tara's mind. "And you're welcome to spend the night. No charge."

"I'll be there," Tara said.

"No," Danny said when she hung up. "I have to be back in Galway. I have an early run in the morning." Tara turned to see Andy loading his SUV. "Tara," Danny said. "Don't do this."

"I'm sorry. I have to." Danny followed her gaze over to Andy. He was in his usual spot, leaning against his vehicle. Veronica's vehicle. Most likely Cassidy's now, or Elaine's. The will might even be contested. Tara was relieved she wouldn't have to be involved in any of that drama. Andy was definitely the loyal sort. He could have taken off already. Tara wondered if he was lonely. Leaving this gorgeous castle and its grounds wasn't going to be easy for any of them.

"He's off duty, remember?"

"I'm sorry," Tara said again. She approached Andy, filled him in, and asked for the ride to the ferry.

"No," he said. "If you're doing this, you're not going alone. I'll drive you to the ferry, but I'm also getting on it with you." Danny met her eyes, then nodded. Tara ran up and hugged him.

"Please don't be mad," she said. "I like the space we're in."

He chuckled. "Do I fit?" he asked. "In the space we're in."

"You do," she said. "You definitely fit."

"Be safe, Miss America." She leaned in and kissed him.

The red-and-white vessel churned across the water, steadily bouncing them toward their destination. Tara and Andy stood out on the deck, and the wind knocked them back. They were instructed to come back inside as the waves leapt higher, covering the windows. "We're lucky," Andy said. "I bet they would have canceled this ride if they knew how much the waves were going to kick up."

"Lucky," she repeated, as her stomach roiled.

"You don't want to know the nickname for this ferry."

"Probably not, but now you'll have to tell me."

Andy grinned. "The Boffin Coffin."

He was right, she didn't want to know. "Because in weather like this we might capsize and die?"

Andy laughed. "No. Normally because the night-life on the island is so much craic you might be dead leaving."

"We won't be in that boat," Tara joked, half wishing they weren't in this one. Tara had researched the island, Inis Bo Finne, Island of the White Cow, and wished she was going there for the first time under happier circumstances. Tara shivered as the cold seeped into her bones.

"Here." Andy removed his jacket and put it around Tara.

"I couldn't."

"I have a thick jumper. Besides, I'm used to this."

"You've been to Inishbofin?" she asked Andy.

"I spent nearly every summer there as a child," Andy said. "My grandparents are from Inishbofin."

Sandy beaches, three looped walking treks, and birdwatching were a few of the reasons people flocked to the island. But they would see none of it today, and not just because of the mission they were on, but the skies left no doubt that a storm was fast approaching. "How will we get to the inn?" Tara asked. "Are there cars on the island?"

"There's one main road and a few cars. But the inn is walking distance from the ferry. We might have to make a run for it before the rain starts pummeling us."

This had been a bad idea. Tara should have waited, or sent the guards. It was too late now. Hopefully Alexis had nice accommodations and maybe even a few good paperbacks left by previous guests. She wanted to cozy up with a cup of tea and a compelling read, then, if weather allowed, get the first ferry out in the morning. Not that she didn't want to explore the island sometime, but she was ready to get back to her life in Galway. Her new life. Her first salvage outing. She gazed around the other passengers, wondering if they were as seasick as she was. It was then that she saw him. Sitting in a back corner, scrunched down. All that was visible was a bald head. She stared until he lifted his chin just enough to get a good look.

Bartley? What was he doing on the ship? Tara averted her gaze as she tried to make sense of it. Andy edged closer.

"Everything okay?"

"Don't look." Andy started to turn his head. She grabbed his arm. "I said don't look."

"What is it?"

"I think Bartley is on the ship."

To Andy's credit, he did not turn his head. His face registered the same shock she felt. "What are you thinking?"

"Do you know if one of the guests bought flowers for my opening?"

"Bartley did," Andy said. "I picked them up myself."

Why would he take it upon himself to get her flowers? And then not sign the card? She turned this over in her mind. "Did you deliver them to my shop?"

"I left them at the door." He cocked his head. "Is it important?"

"I don't know." Why was she thinking about the flowers? Because something—someone—made Mimi think there was something at the bottom of the vase. And the only thing Tara could think that would fit in a vase that would cause Mimi to go mental—was her new diamond watch. She glanced at her phone. The signal was gone.

"I wouldn't expect much use of it with the storm coming in," Andy said.

"I know." She hoped it was nothing. "We need to get ahold of Sergeant Gable."

"Do you want to tell me what you're thinking?"

"If Bartley sent me those flowers . . . It's probably nothing." *But it could be something.* Tara felt unsettled. All the pieces were not in place. She knew it.

Andy frowned. "We can see if any phones on the island are working."

"What about the music box?" Tara asked.

"What about it?"

"Uncle Johnny said you picked up the items from the Clifden antique shop and dropped them off to the mill."

"I did. Bartley asked me to."

Bartley again. "Did you pick them up directly from the shop?"

Andy rubbed his chin. "Just outside the shop. Bartley was waiting on the footpath." Because the items had left the shop way before that? Leaving Bartley enough time to have the music box doctored? "You're starting to worry me. Do you think Bartley is the real culprit?"

"Why else would he be following us?"

"Listen." Andy leaned close. "We have an advantage."

"Tell me."

"I know this island like the back of my hand. I doubt that's the case with Bartley. As soon as we get off the ship, take my arm. We're going to run."

"Okay." Her stomach roiled. At this point she didn't know if was from the ship, or fear, or both. Andy maneuvered them to the front of the ship. "He's in the back. We'll get a good head start."

The ferry finally docked, and when Tara disembarked, she was nearly knocked down by a gust of wind. Andy grabbed her, his strong arms kept her upright. "This way." He took the lead at a fast clip, and she followed. She briefly noted the rolling hills, and stone, and water, as they hurried toward their destination. She could see where Nancy was coming from: Despite the turbulent weather, Tara could imagine the slower pace of the island was comforting. They kept up their pace along the road until Andy turned off and headed toward a detached stone cottage. It was white with blue trim, and an old stone wall delineated a path to the entrance.

A hand-painted sign read: WELCOME INN. Tara threw a look behind her. Nothing was visible in the thick rain. The door opened before they could knock, and Alexis stood, her red hair blown back by the wind. "Hurry," she said ushering them inside.

"We might have trouble following us," Andy said. The wind howled and rattled the windows. "Lock all the doors."

"What's going on?" Alexis slid the deadbolt across the door, and checked the other locks.

"We think we're being followed," Tara said. "I hope we aren't putting you in danger."

"I don't have any mobile signal," Alexis said. "But the doors are locked."

"I'll keep watch," Andy said, taking off his cap.

"The kettle is on, who wants tea?" They both did. "Sit, and relax."

"I don't know if that's possible," Tara said.

"Why would Bartley be after us?" Andy said. "The killer has been caught."

Maybe Tara was being paranoid. Maybe he had other reasons for being on Inishbofin. "I don't know."

Andy removed a poker from near the fireplace. "This should do."

Alexis's eyes widened. "What are you going to do with that?"

"Whatever I have to."

They sat. Waiting. Watching the door. No one came. Tara finally allowed herself to relax.

"How many rooms does the cottage have?" Tara asked when they were settled with their tea and biscuits.

"Three," Alexis said. "My room and two doubles. Nancy had a double to herself."

"Do you get many guests?"

"Enough to get by. There are three hotels on the island, but some tourists prefer the cottage experience."

"I don't blame them."

Alexis's smile quickly faded. "I'm afraid Nancy's death may be the end of my run."

"But she wasn't even here when . . ." Tara left it hanging.

Alexis crossed herself. "Thank goodness. But the locals do talk. And with her things still here . . ." She shivered. "I'll just be glad to have them gone. Nip of whiskey?" Alexis asked Tara.

"No, thank you." She was exhausted, and it was only now that she realized she'd probably be the one sleeping in Nancy's room, since she was here to gather her things. There was something a bit eerie about it. But weariness won over, as did a clawing feeling that she wanted to be alone. "If you don't mind, I'd like to turn in."

Andy remained staring into the fire, gripping the poker. "Sleep well."

"I hate to think of you standing guard all night."

Andy grinned. "I'm used to it. Besides, I'm just going to wait until my mobile has a signal and then call the guards."

"Thank you."

Alexis showed Tara to a small room in the back of

the cottage. It barely fit the two double beds, but it was quaint, with a dresser, and windows.

Alexis pointed to them. "You wouldn't know it, but there's a view of the hills and ocean." Wouldn't know it was right. The rain was relentless and thick, while the wind continued to howl. "Her things are all here." Alexis pointed to a large ottoman in the corner, piled with items. After showing Tara the restroom, towels, and even providing her with a nightdress, Alexis left her alone. Tara approached the ottoman and stared down at the items. A hairbrush. A necklace with a peace symbol. A few blouses, and a skirt. She didn't see a prescription bottle for Savage. Maybe Alexis had put it somewhere else. Tara picked up the hairbrush, and just held it for a minute. It was hard to believe that objects outlasted people. There was something haunting about it. Without thinking she slipped her hands into the pockets of the coat Andy had given her. Something round and hard was in the left pocket. She pulled it out.

A coin. Or should she say a sobriety chip. Like the one Veronica had been flipping around.

Tara felt a wave of dizziness hit. She sank down on the bed, wondering what that was all about. Was this Andy's chip? Alexis offered Tara a nip of whiskey. But she didn't offer it to Andy. Why not? Wasn't he a big drinker? She could still feel the movement of the ferry even though she was sitting down. Why did she think Andy was a big drinker? Had she ever seen him drink?

No. But she'd once seen him with red eyes. Assumed he was hungover. And the other valets laughed at how he was sleeping it off in his vehicle—his alibi . . .

She didn't know where she was going with this. She was tired. She stumbled to the restroom down the hall and changed into the nightdress, used the toothbrush and paste from her handbag, and splashed cold water on her face. When she was finished, she felt it again, the movement of the ferry, and she had to hold on to the sink to keep her upright. She waited for it to pass, then padded down the hall toward her room. A crammed bookshelf on the way caught her attention. Family pictures in frames dotted the top. In one, Tara could make out an older man standing at a quarry. Tara picked it up. Why did this seem familiar? Was this one of the marble quarries?

She began to hunt through the books, hoping to find something to read before bed. She stopped cold at the second shelf.

Places to See in Ireland Before You Die. She stopped and held her breath. Just down the hall was the sitting room. She could hear Alexis and Andy speaking, their voices a whisper, the crackling of the fire obscuring their words. Heart thudding in her chest, Tara picked up the book and opened it. The owner had written his name.

Martin Bixby. A memory rose before her. Bartley's voice. Speaking to Veronica. *Martin Bixby, your previous driver.*

Mimi. What was it she said about Veronica? *She drove her previous driver to an early grave.*

The suicide notice in Mimi's notebook. The rest of the article ripped out.

Andy. What did he say about his father? That he loved that book. Andy said that was the reason Veronica had chosen the book. She saw Andy with it. But what if she didn't? When she saw it in the shop she called it morbid. There was no recognition there . . .

What was Andy's last name? Tara leaned down to get a better look at the pictures. Many of them featured a boy and a girl smiling with grandparents. Tara's stomach clenched, and she had to stop what she was doing as the pain gripped her. A loose photograph of the boy and girl was wedged into one of the frames. She turned it over.

Alexis and Andy.

Behind the largest frame was a mass card. She picked it up with shaking hands.

In loving memory of Martin Bixby.

He died two years ago. The date matched the article in Mimi's notebook. The suicide.

Veronica's driver. Drove him to an early grave.

Tara hurried to her room and dug through her handbag for her smartphone. No signal. The storm had made sure of that. Her stomach clenched again.

Had her tea been poisoned?

How could they think they'd get away with it? Danny knew where she was, and that she was with Andy. The guards had already brought Eddie and Cassidy in for questioning. Was Andy trying to make sure that Tara didn't suspect him? What had she said that might have worried him?

He overheard her talk to Danny about the sofa. How it didn't fit. It was shortly after that that she received the call from Alexis. His sister. On the ferry he seemed eager for her to accuse Bartley. It was only his word that Bartley picked up the items from the antique dealer. And that the flowers came from Bartley. It was Andy who resembled Eddie. Andy who could have pretended to be Eddie when he took the music box into the shop to have it doctored. Bartley wasn't on the ship to come after Tara. He was there because he was suspicious of Andy.

Alexis told her that Nancy had been a regular. Everyone on the island knew her. That's how the two of them found out about Veronica's plans. Her big amends. And their father, the man Veronica drove to suicide after forty years—wasn't on the amends list. Was that why they decided to take matters into their own hands? Did they suggest Nancy convince Veronica to do the amends here, where they could dream up the perfect revenge plot?

Tara hurried back to the room and sat on the bed. Something was wrong with her. She felt sluggish. Had she been poisoned, or given sleeping pills, or was she just paranoid? Did she stay the night, pretend everything was okay? Try to sneak out in the middle of a storm? Where was Bartley now?

That tweed cap. Eddie had a similar one. What if it was Eddie asleep in Andy's vehicle? Andy could have picked him up at a bar that night. Sauced. Slipped him a few sleeping pills. Arranged him in the driver's seat. Alibi sorted. Where had Eddie woken up? He would have said something if he'd woken up in the car. Did Andy move him after returning from Clifden Castle? And how did Andy get there?

Questions. Always more questions. But one thing was for sure. Andy was friendly with all the valets. He could have easily taken another car to the castle. Tara wanted to lie down and just sleep. Just sleep. She bit the side of her cheek. *Focus.*

Alexis said there were three hotels on the island. They were walking distance to the ferry; one of them must be close by. But first, she needed to make herself throw up, something she loathed the very idea of. There was no choice, she couldn't take the chance that she'd die in her sleep. *The Boffin Coffin*. She tried to tiptoe as she made it to the bathroom again. Just as she shut the door, she heard creaking in the hallway.

"Are you okay?" Alexis's voice filtered through.

"A bit seasick," Tara called back, hoping her voice wasn't shaking.

"Oh no. Is there anything I can do?"

"I'm afraid not. I'm sorry I'm occupying the restroom."

"Don't worry about that, luv. Feel free to check the cupboard for anything that might help."

"Thank you." *I bet*. Tara steeled herself, looked into the mirror, and did something she hadn't done in many, many months. She called on her mam for help.

Chapter 34

Tara felt better after expelling her stomach, and drinking water from the sink. She exited the bathroom to find Alexis standing in front of her with a glass of milk. Tara let out a yelp.

"So sorry," Alexis said. "I didn't mean to frighten you."

"It's okay."

Alexis held out the milk. "This will help."

Tara's hands shook as she took it. "Thank you." She slipped back to her bedroom and shut the door before Alexis could watch her drink it. She set it on the bedside table and wished she could take it with her as evidence. She pressed herself against the door until she heard Alexis walk away. With no visible lock on the door, Tara pulled a chair up to it and wedged it underneath the knob, her heart thudding so loud in her chest she feared they would be able to hear it.

Working as quietly as she possibly could, she put her clothes back on and clutched her keys in her hand, each key poking out between the knuckles like she'd done in her early days in New York City, feeling at least she had some protection if attacked. No matter what, she would not fall asleep. She pulled the second chair in the room near the window, and examined the window's mechanism. Opening it would definitely make noise, but she could see how the window latched, and that if need be, there would be room for her to crawl out, and jump. If anyone came in, she'd hear the chair turn over, climb out the window, and run.

Thinking through the case helped keep her wide awake, as well as listening to every creak and groan, a difficult task given that the rain and wind had kept up their unrelenting campaign. Her mind kept returning to the day she met Veronica.

Eddie's portfolio. In it he was wearing that tweed cap. Then Andy comes in wearing the same cap. Even Tara mistook them. When Andy first came into her store, she thought it was him on the portfolio Veronica insisted she take. Veronica of course laughed at the very idea that Andy and Eddie looked alike, but from a distance they did. Up close it was obvious Eddie was older. But from a distance . . . It must have been Eddie sleeping it off in Andy's car. And Andy who came in to doctor the music box, but was mistaken for Eddie. The clerk must not have looked very carefully. Tara's thoughts returned to the first time she met Andy. He rushed in to use the restroom. He knew exactly where the restroom was. Tara didn't think anything of it at the time. After all, it was a small shop. But Andy knew where the restroom was because he'd been there before. To drop off the book. When Curly and Moe were up on the ladder.

Tara remembered commenting on Andy when he came out of the restroom. Comparing him to Eddie's portfolio picture.

You think Eddie looks like my driver?

Bartley pointed out the cap. That it was also the "uniform" of Martin Bixby. Veronica went on about uniforms, the necessity of keeping the working class apart from the rich.

Uniforms . . .

Tracksuits. Oh God. He dressed Nancy Halligan and Veronica in uniforms. The marble stones represented his father's work in the quarry. After Martin spent most of his life working in a quarry, he went to work as Veronica's driver. And then he took his own life. Andy and Alexis blamed Veronica for it. Andy took his father's old job, probably to investigate her. Cassidy was right. Andy did steal her sleeping pills. And her marble stones. To knock Eddie out and create his airtight alibi. It must have felt like a touching tribute to his father, placing the stones on Veronica's face. Not Nancy's.

Why had he killed Nancy? She must have figured out who he was. The sobriety chip. Did Andy meet Nancy in AA? Imagine Andy's reaction to learning that Veronica was going to make amends. But it was too late for his father—a man Veronica seemed to barely remember.

What else had Veronica said about Martin?

His poor bladder condition.

The bathroom routine. Veronica wasn't testing Tara by having Andy come in and ask to use the restroom. Andy was testing Veronica. Because of what she'd done to his father. How she treated him. What she drove him to.

It had only been Andy's word that Eddie and Cassidy were kissing and went up to her room. Somehow, Andy had convinced Veronica to go to Clifden Castle early. He must have had access to another vehicle.

Had this entire amends scheme been his idea? From the stone cottage sale to the article on Renewals?

She could no longer hear Andy and Alexis talking.

They were going to come for her. To see if she drank the milk.

She was going to have to go soon, no matter what the storm was doing. *Please, Mam. Please help.*

Tara wished she could text Danny. He wouldn't be able to get here in time, but she could tell him everything. She could say goodbye. She had to go. It was now or never. She stood and unlatched the window. Wind and rain rushed in as she opened it, sending the window flying back against the wall with a loud bang. The doorknob rattled as someone tried to push it open. Tara hauled herself up to the window and began to crawl out. The chair fell to the floor behind her. She was only halfway through the window. Footsteps pounded toward her. She squeezed out another inch, as rain pelted her face, stinging her cheeks. Hands grabbed her ankles and began to pull.

"No!"

"I've got you," Andy said. "I've got you." Tara kicked and screamed, but his grip was strong. As he pulled backward she clung to the window frame. "Don't fight me."

"Let me go."

Her grip weakened, her hands were too wet, he was too strong. She was yanked back into the room and fell to the floor. Andy towered over her. On the bed behind her sat the fire poker.

"You weren't supposed to be involved in this."

"Mimi tried to tell me." *I always had the notebooks with me. How could I be so stupid?* She meant that she'd had them in the vehicle. "You were the one who messed with Mimi's notebooks."

"She was rather organized," Andy said. "Made it easy to learn about all the guests."

"Bartley said he knew nothing of this game Veronica was playing. Because it wasn't her game. It was yours."

"Hardly a game." He flashed with anger. "Rather a well thought-out plan. Can you imagine, Nancy coming to stay here? Best friends with Veronica back in the day. She didn't even realize Alexis was Martin's daughter. Not until it was too late."

"When she did realize who Alexis was—who *you* were—it must have come as quite a shock."

Andy's eyes danced. He looked as if he'd gone mad. "It was my fault. I carried around the article on my father's suicide. It was to motivate me. That was stupid of me. She found it. Started asking me a bunch of questions. She planned on telling Veronica that her new driver was her old driver's son. I couldn't have that. She was going to destroy our plan."

Tara stood up from the floor, which wasn't easy. She stumbled. Andy pushed her onto the bed. She reached for the poker.

"Don't be stupid." He shoved her hand away, grabbed the poker, and flung it across the room. "Do that again, and I'm using it on your head."

She believed him. He didn't plan on letting her leave this inn alive. The only question that remained was whether she'd choose a peaceful death or a violent one. She didn't believe she could talk him out of it. He'd already killed three people. But talking was her only shot. "It's over. You got your revenge."

"I'm not going down for this. It was justice."

"I won't say anything."

"I'm afraid I don't believe you."

"Danny knows I'm here." She stopped. Looked at the window. *Bartley. Where was he?*

Andy sighed. "It was a terrible storm. The branch fell directly on you. I tried to save you."

"They'll find evidence I was in the cottage."

"This isn't *CSI*."

He didn't know she had the keys in her hand, ready to stab. Should she aim for his eyes? Groin? "Your father wouldn't have wanted this."

"It's not as hard as I thought," Andy said. "Killing someone."

"Because you think they deserved it," Tara said, winging it as she went along. "Do I?"

He grabbed the glass of milk from the bedside table. "Just drink it. You won't feel a thing."

"How did you pull it off? Don't I deserve to know?"

"Drink it and I'll tell you."

"Tell me and I'll drink it."

"I had two years to watch them. Learn their habits. Eddie was always drunk. Veronica always lost the brooch. It slipped off in the car, right after we left your shop. I knew it was that night or never. I'd just been notified that Eddie was arriving by bus. Easy enough to suggest I drop him off at a little trad session first. It was actually you who gave me the idea to use Eddie as my alibi."

"Me?" She hadn't expected this.

"You're the one who commented that we looked alike in the cap. What a gift you gave me."

"We should be even then."

Andy laughed wryly. "I honestly didn't want you to figure it out. But you have. It's out of my hands."

She needed to keep him talking. She took a tiny sip, trying to keep as much in her mouth without swallowing. "You're the one who wound Veronica up that evening. Made her think Nancy was murdered by one of her guests."

Andy laughed. "Nancy *was* murdered. I was only telling her the truth. But yes. It was rather easy to wind her up. When she saw the bottle of whiskey in my glove compartment, she was so upset she couldn't resist."

"You're evil."

"No," he said, the anger flashing through him once more. "She's the one who ruined our father. Our childhood. She treated him like a thing. Not a person. A thing. Never could relax a day in his life. Who do you think he took it out on?" He let the inference hang. Tara shuddered. "She made him that way. She's the evil one."

As long as he was talking, she was still alive. "How on earth did you get her out to Clifden Castle the next morning?"

"It was easy to steal keys from the valet. I took a car parked the furthest from prying eyes. Could have been caught. But I wasn't. Now drink."

Tara took another sip. "But how did you convince Veronica to go to the castle that early?"

"I told her someone with information about Nancy's death wanted to meet her." He grinned. "I wasn't lying. It just happened to be me." He gestured to her glass of milk, now shaking in her hands.

"Nancy didn't deserve to die."

"She was too nosy for her own good. She had a peaceful death. Her own sleeping pills made her drowsy. The sun did the rest." A shiver ran through her. Once she fell asleep, how would he kill her? Where would he hide her body? She'd never know.

He pointed to her glass. "Drink. All of it."

"If I don't?"

"Then it will be very painful. Don't bring that on yourself."

"Mimi put it all together. Realized you had been going through her folders that sometimes she left unattended in the vehicle."

Andy nodded with a smirk. "Those stupid note-books. She had me father's obituary. An article that was written about his suicide. It mentioned he was found with the book. I guess dat's when she put it together."

"*Places to See in Ireland Before You Die,*" Tara said. "It was you who left the book in my shop. You who put the red X in the books, luring the guests to certain spots. You who planted the amends at the locations."

Andy nodded. "Mimi figured out I had a sneak peek at the amends. She was too organized. I must have tipped her off. I honestly don't know how she figured it out. Next thing I know she's asking me all sorts of questions on the sly, asking to see me motor license."

"To see your last name."

"Aye."

"Didn't you have to fill out paperwork to get hired? Didn't Veronica know your last name?"

"I used a fake ID for dat. But me motor license has me real name. I wouldn't let Mimi see it. I could tell—she was going to start digging. Now drink."

Tara took another sip, holding it in her mouth as long as possible. "Why did she throw flowers out of my vase?"

The question took Andy by surprise. He threw his head back to laugh. Tara let milk dribble out of her mouth. "I told her you'd hidden her watch in the vase. She freaked out."

He was laughing over a woman's death. He was a psychopath. Andy pointed to the milk. "All of it. Or what I'm going to do next is really going to hurt."

Tara brought the glass up to her lips, then when Andy relaxed for a second, she threw the liquid in his face. Then, before he could react, she drove her keys into his right eye. He screamed, clutching his eye as he stumbled back. Tara ran for the window. From the hallway, she could hear Alexis. "What's going on?"

Andy stumbled toward her, but this time Tara was out the window, in the rain and mud, and running for her life.

She'd made some progress, but slipped for a third time, and that's when she heard his voice.

"Come back here."

She scrambled to her feet, and reached the road. In the distance she could see headlights of an on-coming car. Just then, someone materialized beside her. A large man. Bald. "Bartley." He grabbed her arm and they ran across the road. They slipped in the muck on the other side and both slid to the ground. "Stay down," Bartley said. "I knew he was no good." Tara lifted her head. Andy was directly across the road from them. The poker was in his hand. His eyes were fixed on them when he stepped into the road. Didn't he see the oncoming car?

"Hey," Tara said.

Andy spotted Tara on the ground and grinned. He headed for them. In his rage, he either didn't see the car, or thought he could beat it.

"Don't look," Bartley said. Tara bowed her head. She winced as she heard the thud of Andy's body on the car, and the screech of brakes. A woman's scream rang out. Alexis emerged, appearing before the car, soaking wet and screaming. She threw herself at Andy's side.

"He came out of nowhere," the driver said, stepping out. "I swear, he leapt in front of me car."

"He did," Tara said. "He came out of nowhere."

Chapter 35

Tara felt the sun streaming in on her face before she felt the little paws knead her chest. She opened one eye and found Savage staring at her intently. Beside her, Danny groaned. "What time is it?"

"It's dog time," Tara said.

Danny pulled a pillow over his head and groaned again. "I hate dog time." Tara scooped Savage into her arms and padded out of bed, as Hound approached, tail wags whacking her thighs.

"I need a better set of friends," Tara joked. "Party animals instead of you morning people."

"Do you want me to go with you?" Danny mumbled from underneath his pillow.

"Nah," Tara said. "I got this."

And she did. The morning air was fresh. She took in the bay, her dogs at her heels, and realized with a touch of irony, now that she'd be going on salvage trips, she would be seeing much of Ireland. Just like

Martin Bixby's book. Andy survived the accident. He was in the hospital, with a long recovery ahead of him before he could be transferred to a jail cell. Alexis had been arrested as an accessory. She was talking, trying to reduce her sentence. Eddie and Cassidy had been able to add to the picture as well.

The morning of Veronica's murder, Eddie had woken up on the grounds of the castle, and assumed he'd blacked out. He was terrified that he wouldn't be believed. A part of him was convinced that he may have killed Veronica in a blackout. He and Cassidy had never kissed, never had an affair—and that's why neither of them came forward as each other's alibi. The valets had all seen Eddie sleeping in Andy's vehicle, but because of that tweed cap, and the way Andy had positioned him, there was no reason to think it was anyone other than Andy.

Nancy Halligan had no idea Alexis was Andy's sister. Which is why she felt completely comfortable confiding in Alexis. How she'd heard some island gossip—that Andy Bixby had taken a job as Veronica's new chauffeur. Her mistake was confiding in Alexis that she found it suspicious and was about to tell Veronica. *Calm down, Eddie.* Andy had pretended to be Eddie on the phone, worried about this Andy character. Didn't Nancy think it was strange that he was Veronica's new driver? What if he was up to no good? It was how he'd lured Nancy to the old stone house.

Alexis and Andy Bixby had planned one murder, but ended up killing three. *What a tangled web we weave . . .* And Tara had almost been number four.

But she was here. Alive. Bartley was partly to thank for that. He'd been doing his own snooping, and she'd learned he'd suspected Andy all along, he just didn't have the proof. When he heard Tara was going off with him to Inishbofin island, thankfully, he followed. And she was ever so grateful for it.

She took a deep breath and sent up a prayer for her mam, Thomas, Veronica, Nancy, Mimi, and even Martin Bixby. Veronica had been a mean drunk, but she wasn't to blame for Martin's suicide. She didn't deserve to die. None of them did. Hopefully, now that their killers had been caught, they could all rest in peace.

Savage barked, knocking Tara out of her reverie. Hound lifted his head and howled. In concert, they whined and tugged on their leashes, dragging Tara forward. "Bunch of babies," she said, picking up the pace. "A pair of freaking babies." They wagged their tails and pulled her along. She laughed. This was life. This was one day at a time. And she was going to appreciate every fleeting moment of it.

Author's Note

For each book, I do as much research as possible. For this one I had the pleasure of visiting Clifden Connemara with my father. We had an amazing time. The scenery was jaw-dropping. Clifden is a beautiful and vibrant town. We loved taking the trek to the Clifden Castle from downtown Connemara, and I was especially thrilled to see a rainbow along our way. What a fabulous set of ruins, set back amongst the mountains and bay, and pasture, and rolling hills. We also hiked the blue trail at Connemara National Park, and took a bus from Galway to Clifden along N59. I was amazed how the drivers handle those narrow, winding roads. Unfortunately, I did not get to Ballynahinch Castle as they were booked solid. From the research I've done, it looks like an incredible place to stay, and I hope to be strolling their grounds one day soon.

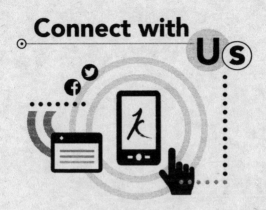